ALSO BY S

The Insect House

REAP WHAT YOU SOW

SHIRLEY DAY

BLOODHOUND
— BOOKS —

www.bloodhoundbooks.com

Print ISBN 978-1-5040-7256-4

For my husband, always.

PROLOGUE

You don't know me. We've never met, but I wanted to warn you that your life is in danger. If something happens to you, some kind of invitation, some kind of gift from the gods that seems too good to be true, it probably is.

W as that enough? How do you warn someone you've never met that they're on a list? That names are being worked through systematically, one by one, and that their days are numbered. To be honest, they'll think I'm a nutcase. That's what I'd think.

I'm standing in the post office with a sack stuffed full of letters, all containing the same message. Each and every one is written by hand. Because I want them to know that they are not just a number on my list; that they are real, that they matter. And maybe, just maybe, one of them... one of you, won't end up dead.

1

LAST YEAR

A young woman, found floating in the Ionian caught in the net of a fishing boat. If this were a film, she'd look pretty, because she was. They'd have her hair flowing out around her pearly white skin like dark lacy tendrils. Kara Jarvis, a once beautiful brunette: slim, delicate-featured with piercing blue eyes. They've gone now, of course – the eyes. By the time they found her, the eyes would have been empty holes in her skull.

'It doesn't take long for the tasty bits to go,' Geoff says as he folds the newspaper, tying it into the top of a bundle he keeps under the sink. His old hands are deft and easy: he's done this a million times before.

About the eyes? Geoff knows things like how long it takes for a body to decompose in sea, sand or soil because he's ex-police, retired. We don't speak about Kara again. She's just one of those tragedies to be passed over. We're good at that kind of thing in the West. It's built into our cultural ethics – *turning the other cheek*. Besides, we were talking about life, not death. His life and, more specifically, we were talking about love.

Geoff's kids, all grown up now, had commissioned a

biography. That's what I do. Have my own little business registered through Companies House, complete with a logo of a swirly book. Designed it myself on the back of a napkin. Had three different company emails too. All set up when I'd been figuring out a name for the business. Eventually, I came down on just one – mystory@gmail.com.

Aptly enough, I only have the one client as well – Geoff. But things will pick up. Everyone's doing it these days: vanity publishing, and double the vanity – why not talk solely about yourself?

I'd always known my clientele would be older; you need the years to have the story and (let's face it) the disposable income. So I was after the retired, silver-surfer generation: those who wanted to get their lives off their chests before the coffin lid came down swift and sure. A lucrative market, one would have thought, but six months in, and Geoff's still the only one buying. I reckon I can survive another three months, then my savings will run dry.

Eighteen hours, that's all the clients get. So it should be possible to pick up some casual work if I get desperate. But Christmas is coming, and surely, surely if you had pennies to spare and a loved one you wanted to get that extra special something for, well surely that something special would be me.

Geoff hasn't put the papers away yet. Instead, he's staring intently at the corner of the top sheet.

'Curse rock pieces in middle of the patio.'

So that's it. I bite my cheeks, trying to stop a knowing smile hijacking my face. We're in a high-rise. There's not a terrace, patio or crazy-paving-stone eyesore in sight. Not one thing to trip us up, but where Geoff's concerned, there's always a little something to slow us down.

'Seven across,' he says, a note of irritation in his voice. He's trying to be casual, but I'm willing to bet this one's been driving him up the wall for the past few days.

'We're supposed to be talking about you,' I tell him. Because, although I really like Geoff, I have to be honest here – he's on the clock. First rule of the self-employed – no freebies. I glance down at the notebook open and waiting on my lap. 'We're on love life, Geoff – your love life. This...' – I glance across at the paper – '*rock garden* is a path to nowhere.'

'Would I do that?' He laughs, and we both know that he would.

'Okay.' I sigh. If he's not going to concentrate, I'm going to have to tidy this up before we start. 'What have you got?'

'T?R?E?T?'

'Middle of paTio, got to be a T.' I smile, trying to tone down the smug. I genuinely love this kind of thing. Cryptic puzzles are as infuriating as a bad itch, crying out to be satisfied. The sort of beast that is so obvious when said out loud, it makes you want to kick yourself. 'Rock equals Tor?'

He nods.

'And pieces, try chess pieces?' I take a stab. 'Could be Men? So...' I smile. 'T o r...' I draw the word out to give him a clue, a chance to catch up.

'Torment.' He laughs. 'You, Sophie, are a godsend.'

I do a self-deprecating shrug, but in truth, the way my career is going, I'm sponging up all flattery on offer. 'I got the patio T first. Then the tor.' I explain. 'Not sure *men* really works?'

'Well... mark my words,' Geoff has a twinkle in his eye, 'where there's men, there's always torment.'

He double-knots the bundle of papers, stashing it under the sink; mystery solved.

'Now, where were we?'

'Love life,' I say. 'Yours.' And that's it; he's off, transported to another time. Telling me how he met the love of his life in a little Spanish place on Greek Street. This woman, *a goddess* he calls her, and smiles. This goddess stormed out of the kitchen shouting angrily back at some chef standing framed in the kitchen swing doors. Standing in his pressed whites, in a doorway that was blinking fast: open, closed, open, closed. The woman's apron suddenly goes flying up out of her hands landing over Geoff's table.

'Lecherous pig,' the goddess shouted. 'Drop things so you can look up my skirt!' A titter of embarrassed laughter started to run through the restaurant – 'Spanish meal, Spanish passion. But...' Geoff adds ironically, 'English diners – English discretion, or apathy. Whichever you think best fits. In less than a minute, people were getting back on with their suppers.'

All but Geoff, he was folding up the woman's apron – the police had him well trained. Then suddenly, he felt something hard and round in one of the pockets: her watch, and that was it. He shot out into the cold November night hot on her heels.

'Maria,' he says, 'the love of my life.' And, no time machine needed; he's back there. I don't mind saying I have a tear in my eye. It's emotional sometimes this kind of stuff. You get seventy-plus years boiled down to just the good bits.

Then it hits me. I pick up my notebook and flick back through the pages.

'So you called her Maria? Not Mellanie?'

He shoots me a baffled look. Then every inch of his face does a light-bulb ping. 'Mellanie, no.' He laughs. 'Mellanie was my wife. Maria... Maria was the love of my life.' Then he adds, like it's an afterthought, 'Better not go putting that in the book. You see, I was already married to Mellanie. It was... What do you young people call it now? Complicated.'

'Actually, Geoff, I think that's called adultery.'

He laughs again. 'You got me.' But the laugh doesn't last long. 'I can see how it might seem sordid, but it wasn't. It was the best thing that ever happened to me. Just... the timing happened to be, off. You know, Sophie, you only get one soulmate, one real love,' and he fixes me hard with eyes as sharp as flint. 'You search for it, young lady, and when you do find it, don't you ever let it go.'

2

LIFT HOME

After work, I go for a swim, but I can't get Geoff's words out of my head. Is he right? Do you only get one shot at love? If so, do you have to search for it? Or does it get delivered, served up when the time is right? Currently, I have to face it, I'm not doing well on the *love* front. There's Jed. Yes, there's Jed. I dismiss the thought and slip into a steady crawl attempting to leave Jed in my wake. I am twenty-eight. I have two failed careers behind me and my first failed company on the horizon. In two months my gym membership will be up, and that's bad because swimming is my life. Well, maybe that's going too far, but it's something I need. If I don't swim, I get grouchy, which is not pretty. And now, I have Geoff's prophetic words beached up in my brain. One man in this big bad world; one man that's cookie-cutter tailored to fit yours truly. Fuck. I am a woman who needs a break.

Geoff says that part of being human is to never value life. To take everything for granted: we don't value our own bodies until we get sick, we don't value our easy lifestyles, we just want more, and we don't value those we love, until they're gone. To be honest, some of us are so monumentally dim we don't even recognise love when it's staring us up close and personal. Then again, it seems like Geoff fell into the same trap. Despite Maria and Geoff's notions of 'true love', what about poor old dependable, faithful Mellanie? Mell: the glue that held his family, his life, together. What's so 'untrue' about that kind of love?

But back in London 2018, hair still wet from my swim, I happen to be struggling with my own conscience and losing fast. I know I shouldn't do it. I can easily walk the mile home in the rain, but I glance at my canvas Vans and think, *sod it, Jed won't mind* because he never does. He'll come pick me up.

I stand gazing out of the gym's wall-wide windows at a London that is dark, cold and oh-so very wet. Outside, buses slither through traffic like whales easing out of the darkness. It's only four o'clock, but it's already black as a deep-sea station out there. If there were no street lights, no electricity, the world would be sleeping. But it doesn't do that anymore – we keep the lights on and the populace strapped to their own private, individually-crafted hamster wheels. I stare through the yawning glass frames watching headlights dip in and out of the off-road parking: gobbling up kids in school uniforms, bags slung carelessly over shoulders. Sticky hands clutching vending machine offerings. Hair dripping wet from that all too brief encounter with the gym's asthmatic hairdryer. Welcome to London.

Another car comes to sit behind the mummy mobiles: a bashed-up red Volvo, circa 1980. I step through the swing door in the foyer and go for it, leaving the smell of chlorine clinging to the air behind me. Jed is already pushing the passenger-seat door open, engine on, windscreen wipers frantically trying to slush away the endless rain.

'Thanks. You're a star.' I ram my bag backwards through the gap in the front seats, grabbing the towel that's ready and waiting for my hair.

'Hungry? There's pita in the back.'

Underneath the towel, there's a wicker basket with pita breads, still warm, neatly cut, wrapped in a napkin and nestled up close to a small tub of hummus. I take the basket and belt up. Jed knows the routine so well: towel, food and transport. I always leave the pool starving and damp. The vending machine only offers chocolate and crisps, and the driers are excuse-my-French crap. My hair's long. Sitting just above my waist. Natural blonde. The chlorine wouldn't tolerate anything less. Chlorine messes up a woman's bonnet sure as paint stripper but none of this is the point. *The point* is: my hair is *always* wet when I leave the pool, and Jed *always* has a soft fluffy towel and food because Jed is *always* thoughtful. It should all be easy. Once upon a time, it was. The wedding bells were ringing so loud we were both in danger of winding up with tinnitus. Jed's my age, good-looking with wild floppy dark hair and blue eyes you could bathe in. So yes, it was easy, only now it's not. Because I'm not so sure I deserve the happy ever after.

As though he can tell what I'm thinking, Jed places one hand on mine. Instinctively I pull my fingers free.

'Sorry,' I mumble. 'Boundaries.'

He says nothing.

It seems stupid I know, but sometimes I feel like it's only the boundaries that are keeping me sane. Remove the scaffolding that they create, and I'd dissolve into some kind of ectoplasmic mess.

'So... how does the boundary thing work when it's raining, and you don't want your shoes to get wet?'

He hasn't totally lost his bite then.

Although the answer's kind of simple. 'None of it works

anymore, Jed. You know that.' I feel myself squirm in my seat. This is all old ground. 'The only thing that's not broken is you. I can't promise I won't drag you down too.'

'I'm willing to risk it.'

I nod. 'Maybe I'm not.'

He sighs.

'I need to get myself...' I stare out of the window into the darkness. My life is like a two-way mirror these days. I can almost see back into the past: see the caving building, the flashing beams of light. Feel the panic as again and again and again I play God and come off burnt.

'Okay. Boundaries.' He flips the indicator, pulling out into the rain.

As Jed drives, I try and leave the past behind me, biting hungrily into the pita, letting his voice wash over me. He sticks to the neutral zone: conversation that does not involve *us* or what we've chosen to call the *incident*. He settles for the weather – obvious – shitty for the time of year. A quick rundown on the bar – a private member scandal. Staffing problems – a chef with no idea of portion control. Which leads us on to a whole wider issue – people with no concept of portion control, and we *discuss* are we a nation with no idea as to how much is simply enough? Is that the problem? Not that Jed sees that there is a problem with the world. Even when it's raining cats, dogs, and labradoodles, Jed is an optimist, the exact opposite of me. He tends to believe that things can always get worse, so best hold on to the good stuff before it slips through your fingers. He's trying to hold on to me. To Jed, I'm part of 'the good stuff'. But seriously, since that terrible day, since the darkness and the dust and the muffled cries, I'm not sure he's got that right.

The best thing I could do would be to get away from everyone who knew me pre and during my meltdown. To sever ties with everyone who knows about the tectonic cracks running through me. That's why we need boundaries. That's why me and Jed can't ever do the happy ever after. He had to live through the aftermath. Our relationship is one big bundle of PTSD.

3

THE MAGAZINE

'And then Geoff said, *but this can't go in the book.*'

Back at my flat, I replay the conversation I'd had at Geoff's place. In my defence, I am not a priest, and Geoff did not say that it was confidential. He just said that it wasn't for the book.

The cat curls around my legs as I slip her a bowl filled with what looks like dried cardboard.

'The old inspector, hey?'

'Detective, he was a detective. And know what, Jed? He is such a lovely man.'

'He cheated on his wife.'

'Yeah, but he was in love.'

Jed eyes me scornfully.

'Don't judge.' I squirm. Trust Jed to find the loophole in the beauty, but I'm not going to let him have it completely. 'Geoff said that for every single person there's a soulmate, just one.'

Silence. The comment hangs in the air like an unexploded grenade. I could kick myself; what a stupid foot-in-the-mouth idiot I am. Because if you were to ask Jed who his soulmate might be, well it wouldn't take a genius to guess the answer.

Only one thing for it: I motor-mouth forward. 'But, I mean him meeting this woman, Maria, in the restaurant. It's such a random sequence of events. It's... it's like me doing this job just because I happened to meet some guy on a train who was doing it and he told me he was making a mint. Fate.'

Jed's looking a mixture of amused and something else. Something I can't quite put my finger on. Superior? Possibly. If I wanted to be completely honest, a first at Cambridge can do that.

'Everything's random,' he says.

You can tell his *first* was in Philosophy and Classics, which only serves to make the whole thing even more irritating.

'There is no fate.' He's on a loop now. 'It's just the human brain likes organising things into narratives.'

Personally, I quite like the idea of fate. I am a huge fan of the notion that at some point in time my chaotic life could get sucked up into a sense of purpose; one with a brilliant rosy destiny shining bright at the end. Because that would mean that somehow all the mess I had to wade through a couple of years back, had one overarching meaning that made everything all right, but for tonight I let Jed have the argument. I'm tired, and he did come out in the rain to pick me up. So I let the fate/destiny/human disposition thing dissolve, and grab a large glass of ice-cold white before hunkering down on the sofa.

Jed stares out through the window into the weeping blackness. 'No sign of a let-up.'

It's been two days now. Continual rain, buffeted in by ice-cold winds that rumble under everything: every thought, every word, every door slam and car horn. Outside, there's a cherry picker with a man in a hard hat valiantly trying to fix Christmas lights to telegraph poles. There is nothing even remotely cheery about the scene. Suddenly, as I stare from the window into the street below, I get the oddest sensation: a primal gut-wrench of absolute terror. Instantly, the lights flicker out. It's just for a moment, but I'm left with this crushing sense of dread as I stare out at the inky black pavement. *Death hunting.* I hadn't thought of that in years. The expression must have got caught up with all those other things I'd walled up and plastered over after the *incident.*

Death hunting. It was what Dara, a woman I used to work with, said. Her last words, in fact, before my life shattered. Dara was Indonesian. Quiet type. Quiet, like she was in possession of some kind of inner spirituality. Not quiet like she had nothing to say. She worked in intensive care. It's an odd place; life and death laid out on slabs. Some nights she'd come in for her shift and say 'death's hunting tonight'. By the next morning, four beds would be empty. And she had said those exact words right before everything blew up in my face. Well, not literally. It did literally blow up in some people's faces, twenty-one people to be precise. The *one* is important, because the *one* tagged on at the end like an afterthought, that's my own personal tragedy. My *incident.* A little girl. Sally-Anne. *Death hunting,* and then I see it. Something? Someone? Slips out into the road. Pulling itself from the dark bulk of Jed's car like a spirit that's been lurking there waiting, always just out of sight.

'Sophie? Soph?'

The lights flicker back on. The shadows are gone. Dispatched. Rationality restored. Only my skin holds the memory: cold and puckered as a dead turkey.

'You okay? You're white as a sheet.'

'Blood sugar,' I say. Not sure how I'd explain anything else. I take a slug of wine but the sense of horror doesn't dissolve. It must be the wind that's creeping me out. It's clawing away at the sash windows. Rattling the locks like a predator. The wind has the power to unnerve. I glance down into the street. There's nothing out there now. Just those poor old council workers.

'I guess I'm tired.'

'You need to take it easy.'

God, I hate it when people say things like that. Besides it's not as if I'm exactly rushed off my feet. Jed must pick up on my irritation, because he goes for a subject change.

'So what's the verdict?'

'What?'

He stares back outside, and I follow his gaze to a four-foot construction of Santa: wrapped in wire and lights, dangling down the side of a crane, grinning a fixed metallic grin.

The holidays, of course. That million-dollar question – where am I spending it? To be honest, I wish I could just hibernate.

'I should go home. I didn't go last year.'

'You could stay in town?'

I shrug.

'I'm off Christmas Eve to Boxing Day. No strings.'

But there are always strings.

'Up to you. I'm here if you need me.'

'You know you're lucky not having a mother.'

'What!' He laughs. But it's more laughing at the whole audacity of the statement-type thing, than laughing because he thinks the comment is genuinely funny.

'Philip Larkin. *They fuck you up, your mum and dad.* She was on the phone earlier, berating me for giving up medicine.'

'Your mum?'

I nod. 'She says it wasn't a big deal. Everyone has a *wobble* occasionally.'

How can she reduce what happened to a *wobble*? I was responsible for the death of a child.

'She also said the personal history market is a road to nowhere.' I sigh. 'Maybe she's got a point on that one.'

'I'm sure she didn't mean to...'

'I'm not.'

'She's just got big feet, Soph.'

'And one hell of a sharp tongue.' I don't bother to tell Jed how my mother went on to say he was a waster, and that he had *'no people'*. Whatever that's supposed to mean. I don't tell him mainly because it's not nice, but also because he probably knows: she's that kind of a mother.

'Kathleen.' He smiles ironically. That same lopsided grin that reeled me in so effortlessly at uni, but now just leaves me painfully aware that something's dead inside. 'She's a classic. Well, just remember. I'm still here.'

He grabs his coat and bends to stroke the cat: a quick one-for-the-road smooth of the fur. He looks so natural in my flat, so much a part of it. We were seeing each other for eight solid years before the *separation*. We kept our own places even after we got engaged, but he helped me set up. We bought the sofa together: an antiques shop in Camden. The lamps: a charity shop on Gloucester Road. He even watched as I crackle-glazed a surprisingly indestructible MDF table, watched, passively inhaled the fumes, and made tea.

'You know, this is kind of an odd separation.'

I sigh. 'I just need...' I don't mention the *incident*. I don't mention how I fell apart. I suppose that is the one good thing – he doesn't need me to.

'... space.' He smiles. 'Finishing your sandwiches. Can still do it.'

'It's because they're so pedestrian. Marmite, not watercress.'

'Oh, and the article.' He holds up a rolled copy of *Marie Claire*. 'Page twenty-eight.'

The cat scarpers as I make a dash towards the magazine.

'Is it good?' But I'm not waiting for a reply. I flick through the pages blinded by the bling.

'Near the back. Good spot. Nice layout. Great picture. Bit

late for the Christmas season. It's the January issue, but it's out now, so...'

It is a good spot; a bloody good spot. Half a page with yours truly's face shining out: '*What do you buy the man who has everything?*'

I scan through the article, drinking it all in. '*Personal histories. Immortalise a family member.*'

'It's perfect. It's bloody perfect.'

'Yeah well, like I said, the editor owed me a favour.'

Yet again, Jed's pulled out all the stops and made something magic happen. I grab him into a tight hug.

'Thank you, Jed. Thank you so much.'

And then there's the problem, which I realise as soon as I feel his body pressed up against mine. When you get physically close to someone you used to love there's a kind of natural fit. It's like two magnetic pieces of the same jigsaw locking back in. If I rest here too long, I know I'll just fall into the same placeholder again. I can't let that happen. I need to find myself first: the me that got shattered, or maybe a new one. I need to do something. Because if I don't, it's like I'll be that hard old pea in the princess's bed: awkward and digging into Jed and myself for the rest of our days.

4

THE CALL

At ten o'clock it's still raining. The guys outside are *still* valiantly struggling with the lights, and the wind is *still* not helping. Instead, it's wilfully lifting the strings of bulbs into curious shapes or blowing hard blasts of rain full frontal into the men's faces. I gaze down at them, although I realise it's not them I'm interested in. I can't help myself; I'm scanning the shadows looking for... I'm not sure what. Besides, there's nothing. It was all just a trick of the light. I draw the curtains, so I'm not tempted to keep checking. *Death hunting*, I think to myself... I need to get out more. Sadly, on my freelancer's handful-of-peanuts pay cheque the chance would be a fine thing.

Despite 240 channels, there's nothing on the telly, and the book I've been trying to read for the past month is still boring me. Maybe it's the book, maybe it's me. I'm not in the mood for dissecting the problem. The only option is an early night. I stare at my reflection in the darkened windows. Then I do something I've never done before, not since the incident. I unclip the silver clasp on the chain around my neck; the chain that holds Jed's ring. Around two months after my world imploded, I broke the engagement off. I tried to give the ring back, but he wouldn't take it. I tried putting it in its box, but that didn't seem right. I tried leaving it in the medicine cupboard, the soap dish, and even in the bedside drawer. But engagement rings are like skin: they only thrive when kept close. I imagined it shouting abuse at me every time I was within a metre of where it was stashed. So I strung it on a chain, but the time had come, surely. I couldn't keep both myself and Jed on hold. I slip the ring off its silver chain, wrap it in a bit of toilet paper and bury it at the back of the bathroom cabinet. Tomorrow is the start of a new day. Well, it's as good a catchphrase as any other. Face cream on, I hit the sheets.

———

It's very dark: a pit of oily black, where there's no up, no down, no gravity, no sound, only me. The air is filled with dust and particles, of what? Wall, plaster and brick. Beams from torches flash. I can hear people moaning. A building lies in pieces around me. I can barely walk forwards without something crumbling under my toes. I have to climb over girders. There may well be bodies under the debris. I try not to look down as I head for a small rectangle of light. A doorway, I think. I can just make out someone standing beside it. An attendant, like the ones you get at posh toilets handing you out toilet paper and squirts of perfume for the price of a pound. But the attendant here doesn't look posh. She's bloodied and bashed, wrapped in bandages. I dig into my pockets, but they're empty. I don't have any change. If I want to get out, I'm going to have to give up something.

I turn my wrist, hold up my watch. That would do. Maybe? It's all I have.

The attendant's mumbling incoherently. Is she talking to me? I'm not sure. The sound swells in my ears, and then I understand. It's not mumbling; it's chewing. The attendant is eating the bodies, the leftovers, the bits that didn't get blasted to Kingdom come. And I realise with a sickening gut-clench that the door, that rectangle of light, is getting narrower. I need to get out, but I don't want to go near the attendant. I get the feeling that if I touch her, those bruises will sink into my own skin.

I start to unbuckle my watch. If I do this quick...

But when I glance back, the door is smaller again, narrower, almost closed. I lurch forward. The ground under my feet rolling away, making me stumble. Beneath my bare toes something is shining white: bones, femurs, skulls, ribcages. Every one picked clean and glowing in the dull light.

My foot slides from under me. I only just manage to stay standing. The munching swells. I look up again as the bandages fall from the creature in front of me. It has wild eyes and blood all over its face; a face that is melting like cheese, dissolving into holes around its cheekbones. And the mouth! Gaping and terrible as a scream with bits of meat, person and bone sticking out from between yellowing, cracked, crooked teeth. Suddenly, I know. I know exactly what, who this is. It's chewing and chomping and dripping saliva, as it reaches one clawed hand towards me. Death hunting. I think. Death. I got away once; it's not going to let me do it again. A hand comes up out of the debris, grabbing my ankle. I'm lost...

I sit bolt upright in bed, sweat pouring off my body. Something is ringing, but not my alarm. It's pitch black. Home, I think. *You're home.* The street lights must have been switched off or blown on account of Santa's unreasonable demands. I hit the alarm, even though logically I know the ringing can't be my wake-up call. It's not the right tone, not the right time.

I hardly ever get nightmares, not even when I was neck-deep in all the middle of the *incident* shit. That thing, whatever it was, whatever I thought I saw earlier today in the dark street, it must have really spooked me. *Death hunting*, I think yet again. It's like some earworm that won't sit silent. I need to get a grip. Meanwhile, the ringing continues. Must be my phone. I throw on the lights and squint, blinking like a baby badger at my handset, which tells me the call is international. Why would someone be ringing me at this hour? I slide the button to *accept*, readying myself to give whoever it is a mouthful, when I hear an accented, melodic voice.

'Sophie Williams?'

Eastern European, I think.

'Yeah?'

'I hope I didn't wake you.'

This is a stupid question and deserves a pissed-off answer. 'I'm always awake at four in the morning.'

There's a pause: a pause in which I realise that the irony of my statement may well have fallen outside of the linguistic ballpark we're working with here. To put the stranger out of his misery, I clarify. 'You woke me.'

'I'm so sorry.'

'Could you cut to the chase?'

'I'm sorry?'

This is super-fast going nowhere.

'What do you want?'

'Oh. My client read an article in a magazine – personal histories? We were wondering...'

'Tim Henderson?'

Jed again, and yes he's in my flat again, and *I know yes* this is odd. But actually, it's kind of normal. It's Saturday. We always watch a film together on a Saturday. And yes, again, I am fully aware that this is not your regular separation. Though it might get one hell of a lot more permanent if he doesn't stop looking so gobsmacked at my news.

'Yes. What I said – Tim Henderson.' I stop myself short of putting in a 'duh' for good measure.

'The geneticist?'

'Yup.' I realise I'm playing with Jed just a bit: trying to be oh-so cool about the whole Henderson thing. But cool is not exactly how I'm feeling: this is big.

'And he rang *you*?'

There's a tone in Jed's voice that I'm not wholeheartedly delighted about.

'Yes. Well no, actually his butler rang me.'

Jed laughs at the word *butler*. Understandably, I guess.

'But why not? Why shouldn't he ring me?'

'Because,' and Jed's voice slips down a tone as he knuckles into explaining mode, 'Henderson was the main man in genetics for about twenty years. Nobel Prize winner. That fertility clinic – all him.'

'There was Grayling as well…' I've been googling most of the morning.

'Pfft, no one remembers Grayling. Then there was some kind of fire in the late nineties and the clinic closed? But why would…?' He shakes his head. 'I'm still not getting this.'

'Henderson's got a great story.'

'Undoubtedly.'

That must be a Cambridge affectation flaring up right there. *Undoubtedly* pulling that one out of the bag if you're under fifty sounds all wrong. But it's too late to pick him up; Jed's steamrollering merrily along on his it's-oh-so-incredible trajectory, and I realise we're heading straight towards salt-poured-open-shaker on wounds:

'But why get *you* to write it?'

'Jed!'

He goes for a quick retreat. 'And... and flying, Soph? You don't like flying.'

I'm not sure if he's glossing over the fact that he's just dragged my skill set into question, or if his concerns re my dislike of anything over twenty feet above ground level are genuine. A mix of the two perhaps?

'It's heights,' I protest. 'I don't like heights. I'll book an aisle seat, and I won't look down.'

Because Henderson not only wants me to write his personal history, he wants it written on his own private Greek island. After what I've been through, this is just the fresh-break, *time-to-think* kind of thing that I've been waiting for.

'Look, I'm not being rude.' Mr down-to-earth is proving tenacious: injecting a pair of gravity filled boots into my dreams. 'Henderson's been a recluse for the past five...'

'Ten years. I googled it.'

'Okay. He's been a recluse for the past ten years. No one gets an interview out of him.'

'I'm a good fit: got a degree in medicine. Masters in journalism.'

Even to my own ears it sounds daft. I spent all those years training to be a doctor, and then I just jacked it all in. Only, I had my reasons: exploded bomb in my life, those kind of reasons. Although when people ask, I keep it short and sweet. I go for lightweight, bordering on anorexic explanations. The truth... it's still too emotional, too raw. My rule of thumb is to tell anyone who asks that I don't like sick people. I like people, but sick ones? No, not for me... I don't tell them about Sally-Anne. I don't say that maybe having life and death resting continually in your own two hands can be too much of an ask.

'Know what, Jed? Maybe it's my time. I could do with a bit of luck.'

'Your time?'

As soon as it's coming out of his mouth I realise I sound like a five-year-old stamping her foot. *My time,* what does that even mean? But there's a part of me that will not let the idea go. Surely I've been through enough? Eventually, my luck has to come in.

'But Henderson doesn't need to pay someone to...'

This is beginning to irritate. 'It's a present,' I say, trying not to sound defensive. 'Someone saw the article.' It's out of my mouth before I'd had time to think it through.

There's silence; someone saw the article that Jed had worked so hard to fix for me.

'Sorry,' I mumble feebly as Jed's Christmas with 'no strings' slides big time off the table.

It's quiet in the car on the way to Heathrow. Even with the radio on, Jed barely speaks a word. It's the kind of quiet that weighs heavy on a person. Outside, it's dark, the early hours, and still raining. We get stuck in traffic on the M4. Nothing unusual on that front. Eventually we arrive at the seasonally surreal bit: a massive Christmas scene: Santa, elves, reindeer, overlarge frosted-white tree. Everything stranded on a diesel-choked strip of roundabout serenaded by the sound of departing 747s, and I know as soon as I see the lights from those heavy birds lumbering through the sky, that there's no turning back.

Jed pulls neatly into the quick-drop lane. The indicators sound way too loud, like a metronome striking off our last minutes. We say nothing, waiting as the family in front extracts itself from their car, watching silently as copious amounts of bags and people spill out. There are pavement hugs, kisses, and waves. Then the driver jumps back into the car. The Fiesta pulls away a whole heap lighter, and Jed slides the Volvo into its space.

'That wasn't so bad,' I say brightly, unfastening my belt. But Jed remains mute. I sigh, glancing in the mirror at a captured slice of my face. I should have taken the Tube. This was a mistake. Despite the fan heater busting a gut to deliver warmth, the temperature in the car is full-on frosty.

'It looks busy,' I say, deciding small talk is probably the best plan, but Jed's not listening. He's rooting through the pockets in the car, switching his attention from side pockets to wallet, wallet to pockets, in the hunt for change.

'Jed?'

He grunts, not wanting to talk. I glance out of the window again. All those people abandoning the ship for a Christmas with loved ones, and suddenly it hits me hard: a sense of being alone, of being way out of my depth. In truth, I'm apprehensive about everything; the trip, Henderson, the bluff that I'm going to have to pull off – big-shot journalist. Two years ago, my life fell apart. How can I be sure I've got all the pieces of me back together again, together enough? This is a big job and I have a stellar track record on the mess-up front.

Outside, a man collides into the Fiesta family. The youngest member goes flying. But the man doesn't stop, just disappears into the building. He's like a black sliver of oil, like the figure I'd seen that night beside Jed's car: like *Death hunting*.

'Jed, did you see that guy?'

But Jed's not looking, not interested. Instead, he's sitting there facing forward, seeing nothing, money on dashboard ready to go, steering wheel threaded through his hands.

I glance back out at the pavement. The father's been called back to the mess: the cases, the kids, everything is all over the pavement and getting wet. The dad gathers up the whimpering child, muttering reassurances. I stare at the family dusting themselves off, the incident forgotten: just a few wet patches, maybe a scraped knee. It's all part of the Christmas fun.

'Did you see... that man, he was kind of... odd?'

The way he walked, the way he slithered, his painfully thin frame.

Jed turns to face me, but he just looks blank.

I hate flying. All these bad omens, these wobbles, it's just my brain conjuring up avoidance tactics.

'I'm sorry,' I say, willing everything to be all right, trying not to think about the parking meter ticking merrily away, racking up time at an exorbitant fee that Jed will have to settle. Should I offer to pay? Or is that sliding into insult-to-injury territory?

'Maybe you were right,' Jed says, facing away again. 'Maybe it is all for the best, us separating.'

His voice sounds flat as if it's had the life washed out of it.

I watch the wipers going left to right. I'm about to leave all this behind. Provided I don't freak out on the plane because of the height thing, my future is looking... Well, to be honest, my future is looking like a future, and that is so much better than before. And although it breaks my heart to think it, my future is probably better without Jed. He saw me broken. How can he ever see me whole again? Besides, Jed will probably, possibly, definitely be better off without me. Someone else will watch videos with him on his Saturdays off. He could be happy with someone else, someone nicer, someone who didn't try and top herself, but there's a part of me that still doesn't want to let go. Emotions are so much more complicated than right or wrong, best or worst. They don't do binary. They don't do dichotomies. They do texture and uncertainty and that's just one reason why they drag you all over the damn shop.

'You know I've had offers,' Jed's voice breaks into the quiet. 'There was a bar in Greece. I could have gone out and run it. It was really good money. Only...' – he pauses, letting the wipers beat time – '... I didn't.'

'I wouldn't have stopped you.'

He doesn't want to know this. Because this is part of the problem. Jed wants the pipe-and-slipper life, the mortgage, the kids but I'm not sure I can do that now. I need some kind of experience that can take away the bad taste life's given me. After my breakdown, I tried to get Jed to do something... something different. We could hitch-hike across America, or Europe, or anywhere. Anywhere I could start fresh. But he was worried. I guess he had cause. The part where they pumped my stomach, well that was enough to make any sane person cautious. I know it won't happen again, seriously once is enough. But for Jed, he's much happier if he can keep a crack medical team within shouting distance.

5

FLY AWAY

I've never been in an airport for the Christmas run-in before. The whole panic-stricken sale-time-at-Oxfam vibe is enough to murder the season's greetings out of St Nicholas. There's still a week to go, but the panic is palpable. The terminal's packed with tribes of people carrying suitcases so big you could fit a reindeer inside, and not one person is wearing their Christmas smile despite strands of tinsel decorating desks and wrapped around the long slim necks of the flight attendants. It's true there's a smattering of Christmas music being squeezed apologetically out of a tannoy system somewhere. But whatever joyous undertone the soundscape is attempting to induce, the men and women flack-jacket clad and toting guns that would scare the bejesus out of Liam Neeson, are managing to neutralise all season's greetings.

I move forward, tugging my case into the mayhem, and discover I'm unable to get past a stewardess doing triage. Major-league pissed-off people are directed back outside to a long queue snaking around the building and exposed to meteorological conditions that would prove trying for a woolly mammoth. I am wearing far too little for this. I've left my wool coat at home. Clad only in my tan leather jacket and denims, I will freeze within ten minutes if left outside.

'It might be worse,' the stewardess says to a woman whose face is screaming out to be used as an emoji for *pissed off*. 'It could be snowing.'

To be honest, snow would be preferable to this eternal grey drizzle.

The emoji-woman pulls away from the stewardess, defeated. The stewardess has been trained and set to react only at surface level. Large protestations will only incur flak-jacket attention and possible permanent eviction, or a Christmas dinner courtesy of Her Majesty.

I walk purposefully towards triage, holding my ticket in my hand as if for validation.

'BA flight 770563.'

Her eyes glaze as she steadies herself to address the situation, before launching in without even the merest hint of a 'sorry'.

'We're having to ask everyone to...'

But then her eyes catch sight of the ticket. 'Sorry...'

I smile to myself – really?

'First-class passengers can go straight to check-in.'

I glance at my ticket, held aloft in my hand, feeling more like Gandalf wielding a magic staff than a punter with a seat reservation.

'First?'

She smiles, in a but-of-course way, before stepping back and allowing me passage.

The concourse beyond the guardian is empty and serene. I go straight for the desk. There's only one person in front; a man clad in a piss-tea mackintosh that matches his skin tones so perfectly I would not be surprised if he was born in it.

I'm still clutching my ticket, tighter now that I realise the thing has actual power. First class, I have never travelled first class. By the time I get to the desk, the man in the mac has been well and truly processed. He's turning towards me as his bags are ferried off down the conveyor belt. Suddenly it hits me: I know him. I'm not sure where from or how, but I definitely recognise that face.

'Fancy seeing you here.' It's the best I can do at short notice.

He shifts awkwardly. He's not giving anything away.

'We met at...' I'm stalling for time.

'Ma'am?' The ticket lady has a queue of cold travellers trapped outside the door. She wants first class processed and out of her hair.

'I'm sorry. I think you must be mistaken.' He nods his head, as if it's a full stop, then walks away.

'Ma'am, your ticket and passport, please?' The lady behind the desk is sounding a little less polite and a lot more insistent.

I hand over my documents, while all the time looking back over my shoulder at the guy in the mac disappearing up the escalators. Faces are my thing, and I've definitely seen this one before. So who is he and where did we meet? Only as I watch, I catch sight of something else; someone, something right behind him, and the hairs on the back of my neck begin to bristle. It's the same figure: the death hunting figure, not so much a person, as a shape. The way it moves: fluid, almost as if this being is liquid shadow. And I know now, in my gut, that this guy, this creature, this is the third time I've seen him. It's the shadow man; the thing I saw lurking by Jed's car. Now he's weaving in and out of the crowds, just behind Mr Deny-All-Knowledge. Keeping just far enough back so he's not noticed. He's got to be following the guy. Moving unobtrusively pillar to pillar, body to body, blocking himself from sight. He has no idea that I'm also in on it now; that I'm behind him, watching the cat trail the mouse.

'Enjoy your flight.'

My suitcase disappears down the conveyor belt. But I don't stop staring up at the raised gallery. Then, as if aware that someone's watching, the man in black turns and looks straight at me.

'Miss, are you all right?'

It's the stewardess again, jolted out of her sales patter by my involuntary gasp – he doesn't have a face! All the regular details appear smudged, rubbed out. Then he's gone. It was just for a moment, just a glimpse.

'Miss?'

I can't have seen what I thought I saw.

'Fine,' I mumble, 'just...' It must have been a trick of the light. After all, he was a long way off. 'Absolutely fine.'

Stupid, I think to myself as I trundle up the escalator. One thing's for sure – everyone has a face. It's standard issue. You need one for your passport. This is all just a bad case of nerves on overdrive. I don't like flying. I'm conjuring up monsters so I don't have to get on that plane, but nothing is going to stop me from taking this job.

On the plane, I stretch my feet out into first-class space; there is so much of the damn stuff. A stewardess is fumbling past, handing out little menus printed on cards – choice. Space and choice. I can tell already that I am going to enjoy this.

I notice Mr Deny-All-Knowledge sitting across the aisle. He catches my eye, and I smile, leaning towards him to say something, but deftly he shows me his back.

I scan the section where we're sitting. The man in black doesn't appear to have deep pockets. He's not in first.

The stewardess retreats past Mr Deny-All who's stowing his

briefcase in the overhead. As he does, his sleeve rides up, and I catch a glimpse of what can only be described as one of the worst skin grafts I've seen in all my medical training. I look quickly away, bury myself deep in the in-flight perfume section. The engine is revving, the lights are on, and my window to the outside still has the blind up. I pull it down. It may be daylight, but if you can't see that you're high, you can't get scared.

6

ARRIVAL

I swear to this day I have never seen anything so brilliantly blue. It hits me as soon as I get out of the airport, following in the wake of some guy that has HENDERSON printed on a laminated board. The sky is bright as a kid's paint palette, and that's despite the diesel fumes belching out from the traffic. If you could just pull yourself above the cars, that sky is where the gods must be.

I get into the back of an unmarked Ford that's seen better days, deciding to try a few words in pidgin.

'Nice sunshine,' I say, with a smile.

The driver looks blankly at me via the mirror, and I'm not a hundred per cent sure if his lack of conversation is down to an understanding, or an attitude thing?

'Henderson,' he states simply.

'Henderson,' I repeat, as we pull away from the terminal.

Luckily, the signs are in Greek and English. We're heading towards Delphi.

'The Oracle,' I say, pointing to the sign as we pass.

My driver nods, repeating the word twice as if conjuring the woman into life.

'Oracle. Oracle.'

'She still there?'

But the conversation's already way too much.

'I could do with some answers,' I mumble. Wouldn't that be great? Wouldn't it all be oh-so easy if you could just hand over a tenner and have your life mapped out? Think of all the mistakes you could avoid.

I grab my phone, take it off flight mode, and stare at the screen. No word from home. No word from Henderson. Suddenly, I feel completely alone, and I'm not sure if this is exactly a good thing. Tired after the flight and my hasty London escape, I lean my head back on the leather seats and shut my eyes. Five minutes I think.

When I wake, two hours later, my mouth is dry, and my neck feels cramped; it must have been throwing my head around like a Swingball. My driver grins at me through the reverse mirror, and I see that his smile is more gap than tooth.

'Sleepy. Sleepy.' He grins.

'When will we be there?'

'Sleepy, sleepy,' he repeats, caught in a groove.

'Arrival?' I ask.

There's not one ounce of understanding in those eyes, just amusement at the fact that I've been snoozing like a baby. To be honest, as a joke, I don't personally think it's got legs, but pidgin English jokes are more about repetition, than content. So I play along. Briefly.

'Yeah, sleepy, sleepy.' I stare out of the window. The industrial landscape has disappeared, replaced by emptiness: a rocky ancient Greece sheltering under a vast blue sky. I stare at the road signs. The English has also gone. The letters mean nothing to me. It's like being spun on one of those fairground wheels, the ones they stick the knife thrower's assistant on. I don't even know which way is up. Then I remember – Kairos

– it's an island; there would be no direct signs. But why hadn't we gone to Piraeus? Okay, so geography is not my strong point, but I do know that the main port in Athens is Piraeus.

'No Acropolis?' I ask, knowing he should manage to get this.

But, nodding his head inanely, he simply repeats my last phrase, switching it neatly from question to statement.

'No Acropolis.'

I'm beginning to feel uneasy. How do I know I'm going to Henderson's? Okay, so the driver had a sign, but not one with my name on. It was Henderson's name on the card. The only previous contact I've had is a phone call at some ungodly hour summoning me to Athens. I had to fill in some forms, non-disclosures, but all of these arrived by courier, and now a man who looks like he's straight out of central casting (category: henchman) is taking me who knows where.

By the time we turn off the main road I'm beginning to get twitchy. Suddenly the car rattles into a steep descent, and I feel my stomach hit the back of my throat. Instinctively, I clutch the sides of my seat.

'Hey. Where are you going?' I shout, trying to sound assertive but managing only scared shitless. None of this is important anyway, because the noise of the pockmarked road is so loud I can barely hear my question. But I can see the driver's lips moving in the mirror, and don't need to be a lip-reader to know my own question is just being repeated back with a shrug. Ironically, I remember this was the story of the Oracle. She would only ever repeat questions back, placing stress on different elements, because the answers were always invariably locked somewhere deep within the seeker.

The car hurtles downwards. The lane closing in on either side. Contorted trees twist above us as the wheels bounce off stones and I'm jolted across the back seat like a forgotten crisp packet. I look at my phone; there are still no messages. What the hell have I got myself into?

'Kairos?' I ask nervously.

'Kairos. Kairos.' The driver nods in reply, jerking the gear lever back in order to give the brakes a bit of a helping hand. I grab my phone from my bag, and switch it on, comforted momentarily by its dim light. I need to get a message home, tell them where I am. I attempt to tap in a quick note to Jed, but my fingers are all thumbs, and what with the bumping and the impending sense of panic I can't get anything to function. I feel a sickening sense of despair drain through my body top to toe. What do I honestly expect anyone would do? I stare out of the window, at the trees, at the endless twisted foliage. Everyone who is even remotely interested in my well-being might as well be on a different planet. Just at that moment, the car pulls onto a clear, flat stretch of ground – the sea lying wide and open in front of us.

We draw up next to a small private dock. I don't wait for an invitation. I slip out of my belt, yank the back door open and set my feet firmly on gravel. I'm standing in a natural cove, a small but perfectly formed crescent. Directly ahead there's a wooden sailboat nestled in the harbour – just one boat. I guess, from the torturous approach and state of the road, not many people know this place exists. The slap of the waves washes over me doing a damn good job of easing away my abduction theories. Now I just feel foolish. It was all an overreaction. Standing on this deserted bay, I can't help feeling special, chosen somehow, like when you plant your foot in a field of unbroken snow. This whole trip is going to be amazing. It's all beginning to fit together; Henderson is a recluse for God's sake. He isn't going to want the press watching his every move; who comes and who goes.

Sadly, my driver is hot on my heels. He's out of the cab

grinning like a fool. I hope to God he's not going to be driving the boat as well. He heads around to the back of the car, opens the boot, and grabs my bags.

'For me?' I ask, partnering my words with a basic form of sign language – a point at the boat, followed by a finger aimed at my chest.

My driver grins his toothless grin, pushing his index finger into my sternum.

'Henderson,' he says as if marking me.

I give his finger a withering look. He withdraws it, but the grin doesn't fade.

I'm so relieved when he places my case on the ground. So he won't be ferrying me. Fantastic. I grab the handle, maybe just that little bit too eagerly. Does he know that he spooked me? Is it intentional? He's still standing there grinning. My case feels light in my hands. It was hastily packed, enough underwear for ten days although I'm only planning on staying for six.

He doesn't move. Should I give him a tip? No. No way, and maybe he picks up on the fact I'm not going to play ball. Maybe me being some tight little rich kid fits into whatever story he's built for himself, because grinning like a monkey he offers some kind of strange salute, closes the boot with a fierce slam, jumps into the driver's seat, and disappears in a cloud of dust.

I couldn't be happier to see the back of him, even though I'm now all on my lonesome and have not one idea as to how I could personally make that boat in the harbour do anything more than sit and look pretty. Though it has to be said, it's managing that by itself: nestling in its bright-blue cove as if posing for a postcard. Well, I'm impressed. Then again, I don't get out much: out of the country that is. There had been driving holidays to France, always Provence. Small, tattered, lavender-edged villas with no phones for my father, a pool for me and a sunlounger coupled with the latest 'must-read' paperback for my mother.

Maybe they were worried that because I loved swimming, if they gave me a beautiful ocean I might swim right out into the sunset. I've always had my own way of doing things. We didn't need the sea – so the wisdom went – because didn't we live right by it at home? Leiston to be precise: the East Anglian coast. Only, as I was rapidly beginning to understand, there is sea, and there is brown stuff sheltering beneath a nuclear power station. In Greece, you can look right down twenty feet or more to the bottom. You can see till the light runs out, and it's all blue and green, fractured and beautiful.

I pick up my case, walking cautiously towards the boat. Could this really be for me? If so, I'm not disappointed. It's not a yacht, but then I've always felt acres of moulded fibreglass are only aesthetic for people impressed by money. This boat, my boat, is a beautiful wooden fishing boat; its planks are polished, perfect, and glisten like honey.

'Hello?' I call nervously as I walk slowly forwards. Silence. Maybe this isn't my boat? Suddenly there's a clatter of bare feet on wooden boards. A man emerges from below, an easy smile written all over his face. It would be all too predictable to call him a Greek god, but my first coherent thought is simply: they don't make men like this in the UK.

He's charmingly apologetic for missing my arrival. Apparently, he'd been fixing the engine. He hadn't heard the car. He practically pulls my arm off in his eagerness to take my case. He is the absolute and polar opposite of the monosyllabic goon who drove me here. His name is Achilleas. There's a schoolboy joy to his conversation. A kind of wonder, it feels so refreshing. Such a change from the cynical world I've left behind, where money, mortgages and monotony rule. This trip was the right thing to do.

We chug out of the cove into the glistening blue sea. There's a bench in an open cabin, laid with cushions so soft, sit on them once, and you never want to stand again. Just like all those ancient Greek myths about people being bewitched: people falling in love with a place and never wanting to leave. I could see how stories like that would come ten-a-penny in a place like this.

There's food laid out on a small polished table, a light meal: just fruit, roasted veg, a rustic loaf and a few dips. All vegetarian. Did I tell Henderson's guy that I was veggie? I didn't think so, but couldn't remember. Maybe they were just playing safe.

After I've eaten, I head out onto the deck. We've been going around an hour now; there's no sign of land. Achilleas stands behind a large pirate-style wheel, smiling easily as I come up from the cabin. I had thought he was younger than me, but I'm guessing now that maybe we're around the same kind of age. The boat, apparently, is his, and he's so proud of every rope and nail, it's endearing. It makes me realise how our lives back home have become overfilled with mountains of disposable tat.

He has his back to me, smiling out over the sea, so I have the luxury of a little forensic analysis. He has a slim muscular build, the kind of shape you might get from daily gym visits, but there's not a doubt in my mind that his outline is more organic; he's toned by work rather than reps. When he turns and smiles, I feel instantly foolish.

'The sky,' I say to Achilleas, looking up into its wide blue emptiness, breathing it all in.

'You have no sky in England?'

'Apparently not.'

He points into the distance, at the even horizon where the sea kisses the heavens, fifteen miles off I'd say.

'Kairos.'

I squint, seeing nothing.

'Henderson's island?'

Achilleas nods.

'And he actually owns it, yes?'

Achilleas looks a little amused at this, and dusts off that brilliant, shy smile once again.

'The land, the sea, the fish, the sky,' he says.

I laugh.

'And you?' he asks.

'It's just a job, a very well-paid job, but just a job.'

He smiles again and points into the distance.

'Kairos.'

Then I see it, a small dot drawing closer over the waves.

7

KAIROS

Kairos rises out the sea like a fortress; a wall of elephant-grey granite towering above a thin pavement of rock. We sail into the shadow of a large crinkle. As *crinkles* go, it's big. I'm guessing you could fit at least five large yachts in here, no doubt that's the plan. There must be parties for the great and the good, selected stop-offs and stay-overs for the world's fabulous and famous. But one thing's for sure I think, as I stare up at the cliff face, no one gets into this place without an invite.

I'm off the boat before I remember my case but Achilleas is already behind me carrying my bag, depositing it neatly onto the floating pontoon.

'You leave this here.' He indicates to the bag with a nod of his head that sets his dark hair cascading forward over his eyes. 'They send someone.'

He stares up at the great terraces of rock towering above us, and despite the sun, and the late warmth of the day, he shivers.

I look up at the cliff – it's high. At a guess, I'd say two hundred feet and it is cold here, standing in the shadow of the rock face but even though I hate heights, I get this curious feeling that there's more to dread about this place than just fortress-style cliffs. There's something brooding about it that turns my stomach to jelly. It's like coming up against the face of a god, immortal and uncaring. Our lives in comparison to something this solid, this eternal, are just dandelion clocks floating on the wind.

'Where do I go?' I ask nervously, and the answer I get is the exact same answer that I do not want to hear.

'Up.'

The muscles in my face flinch.

'There's a path,' he says, pointing to a steep line climbing up the cliff face. 'Someone... they will find you.'

Someone? I think staring anxiously towards the path. There's not a sign of life.

Achilleas gently touches my upper arm. His hand lingering for just one moment more than is strictly necessary. He could be flirting; I'm not entirely sure. With looks like his, it's probably difficult to stop yourself, but I don't brush the hand away. In truth, I'm one hell of a lot happier with him holding on to me.

'Great,' I say, which is not exactly what I'm feeling.

Satisfied, he removes his hand. Looks like this next part, I'm going to have to do on my own. I give Achilleas a short, swift smile, which he matches before waving goodbye, grabbing the mooring line and leaping back onto the boat. Despite the hand on the arm, the flashing smile and the possibility that Achilleas might have been attracted to me, he's moving fast, and I can't help but get the feeling he's relieved to be making a hasty exit.

Initially, I make no movement, hoping someone will appear. Tackling that cliff face on my own holds zero attraction. I would be so much happier jumping on the fast receding boat and heading back to the mainland; once-in-a-lifetime opportunity with Henderson, be damned. But, that kind of attitude will get me nowhere.

I decide to stall. So, like a love-struck teenager, I stand on the dock and watch as the boat chugs away. Achilleas waves as his form gets smaller, eaten up by the edge of the cove. I wave for much longer than needed. I wave for so long I begin to feel a bit of an idiot with my hand stuck in the air. Surely someone will have seen our arrival and be heading down towards me. If I just give them a little time... But when I look back at the cliff face – nothing.

I take my phone out of my bag and text a quick message to the number I've been given for Henderson.

Arrived.

I press send and wait a moment longer. Nothing and no one. I flick to Jed's thread. Not a dicky bird, just a string of stale messages from a life I'm no longer a part of.

On the island. I text, but that seems hopelessly inadequate. *Miss you* I type, and the obligatory x escapes from my thumb.

It's okay. It's not a problem. We are a culture of x-ers. We've all been emboldened by technology into digital shows of high emotion, emotion that we have absolutely no intention of physically reconstructing. But I wish Jed was here. I wish Achilleas was here. I wish anyone was here.

I am a woman who is nearing thirty. I'm not sure where prime comes anymore. Geoff insists seventy's not what it used to be, and I have to say that I think he's onto something there. The swimming means I'm reasonably fit, but I haven't exactly cut my teeth on hill climbing – because of the heights thing. But Henderson, he's not exactly a spring chicken, and his guests, they must all have to join in on this goddamn *Jurassic Park* journey up the cliff face. I give a brief note of thanks that I am, at least, wearing flat boots.

There's the path Achilleas pointed out. It's cut into terraces. So you go up and along, up and along, and the path is edged by a wall. If I'm going to fall, I've got to get over the wall first. So that's all positive, kind of. If the others can do it... and I'm imagining strings of rich ladies dressed in impossible frocks and ridiculous shoes, laughing in champagne-soaked trills: the glamorous women who spill off their big yachts... If they can manage it, I've sure as hell got to try.

I take a photo with my phone and tag it with a message to Jed: *Where's the Minotaur?*

8

HENDERSON

I must be fifty feet up when a piece of the cliff crumbles, sending a skittering of stones cascading down. They land just ahead of me. I don't suppose they would have hurt much if I'd been caught in the shower but anything bigger could have done serious damage. A bird above me lets out a long, lonely call, sweeping out and around the cliff. I glance down. It's the first time I've given myself permission to look, and I wish I hadn't. The sea that had seemed so inviting back on the mainland is now looking cold and unforgiving as concrete. As my palms begin to go clammy, I vow not to look down again. Glancing up, the bird soars into the blue sky, and suddenly I feel unsteady. I should know all this by now. There's only one place to look: keep my eyes fixed dead ahead at the cliff face, and I'll be fine. Fifty feet or two hundred, the end result of a fall would be the same. I step forward once again.

Not much further on and I find myself a problem; there are two paths. One appears to go directly up the cliff, climbing high in quick short terraces, only there's a narrow section with no barrier. Then there's a second path which goes into a dark tunnel; no clues as to where in the hell that one comes out. I glance fearfully up at the direct route, with its lack of barrier – tunnel it is.

It's dry inside, which I suppose is a good thing. It's around six feet high by two feet wide. Luckily, claustrophobia is not my problem. I switch my phone to torch mode, wondering how people lived before smart technology. Maybe they had to be smart themselves. I continue into the gloomy tunnel, running one hand along the rock wall. A precaution – just so I know the path doesn't branch off. Despite the thin beam from my torch/phone and my hand on the wall, I'm also feeling with one foot: sticking it out gingerly ahead of me. Although I can't really see where I'm going, I reckon I'm safe as long as there is only one tunnel and no sudden dips. If there are two tunnels I'm snookered; I could easily lose my way and do they even know that I've arrived? They had all my flight details. They'd sent someone to fetch me. They must have been able to make a half-decent guestimate as to my arrival. I'm feeling kind of just the tiniest bit pissed off. I didn't want adventure. I was after a fresh start. Going it alone is wearing thin. Surely if Henderson is that rich (which he is) he would have people to meet me? There are steps in front, steep and narrow. Irritated, I begin to climb. Why hadn't anyone been there at the pontoon? Should I have stayed back on the beach? But Achilleas had kind of said I should go up, or had he? There was that whole language problem thing going on. Maybe I should go back?

If there are two tunnels I'll just have to retrace my steps: try the path without the barrier. No, not that. I'd go back to the cove. Eventually, someone will have to come looking; he's paying me a small fortune. I've been climbing for what seems like an age; my heart filling my ears with a persistent beat. There's one hell of a lot of self-doubt banging around in my brain. I shouldn't have done this. I should have waited on the beach with my luggage. I'm about to turn back when suddenly I see a small glimmer of light piercing the darkness. Daylight? I walk faster.

The relief as I get closer to the end of the tunnel is coupled with a smattering of nagging panic – what if there's no wall? I'm higher up now than I was. I've been climbing the whole time in this damn tunnel thing. Even at the thought, my palms begin to sweat. Vertigo is so uncompromising. Stand over thirty feet up, and you feel that good old dependable gravitational tug pulling you towards the edge. Your mouth dries up faster than a puddle in a desert, and words (however mouthy you are) will evaporate smartly on those dehydrating lips. Then your knees give, and as soon as your knees slide, you're lost.

But when I come to the end of the tunnel, there is a small narrow barrier wall. I don't look down. I keep my eyes fixed on the cliff face to my left, but I can tell, because the wind is more intense here, that now I'm high, really high, and I'm having to concentrate hard: trying not to listen to the sound of those hard waves hitting the rocks below. I continue on. My palms are now wet. Not dripping, but certainly not the kind of texture anyone would enjoy grabbing hold of. I know my face will have gone luminously pale. My jaw's already hanging open and slack. It's a race against time now until my knees give up the ghost. The path beneath my feet is loose; scree keeps rolling away from under my shoes. I can see now why the bird brought some stones down when it took flight. It would be difficult to leave the nooks and crannies that litter the cliff wall without taking a few souvenirs. None of these thoughts are helpful. I go a little faster. It's then that I feel something hit the back of my leg. A rock the size of a fist kicks back under my heel, rolling steeply down towards the tunnel.

I stumble, ending up on my knees, face in the dry dirt, hugging the cliff. I watch as the lone rock rolls back into the darkness. I was lucky. I could have fallen, could have tripped. Suddenly the thought dries in my head because something odd just happened. The rock has rolled back out of the tunnel; it's rolling uphill towards me. You don't need a degree in science to know that this just does not happen.

'Hello?' I manage to squeak out of a mouth as dry as the Sahara. No reply. I remain sitting on the path, body pressed against rock, wishing my voice sounded a bit... more.

'Hello?' Still nothing, but the words give off a faint echo around the cove, a sound that rubs in the blatantly obvious: that I'm really high. I think of Sisyphus doomed to roll his rock uphill for eternity. It doesn't make me feel any better – regurgitating Greek myths. It just makes me feel as if the island itself is alive. Riddled with mythical structures that work beyond my understanding.

I know I'm beginning to lose it. My breath is coming in short ineffectual bursts. My lungs are starting to burn. I have to get out of this. Have to get to safe ground.

I continue on up the path going quick, quick, quick, practically running, feet skidding on scree. It's a matter of time, only time before I dissolve into a jabbering mess. I round a corner, go up a few tight corkscrew steps, and suddenly find myself standing beside the most amazing pool terrace. I step right out onto it. All the panic of the path, the dark tunnel, the mysterious rolling stone, the waves crashing on the rocks below, all of that falls from my shoulders.

My *wow* is audible.

I've always had a thing about private swimming pools. They're not really made for people who *swim*; they're made for rich people who dunk. Any decent swimming pool has to be a bare minimum of twenty-two metres long. Anything less is not a pool; it's a puddle.

Okay, so this has to be eighteen, so not perfect. But seeing as how it's open-air, private and set in the most incredible terrace with views falling away into olive groves and sparkling blue water, this pool is well worth getting wet for.

I drop down and dip one hand into the water. I can't resist. My guess would be it's around twenty-eight degrees centigrade. Too hot for a training pool, but for an outdoor pool at Christmas? Perfect. I smile at my fractured reflection in the clear water, feeling a bit like Goldilocks must have felt when she discovered the best chair in the building. Then I realise, there's someone else, someone standing right up close behind, and their face? Well, they don't appear to have a face! I gasp. It's out of my mouth before I've had a chance to strangle it. I jump round expecting to see someone standing behind me, but there's no one.

'Hello?'

Nothing. Just the sound of the gate I came through swinging gently back on its hinges. Someone was following. The someone who rolled the rock uphill? But why, who would follow me?

A cloud passes across the sun. Suddenly I feel cold. I have no intention of going back through that gate. Whatever is down there can stay down there. There's only one direction for me now, and it all involves flat ground and terraces. I glance around, taking in the rattan chairs with their soft, inviting cushions. This terrace is worked by invisible hands: not a leaf out of place. The area is edged with low, immaculately pruned, lines of rosemary. The smell is just amazing. It's heaven. Directly ahead of me is a small bougainvillea-covered building. I guess that must be the villa? It's not as big as I'd imagined. Perhaps it's some kind of pool house? There's no one around – not a soul; the terrace is draped in silence.

I look down the cliff from behind the safety of a wall. I can see the jetty far below. I have to admit that I'm secretly amazed I managed to get up that path, and worryingly, I have no idea how they're going to get me back down again. Perhaps I might have to hole up here for the rest of my days? Then it dawns on me; there must be another way up because my bags are gone. Unless the stone roller carried them up? I glance towards the gate. But if that were the case, the bags should surely be on the terrace, and why the hasty exit?

'So, are you?'

I turn sharply. There's a man behind me. He's backlit, so I can't see his face, but I know from his straight posture and the expensive cologne emanating from his clothes that this isn't my Sisyphus. I squint in his general direction.

'I'm sorry?'

'Wise.'

Sun in my eyes, I still can't see the bugger.

'Sophie, it means wisdom in Greek.'

'You don't say.'

He laughs. 'It's a long time since I've heard a bit of sarcasm. People tend to be on their best behaviour with me. To be honest,' he says, 'I miss a bit of sarcasm, a bit of wit. Tim Henderson.' He shifts ever so slightly so his body clips the edge of the sun and extends one large well-manicured hand towards me.

'Right,' I bluster. 'Mr Henderson, I just wanted to say that this is... It's such an honour.'

He shifts slightly again. The sun comes flooding right back into my eyes. Praise apparently makes him uncomfortable, and with his shift he's dragging me into the discomfort zone. I angle my body in line with his. There, I think to myself, that's better, and I see a fleeting smile cross his face. I've seen that smile so many times before, it's always apparent in the photos, newsreels,

TED Talks. He's permanently press-ready. A smile, like a handkerchief, carried for emergencies. It's a little thin, if I'm being perfectly honest, slightly all-knowing, slightly smug. The kind of smile that people use when they've got dirt on a person but they're not sure if they're going to use it.

'I did my thesis on you,' I bluster like a schoolgirl.

The smile drops, his forehead creases into a frown, and I realise he doesn't understand. For a moment I'm not sure what it is that he doesn't get. Then it comes to me – he has no idea I studied to be a doctor. The only reason I'm here is because of an ad Jed happened to put in a women's magazine.

'I studied medicine,' I offer.

'Of course you did.'

But I can read people better than he can act.

'At UCL. I went on to do journalism later.'

'Oh?'

God, I hate that question. We've come to the *oh, so what happened?* bit. Luckily I have my stock answer ready and waiting. 'Don't like sick people.' There it goes. I've used it so much I'm beginning to think that it's true.

Henderson leans back his head and roars with genuine laughter. 'Exactly. Neither do I, young lady. I can see we are going to get along famously.'

Famously? He has more than a touch of the Henry Higgins about him.

'You must be tired after your journey?'

'Actually, I slept in the car. I guess London living finished me off.'

'It does that.'

'Amazing pool you've got there.'

He smiles proudly as if I'm heaping praise on a favourite child.

'I used to swim a lot. The villa's been in my hands for almost forty years, but really I've done very little to the house apart from this.' He reaches down to the water with the agility of a much younger man, no knee creaks, no groans as his stomach sinks onto his knees. I guess that's what extreme wealth buys, a kind of immortality.

'Good temperature. Twenty-eight degrees?'

He smiles, amused. 'A little hotter – thirty – now that I'm not as young as I was. And of course, the winter.'

I stare around the terrace, now bathed in sinking golden sun. 'Believe me, this is the kind of winter you want.'

A leaf floats across the pool, a curled brown reminder of the season despite the warmth. Henderson reaches out one arm and skims it from the surface.

'Deciduous, you see.' He glances up at the trees surrounding the pool. 'There's really no need. I could easily have planted something... less fickle, but I can't help myself.'

He drops the leaf back into the water. It goes floating off in the opposite direction, away from the filter. I guess pool cleaning's not on his to-do list. A light wind rustles across the terrace, stirring the rosemary in its wake, releasing perfume into the air.

'That smell is just incredible.'

A dark cloud crosses his face.

'It's so strong,' I add. Not sure what I've said wrong.

He blusters for a moment, seemingly knocked off guard. 'The kitchens... We bake our own bread.'

But no, there's no smell of bread. How could he not smell the rosemary? I'm about to correct him, correct myself, cover the moment over, but he moves on seamlessly.

'You'll join us for dinner?'

From his tone, I'm left in no doubt; this is not a question.

'For once I think our party will be greatly improved by a new presence. Another medic is always welcome.'

'Well... I...'

'Eight thirty. We tend to dress.'

Dress? Mentally I flip through everything I have in my case. There's the emergency black jersey wrap, but with boots?

'There are clothes in your wardrobe. Ellie will help you get your bearings.'

And there she is, Ellie, dressed in black and white, complete with an ironed apron. Summoned as if she had been there all along, waiting in the wings, my case already held firmly in her pretty olive hands.

'And Sylvie. You may well need Sylvie.'

This is addressed to Ellie. Which is good, because I have no idea who Sylvie is, or where to find her.

I'm about to step forward, to follow Ellie from the stage when I glance to my left, and the gate standing open, leading back down the cliff path.

'What was that I came up through? Some sort of maze?'

He smiles as if I've stumbled unwittingly onto one of his favourite subjects.

'Did you like it?'

I glance back towards the gate. I remember the height, the drop, the wind on my face.

'Not really my kind of thing.'

He looks mildly disappointed. 'Best time yet. Most people miss the tunnel. And for supper, Sophie, please do remember, not to be late.'

I've been dismissed. Ellie smiles sweetly at me. I'm not sure if she speaks English. She's nodding a lot, so I'm guessing maybe she doesn't? She indicates towards the building, and I follow, taking the wide row of steps up to the low-line structure that I'd already seen. As we grow closer, I realise this is not the house: it's just an entrance. An entrance with floor-to-ceiling windows and sofas positioned ready and waiting for guests to admire the view.

The house itself is a different story altogether: larger and more sumptuous than most five-star hotels. This is going to be a bit of a holiday for me, I think, stepping into what must be the main entrance hall: going from the size of the door, which could accommodate a small Trojan horse.

9
SYLVIE

Effusive adjectives gush from my mouth faster than a tap with the stopcock broken. I am so over the moon about... well... everything, I'm fast running out of praise. My bedroom – bedroom! Suite. Small apartment. It has a sofa, a desk, a bath I could swim in, and the bed. Even diagonal snow angels are a possibility. Then there's the smell, it's like walking through a rose garden.

Since my arrival at the villa, I haven't been able to hold back on the 'wows'. I soon realise I'm going to have to rein it in. It may have amused Ellie the first fifty times, but even to my own ears, my constant excitement is beginning to sound a tad on the moronic side. Luckily Ellie hauls me back on track with her understated reserve – it needs two to bounce on a bed.

She reminds me simply that we have dinner to prepare for. I suggest I iron my little black dress, but Ellie says no that's her job, and where there is an ironing board involved, I'm not going to argue. I let her place my tatty case on the immaculate satin eiderdown, and though Ellie manages to keep a lid on it in reference to the case, when she sees the state of my crushed

black jersey, she does a classy eyebrow raise and says one word –
'Sylvie.'

Sylvie, well what can I say about Sylvie? French and
gorgeous are the only words that fit. Forty to forty-five, but
wearing her age in that way that makes you feel that hers is the
only true age for a woman to be. On her instructions, I find
myself standing in my suite, arms held high over my head, as she
thrusts me into a series of cocktail dresses: tulles, silks, organzas.
I've never felt such beautiful fabrics. But it's only when Sylvie
slides a crushed raspberry velvet wiggle dress over my head that
she begins to smile.

'Now, I think this is going to work.'

'Work? I love it.'

'It's well-cut, but this...' She squeezes an inch of material
from my waist into her right hand. 'This does nothing for you.
Off,' she instructs.

'Maintenant. Now... brush.' She ruffles my hair with one
spare, tiny French hand. 'And while you do that, I'll fix the
dress.'

I slide it over my hips and step out.

'I've never worn anything so...'

'No.'

'And he just has these things hanging around?'

Sylvie shrugs, jaded: as if the dresses are all simply part of
the lifestyle wallpaper. 'He has a lot of parties, a lot of people in
and out over the years.'

'So you work for him?'

Taking her sewing basket from the bed, she examines some
bobbins, searching for the crushed raspberry match.

'I style for him: the people, the rooms. He likes... Well, I
have a flair.' Suddenly she stops, running a critical eye over my
face. My hair is hanging brushed, but limp, around my

shoulders. She frowns, not happy. 'You need to do something more than just comb through.'

I pick up the hairbrush again and pull it through to the ends. 'I could wear it down?'

'With a neckline like this, it has to be up.'

'So you just "style"? This is a new one on me. I know some of the fancier shops have personal stylists, but to have your own stylist on call day in, day out?'

Sylvie smiles. 'Some rich women pay people to cut their toenails. I don't make judgements, just bank the cheque.'

I take a couple of mother-of-pearl hair slides from the dressing table. They're delicate, edged with seed pearls and diamanté.

'Is it okay?'

She shrugs again. 'The room is yours.'

Then I guess that's a *yes*.

I pull two front sections of my hair back into the slides, leaving a tumble of curls to fall neatly around my face.

'Better,' she says simply.

'How long have you been on the island?'

She stops for a moment, almost as if she were an automaton being asked a question it doesn't want to compute. When she speaks again, there's an edge to her words that I can't quite place. Sadness? Surely not.

'I've been here so long I've forgotten what it's like – the real world.'

'The real world?'

But the moment has passed. Sylvie the professional is back.

'Now, you are distracting me. If I don't get on, you will have nothing to wear.'

'Nothing?' I smile.

And she laughs. 'Now there's a thought.'

'Well, I appreciate the help.' I glance at my black dress lying humiliated on the bed, like a scholarship kid at a fancy party. 'It could do with being retired,' I say, wondering if I'll ever get around to it, but Sylvie's a woman of action.

'Ha!' She picks up the dress, crosses to the en suite and plants it in the bin. 'When you leave, you take this one; it's much better.'

I can't argue with her there, but it seems like a ridiculously good trade.

'It doesn't suit Henderson.' Sylvie smiles mischievously.

I look at myself in the mirror. Jed always says I brush up okay but I don't tend to invite compliments; they embarrass me, guess that's just part of being British.

'I appreciate this. Thank you.'

'I enjoy it.' Sylvie smiles proudly at me as though I'm her creation. 'I am always styling for Alice.'

'Alice?'

'Henderson's sister.' Sylvie gives me a wicked smile and whispers in my ear. 'Younger, but you wouldn't know – a stick insect. I could cut the top off a sock, slip it over her head et voilà. You know a secret, Sophie – a stick insect will only ever look like a stick. Now, what time has he called you?'

'Eight thirty.'

'Eight thirty!' She screeches in mock despair. 'He called you for eight thirty, and you have me chit-chatting.'

When Sylvie leaves, I stand staring at my reflection in the mirror. It's not vanity. It's amazement. Every woman should have this kind of fair-lady treatment once in a lifetime.

I glance down at my wrist. My watch is far too bulky, suitable for extreme sports, not designer dresses. I unbuckle it, taking a moment to examine the face. It reads eight twenty-five. I'm cutting this fine. I lay the wristband on the washstand. As I do I happen to notice the overflowing bin; the arms of my old jersey dress crumpled sadly into its body. Carefully, I pull the dress out, folding it swiftly before stashing it in the bottom of a drawer. We had some good times, once.

Suddenly my phone, which I have plugged into the socket by the bed, buzzes. I don't have time for this, but it doesn't stop me from looking. It's a message from Jed.

What's the great man like?

I grab the phone towards me, knocking my Kindle off the bedside table. I'll grab it later. I'm about to text Jed back when I realise – I'm not entirely sure how to answer his question. After supper, I think, I'll know more about Henderson then.

10

SUPPER

Eight thirty. I move quickly through the house. Ellie's already told me where the dining room is, or at least pointed me in the right direction, which is lucky because this place is as sprawling and quiet as *The Shining* hotel. There's not a soul out here. I fly around the bottom newel and step quickly through the large entrance hall, my footsteps keeping me company as I hammer over the white marble tiles. There's an open doorway. I head through and stop. It's dark. My eyes take a moment to adjust. The entrance hall was all illumination, a large chandelier, floor-to-ceiling lamps and orangery style windows that must catch the daylight in summertime certain as a dragnet. This second room is more like a dark rabbit hole: very little light, not an ounce of fresh air and circular in shape. The walls are painted black, which gives the curious impression of infinite depth. The effect would be unnerving, like stepping into a black hole with space and time snuffed out. But to counteract the formless nature of the room there's a series of alcoves set into the curved wall, each indent edged with bronze piping and illuminated in a soft, orange glow, and in each alcove, there's some kind of artefact: Greek or pseudo-Greek.

Some of the stuff looks old: valuable old. There are the usual Greek busts staring out indifferently with their cold, blank eyes and a few shapely urns chipped with accidents or years (or possibly years of accidents).

If this stuff is original, it must be worth millions. I glance up at the ceiling looking for cameras; nothing. I guess this is an island. Taking anything out of here, you're going to get spotted, but if you were the owner of all these priceless antiquities would you risk it? Surely prevention is better than high-tailing it James Bond-style after some cat burglar with a sack full of Hellenistic treasures. You have to be pretty sure of your security to decide CCTV is redundant.

I turn and realise there's a large centrepiece looming behind me: a statue of Laocoön – the priest who attempted to unmask the Trojan Horse. The gods didn't like Laocoön's interference, so sent out a couple of sea serpents. It's easy to guess the rest – no one gets out alive.

The statue is incredible. I've seen it before, well one like it; in the Vatican one summer on a road trip from Provence. Only this one isn't marble. It's bronze. People like to believe art is only ever about one-offs and individualism but high art's often wholesale. There are at least eight 'originals' of Rodin's Kiss. And bronze, well, make yourself a mould, and you can churn art out faster than Nissan Micras.

This has to be a copy, but it's a beauty. The one everyone thinks is real, the one in the Vatican, is also a copy but it's so old people just assume it's original. The real one, the lost one, was bronze. So, nice touch, I think to myself as I stare into poor Laocoön's face.

'Always thought he got a bit of a rough deal.'

I turn sharply to see a small, thin, spectacled guy. An academic, I'd have said if forced to make a judgment call.

'Laocoön. Classic case of shooting the messenger, or rather…

strangling him and his offspring with some handy sea serpents. Alfred.' The man says, offering his hand.

'Sophie.'

'Sorry. I didn't mean to intrude. We were worried you might have lost your way.'

We? But I don't get a chance to ask. Because it's then that I see the mask. Laocoön may be stunning, but the mask is altogether in a different league. Laocoön is a depiction of horror. The mask, well this mask... it kind of *is* horror. It's haunting. Primitive in construction with two large, sagging holes staring out of its wooden flesh, like tears, and a set of dark twisted horns rising from the sides.

'What on earth is that?' My hands reach out instinctively to pick the thing up, then freeze mid-air.

Alfred nods in an amused fashion, giving me permission to touch, but I still hesitate, so he reaches forward taking the mask from its plinth.

'Despite the distressed appearance, this is only around thirty years old.' He taps the wood. 'Damien Hirst, so I understand, or probably. It's difficult to know. There are so many stories circulating here. One thing I do know, it's valuable, but not fragile.'

He places it into my hands. It's heavier than it looks. Curious, I lift it into the light.

'A helmet?'

I glance into the eyeholes. There's something glistening inside. Through the empty sockets, I can dimly make out a thin spike, half an inch long. Anyone wearing this mask would be pierced by the spike. It wouldn't kill you, but as far as comfortable goes, it doesn't work.

'This is our Minotaur,' Alfred informs me, indicating towards the mask.

'Minotaur?'

'When in Greece...'

'It's horrible.'

'Yes,' he smiles amiably, 'isn't it. It's part of the whole... labyrinth thing.'

For a moment I have absolutely no idea what he's talking about. Is he referring to Crete? Like I said, geography is not my strong point. Then it dawns on me. 'You mean the maze?'

His eyes light up with all the excitement of a fifteen-year-old who's just discovered a soulmate in the no-hopers corner of the playground. He leans his head towards me, as though we're co-conspirators. 'Exactly. Maze. But Henderson is insistent, and it's hardly for me to say that Tim Henderson has it wrong.'

Now Alfred's lost me completely. He must realise because his look suddenly falters. He's coming down to earth Icarus-style: in short – hard. He's not speaking to an educated academic with an opinion here, just some blonde stumbling around a rich guy's mansion who inadvertently used the wrong word.

'It is a maze. A maze is a complex, branching, multicursal puzzle that includes choices of path and direction. It may, as ours does, have multiple entrances and exits. A labyrinth is unicursal – it has only one single, non-branching path leading to the centre and back out the same way. The point is: it has only ever got one entry/exit point. We have four. It's my speciality,' he says, beaming. 'I've studied them for over twenty years.'

For me, this is seriously impressive: his dedication, not necessarily the maze/labyrinth distinction. With my multiple career choices, I'm always impressed by anyone who finds it possible to settle on just one thing.

'Of course, ours is unique. It has maze-like elements because of its construction. Not another like it in Greece, arguably not in the world. The site was modelled on the intestines of the Minotaur. The bovine stomach having four chambers.'

'I'm not sure I understand.'

'No doubt that's the intention. You must have seen it when you came up?'

'The tunnel thing? There's more to it?'

'A lot more. I've explored some of the veins; principally the one you came up through and a second one to the north side of the villa. That one is kind of like the front door, links into all the others. For a relatively small island, the underground construction is vast: miles and miles of tunnels constantly doubling back on themselves. Some sections date from as far back as 200 BC, possibly older. Though I've only been allowed entrance into the more modern additions. So far,' he adds with a determined note. 'And at the centre,' he continues, 'so the myth goes, the seeker will find their true self.'

'Can't be bad.'

Alfred shrugs. 'The seeker is supposed to wear the helmet to help them navigate.'

I look at the helmet, gazing once again through the darkened eyeholes at the spike. 'Ouch.'

'Ouch, indeed. Not the original, as I said, but close enough, so we hope.'

'Your specialist subject.'

'I like to think so. I'm an archaeologist. I used to have a seat at Princeton. Currently, I'm here at Henderson's goodwill.'

Somewhere in the house, I hear a clock strike and Alfred begins to look a little nervous, which sets me wondering if *goodwill* might be tested by tardiness.

'Perhaps we should...' He lifts the helmet carefully from my hands, placing it back onto its plinth.

'But what about the ball of string?'

He looks puzzled.

'The Greek myth – in the story Theseus goes into the labyrinth to kill the Minotaur. Ariadne gives him a ball of string so he can find his way back out. If it's one way in, one way out, why does he need a ball of string?'

I've won him back. Alfred smiles, momentarily losing his sense of time.

'A couple of theories: one, it was never a true labyrinth. It was only ever a maze. But my favourite school of thought is that, just as in our labyrinth, there's madness at the centre. You need something to pull you back. Find your true self and where is there left to go? We have our helmet, Theseus had Ariadne's string.'

'And then he left her,' I say. I remembered talking about this with Jed. Theseus is not exactly my kind of hero. 'After Ariadne put her life on the line, gave him the string which got him out of the labyrinth, Theseus forgot his promise and abandoned her on a beach.'

'Not the most chivalrous of actions I agree, but then Ariadne did go on to marry Dionysus, the only god who remains faithful to his wife.'

'And fun to boot, I guess.'

Alfred smiles. 'No doubt.'

I glance back towards the helmet.

'Maybe it never was Theseus' story,' Alfred says wistfully. 'True, he slays the Minotaur, but he doesn't actually overcome the labyrinth, only Ariadne does that. Perhaps he's just her ball of string, her way of getting off the island.' And with that, he smiles what is, despite his years, a schoolboy grin. 'Now we should be getting into that dining room before we ourselves get fast-tracked off the island.'

As we walk through the villa, I'm glad to have Alfred at my side; you don't need the excuse of a maze around here to get lost. Eventually, we find ourselves in a large dining room. A fire burning hungrily in a yawning grate. A tall, well-dressed man has his back to me, warming his large hands against the orange glow. There's a woman sitting at a wide oval table. In her forties, I'd guess. A glass held loosely in her hand, long red hair tumbling over her shoulders.

'Ah. Another butterfly for the collection,' the woman with the red hair says. Instinctively I look behind me, but there's no one there. I guess that makes me the butterfly.

'Sophie,' I say.

'We know. He told us this morning,' the redhead replies, raising her glass towards me in a toast. 'I'm Clara. Married to Numbers.'

'Numbers?' I look blank.

'Accountant. We're all known by our occupation here, rather than name.'

'So you're all interchangeable?'

Clara laughs. 'Yes. The Doctor...'

She indicates the man beside the fire.

As he turns to face me, I realise – it's Mr Deny-All-Knowledge from my flight.

'Now this time I do recognise you.' He's walking towards me, hand outstretched. 'We met at the airport.'

But as I take his hand, I feel an irritating gnawing deep in my brain. I'm missing something. I've seen his face before, and it's not from earlier today. But where? His sleeve slips momentarily, and I get another glimpse of shiny, grafted skin. He catches my eye but says nothing, just shakes down the sleeve.

'Beavis,' he says.

The name rings no bells.

'I'm media and communications,' says a bright woman with a stiff smile and a blonde bob. 'You can call me Mandy if that's easier. Henderson was keen to call me Medea, but I put my foot down.' She smiles. 'My husband, Trevor, is on tech.'

'Alliterative.'

'Pleasure,' Trevor takes my hand. 'Hope the journey was okay, understand you're not keen on travelling.'

'I...' How does he know this?

'White as a lily,' Mandy says easily, shooting Trevor a look that I don't quite understand – a reprimand?

But Mandy continues, unfazed. 'You don't get to spend your days in the Med, and keep alabaster skin like yours, Sophie. Sunscreen tomorrow. Never mind the fact that it's winter.'

I feel like I'm missing something here.

'True, I don't travel much, but I'm kind of turning over a new leaf.'

They all nod, as if all this is only to be expected.

'And believe me, it's great to escape.' I think of London and the rain, and the cold and the electric Santa smiling grimly into the wind.

There's a sound from the hallway. We all turn together. Curiously, it feels as if our lives are not entirely justified without Henderson, but we're disappointed. A small, timid-looking woman enters, her dark hair held in an apologetic bun. She's talking nervously to a large man with the body dimensions of a Wetherspoon's bouncer.

'Ah, Sophie, this is my wife, Mia.' Alfred assumes the role of master of ceremonies.

Mia is exactly the kind of woman Alfred would be married to. They're of the same mould: same height, same kind of weight, same thin slightly worried faces.

'Lovely,' she says. Unlike her husband, she seems to have fewer words at her disposal; perhaps it's difficult to get them in?

'And Gorski.'

Gorski is dressed in an overly formal DJ, and I wonder if somehow he slipped through Sylvie's net. Then I twig: Gorski is the butler.

'We spoke on the phone, ma'am.' The Slavic tones are there,

despite the fact that the dialogue is straight out of *Jeeves and Wooster*. He gives a quick, sharp bow.

'The butler, and don't ask him...' Clara says, unable to suppress herself. 'He most certainly did it.' She roars with laughter, and I can't help it, it's so corny, I like her already.

'If you would please take your seats...' Gorski continues, seemingly oblivious.

He pulls a chair out for me, and I sit like an obedient dog. Everyone else is seated in much the same way, and I realise, as Gorski manoeuvres himself effortlessly around the table, that this is normal. The chair game is played out each night. I wonder if position is random boy/girl, boy/girl, or if Henderson oversees the seating plan: keen to extract the best conversation.

'Doctor?' Gorski asks, pulling back the chair next to me.

Again, I feel the frustratingly fruitless grind of mental cogs; where do I know this man from?

'After five...' Beavis the doctor says to me firmly, as if laying down ground rules, 'I don't look into people's mouths, feel glands, or set bones. And if you're dying of a virus, it's my night off.'

I laugh. He's a man after my own heart. 'I promise I'm healthy, no ailments.'

'So you found your way through the maze?' Mia asks.

'Labyrinth, sweetheart, Mr Henderson likes *labyrinth*,' Alfred says curtly as if trying to smooth over some terrible faux pas.

'I wasn't exactly keen on the height, but the route, well I didn't find it too tricky.'

'Lucky you,' Mia says with a tone of bitterness. 'We got stuck in it for hours.'

'Not hours.' Alfred laughs nervously.

But Mia's not backing down. 'It's perverse,' she whispers. 'There are far easier ways to get up here.'

I find this reassuring; I'd been dreading having to go back down, but...'Perverse?' I ask.

And I swear Mia jumps out of her skin. I'm wishing I'd kept my language a little less inquisitional, then I realise the fact that she's blanched has nothing to do with me. Henderson has arrived. He's dressed in a DJ but it's in a different league to the one sported by Gorski. There's no mistaking who's boss here. I'm not sure why, but the whole thing is beginning to make me feel uncomfortable; we're all looking way too much like the cast of an Agatha Christie for my liking.

'Perverse?' Henderson repeats Mia's comment into the absolute silence of the room.

'I was just...' Mia stutters, and I feel sorry for the woman.

'I didn't build it, most of it was built by my predecessor.'

Henderson must be referring to his labyrinth.

'He was an eccentric.'

Like that explains everything, and I wonder why it is that eccentrics always have mountains of cash? Maybe they don't. Maybe it's only the ones with the money mountains that do truly ridiculous things and get noticed. Eccentricity is a question of scale, I guess.

'The path was... interesting,' I say. 'I hadn't realised it was part of a much bigger complex.' I avoid the whole labyrinth/maze distinction. 'I liked the covered bit.' Well, that's not a complete lie.

'Most of the sections are, in fact, covered,' Alfred interjects eagerly.

Henderson smiles. 'Have to keep the sun off my Minotaur's back.'

There's a small titter of amusement. It feels forced. So forced I wouldn't be surprised to find 'laugh-buttons' beside each place setting, with green and red action cues. Nothing here feels genuine, apart from maybe Alfred's enthusiasm.

'Myths are important, wouldn't you say, Alfred?' Henderson asks, though the question feels rhetorical. 'Myths and superstition, we must continue to feed them to the masses. It's through these 'stories' that we maintain the status quo.'

'Keep the old *band* together,' Clara mutters.

'Flippancy can grow very wearing, my dear,' Henderson says, without bothering to look at her.

There's an icy silence. Clara glances nervously at her napkin, and I'm wondering if she's going to make some excuse and dive out.

'I'm sorry.' She doesn't look up. 'It wasn't funny.'

'No.'

Silence falls once again, and I find myself feeling thankful for the waiters as they close in around us.

The starter is scallops in a pool of creamy yellow sauce. It's all so effortlessly placed on the table that I have to check with the staff that they know I'm veggie but of course, everything has been handled. The veggie option has the same look, minus the scallops.

'Leave it,' Henderson barks suddenly.

Gorski was about to clear an untouched place setting.

'Your sister won't be joining us?' I'm guessing that Alice must be the one that commissioned the personal history, probably a Christmas present. I was hoping to meet her.

'No. My sister doesn't often dine in the evening.'

So Sylvie's hints held a smudge of truth. You don't get to be a stick insect without shunning the dining table or making regular appointments with the porcelain goddess.

'The place was for... my son, Cal. He can be... difficult.'

Henderson doesn't need to spell it out. I can tell from the gathering, the lowered heads, the awkward silence, a couple of throats being cleared, that the topic of Henderson's son is a sensitive one.

'He knows I value punctuality, yet insists on being late.' Henderson wipes his lips on a napkin as if something tastes bad. 'Cal has perhaps been indulged too much.'

Suddenly I remember – Cal Henderson. He was in all the papers recently. I hadn't put two and two together. The guy was a playboy, a waste of space. Not even a toenail clinging onto the Henderson intellectual vanguard. No wonder I'd missed the link.

'There was a car? An accident?' I run my mind back quickly over the newspaper reports. It was gossip. Not the kind of thing I normally go for, but it had been unavoidable.

'He's having a quiet few months,' Beavis offers.

'Perfect place for it,' I say.

Henderson smiles, and this time it's genuine. I realise that this island is his haven.

'A point of order in a sea of chaos,' he says. But his smile fades abruptly, halted by the sound of clapping. Clapping that is so slow there's no doubt that it's driven by sarcasm. It's coming from the corner of the room.

I recognise him as soon as he steps out of the shadows: the face from the papers. He's my age, good-looking in a silver spoon kind of a way, with dark, tight, cropped hair. He looks so clean, so fresh, as if he's only just peeled himself off the ironing board. It's only the super-rich that ever get to look like that.

'Quoting Schrödinger, Father?' Cal drawls in a soft American lilt. 'Philosophers. The cat in the box, is it dead, is it alive, does it matter? Life and death as theoretical constructs. And the cat? How does the cat feel about it all?'

Henderson sighs in a bored fashion.

'You missed the starter,' Beavis says, as our plates are whisked away.

'I'll live.' Cal's staring straight at me, in an unnerving way – eyeing me up as if I'm fresh meat. I've helped out in Jed's bar on the weekends. I've had to deal with desperate men, drunk men, men who can't keep their minds out of their trousers, but I've never had anyone look at me in quite the way that Cal Henderson does: like I'm an ornament for his amusement.

'No one told me you were pretty. And blonde? Different.'

I have no idea what he's talking about, but to make myself feel less like the latest offering on the Harvey Nichols food counter, I offer him my hand. He takes it gently, raising it straight to his lips and kisses it. Actually kisses it. And I can't help myself when he flashes those bright blue eyes, I get the oddest sensation. It's as if time has been caught on a loop, and somehow I've found the exact place in the universe that I'm supposed to be. I'm willing to bet that I've gone bright red. I'm so annoyed at myself. I pull my hand back as if I've been stung. But he just smiles in a way that can only be described as super-supercilious, before throwing himself down into his seat.

'Gors?'

Gorski looks up. He's pouring wine into Mia's glass, right arm folded behind his back as though he's just stepped in from the Café Royal.

'Get Sophie a glass of my favourite wine.'

'It's okay,' I bluster. 'I'm fine with this. It's good.'

Gorski hesitates, waiting for a word, but the *word* doesn't come. Henderson says nothing, just a swift nod of the head. An authorisation? Gorski exits.

'Great,' Cal says, shaking out his napkin. Smiling at me as though we've got some big secret joke to keep us warm all winter. 'Christmas suddenly got interesting.'

11

THE SCREAM

Thankfully, the meal is done and dusted by eleven. Six courses had come and gone. The portions small, but perfect: a neat stack of dauphinoise, a jus of something delicious, salad so fresh it practically had dew on it. Followed by a tower of berries mounted on an intricate chocolate stack. Each course could have been prepared in a Michelin-starred kitchen. Not that I'm an expert on that, but like everyone else I've seen a bellyful of photos in the Sunday supplements.

Over the meal, I discover that Beavis and Henderson met through their shared interest in collecting. Collectors, Beavis told me, gravitate towards each other. At the top of the pyramid, which is where I gathered he thought himself and Henderson were sitting pretty, there was a mutual respect; a gentleman's understanding that not all collections were for public consumption. I didn't bother to press. If there was anything more disturbing than the mask, I was glad to be kept on the outside of the *inner circle*.

I liked Clara. She had kind eyes and was constantly cracking jokes. Not funny ones, but she deserved a gold star for tenacity. Mia hardly made a sound. It wasn't that she didn't reply when I spoke to her, or wasn't polite, or at least polite enough, but her conversation seemed hollow. Even her movements were measured, nothing sudden, nothing out of line, as though she wanted to crawl through the evening under the radar.

Surprisingly, after his scene-stealing entrance and insisting I try his *special* wine, Cal shut right up. I got the feeling he wasn't worried about passing for *polite*. Occasionally he flicked me a – *all these other people are idiots* – look. To which I would double-blush, or jump awkwardly into any conversation I could slither myself into.

In between the awkwardness and the constant assault on the fine foods front, I found myself wishing that Geoff hadn't told me the – *one true love for everyone* – thing. A world with 7.7 billion people in, surely the odds have to be better than one on one? I didn't even like Cal. He's everything I detest. But then, as soon as I heard myself protesting full volume in the privacy of my head I realised – isn't that exactly how this kind of thing always starts?

I hang my clothes in the wardrobe, allowing my fingers to slip briefly over the dresses Sylvie's left. My meagre offerings have been taken from my suitcase, ironed crisper than cardboard, and arranged at the far end of the rail. In spite of the on point ironing, they are one hundred per cent the poor relations.

A silk nightdress lies draped across my bed. It's not mine, but the material feels new, and it's my size. Was it bought for me? I can't help feeling unnerved. It's as though the contents of this room have always been here waiting patiently on the island for my arrival. As though I'm stepping neatly into a placeholder that life/fate has created for me. Cal, again, those blue eyes, that dark hair. It's the exact look I go for. Is he my soulmate? The person I've been waiting for? There's an element of escape here that I like. How different my life would be if... No. The whole thing is so way off-mark. I have to get myself back on stable ground before I go inviting anyone else into my mayhem of an existence. Let's face it, I can't even manage a relationship with Jed, and he's as comfortable as an old armchair. Cal, on the other hand, is an atom bomb of a person.

I pull the nightdress towards me. It's like cool water against my skin. It is beautiful... but somehow, not quite me. I hang it on the side of the cupboard and pull on a cotton vest. I check my phone. The text from Jed is still there, anchoring me to reality – asking about Henderson. What is Henderson like? I could write a polemic on Cal, with a warning note for the women of the world. I could talk about Alfred with his passion for Greek archaeology, or the Doctor and his obsession with collecting. I could tell Jed about Clara, who had drank her way through a good bottle and a half of red, and who I left working her way merrily to the bottom of a dry white. I could talk of her husband – Numbers. Who, like Mandy on Media and Trevor on Tech, had somehow lost their names in favour of an employment description. Or Mia, with that mysterious air of sadness. But Henderson? A rich guy with a belief that myths were important in controlling society, and his own take on a Cretan funfair? I'm not one step closer to understanding who he is.

I cross to the window and gaze out over the garden. It's so peaceful. The lack of light pollution, and the absence of clouds, means that the heavens are on full view. As I stand looking out on to the moonlit courtyard, I can see why Henderson never wants to leave. I take in a deep breath, filling my lungs with the clear, fragrant night air before I pull the shutters closed.

Within minutes I'm asleep, falling, falling down, deep into a bottomless soft pit where there are no sounds, no people, just crushed-velvet nothingness.

Isn't it always the way? You have an amazing room, a fantastic bed, and you're tired as hell, but something wakes you. And isn't it twice as irritating when the thing that pulls you from the arms of Morpheus is your lack of attention to detail? One o'clock in the morning, my phone cuts like a knife through the air. PING.

All okay? A text from Jed. It's eleven o'clock in London, a Thursday night. He'll have called last orders and be waiting for the punters to down their drinks and clear out. He would know that there was a time difference, but he would have expected me to have my phone on silent if I wasn't awake. I don't bother to reply, not wanting to wake myself even further. Switching the phone off, I lay back in bed; my face disappearing into the deep, soft pillows. I close my eyes, and I wait. I wait as time yawns open before me: Sally-Anne is running through my brain, her eyes, her half-smile, her hope. She followed me here? Did I really think she wouldn't? I sigh and roll over.

I wait until I decide there's just no point, sleep is not going to happen. I let my eyes roller-blind open. My lungs pushing out an overdramatic sigh. Throwing the thick blankets from my body, I pull myself up and, heavy-footed, cross the cold tiled floor.

In the darkness of the bathroom, I pour water into the waiting crystal glass. Everything is at hand. Everything has been thought of. If I were to sneeze, I wouldn't be surprised to see Ellie materialise out of the shadows and wipe my nose. Leaning my hips back for a moment into the double sinks, I gaze into my darkened bedroom. I don't want to do a whole rerun on the *wows*, but this bathroom is practically the same size as my London flat. Ironically, I note that my attitude appears to have switched from 'isn't this life fantastic,' to 'isn't my life at home such a crock of shit.' It's clear as day to me now that I have been living in a rabbit hutch. Don't get me wrong, this is a great job; it will easily pay for twelve months of rent, food and gym pass, but what then?

My chances of going back to sleep slide steadily down night's plughole. Despite the time of year, the room is hot. Underfloor heating pumps out the kind of greenhouse-living a tomato would be proud of. I'm not keen on opening the windows; the temperature outside is unpredictable. I'm tired and don't want to be disturbed. I want to sleep. I make a beeline to what I am guessing is a control panel. In the dim light, I squint irritably at a digital gauge.

I could turn the lights on, that would help me see, but ironically I'm against it on the grounds that – it would also wake me up. I can sort of see. Besides, I have no idea what I'm supposed to do. I decide, despite my reservations, I'm going to have to go old school. Drawing the shutters, I open the window. A delicious honeysuckle scent wafts in on an ice-cold blast, and despite the fact that all I want to do is sleep, I find myself lured out onto the balcony.

Outside it is beautiful. Blue light bathes the villa, and the olive groves that I can just make out beyond the compound walls, cluster like dark shaggy sheep in the night. Everything is either dark or light; all colour leached away. Only the cold blue moonlight remains. I am entirely, deliciously alone in all this space. I glance at the plant trailing up around my window, dotted with persistent winter flowers. A pale yellow perhaps? Difficult to tell in the blue wash of the evening. I take a bud gently between my fingers and inhale. A light Jasmin-style fragrance fills my nostrils. This world feels and smells so good.

Maybe the job will last longer, not just a few months, perhaps a few years? Henderson is a man with an amazing story. I could certainly get used to this, I think to myself gazing out over the courtyard. Then a nagging doubt begins to gnaw. Yes, I could get used to it, but there was also Cal. Everything about Cal is upside down. It wasn't like I felt with Beavis: that I knew him from somewhere. I know that I do know Beavis and it's driving me up the wall. But with Cal, it's kind of like he's... part of me. God, what does that even mean? Despite myself, I feel my shoulders rise. I'm actually getting up my own nose here: how could I fall for... for that? The man is so arrogant, so entitled, and more... there was something in his words. Something in the way that he had spoken about me: almost as if... and suddenly I know what it is. What's making my teeth stand on edge. The way he spoke, it's almost as though I've been brought here solely for his amusement. Which is stupid, but...? Where are the other young people? Surely in an environment like this, a house with so much space and opulence, there would be others of my age?

Still, that uneasy feeling, I just can't shake it off. What did he mean when he commented on my hair colour? Blonde, he'd said, and then 'different'. Different than? He must have met millions of blondes. If I googled him now, I'd bet I'd find hundreds of pictures of Cal standing smiling next to multiple golden-haired women. So why would I be *different*? And why the hell does my heart race every time I look at him?

Suddenly, a sound pierces the night. I freeze, my hands gripping the edge of the balcony. It echoes for a moment, finding pockets in the night to ricochet off. Then, just as suddenly silence descends. Was the scream in my head? Could it be that my own brand of personal persecution has stepped up a notch? It was a child crying out in pain. Sally-Anne? No, that's stupid. The sound can't have been in my head. The remnants of it are still ringing at the edges of the night; a child's terrified scream. I feel sick. I shouldn't have come all this way on my own. I'm not ready, not emotionally stable enough to be globe-trotting away from my support network. I peer into the darkness, my heart thumping hard in my chest. Listening again, I strain my ears into the now deafening silence, straining till my ear canal feels scraped red raw. But all I can hear is the pulse of my own heart, pressing up through my body like it's about to burst.

I know what I heard. It was not in my head. It was definitely a child screaming in terror. But every second that the silence slips over the villa, settling the night back into sleep mode, makes me doubt myself. Could it be something else? Foxes scream. Do they have foxes on Kairos? They have foxes everywhere.

I'm about to shut the windows when the scream shatters the night again. This time it's unmistakable, a sound of such distress: a child in terror. It's coming from the far side of the complex: the north side. The main entrance to the labyrinth, that's what Alfred had said.

I peer into the darkness, my eyes growing more accustomed to the light, and then I see something, a shadow. Someone is out there: someone moving through the inky darkness. I lean out over the railings trying to get a better view. There is no way I'm going back to sleep now. If there is someone moving through the shadows searching for a terrified child, I figure I'm going to throw my hand in. If I help, if I can at last do something worthwhile, maybe I can put Sally-Anne to rest.

12

THE LABYRINTH

The house is locked in sleep. I find myself walking on my toes, trying to make as little noise as possible. I shouldn't, I know. I should wake someone: sound the alarm, but if I wake anyone they'll send me back to my bed. The journalist in me is reluctant to let that happen. The doctor in me should surely be able to cope with whatever carnage I come up against. Besides, I take enormous comfort in the fact that I have a fully charged phone in my pocket.

Creeping towards the door, my hands reach out into the darkness, clutching the large ornate handle. I stop, dead, wondering if the house is alarmed. If I pull the door open, will a barrage of security men come bundling out of the shadows? I glance up at the ceiling, scan the corners of the room. There's no blinking black box. I push hard on the door, the fresh night air engulfing me. Silence. So far so good.

I put the door on the latch, and as I cut across the courtyard to the northern corner, I offer up a silent prayer that no one is loitering in the vicinity with a crack team of weightlifters, a JCB, an empty haulage container, and a desire to abduct a few million pounds' worth of Greek artefacts.

The night air wraps itself around me like a cool blanket. My feet echoing off the walls of the villa seem almost surreal, sharp and insistent as hammers. Again, I press up on my toes. As soon as I reach the shadows, I swipe my phone to torch mode. Alfred was right; the northern gateway does look like a grand entrance. A rocky arch at least eight feet high leads into the mouth of a tunnel, the path winding steeply down into darkness.

'Hello?' I whisper into the gloom, but there's no reply. Whoever I saw skulking in the darkness is way ahead. Cautiously, I move down the ramp.

Over the years, I've developed a method of navigating from festival to car park. I count. Two hundred steps left, one hundred forward, fifty downhill, that kind of thing. It amuses Jed. He says that steps are all different sizes; they're not uniform enough as a 'mean' form of measurement. Yet, surprisingly, the steps are always accurate. Perhaps some steps might be slightly smaller or larger, but over time they average out. We all walk with a kind of inner rhythm and over maybe twenty steps or so the *mean* presents itself. As I achieve each distance, each turn, I recount, mentally mapping the journey. On the journey out, I am a cartographer, committing measurements to my inner map. On the way back, I simply have to follow. So in this labyrinth, just as Theseus pulled out Ariadne's string, I lay my footsteps. I have no intention of getting lost. The labyrinth, I soon discover, is a mixture of tunnels and walled pathways. The walls are always a minimum of eight feet high. So there's no chance of peeking over to get your bearings.

For the most part, there's only one path, and I can't help but feel I'm being led step by step towards an ultimate goal: a Minotaur? Suddenly I don't feel quite so confident. I remember the *something* that followed me when I arrived on the island. I stop short. I'm going to get nowhere if I keep spooking myself. Minotaurs are mythical. Might as well believe in unicorns.

Besides, it wasn't supposed to be a beast at the centre. Hadn't Alfred told me that it was a person's *true self*? That's what the seeker is supposed to be hunting for, but what does that even look like?

Mind monsters vanquished, I set off again down the passage. People just like stories with a prize: they like a pot of gold at the end of every rainbow, and a pub at the end of a walk. There are no beasts, no unicorns, no lightning-bolt revelations. Here, I have only a maze to follow, and somewhere, maybe, possibly... a child in pain. A child that this time, I fully intend to help. All I have to do is follow the path.

I've been going maybe ten minutes, only my footsteps for company, when I hear a new sound in the darkness: the gentle trickle of water. My tunnel opens out into a walled quadrangle. The quad is around twenty-five metres wide, edged with narrow gullies of running water, but this is no random rainwater overspill. It's all too planned, too ordered. Somewhere there must be a pump powering this 'effortlessly' babbling stream.

The ground inside the gully is covered in a chalky white substance so the entire quadrangle shines in the moonlight. Clever. I step over the water. It kind of reminds me of a footbath, the sort of thing you might find before entering a temple. Is this some purification ritual? The sound of the water echoes gently around the courtyard, and I feel an overwhelming sense of calm as I move away from my dark tunnel into the open garden lit by a harsh moon. I get the feeling that this is supposedly a place of peace, a respite from monsters. Or maybe, like in all good horror movies, the calm before the jump-out-of-your-seat moment. With that fixed neatly in my head, I remind myself that I need to keep my wits about me.

There are four mini-terraces within the courtyard. Each one is marked out with a smaller quadrangle of lavender, and each inner courtyard contains a small stone bench, flanked by an arch of honeysuckle. The smell of rosemary wafts gently into the air, tricked into action by the unseasonably warm weather. I remember the strong scent on my arrival at the terrace earlier and yet again feel my forehead crease into that vertical puzzle line that I'm trying so hard to keep at bay. Henderson had seemed oblivious to the smell. In fact, it had kind of caught him off guard. His story of the kitchens, the baked bread? I'd smelt nothing, nothing but rosemary. I bend down to the plant, run it through my fingers. Rosemary, that was what Aphrodite was supposed to be wearing when she stepped out of the waves. Rosemary for remembrance. Is the courtyard somehow dedicated to her? The smell blossoms into the air. The plants circle the pool in the centre. Just like before, each bush is short, stocky. Not woody as it tends to get when left to do its own thing. I know very little about gardening, but I do know that plants don't grow themselves in neat, cropped lines. So, this courtyard, well it's not exactly a secret garden. All of this must be on the groundsman's rota.

I glance around, taking it all in once more. Feeding each corner, I can make out yet another dark tunnel. Just like the one I arrived through. And then I notice, each of these 'doorways' is decorated to look like the mouth of a giant serpent. The more I look, the more detail I see. In contrast to the dark shadowy exits, this place feels more at peace, and yet... restless. Because it feels as though the moon is trapped in the courtyard. So maybe this is not about Aphrodite. The sparkling white paths, and the shallow pool directly in the centre of the quad, all of it leads to the moon bathing naked in the central pool: sitting like a proud queen in residence. I bend down towards the reflection wondering – is she ruler here or prisoner? Difficult to tell, but I don't get a chance to mull it over. The tranquillity of the courtyard is shattered. That terrified scream rings out again. Only this time, it's much closer.

'Hello?' I call. Silence. 'Hello?' I call a little louder. It makes no difference. My voice bounces aimlessly off the walls.

It's impossible to guess which of the serpent's mouths released the scream. There's only one thing for sure; it can't have been the tunnel I came down. I would have noticed if I'd passed anyone. I move towards the easterly tunnel. It's just a guess; if I entered through the northern doorway perhaps, I should be travelling clockwise? I stand, listening hard. Nothing. This is madness. Alfred said the tunnels were miles long. It's easy to follow a unicursal route, but now I have three passageways to contend with.

'Hello?' I call anxiously into the serpent's mouth. Nothing.

I can tell Henderson tomorrow, ask him to investigate. The night is getting colder. My overwarm room seems more attractive by the minute. It's then that I hear it. The noise is unmistakable. Coming from inside the passage in front of me, someone is walking away. I enter and begin to count my steps.

The tunnel seems identical to the first: the same height, the same width. It even appears to twist and turn at the same intervals. I quicken my pace, keen to catch up with my nightwalker. As I increase my speed, the footsteps in front also get faster. I break into a light jog, but almost at that exact same moment, the person I'm following begins to run.

I near a fork in the path. This is new. I listen, but it's impossible to tell which fork leads to my runner. If people are left to walk in a straight line through a desert, they tend to veer to the right. It's a behavioural asymmetry. Right tends to feel 'right' unless you're left-handed. But this labyrinth is a giant puzzle, designed to keep a person on their toes. I cut off to the left. No sooner have I made my choice than I know my hunch was correct. The steady pace of my runner echoes out in front of me. I have to push forward. I have to make just one last burst, but again, the faster I go, the other footsteps do just the same.

My heart pounds in my ears. My breath fills the tunnel with noise: whoever is in front must be aware that I'm following. So why don't they stop? Why... Suddenly I realise the sound has changed; the footsteps altered. I listen hard, slowing down, to lean against the wall, trying desperately to quiet my breath. Then with a sickening lurch of panic I know why everything sounds different – the footsteps are coming from behind. I'm being chased!

Isn't this kind of what I wanted? To catch up with whoever I was pursuing? Now all I have to do is wait and in a few moments, all will be revealed. But nothing about this feels right. My heart thumps loud in my chest. I can hear the pounding of heavy feet, thud, thud, thud. And then... something else, something so hideous it makes my flesh creep. A scraping. An intermittent high-pitched nails-on-a-blackboard zeeek, zeeek. Thud, thud, zeek, zeek. Thud, thud, zeek, zeek. Blind panic grips me. I run.

I can hear the thing gaining on me, breathing heavily. Thud, thud, zeek, zeek. Getting a little closer with each twist, each turn. Thud, thud, zeek, zeek.

Suddenly it's worse, so much worse: now there are two tunnels running parallel. There's no time for rational thought. I enter the smaller one, bending my neck awkwardly as I squeeze through. It has window-like holes punched along its side. Patches of moon stream in. I want to stop and look, but the footsteps are gaining on me, and as I sprint down the tunnel through the strips of moonlight, suddenly I see the shape of the thing. It's silhouetted in the half-light. Its shadow bearing down on me with each and every turn. I squint, trying to make out what it is. Shadows of dark limbs stretch and distort across the walls. It's bigger than human, and as I look, I realise with absolute horror what the scraping noise is: it has horns. Long, twisted, devilish spikes are being drawn across the tunnel roof.

Thud, thud, zeek, zeek. Those horns could impale a person with one twist.

I come to another fork and take a turn to the right. I have to shake this creature off. I don't believe in monsters. I don't believe in Minotaurs, or devils. But I do believe in fear, and fear is chasing me, filling me, spreading through my body with every thump of my heart. There's a small recess. I push my limbs inside. If the thing goes past, it might not notice me. Putting my hand over my mouth to silence my breath, I wait as wild thoughts scream through my brain; say it can smell me? Say it can hear me breathing, sense my heart thumping? Say it's lying in wait for me even now, plotting to trick me?

From the fork in the passageway, I hear the creature thunder past. I don't move. I don't get out. I wait in my recess until the sound of footsteps fades; till I know there's no chance of it getting back to me. Then, I pull my shaking body from my hole. Hands fumbling, I switch on the torch on my phone and begin to retrace my steps.

When I arrive back in the moon terrace, the moon is shrouded, hidden in the pool beneath a veil of clouds. I don't venture into the centre of the quadrangle. Instead, I hug the shadows of the garden, pressing myself into the wall. If the creature is still around, the darkness might hide me. With relief, I reach the serpent's mouth at the northern edge, when suddenly the clouds shift, light floods across the garden and out into the courtyard stumbles the beast. Its horned head held high, the creature bellows like a bull at the moon before falling away into one of the other tunnels. I run. I don't look back. I don't think once of the child I heard screaming, or my belief that monsters don't exist. I count my steps and fling myself through the tunnels as if the devil is on my back.

13

BREAKFAST

The next morning I wake with a splitting headache. It takes me a full five minutes to get to grips with the head-mess that is last night. It just doesn't make sense. There are no monsters, no Minotaurs, and why would a kid be screaming out in horror on this picture-perfect island? But despite the cast-iron scaffold of rationality morning normally brings, there's a cold chill running down my spine. I can still hear it in my head, that thud, thud, zeek, zeek, thud, thud, zeek, zeek and feel the hot breath on my neck as the thing drew closer. Nausea starts rising in my throat. I'm a mess. I grab an aspirin from my bag, chasing it with a slug of stale water from the glass beside my bed. Just hang on a minute, I tell myself, pushing my hands through my hair as if trying to root myself to reality by the follicle. There has to be at least a few threads of sanity here that I can somehow knit together.

I pull open the shutters. The bright light hits me hard, and my brain shrinks. Seriously, I feel it pulling away from the edges of my cranium like a poked limpet. But that's not all it does. It's on overdrive; throwing up images of the mad and macabre. I remember the beast, the shadows, the sound, the blind terror. I squint into the daylight, rubbing my neck with the flat of my palm as if hoping to cool some scorched imprint, but that's ridiculous. Even if I did see this... whatever it was, the thing was too far away for me to actually *feel* its breath. Yet even though I know all of this, even though I can rationalise at least some parts of the experience, I can't wash the horror out completely. I think of the beast lowering its head as if it's going to charge right at me; sink the blade of its horn straight through my intestines.

'For Christ's sake.' The words that were meant for brain circulation only, spill into the cold morning sunshine. What an idiot. Wilting with embarrassment, I glance quickly around. Luckily, the courtyard is empty.

Deep down, I know that there has to be some explanation. I may not know exactly what I saw last night. But I do know one thing: none of it was anywhere near normal, and anything out of the ordinary can usually be wrestled into context once you get the facts. That's what I'm lacking here – facts.

The courtyard below is bathed in sun, and all the colours are out: the terracottas, the green of the shaped bay trees, the bright purple hellebores drooping their heads demurely. Paradise appears to have returned. I am not complaining but it's ten o'clock already and the best part of the morning has been slept away. I shower quickly, pulling my wet hair back into a tight ponytail. My head, despite the shower and the aspirin, is still banging against my skull like a disgruntled jailbird. I'm not a big drinker, but a few glasses shouldn't have floored me like this, and a few glasses was all that I had. Something's not right. My wine, the wine that Cal was so insistent I got to taste, could it have been drugged? He barely gave me the chance to refuse. Not that I would have sent it back. It tasted amazing, but... drugged wine? It all figured. The killer hangover. The paranoia. Cal. It had to be.

I grab my notebook and head down to the terrace. One of

the few things I'd managed to glean from Ellie was where and when food happened, and I knew that the terrace was where I was supposed to grab breakfast. Not that I was hungry. In fact, on this rare occasion, food is the least of my worries. If I see Cal, I intend to give him a piece of my mind. But there were other questions, questions that wouldn't totally be sent packing by the fact that my young host was a narcissistic pusher. The scream, that had to be real. I had heard something screaming in the garden. Sally-Anne, I think to myself. She's always popping up in my brain when I least expect her to. But then... Sally-Anne didn't scream, not in the end.

The large windows that had yesterday been filled with flat slices of darkness are now full-on illuminated, looking like wide surprised eyes – throwing stark reality into the room. My head complains, but thankfully it's getting a little less insistent. I'm about to go out through the side doors towards the terrace when I remember something: the mask. I can still picture the shadowy beast of last night, not an image I'll forget in a hurry. Had the beast somehow been conjured up from things I'd seen earlier in the day? Isn't that how dreams work? Reality spilling like an oil leak into the subconscious; rearranging itself into chimaeras for our entertainment or horror.

Instead of going to the terrace, I head for the artefact room and there it is, staring out from its plinth: the mask. It's the same kind of shape as the beast in my nightmares. The creature was bigger, but one thing all nightmares have in common is the need to exaggerate. I glance around me. I'm alone. I know there are no sensors attached; I've already seen Alfred pick it up. Taking the helmet firmly in both hands, I lift it carefully from its mount. It is so much heavier than it looks. The wood may have the appearance of a kind of driftwood, but it's solid. This is probably a lifetime's worth of salaries for a Ms Average like myself, and then some. I turn it upside down, my breath catching in my throat; the helmet is covered in red streaks. Blood? I push a finger towards the spike, but then hesitate, unwilling to touch. Quickly I right the mask, putting it neatly back just as it was. I hadn't closely examined the insides of the thing yesterday. Possibly, the blood has always been there. It glistens as though fresh, but a glaze could do that. The blood could be an affectation. What was it that Alfred had said about the island's stories? Hadn't he implied that it was difficult to tease the fact from the fiction?

Suddenly the room seems to be closing in. Pulling its dark, black walls towards me, as if hoping to squeeze every inch of breath from my body. And I don't care anymore. I don't care who sees. I'm freaked. I run back into the entrance hall, standing for a moment in its vast emptiness. Only that brooding sense of danger doesn't evaporate. The vast windows open out, all-seeing, all-knowing, like some kind of sick smiling Cheshire cat. *For Christ's sake, Sophie*, I think to myself. *Get a...*

I turn sharply, not exactly sure why. There was no noise, just a sense, a sense that someone was watching. It's Ellie, standing in the shadows of the circular room. How had she got there so quickly? Why hadn't I heard her footsteps? She points, raising one long slim arm slowly, indicating the direction of the terrace. I don't even bother to say thanks. I need to get out.

The French doors are open, and the dining area on the terrace is only partially exposed. A low, clear glass wall protecting diners from the elements. I stride into the winter sun, a gentle current of fresh air proving a welcome contrast from the oppressive house. It's silly, an overreaction, I got spooked. I can hear the sea murmuring far below, and the air here tastes so clean: as if freshly minted this morning. *Beautiful*, I think to myself. I just need to make sure Cal doesn't mess with my head, and stay off the booze. There's a small table beneath a bank of patio heaters. Henderson's sitting on a bench, immaculately dressed, a scarf wrapped around his neck against the chill. A paper is generously spread open in front of him. In this full morning light, I can't help but be struck by how young he looks. He could pass for fifty. I think of my sorry face in the mirror this morning – the frown lines, the bags. I'm growing old without ever managing to grow up. Whatever scrap of immortality Henderson is on, I would love a bit of it. Slow the whole thing down, while I catch up with myself.

'Morning.'

He nods without glancing up. 'I hope you slept well?'

It's not a serious question. He's a man riddled with politeness, so he's not ready for my answer.

'Not really.'

Now he looks up, peering into my eyes shrewdly. 'Oh?'

But what can you say? *There's a child screaming in terror in your labyrinth. There's a beast haunting my dreams. I strongly suspect that your son is a pusher. Oh and by the way, I had a nervous breakdown about two years ago, so you'll have to excuse me if I continue to segue into the odd freak-out.* Best to stick with tailored questions and facts, avoiding all mention of the breakdown.

'Are there staff quarters at the north edge of the compound?'

Henderson shakes his head, but there's a quizzical look on his face.

'I thought I heard a child screaming.'

For a moment he says nothing, just lets my words hang between us.

'The island has peacocks.' He glances down at his paper. 'Not my idea. Something I inherited.'

Peacocks, could that be it? They do scream. But the sound... I was convinced it was a child: a child filled with terror. Besides, I hadn't seen any peacocks.

'Anything else?' He looks up again, scrutinising me carefully.

I think of the mask and the blood and my sore head and the sound, the thud, thud, zeek, zeek.

'I... I thought there was someone in the labyrinth last night.' This much has to be true. I had definitely woken at some point in the night and seen someone from my window.

He holds up one hand, silencing my stammers. 'Please, sit.'

Like a dog, I do exactly as he tells me.

'My door, Sophie, is open all night. My guests are free to wander the labyrinth if they wish.'

'Seeking their true selves?' I ask, the blood from the mask still at the forefront of my mind.

'Seeking... whatever they wish to seek.' He lets his eyes sparkle mischievously. 'The labyrinth, dear Sophie, will wait. It's stood there for many, many hundreds of years. It's in no rush, whereas us mortals, well for some of us, time is a little more... pressing.'

But he doesn't look like Father Time is hot on his tail.

'You, Sophie, were engaged to write a personal history. Might I suggest we start with my story?'

'Does the labyrinth figure in it?' I ask. Somehow I find myself unwilling to let the subject drop.

'The labyrinth figures in just about everything I do. But all in good time, Sophie.'

So I sit, drinking coffee in the morning sunlight and listening to Henderson. I am fully aware as to how privileged I am; this man does not give interviews. Which is odd because he's so open about his personal history. The labyrinth is something he doesn't intend to discuss until he's good and ready, but his life story; his career with its jealousies and struggles; the academic bodies, the ethics board, the petty rivalries, he seems more than happy to pour everything out into the open. And as I begin to scribble down my notes, I realise what a unique and valuable document I'm forging here. This is the kind of thing you see sitting in a glass case in the British Museum, or bought up lock, stock and smoking barrel with the rest of Henderson's archive, by some wealthy American institution.

'Class,' Henderson tells me with a sigh, 'when I was younger, it was endemic. Try stepping over the barrier, and they'd knock you back; the way you pronounced a certain word or how you wore your tie even. So many subtle, esoteric rules waiting to catch a person out.' He nods to himself as if remembering the minefield that had been a scholarship at Eton for a shopkeeper's son. 'But science...' he says as if grabbing the Olympic torch. 'Science levels all.'

'You understand it, or you don't,' I add.

A knowing smile darts across his face. 'Sophie, I really do think you will give me a run for my money.'

This is blatant flattery, and if I'm perfectly honest, I think it may have just a touch of sarcasm attached.

'Science,' he tells me, 'can never be just about social connections. It's about so much more. It's about connections of ideas.'

I scribble it all down, extra quick, in my own brand of shorthand. There will be TED Talks. I will be in hot demand. Everyone will want to hear my take on his life. I can see it now: Radio Four, *Start the Week, End the Week, All of the Week*. I'll be there, talking about this mysterious, reclusive man that I cracked.

I flick back through my notes, more for affectation's sake than for any sense of real need; I've done my homework. This fish is far too big to let slip through my fingers. 'You got a scholarship?'

'Two. There was Eton...'

I detect a shudder at the mention of the school. 'Then

Oxford. And now, I have two academic scholarship awards in my name. For disadvantaged young men or women, gender makes no difference.'

'Apart from the fact Eton's a bit of a boys' club.'

He stops dead, and I think for a moment I've overstepped the mark. Henderson's a man who doesn't like to be challenged. Slowly he begins to nod, as if mulling over the problem.

'Of course. When I set the Eton scholarship up, I think it was more because I wanted to stick two fingers at the establishment, rather than support the institution. I wanted to give other young people, serious young people like myself, access to opportunities I never had. You see, I had to focus, Sophie, from a very young age. No time for distractions or games. But then... I wasn't exactly well liked in school. It wasn't an easy time for me personally. Childhood is often difficult, especially for those who don't appear to be... how shall we put it? Playing by the same rules.'

'Tell me about it,' I mumble ironically, thinking of my overbearing mother, her daily etiquette assault courses and endemic snobbery towards Jed.

'Besides, most of the people who...' he pauses, 'made my life hell, shall we say...'

I write down the word *hell*: longhand, and circle it; Jo(e) public loves a victim/success story.

'Most of them did nothing with their lives. In fact...' and he snorts, 'quite a lot of them are dead. Seventy has a way of culling the unwanted.'

Culling? I think. I'm not sure most people would be a hundred per cent comfortable with that.

I look again at his clear, unlined skin. 'Well, you're looking really good... If you don't mind me saying.'

He waves his hand dismissively; he wasn't fishing for compliments.

'It was Oxford that allowed me to... get my wings. Fertility and gestation always fascinated me. You're dealing with the creation of life itself.'

'Like a god.'

He smiles, an if-the-hat-fits, kind of a smile.

'To be honest, the academic world bored me. It was the research opportunities that I valued. After my PhD, I left Oxford and set up the fertility clinic. Small stuff initially, but that was when the light bulb started to shine.'

'With Grayling?'

There's a flicker, a kind of tic to his eye: some sort of dismissal? A twinge of bitterness? I know things went wrong between Henderson and Grayling, though *what* is a mystery.

'Grayling was useful, for a time,' Henderson replies.

Useful for a time? I make a note. It's an odd description, shows a lack of camaraderie and stinks of a bad dose of built-in superiority. Priceless – is the word that sticks in my mind. All of this is *priceless*.

'And you're still in touch?' I can't help myself. I'm watching his face now for any leakage on the emotion front, but instead, oddly, he suddenly goes completely still.

For a moment I wonder if he's heard me. It's like he's frozen. He's sweating: beads of perspiration collecting on that sun-kissed unlined forehead. Maybe I've overdone it. I need to be careful; push too hard, and he'll clam up. I wonder whether I should go forward, or backtrack?

A fly begins to buzz around the table, hungry for the syrupy pastries left untouched on the tea tray. I flick it away. There's still no answer. Did he hear the question?

'Grayling? You're still in touch with him?'

Then, a look of what can only be described as utter disgust sweeps across his features. His chin juts out. There's a slight sneer to his lips as the beads of perspiration break into a small stream. Irritated, he wipes his face with a napkin. It's not hot, I think, glancing up at the patio heater, but should I offer to turn the thing down? I look around for the seamless army of help that always appears to be waiting in the wings, but we are alone.

'Grayling and I...' He stops for a moment, the sneer returning, and I know not to stand, not to fiddle with the heater, not to break the flow.

'... are no longer in contact.'

'Because of the fire?'

I see him bristle. I'm walking on glass here. All eye contact has vanished. I need to push lightly if I'm to find out more.

'You didn't reopen the clinic after the fire?'

He's irritated, but suppressing it. 'There was no point. Grayling made sure of that. We parted company. The work was the important thing, and now it's done.'

'Is it?' I ask, because since the clinic closed, there's been no real alternative. The NHS is painfully slow and underfunded. Most people can't afford to go private.

'For me...' he says, his voice booming, 'the work *is done* for me. I didn't intend to solve the issues of populating the world. It appears to have no problem doing that. The fact that people aren't happy with the distribution, well... that's not my concern.'

He's got a point: the IVF problem. The wanted and the unwanted births of our world, it was all one big intractable puzzle.

I glance at my notes. Time for a conversation shift. 'So then it was on to pharmaceuticals?'

'Where the money is.'

'I guess.'

'We make our own history, don't you think, Sophie? Freedom of choice,' he says, and I detect a touch of irony in his voice. 'Isn't that what being human is all about?'

'I wouldn't even try and sum up the human condition.'

Especially since I'm willing to bet he's thought about this a whole lot more than I have.

Suddenly, Henderson's hand shoots out, squashing the fly. I can't help it, the gesture was so sudden, so unexpected, I jump out of my seat. It's then that I notice his hand is shaking. Henderson clocks my gaze and pulls the offending hand gently towards his body. But it's still shaking. I'm guessing he doesn't like to show any sign of weakness? I'm about to question him a little more gently when a tall, slim woman appears on the terrace. I don't see her face; it's covered in an overlarge film-star hat, but the straight, angular lines of the body would suggest that this is stick-insect Alice, Henderson's sister. I am on borrowed time, and as if to second this, Henderson's phone rings.

'Ex...cussse me.' His words, I notice, are slurred, missing their normal, precise, clipped quality. A drinker? I wonder. He hardly touched his wine last night, and he seemed fine earlier.

He holds up his hand as if to quiet me.

'I mussst take this call.'

Again the slur.

Then he disappears off towards the house, leaving me with the odd sense that something's not right.

'Egg whites. Two. Pepper, no salt,' Alice instructs a maid. Not Ellie, I think, but I could be wrong. They're all unsettlingly similar: petite, dark hair scraped back, deep-pooled eyes that see no secrets. This Ellie departs as stick-insect Alice arranges herself on the seat beside me. Like Henderson, she looks as though she's in her fifties, but I know she must be a good ten years older, and despite being the younger sibling, there's something 'odd' about her youthful appearance. Her skin has an over-shiny, pulled-back look. She's had work done.

'You must be Alice,' I say, squinting into the low sun.

'I must, mustn't I.'

She certainly has the same features, a hard square jaw, deep-set eyes shaded by thick serious brows. But on Alice, it's as though her features have deflated slightly like an old balloon. She doesn't ask any of the usual things; did you sleep well? How was your flight? In fact she appears to have little or no interest in my presence, which is unusual seeing as she's the '*lady of the house*', as my mother would so hideously put it. Henderson had married only once. It seemed like it must have been a mistake from the get-go. A twelve-month entanglement with only Cal and a hefty divorce settlement to show for it. There were a series of affairs, a plethora of rumours, but nothing solid. So Alice is the only fixed female in Henderson's home.

'I hope it'll be okay,' I say, trying to engage her. She must have commissioned the biography, and yet it's odd because we've never actually spoken. 'It's only just under a week till Christmas. He has quite a story, and of course, he's a busy man. Will it matter if it's a bit late?'

'Christmas?'

I laugh. No that's wrong, it's more of an involuntary snort; can she honestly think that's what I've just suggested; proposing we move Christmas because it's a bit inconvenient?

'The memoir,' I state simply. 'I'm guessing you wanted it as a present?'

At this, Alice seems genuinely amused. She throws back her chiselled white face to such an angle that her film-star hat is in danger of pitching off her head. But like the true bit of hard-earned class that she is, she manages to keep the hat securely anchored.

'You don't think I... No. Dear Lord, no. He's the one that wanted you here. You'll have to dance to his tune just like the rest of us, I'm afraid. Join the carnival.'

I'm amazed Henderson felt he was lacking a little sarcasm at the villa. Alice seems more than competent in that department.

'My brother likes to control the action, play ringmaster.'

I'm not sure that I quite follow. I must be looking blank because she leans back in a bored but compliant fashion.

'When we were children, we went to a circus once, just once. Our parents didn't approve of frivolity, entertainment, even books in the house. I think the circus people must have given my father the tickets free. God knows why. He wasn't a likeable man. But we had ringside seats. I don't remember anything about it...' She squints her eyes, tilting her head a little as if trying to recollect, then sighs. 'No. Apart from the colours, red and white, the big top, and the seats, and the circus master. He kept cracking his whip and the monkeys, the horses, the tigers, even the clowns, everything jumped. In the car on the way home, there was some kind of argument. Someone had spilt something and my father was cross. He hadn't enjoyed the entertainment. I think to see all those people sitting in their red seats laughing, and not to get the joke. Not to see anything funny in front of you. I think that made my father feel very...' she pauses, as if trying to fix hold of the right word, 'alone. But Tim was full of it. He was so excited, telling us all how when he grew up, he was going to be the ringmaster. He was going to make everyone dance. My father beat him that night. I suppose you could say we heard a different kind of whip crack. The next day I saw the red welts on my brother's skin. It cured him.'

The silence is deafening. I can't quite believe that she's telling me all this, but then again, I'm not entirely sure what she is saying.

'I'm sorry,' I say hesitantly. 'Cured him of?'

She fixes me with piercing hard eyes, as though weighing me up. 'Frivolity. Though I'm not entirely sure we're not all, somehow, part of the Tim Henderson menagerie. Part of his circus.'

Is she talking about me? Is she taking a dig at my work? What I'm here to do?

And as if to underscore the utter pointlessness of *my work*, my notepad suddenly flies out of my hands. I turn sharply to see Cal, standing behind me grinning ear to ear, the errant notebook held firmly between his fingers.

'Come on. I'll show you the island.'

I'm not oblivious to the fact that Alice, lizard-like, squints her eyes, keeping them just wide enough to manage a disapproving look.

'Actually, Cal, I did want to talk to you,' I say through gritted teeth. My headache may have gone, but the memories of my drug-fuelled night haven't.

'Great. Talk on the way.'

'I'm supposed to be working.'

'It'll wait. He'll be hours.'

Cal glances down at my notebook, which he appears to have no intention of giving up. 'Ahh,' he pretends to read, 'born in a shoebox. Poor little rich boy.'

'It doesn't say that.' I jump to the defensive, but Alice, from her shrug, doesn't appear to care, and Cal is by now having his fun at my expense.

'You've had your Henderson twenty minutes. That's all any of us ever gets,' Cal says, dismissively. 'Come. Follow.'

And so I do, Cal handing the notebook back to me as we walk down stone steps hidden by bougainvillaea, to a neat row of polished cars; a Mercedes, a Bentley, something low-slung and red that I'm not convinced isn't a Maserati.

'Make sure you bring her back,' Alice calls after us. 'Preferably in one piece. He'll be cross if you mess her up.'

Odd to feel I've somehow slipped under 'the great man's' protection, which reminds me...

'I've got a bone to pick with you,' I hiss as I follow Cal past the line of cars.

He laughs. 'Very canine of you, but there's surely enough food at the villa for the both of us.'

'My wine...'

He looks blank.

'What was in my wine?'

He laughs. 'Grapes. I'm not clear on the exact process, but I think grapes is pretty much it. Maybe some fish guts? But they all have that.'

He stares straight at me, then nods, amused. 'Didn't agree with you. Is Sophie feeling a little worse for wear? Come on then. Let's blow off those cobwebs.'

The wine wasn't drugged. I know that. I can tell because Cal has no idea what I'm talking about. He's the picture of innocence, and I get the feeling that innocence would be a harder state for Cal to fake than any other. But if the wine wasn't drugged, what does that say about the reality?

14

CAL

I've never been on a Lambretta. Spend any serious time in A & E, and you get put off anything with two wheels big time. Yet, here I am sitting pillion, trying to stop grinning like a kid come Christmas morning. My night terrors have been put to rest. The wine wasn't drugged, it just didn't agree with me. The whole thing must have been a dream, a vivid dream, but a dream nonetheless. Besides, the Lambretta is fun, and even more so when it's being driven around an idyllic Greek island by a man like Cal Henderson. I know he's trouble, but I need a break, and it'll be useful to get Cal's take on his father. I want a three-dimensional picture, not just Henderson spinning his story.

Cal takes a bend too tight, and I glance down at my bare arms, wishing I'd grabbed my leather jacket before I left. An old biker gave me advice one night in the emergency ward. His leathers had been ripped to shreds, but apart from a broken collarbone, he was still standing tall. He said it was always best to leave a little leather on the road, rather than a portion of skin. A & E might as well be on the other side of the world and Cal is not exactly the most cautious of drivers. I should have brought my jacket.

Despite the charm, I'm under no illusion that Cal Henderson could be dangerous, and not just on the driving front. He is one of the most good-looking, spoilt, arrogant men I have ever met in my life. But... the drive away from the compound is just what I need. I want to leave last night's bad dreams as far away as possible. I could also do with some thinking time. There's something about Henderson that's troubling me; the involuntary shakes? The slurring? Something's not right. It reminds me of... We take another bend too tight. The bike leans menacingly. As we pull out of the turn, Cal laughs. It was deliberate. He's trying to scare me, but this is fun. I press my body tighter into his, letting the wind rush across my face. For the first time in two years I feel alive, and what's even more important – I don't feel guilty about it.

I hadn't imagined there would be much to see: this is a private island, bought and paid for, so I thought it would just be some small rock towering out of the Ionian. But no, we drive down and away from the villa on a wide tarmacked road through twisted olive groves. The island is giving absolutely no signs of running out of space. We're soon out on a cliff road. I hug Cal even tighter, hardly daring to look down into the blue waters below. After a while we drive through a picturesque village. About fifty tumbledown houses clustering into the lee of the hill. I'm a little surprised. I hadn't realised the island was occupied. A swanky looking taverna sits beside the water, its long glass windows creating a wall between tables and sea. The village is empty, as though it's fallen into a deep sleep and is waiting for a magical kiss to call it back into action. There's a village square, complete with what looks like a war memorial: an unadorned grey finger of stone pointing accusingly towards the sky. As if saying, *you were there. You saw all, and yet...?*

A yacht, the size of an English vicarage, shelters in the harbour. The name *Calypso* painted in a flowing blue font on her prow. Henderson's ship, I think, ready and waiting. Achilleas' boat is there too, dwarfed in comparison, but Achilleas doesn't seem to notice. He's washing the deck down, a look of love writ large over his face.

As we pull past, Cal toots the horn, and I wave. So Achilleas must live here, I think to myself, as I press a smile into Cal's broad back. With that kind of alternative close by, I really should be able to keep my attentions off Cal the heartbreaker.

Standing on his boat, Achilleas squints back at us, trying to place me, perhaps. Then recognition floods his face. He smiles a wide, open, easy grin: as though we've been friends for years, and I hear my name being called out on the wind. 'Sophie, Sophie.'

To be in a place for less than twenty-four hours and feel like you're home, feel like you belong: that's some strong magic that this island weaves.

Cal drops the Lambretta down a gear, and we mount the steep road leading us out of the harbour and along a winding cliff road where the coast is less exposed: the foliage heavier. The olive trees no longer bend compliantly with the wind but reach twisted arms up towards the sun. After another twenty minutes or so, Cal pulls the bike into a makeshift car park and kicks down the stand.

'We're here.'

Pulling my helmet from my head, I shake my hair loose and glance around me into the tangle of trees. *Here* doesn't look like much, and I can't help myself wondering why we didn't stop at the taverna?

Cal grabs a bag out of a pannier. 'Come.'

'What?'

'This is the best beach on the island.'

'It's winter.'

'So, I'll light a fire.'

He walks confidently towards the cliff edge. I feel my body shrink back.

'There's a path, idiot.' He laughs. 'I'm not going to jump.'

It's not often that someone calls me *idiot*. It's not exactly a term I like.

'Idiot?'

But it means nothing. Well, not to Cal anyway.

'I'm flying!' Foot to knee, his legs disappear over the edge.

I can't help it: the gasp is out of my mouth before I've had time to... but he's still standing, flapping his arms like he's about to take off. He chuckles, stepping himself back up again to my level; there must be a hidden ledge. 'You know you've got to do something about that.'

'What?' I ask uncertainly.

'Terrible lack of trust that you have.'

'Well, it's not every day I'm out with a reckless playboy.'

'Hey, less of the playboy. In case you hadn't noticed there's not much company to *play* with here on dull-as-ditchwater Kairos – retirement island for the insanely rich.'

There it is again, that niggling question: is that why I'm here? As if reading my mind he's right back in there.

'Don't worry. No. You haven't been imported for my own, juvenile amusement. Sadly, thoughtfulness is not part of his repertoire. He'll have some job for you.'

'Like a book?' I offer.

Cal shrugs, as though he doesn't seem to think this is very likely but then maybe isn't ruling it out completely either.

'You coming?' He turns his back and disappears slowly below the edge.

I sigh, taking one reluctant step forward. 'Wait...'

But he doesn't. I move cautiously towards the cliff edge. As I peep over, I catch sight of the narrow path winding down to the shore. It may not be as high here as the steep cliff I came up, when I arrived at the island, but it's high enough; maybe a hundred feet, no wall and it's all sand and scree underfoot.

Cal's already halfway down.

'I didn't bring my costume,' I call out after him.

'Sophie, we're not swimming.' He laughs and shouts loudly into the sky, 'It's Christmastime; the water is freezing. I bought this...' And he opens his bag, producing a bottle of Dom Perignon.

I guess it's a step up from sharing a bottle of Prosecco on a park bench, but this early?

'It's breakfast time.'

He shrugs. 'Then just wet your lips. We can throw what we don't want in the sea. It's biodegradable.'

Throw a bottle of expensive champagne in the sea? This seriously is a different planet, but I'm still not moving forward, still not taking one step down that path.

He glances back up, one eyebrow raised in a question mark.

'I don't like heights,' I offer nervously, feeling like a child.

I think he's going to say something crass, or dismissive, but no, he bounds effortlessly back up the path like a mountain goat and extends his arm out towards me, hand open for me to take.

'Don't look down.'

'I know,' I say. But my palms are beginning to sweat.

'Fix on a point, and just look at that. You never did ballet?'

'If you have a mother like mine a tutu is kind of standard issue at delivery point.'

'So you must know – to keep your balance you look at something fixed. Same thing here. Back of my head.'

He takes off his baseball cap. 'Just there.' He points to his tanned rugby-player neck. 'I won't let you fall.'

I nod. I'm not convinced I can do it, but you can't spend

your life running away, or sitting abandoned at the top of a cliff path, sometimes you just have to bite the bullet. Besides, he's got a nice neck.

Cal's right about the beach being the best on the island. I don't need to see all the others to get that. The water is standard-issue, Greek-island beautiful; flat, still and clear as a sheet of glass – heaven. The sand is almost white and set like a diamond inside a hug of rocks. He finds a small indent in the rock. He must have been here before; there's the remnants of an old fire and even a metal box with cushions, blankets and glasses in. I wonder how many other women have had the 'explore the island' treatment. But it's daytime, I reassure myself, and I'm perfectly capable of turning down any advances. No doubt Jed would bear witness to that. I've had a hell of a lot of practice over the past two years. But do I want to? If Cal makes a pass... It just feels so natural being with him. It feels like... but I know how it would end. I am just amusement for Cal. He's a sure-fire way to a broken heart. I stare back up the cliff face and feel a sense of utter dread – I have to climb back up. Romance be damned. Probably best not to have a fall-out.

'When I was a kid, I got stuck up a lighthouse,' I tell Cal later as we sit wrapped in blankets beside a driftwood fire, the bottle of champagne half gone. 'I started to hyperventilate. Some guy had to carry me down.'

'Not sure I could manage that.' He smiles. 'You think you'll fall?'

'No.' I shake my head. 'I think I'll jump.'

He laughs.

'Well maybe *jump* is the wrong word. I feel as if I'm being pulled to the edge and I'm not going to be able to resist. I know it's stupid.'

'Everyone's afraid of something,' he says stoically, and I

wonder what his fears might be. Having his allowance cut perhaps?

I run my eyes back over the wide sparkling sea. 'This place, it's like being in some fairy tale.'

He glances at me shrewdly. 'People should be careful of fairy tales, they're difficult to get out of.'

'True. Once you've seen all this luxury, the rest of the world kind of pales, well, apart from the peacocks.'

He looks blank.

'Last night, they woke me.'

He nods dismissively. 'They don't tend to come over our side of the island.'

'They sound like...' I hesitate. 'It sounded like a child screaming.'

He looks uncomfortable. 'Could be the...' He stops, the words drying on his tongue.

'Cal?' He looks away. 'You were saying?'

'Nah.'

Whatever it was, he's decided not to spill the beans. *Could be the...* The what? I lie back on the cushions, pulling the blanket around me and staring up at the cloudless sky.

'Is it natural?' He tugs at my hair.

'Ow!' I sit bolt upright, a look of utter amazement on my face. 'What?'

'The colour?'

Irritated, I pat my hair down. 'Yes.'

'No way.'

'I'm certainly not going to prove it. Believe me, it's blonde.'

'Unusual.'

'You said that last night. It's not unusual. You never been to Scandinavia?'

'Yes, but you're not Scandinavian.'

'You don't know that. Besides, that's not the point. Point is – it's not unusual. London is full of blondes.'

He nods, as if conceding that this is true enough before picking up a small stone and throwing it idly towards the water. 'So, Sophie Williams, let's talk about you, who's missing Sophie this Christmas?'

I can't help it, when he asks me straight out like that, the first thing I see is Jed.

'Oh, look at that, the lady blushes. There is someone.'

'No. Well...' How exactly do I explain Jed? *He's like a brother; I love him, but I'm not sure I'm in love with him.* Worn-out phrases from the cemetery of failed relationships. 'There's a guy...'

'Surprise, surprise.'

'Not a boyfriend. Not anymore. Not...' I find myself wishing I'd used a stock phrase. So much easier than having to genuinely explain a situation I'm not sure I understand. It had been all fine until... Sally-Anne. That changed me, changed everything. But that story is way too much. I decide to give Cal a boiled down version. 'Maybe we just grew apart. We met at uni. We weren't at the same uni, but we...'

'Journalist?'

'No.' I laugh. 'He's way too nice. Anyway, I'm... well, I was studying something else then, medicine, but... it wasn't for me. He runs a bar in Soho.'

'Oh?'

'Private members club on Greek Street.'

Cal nods.

'I don't know. Sometimes it just... It feels as if my life is a string of dominoes. There they are all lined up ready and waiting. Set them in motion – uni, mortgage, marriage, kids.' But my dominoes kind of went wonky somewhere along the line.

'The bored rich.'

That one makes me laugh; I remember just last week – my worries at not being able to afford my one luxury: my gym pass. 'Rich, I am not.'

'A good relationship, but it's not enough. A nice man, but you still want more.'

The man who I described as *spoilt* runs through a shopping list of my first-world failings, but he's hardly one to point the finger.

'Can I remind you that it was you who drove that Lotus off a cliff because you *wanted to see it splash.*' I'd done my homework.

'I was drunk when I said that. It was a harbour wall, not a cliff, and anyway, what are you supposed to say?'

'Never had that problem. Was your father mad?'

Cal raises one eyebrow, in a hard, ironic tilt. 'Tim Henderson pays other people to get mad. I've only seen him mad once.'

'About?'

But there's no reply.

'A lot of people...' I say, 'would claim that the man's heading for sainthood.'

Cal looks irritated at this but it's too easy picking holes in other people. When you've done nothing meaningful with your own life, you're sitting in a glasshouse.

'You say he's not thoughtful,' I plough on. 'But his research, his clinic, it made hundreds of people happy.'

There's a long pause. Cal's hand taps against his leg. There's something he wants to get off his chest, something that he's trying hard to keep down. I say nothing. Silence is the best midwife. Then eventually...

'People like him don't do anything for nothing; there's always a motive.'

'Surely, giving others happiness outweighs any glory/financial motive.'

'Happiness?'

There's a note of disgust in Cal's voice, and on cue, as if to match Cal's mood the sun disappears behind a cloud the size of a continent.

A sandfly lands on my hand; irritated, I flick it off. Suddenly it hits me. Henderson, I think – this morning: the fly, his shaking, the slurring. And when I arrived: the rosemary, the smell, or rather the fact Henderson couldn't smell it. And the sweating.

I fix my eyes on Cal. 'Why did he give up lecturing?' Turns out the journalist in me is never far from the surface. 'Is it Parkinson's?'

Classic textbook symptoms: lack of smell, sweating, slurring, shaking. I could be wrong, but then again... Cal looks uneasy.

'Your father had a muscle spasm this morning at breakfast, and his speech slurred.'

'So, have you ever seen me after a skinful?'

'He hardly drinks. Besides, there are other things.'

'You should drop this,' Cal says, his tone clipped. 'My father likes being Mr Perfect.'

'If it is Parkinson's it's not exactly the easiest thing in the world to cover up, not even on your own personal island.'

'Boring, Sophie. I thought we'd left Dad back at the house?'

'Sorry?'

The conversation is closed. Cal jumps up, spraying a wave of sand over my body.

'Come on; we have to scale that mountain. Get you home for another brainwashing session.'

He's walking away.

'Can I borrow your neck?' I call anxiously after him. Not

wanting to put too much distance between myself, and my only hope of getting off the beach.

'All yours.'

But he's angry now, and I make a mental note that if I'm out with Cal, I'll have to leave his father back home.

15

TRAGEDY

When we get back to the villa, Henderson is nowhere to be seen. I go to my room, grabbing my swimming costume and a thick towelling robe. The sea may be out for a swim, but that pool is just lying there empty and heated.

I take my notepad and pen; after knocking off a few lengths, I can haul up in the shelter of the terrace. I'd noticed an open fire out there, perhaps they light it. Luxury. I could certainly do with a bit more of that in my life, although I can't afford to get sidetracked. This is work. I have to get my thoughts in order. As soon as Henderson gives me the next invite, I need to be ready to push on with the story. No journalist has ever been allowed this kind of access before.

If there are other people in the house, they're keeping quiet. There's not an Ellie in sight, and even Cal has disappeared. I walk through the empty rooms, out onto the terrace (where the fire is indeed blazing) and head down the steps onto the pool patio. It's all laid out ready and waiting with cushioned sunloungers and heaters. It's too cold to sit out, but to dry off beside the heater is a godsend, and one of them is already flaring. Did someone know I was coming? I stare up at the house. No signs of life. You can only see bits of the villa from here, the back entrance, and I can just make out a small tower. It's from the inside that you really get the feel of the place. *Feel of the place.* Even as the thought flits through my head, I find there's something... something ominous about it. I'm not quite sure if I'm getting a feel for it, or it's getting a feel for me?

It's not like a normal house, not just because of the size. It's as though the building has been growing organically for decades like a fungus: putting out a spore here, a spore there. I get the feeling that most of its roots dwell somewhere deep in the soil. The labyrinth? The buildings, the additions, the tower, they're all new forms of fungi erupting out of... out of... something timeless. Something not so much living, as somehow not exactly dead. The thought irritates me. I've got a medical degree. I know there's only dead or alive. But then maybe with inanimate objects? Maybe that's all too simple. I think of the entrance hall. Its great 'surprised' eyes. The way, as I had stood in the artefact's chamber, the building appeared to close in on me, to crush the air from my body. A cold shiver passes over me, and I pull my bathrobe tighter.

Perhaps if I stay much longer there's a guest house I could use? Or the taverna. Because for all its beauty, this villa reminds me of a Venus flytrap: pretty petals resting patiently above a vat of acid.

After my swim, I sit in the screened terrace in front of the fire, flicking through my notes, and yes, I hate to say it, dozing. This is turning out to be way more holiday than work. At about two Sylvie finds me and tells me that we'll be eating at the taverna. An early supper, she says. I'm to be ready by five.

She hands me a bundle of pressed clothes: capri pants, a small round-neck top, a neat fifties-style cardigan, and a pair of slingbacks.

I laugh. 'I feel like your Barbie doll.'

'Not mine, my darling, Henderson's. And you watch out for that boy on the bike.'

'Cal?'

'He collects young girls' hearts. Eats them for breakfast.'

The thought seems to amuse her, and she walks away smiling to herself, swinging her hips to some inner tune.

———

Of course, the clothes all fit perfectly. So perfectly I get that awkward sensation yet again that everything has been lying in wait for me. It should feel great, but there's something more than a bit sinister about it. Although, the shoes are a bit tight. They're that kind of a shoe, but then I don't really have that kind of a foot. I go to the wardrobe to get my boots. It might ruin the crop-trouser effect but...

It's then that my heart sinks, and I feel my skin literally crawl over my bones; my boots are covered in a thin chalky residue. With a sickening lurch, I remember the quadrangle; I remember the white moon shining off the path. I remember the thud, thud, zeek, zeek, and the hot, hot breath.

———

I arrive in the hallway feeling shell-shocked, the ghost of the Minotaur rattling around my brain. Did that all happen? I'm standing around wearing the clothes Sylvie gave me, but feel like I've left myself somewhere else. The nightmare keeps skittling round and around in my head like a pinball looking for a way out. If there were no drugs involved, and no dreams, then what in the hell had I seen?

I'm quieter than before, although nobody seems to notice. Lifts are organised and passengers delegated. I realise nobody knows me here. Nobody knows anything about me, apart from (oddly) my clothes size.

I sit in a car with Mandy and Trevor. I would rather be with someone else. They're surface friendly, but perhaps not the best people if you have questions, and I seem to have a lot of those.

We drive off into the night, Mandy's perfume overpowering us all in the closed car. Musk, I think. Which always makes me think of rutting stags, and stags make me think of... the Minotaur baying to the moon, its horns glinting in the light. Despite the car arrangements and Mandy's overpowering pheromones, part of me is relieved that at least we're out for the evening. I think of that large house, closing in, wrapping me inside itself, digesting me slowly.

The taverna is the same one I'd glimpsed from the road. It's more impressive from the inside: a swanky, ultra-modern space. Designed with a nod to high-end taste, rather than rusticity: minimalist and chic. It has that mid-century sixties thing going on; angular chairs, clean lines, pale wood. A modern take on a jazz club. Part of the building juts out over the dark water, nestling itself amongst a handful of newly arrived, ludicrously expensive-looking yachts. As if the building is straining against its chains, eager to sail away on an adventure. The most impressive boat, the one I'd seen earlier in the day, is Henderson's – *Calypso*. It's moored directly outside. Unlike the building, it's facing inward: threatening to plough through the windows and join the party.

Our group has a large table looking out over the lamplit water. It's the usual suspects from the house: the Doctor, Cal, Alice, Mia, Numbers and his wife Clara, Trevor on Tech and

Media Mandy. But there are others, all of them 'professional' in some way, or linked through marriage to someone commercially useful. I work my way down the line, shaking hands with a tutor, a pension advisor, a banker, noticing how everyone introduces themselves by their occupation, their name getting thrown away like an afterthought.

'Beside me,' Clara hisses, moving her bag so I can take a pew at the long table.

'This place!' I gawp in amazement.

There's a live band playing on stage with a saxophonist who should be headlining at Ronnie Scott's, not pumping out sounds on the island that time forgot. 'And the band!' I realise I'm going to have to rein myself in: once again I'm slipping into *enthuse mode*.

'The musicians are imported from the mainland,' Clara says.

It's an ethnic mix of Greeks and Americans playing effortless jazz that makes it near-on impossible to keep your feet still.

'No one can complain on the entertainment front,' she adds, and I can't help wondering what *front* she would like to level the complaints at? As if reading my mind, she shoots me a shrewd look.

'So, how are you settling in?'

The question is just a little too inquisitorial. Clara's after something, though I'm not sure what.

'The villa is very...' I hesitate. The idea of the house as somehow alive, as shooting out spores and tentacles flits through my head.

'Indulgent?' she asks.

And that's certainly part of it, though indulgent of itself? Or its guests? Of that, I'm not sure.

'Indulgent, yes.' I nod.

'To be honest,' she lowers her voice, 'I find it a bit oppressive – all that *luxury*. It's a little – over-controlled.'

I think of Sylvie scurrying around the house, laden down with piles of clothes for the guests. Yes, *controlled* certainly hits part of the problem on the head.

'We live in one of the cottages now. Those bedspreads at the villa were so heavy I was in danger of being crushed.'

So I'm not alone then; in finding the opulence over the top.

She goes to fill my glass, but I place my hand above it.

'Too much last night, or at least... something didn't agree with me.'

She laughs. 'Tell me about it. You get what you needed for your biog?'

'Think I maybe need a bit more than a hasty half-hour.'

She smiles, a wry sense of irony twisting her features. 'Well, we all have to move fast to keep up.'

I nod. 'He's amazing for his age.'

'Now that, my dear Sophie, is one hell of an understatement. He's *amazing* for a man thirty years younger.' She looks over at Henderson, enviously. He's casually dressed, his figure toned, his hair neat. There's not a hint of the vulnerability I saw earlier: no shaking, no slurring, no sweating. I know from experience that it's all too easy to get carried away with your thesis and miss the important facts. I learnt that the hard way. So I need to rein back on summoning up conclusions when my opening paragraphs on the man are still works in progress. If he has Parkinson's, and this is a massive 'if', he must be at such an early stage; he may not even know it himself.

'I've tried to copy his regime – stave off those wrinkles,' Clara says, as she toys with her wine. 'But it can't be anything to do with what he's eating. I have been a good girl, Sophie. Done everything he asks. *Commitment*,' she says, a note of bitterness edging her voice, as she shifts awkwardly in her chair.

'Anyway...' She nods towards Alice, who's pushing olives around on a plate. Stabbing, then releasing them like she's taunting a kitten. 'He's not told Alice where his *fountain of youth* might be either. Alice's alterations are one hundred per cent knife.'

'Expensive.'

Clara shrugs. 'Take a good look, Sophie.' She sweeps her hand around the room, at the laughing faces, the fancy frocks, the smooth skins that should be twice as lined. 'For they shall inherit the earth. You know they do blood transfusions now? The old buying blood from the young.'

'You think that's what he does?'

She shoots Henderson a shrewd glance. 'All those *Ellies*. You can never find one when you need one then... ping. Mandy used to say... before Mandy stopped being fun...' Clara looks over the table wistfully at Mandy, who is head-locked in a no-smiles conversation with Beavis. 'She used to say that the Ellies were all clones.'

I laugh.

'I kid you not,' Clara continues, but she looks more than a little amused. 'I wouldn't put it past Henderson, nor the transfusion thing. Just wish he'd bring me in on the *immortality party*.' She eyes me up and down like she's giving me an appraisal. 'Still young,' she says. 'Let's hope he's not going to transfuse you while you sleep.'

'It's actually not that simple,' I say. 'It involves a machine the size of a small garden shed. Believe me, I will notice if he starts hooking me up. Besides, there can be reactions, and you have to be the same blood type, not infected...'

'Oh, there's the doctor.' She shoots me an amused, wry look.

The band strikes up a sixties R & B number, 'Hit the Road Jack'. Clara begins humming along, drumming her fingers to the rhythm.

'Clara?'

'Hmm?'

She turns towards me, her head swaying slightly like one of those ridiculous nodding dogs that people sometimes have in cars, and I wonder just how much she's put away already. She had been at the taverna when I arrived, so I'm guessing she's had a head start.

'I thought I heard something last night, a kid crying.'

Clara's head stops swaying. In an instant, she's sobered up. Her face, with all its smiling, flirty looks, is suddenly hard as granite.

She leans towards me, her voice almost a whisper. 'You've heard the story about the children?'

I can barely catch the words over the music; she's talking so low.

'No, I...'

She glances around checking that no one's listening. Thankfully, no one's interested. They're all enjoying the music. Hooking her bottom lip between her teeth, Clara leans in again...

'Hey! No sitting.' It's Cal. He pulls me around by the arm. The conversation is lost. 'Dance,' he says.

So what do I do? I dance. Not quite like a dog being instructed to jump, but I guess not far off. Though I have to admit to feeling a massive sense of injustice when it turns out Cal is brilliant on the dance floor. Money can't buy you rhythm, surely not that. Surely that has to be the one thing. Yet, the boy seems to have it all.

As I circle the room in his arms, I keep reminding myself that if I want to escape with my heart intact, I am going to have to concentrate on the negatives. Keep hold of the thought that he eats young women's hearts for breakfast, that along with the image of a bobbing sea-soaked Lotus, all that should help.

'You're a bit rusty on the dance floor. Usually, they're better,' he says as he pulls me into a spin.

'Will you stop that,' I say. 'Who are *they*?'

Cal shrugs. 'There's normally something "pretty" on the island.'

If it's a compliment, it's shoehorned into the strangest format I've ever encountered. I decide to ignore it. 'Clara thinks your dad's doing blood transfusions on the young: nicking their blood.'

Cal laughs. 'I wouldn't put it past him.'

I get the feeling that Cal wouldn't put anything past his father. I think of the dust on my shoes, the beast in the maze, and Clara's curious words: *'You've heard the story about the children?'*

'Cal?'

'You can't talk and dance at the same time.'

'I swear I can.'

He laughs again. 'You're just going to have to believe me on that one.'

'But, Cal, at the beach when I mentioned the child screaming, you...?'

He stares at me, a curious look on his face. We're no longer dancing.

'You started to say something...'

'It's a story, Sophie. A stupid story. There are no kids screaming out from the labyrinth. It's just things people say. Fuck, sometimes I think people like to scare themselves senseless. Don't ruin the evening.' He pulls me towards him again. The conversation is done but he's covering something up. I've caught him out. He's fallen mouth first into my snake pit – I never mentioned the screams were coming from the labyrinth, but my triumph is short-lived. The faces around me blur, as an icy fist grips my whole being. Reflected behind Cal, picked out in the long glass windows, moving slowly through the fractured reflections, I see a shadowy figure. His clothes are dark. He's slim and angular. I can't see his face, but I know from the way he moves, always in the darkness, staying just out of view. I know exactly who this is – death hunting.

'Lost for words?' Cal pulls me into another spin, and I lose sight of my spectre. When I twist back into place, the figure has disappeared. I stare into the dark shadows.

'Hey?' Cal's voice demands attention. 'You okay?'

'I...' I may be lost for words, but my brain has kicked into overdrive. What was that man, that thing, doing here? So I'd been right that day when I saw the reflection in the pool. He is on the island.

'Sophie? You look like you've seen a ghost.' And Cal laughs, as though seeing a ghost would be the funniest thing ever.

The music begins to wind up. I make my excuses and head back to the table where Clara's methodically working away at a bottle of vodka. All the time I'm looking at the windows. But there are so many reflections thrown up by the glare of the lights battling against the dark winter sky outside. Did I really see the man? Or was I simply projecting my fears onto a collection of random shapes?

'That looked fun.' Clara smiles up at me. 'He'd be quite a catch, though perhaps on the slippery side.'

'Did you see a guy standing outside the window?' I nod towards the dark reflections. 'Odd-looking man, wearing black, really skinny?' Crippled by political correctness I give a wide berth to an accurate description, avoiding at all costs blurting out the one thing I really want to get off my chest – that this man has something wrong with his face. In short, I'm not wholly convinced he had one, but Clara just looks blank.

'Dickensian-looking guy.' If I were to tie it down, I'd go for the Ghost of Christmas Future.

Clara glances around the room. 'Take your pick. We've got the cast for a whole novel.'

The band strikes up again.

'Are you okay?' she asks, noticing that my face has blanched.

I sigh. 'Tired, I guess.' I stare back at the window, the darkness outside, realising that some of the images fractured in the glass are so split, so morphed, you could see anything if you looked hard enough.

'Why don't we dance?' I say. I have to stop my brain conjuring up monsters. Having fun is probably the best way to do it, and Clara is fun. Probably one of the few people on the island I can relate to. But at my request to dance, her body curls back into her chair. She's not exactly jumping at the chance to hit the floor. They're playing 'Tu Vuò Fà L'Americano', which is impossible not to dance to. Its fast rhythmic beat vibrates through the air, and I'm desperate to get some movement, some life back into my veins.

'Come on. They're great.'

'They're always great.' Her voice sounds jaded.

'Clara, come on.' I get to my feet.

'I don't dance,' she says simply.

'How can you not dance to this.' I grab her hand in mine. 'It's good for the soul.'

'Then, I guess my soul will just have to rot.' She gives me a hard, sober stare. 'If you'll excuse me.' Clara pulls herself up from her chair, using the table as leverage, before walking awkwardly towards the washrooms, dragging one twisted, withered leg behind her as she goes.

Shit!

She's standing at the sink when I go in: the hot tap on full, gushing fast into a white ceramic basin. Steam rises in foggy tendrils: like dry ice let loose on a stage. I don't even let the door swing back behind me before the apologies come tumbling out of my mouth.

'Clara, look I am so sorry. I had no idea.'

She nods briefly, before glancing back over her shoulder at the stalls behind. One of the doors is closed: someone inside. Then her whole face does the oddest thing; all the sadness, the humiliation, drops away. She's standing straighter; her lips pulled up at the edges in some kind of weird painted-on smile.

'Oh, please. It's nothing,' she says dismissively, but her voice sounds forced. I'd seen how upset she was, and now this mask of indifference? 'You weren't to know,' she continues as she drags one finger across the steamed mirror.

'You must be enjoying the island?'

'Well... I...' The plastic delivery of her words throws me completely. It seems so unnatural.

'We're from New York, so it's just lovely to overwinter.'

'Yes. I...'

But her eyes fix on me, hard and unflinching. She's trying to tell me something, warning me to be quiet. She flicks her glance towards the mirror. I follow suit.

'Well, it's just...' I stumble because as I speak, I'm reading the letters she's so carefully written in the steam – **LEAVE NOW**.

Then I hear it. So loud and piercing, it makes my heart drop. This time I'm not imagining it: a terrified scream. Clara's face drains white. The music stops. People are shouting. The sound came from the restaurant.

Clara brings her arm back over the mirror, wiping the slate clean.

'Go,' she says quietly, and I'm not sure if she means 'go' leave the island, or 'go' get back into the room. Either way, the scream thrusts my emergency training into overdrive. I'm out of the bathroom, sprinting towards one of the long sea-view windows. Through the dark, fractured panes I can make out a knot of people outside, huddled beside Henderson's yacht.

As I hurry towards the door, a woman pushes past me from the kitchens. She's wailing uncontrollably, it must have been her that I heard, but now it's a mixture of emotion and words – everything in Greek. Although I don't speak the language, I can tell from the panic and anguish in her voice that something has happened to a child, her child? I follow her out as the crowd parts either side. Then I see it: there's a man on the jetty cradling a young boy in his arms. It's a bloodbath. No doubt made worse by the fact that everything is dripping with water; diluted blood goes so much further. The lad is maybe ten years old, and convulsing, barely conscious.

'Stand back. Get them back.' Henderson's trying to move people out of the way.

'Here, hold this.' He pulls something up from the floor. Immediately the crowd cowers; it's a severed limb, an arm. No one's touching it. The woman in front of me screams again. The note is so shrill, so bald and piercing; it's impossible to shake off.

'For Christ's sake, someone take this.' Henderson's furious. It's not his anger that motivates me; it's that sense of pragmatism my medical training tattooed into my soul. I move forward and take the limb.

'Apply pressure here,' I tell the man cradling the child, moving his arms up to the top of the bloody stump, forgetting that he may not even speak English, but he does as he's told. From his blood-soaked white trousers and shirt, I'm guessing he must be crew.

'The propeller, it was some weed. He was trying to...'

He's English. He's in shock, shaking as he relives the moment, trying to pull some kind of sense out of it.

'It's okay,' I say reassuringly. 'Just keep the pressure on.'

The Greek woman is still weeping uncontrollably. She must be the mother because she's fallen to her knees beside the lad, her hands gently touching his face, willing him back to life, but he's out cold now, unable to feel anybody's touch. The outburst is useful only for the mother. For everyone else, she's a problem. Death hunting, I think, the words running around my brain. I saw him – the shadow in the window. I can't help myself. I scan the crowd.

'We need to get the boy to the villa.' Henderson's words snap me back to reality. He's straightening up and moving towards the boat.

I'm not sure how we're going to haul the boy up through the labyrinth, but Henderson's voice has pushed a new dynamic on the scene. The shocked crew member grips the boy tightly and attempts to stand. Henderson is the picture of calm. He's not shaking. He's not slurring his words. He's in perfect control.

The man holding the child stumbles, Henderson pushes him back to his feet, literally pushes him back up.

The woman shouts something else in Greek. Her hands pressed together in prayer. I look at the man next to me for a translation.

'She's asking Mr Henderson to help,' the man whispers.

I suppose that when Henderson moved towards the boat, the woman thought we were all just going to sail away. She's pleading now, and I can't say that I blame her. We're on a tiny speck in the middle of the sea, the mainland is miles away by boat. Even a helicopter would take hours to get here. That limb is not going back on. We'll be lucky to keep the lad alive. I press two fingers against the pulse in the boy's neck; it's getting fainter.

'We need to get him to a hospital. We need a helicopter. Can we call the mainland?' I say. But no one's listening. We're moving forward in our huddle towards *Calypso*. I guess the surroundings will at least be clean. We can keep the boy safe until help arrives.

'For Christ's sake, get on the boat,' Henderson shouts.

'Alice?' I hear Alfred ask nervously.

'Now,' Henderson replies, as our tangle of bodies boards the yacht.

'We need to get him to a hospital,' I repeat weakly. I'm telling Henderson, telling anyone who will listen, but no one is. I take my phone out and start frantically quizzing the crowd about numbers, the nearest medical centre. Is it Athens? Surely, one of the other larger islands has a hospital? But I'm met with nothing but sheep-like blank faces. They're leaving everything to Henderson, and I pray to God he has a plan.

The crowd pushes me forward till I'm on the boat, still trying to extract information, but no one's paying me any attention. 'Hospital,' I mutter.

'It's in hand,' Henderson says simply, and his level stare tells me that, at this point, I need to shut up and get on with, whatever this is.

Leaving the distraught people on the pontoon, the *Calypso* pushes out over the water, the lights of the taverna fading behind us. I scan the boat. We do have the 'Doctor' with us. I pray he's not going to stick to his 'opening hours policy'. From the way he's attending to the boy, I guess not. I find some ice for the limb and pack it. But I'm still worrying: how the hell will we get the kid up the cliff? This is madness.

We sail through the black sea. The journey seems to last forever, but the boat is going fast, cutting through the waves like a knife. It must only be ten minutes before we find ourselves pulling up on another pontoon. The elephant cliffs stand tall above us, black-shadowed angles in the night. Despite the mayhem, I stare up at the rock face jutting high above and think to myself that this is not going to work, but we are all of us caught up in Henderson's relentless drive forward. In total silence we clamber off the boat, still huddled in our knot of horror. Henderson strides on ahead of us into the darkness.

'Come on,' he shouts back, not even attempting to hide his anger.

It's dark, and our footing isn't sure. The guy holding the boy is grief-stricken. It's only the Doctor and Henderson who are treating this more like an inconvenience to a pleasant evening than a life-threatening situation.

I trip on a rock. I'm not dressed for whatever it is we're attempting to pull off here. Eventually, I'd worn the shoes Sylvie had put out for me, and they pinch. My feet have swollen after all the dancing. Dancing? That feels like a different lifetime.

'Okay?' the man carrying the child mutters without looking at me.

'Yes, fine. You just watch yourself. I'm fine.'

And I am, for the moment, but if we are about to start our steep ascent up the cliff in the dark, then I'm going to have problems.

'I've got my torch on my phone, just wait...' I fumble in my bag for it and press it into action. But no sooner is it on than it's superfluous – there's a large clunk and a brutal bank of floodlights illuminate the night.

I squint awkwardly into the glare. Where on earth are we going? We're not even heading towards the terraced path. Instead, we're walking straight towards a deep, dark gully. This is totally insane. There's no way across, but Henderson presses a button on a pole, and a narrow aluminium-looking bridge comes down over the ravine. We cross. The boy is beginning to come around. He's whimpering like a wounded dog.

'It's okay,' I say. 'It'll be all right.' It doesn't matter that it might not be. It's more important to keep the patient calm. The boy continues to whimper.

'Hurry up,' Henderson shouts back at us.

The man carrying the boy is beginning to flag.

'Can I help?' I ask, but he shakes his head, quickening his pace as if he's under orders. Or perhaps he feels that this is some kind of bizarre penance. I'm reminded of plague doctors stumbling through streets, carrying incense and bodies. We are part of some macabre pilgrimage, tied together: a procession of death and destruction.

There are some stone steps heading up towards the cliff face. My heart sinks. This will be my test. I imagine myself sitting dejectedly at just this spot until morning. I can't do that. I have to be brave for the kid, but where in the hell are we going? I can't even see a path. All I see, all around me, is the stone face of the cliff, impenetrable and unforgiving. Then I realise there's a door, like a garage door, cut into the cliff. Henderson brings a key fob out of his pocket. There's an electronic beep, and the door cut into the rock slides up and over.

I've seen some curious things this evening: a strange shadowy man with a melted face; a warning written on a mirror; an incident with a young child maimed by an expensive toy, but nothing prepares me for what I find beyond the door. I'm expecting it to be another portion of labyrinth: a tunnel or cave. Perhaps some primitive boathouse? But in front of me, I see a long, sterile, strip-lit corridor. It reminds me of a hospital. It smells like a hospital. Only this place is far fancier than any private medical facility I've ever seen.

Henderson stops by a door; there's a keypad. He types in four numbers, and maybe it's journalistic nosiness, or maybe just luck, but I can't help seeing the code, and I'm going to remember it. Because, well, because he types in 1.9.9.0. – the year I was born. Maybe the year that Cal was born as well? But my musing stops short when the door slides open, and my jaw practically hits the floor. There's an operating theatre in there, and I don't mean some sterile surfaces, a bench and a few bright lights. This is the real deal.

In awe, I glance around at the equipment. It's so state of the art that some of it, I'm not even sure what it does. Henderson takes the limb from my hands.

'Out.'

'I... I could help.'

'Out,' he repeats. 'Just me and the Doctor.'

I head towards the exit with the other guy. The door slides shut behind us. For a moment we're lost. We're not exactly sure where we're supposed to go. We stand there awkwardly, covered in blood but barely noticing. We say nothing, till it dawns on us – no one is coming, and it could be a long wait.

'Maybe I'll go back to the boat?' I say to the guy. 'I'm not going to attempt the path up the cliff. It was bad enough in the light.'

'You're staying at the villa?'

I nod.

'There's a lift.' He points down the brilliant, white corridor. 'It's first left, then straight ahead.'

So Mia was right when she described the whole *coming up through the labyrinth* as perverse.

'I'm sure the boy will be okay,' I say to the guy, who's looking like he's going to throw up.

'I've only been here six months.' He sounds as feeble as a small child. 'It's a good job.'

'What happened?'

He shakes his head uncertainly.

'There were some kids diving for weed. I think it was a game? I didn't realise. I didn't know there was anyone down there. I...'

His face blanches.

'Oh God,' I say, 'the propeller?'

He nods.

For a moment I can hardly speak. No wonder he looks so drained. 'It's not your fault,' I say. 'And... and surprisingly, it looks like he's in the best place.'

'God, I hope so.' The man rubs his forehead as if hoping to erase away all thoughts.

I wouldn't like to be him. It was an accident, pure and simple. The kid shouldn't have been down there, and the poor guy genuinely had no idea, but I know all too well that guilt tortures the innocent, just as greedily as it lays in to the guilty.

16

THE BEAST

Back in my room, I get out of the capris. They're soaked in blood, and my top is ruined. I take it off and put everything in the laundry basket, then pull it straight back out and cram it into the bin. I have to push it down tight so it'll fit, but I'm determined to get it all in and close that lid. Like a kid, I want to shut the door on the bogeyman, on the nightmare.

I step into the shower. The blood has soaked through to my skin. Not so much red, as black. It's as though my body is stained, marked indelibly in some profound way. All this mess, all this trauma in my life, pretty soon there will be hardly any *me* left. I pump at the soap dispenser till liquid gel oozes through my fingers; holding me in a frothy cloud of orange blossom that seems totally out of place. Carbolic would have been better. Something, anything stronger: more medicinal. The black marks turn red as they chase over my body, down my legs and finally away.

The boy would be okay. Wouldn't he? He had to be. The arm would be lost. There would be no more 'games' with propellers. The crew member would be sacked. I don't even know his name. It wasn't his fault. He was just another cog in the Henderson machine, not for much longer though. Most likely he'd be leaving tomorrow. Trauma always sits easier when there's someone to blame, unless that someone is yourself. It was probably for the best. Every time he turned the key in that engine...

I step out of the shower and dry off, wrapping myself in a bath towel the size of a carpet. For a moment I stand there, dripping onto the mat. It wasn't the severed limb that was bothering me, not really. It was all the other things. The ones that exist in a place so much deeper than the purely conscious: the instinctive gut feelings you can't quite express in words. Those deep layers of understanding that tie you in to something larger than the personal. It's like that Picasso painting – *Guernica*, where you can almost feel the beating of breasts, the tearing of hair. Every mouth is held open in a scream or an anguished cry, and it's difficult to tell where each person stops. Who's responsible for which part of the pain? Which part of the cry? But it doesn't work like that. No one owns the pain. Everybody gets sucked into the whirlpool. *Death hunting* and I think once again of that figure outside the windows.

I can still remember the last night Dara uttered those words. It's not something I'll ever be able to forget. At the start of the shift, she'd said, 'Death's hunting tonight', and although I didn't take it completely seriously, I still wished she hadn't.

It was the early hours of the next morning; we'd lost four people in ICU, not all at the same time, but kind of one after the next. Sometimes it's like that in intensive care; you lose people as inevitably as marbles on a pendulum wave. Click, click, click, one trauma following on from the next. We'd cope with one set of panic, one raw and ripped group of relatives. Then the alarm would go yet again, and the dashing stampede of medics would fill the air. Life distilled into its essence. The only dichotomy that matters: Life:Death. Life:Death. Life:Death. Each moment seemed to be stretching out endlessly. As one by one the monitors would stop bleeping, carving silence into our eardrums with a scalpel, and time, like an elastic band, would spring back in on itself. I thought that would be it. Well, it should have been; my shift was over.

I was sitting in the cafeteria. The breakfast staff hadn't yet hobbled in. It was too early, still dark outside, keeping us in that womblike life/death bubble. Despite the fact that the eggs and bacon hadn't made it out of the fridge yet, the room clamoured with the taint of them. The ghosts of year upon year of fry-ups permeating the soft furnishings, plastic, walls, whatever they could get their hooks into, before clogging up arteries. Arteries that somewhere down the line, me and the team would have to unplug.

I had grabbed a coffee from the machine, the plastic so hot it almost melted in my hands. I wasn't drinking. I wasn't thirsty. I needed the coffee purely for the sense of warmth. I kept my hands circling that cup till the inside of my fingers glowed red.

Dara came up and sat next to me at my Formica four-top. The restaurant was empty, but in intensive care, we always clustered together in the gaps between shifts, close as grave robbers.

She didn't say anything for a long while, just sat there. But then, it was kind of like she sensed something in the air. She looked around, inhaled. Suddenly her eyes became more animated, yet they were looking at nothing, flicking forwards and backwards.

'Something happened,' she said. 'Something bad.'

And she stood up, pushing her cup to the side. 'Sophie, they need us.'

I wish I hadn't gone. It was the end of my shift. I was tired already. I should have been on the bus home. If only I hadn't stopped in the cafeteria.

Within minutes all beepers were bleating and we didn't need to ask what had happened; it was hanging out to dry over every TV screen. The sound was off, but the words have been inked in my soul forever. *Bomb blast. Clapham.*

I stopped *pretending* to be a doctor shortly after. Everyone said it wasn't my fault, but of course, that's a lie. A more experienced doctor wouldn't have made such a rookie error. If I hadn't stopped for a coffee, if I had been on that bus heading home, instead of still on-site, Sally-Anne might have been celebrating Christmas this year. It's a difficult one to live with.

After the incident I started getting panic attacks. Same kind of thing as the vertigo, only now the edge seemed raw and naked: determined to pull me over and down. There were too many pills taken, only once, but enough to make me realise (make everybody realise) I was slipping over into my own personal abyss. Nothing's ever quite as simple as the one-line excuses we dish out when asked. *I don't like sick people.* And know what? It is true. I don't, I genuinely don't. But there's always an iceberg of reasons under just about everything anyone does. Very few people get the full picture, they just steamroller forwards with you anyway, not realising they could well be standing on the deck of the *Titanic*, and if your backstory is bad, really bad, then it's unavoidable; at some point, you'll drag the whole shebang down with you.

I grab my laptop and phone. I don't want to sleep. I want to plant something else in my brain, so the corpse of that young boy doesn't go sprouting in my dreams. One kid's corpse is enough to carry around. Besides, the lad we brought to the villa tonight isn't dead – I tell myself that over and over again although I don't know that for a fact. He'd lost a lot of blood.

Blood. I think of Clara's ludicrous comments: Henderson as a vampire – stealing youth. Well, now I'm hoping he has got some kind of blood transfusion thing going on in that Batcave of his. It just might be the only thing to save the kid.

In an attempt to take my mind off things, I try Instagram, but the posts wash over me in a tsunami of the inane and vacuous. So many pictures of cats, along with smiling faces of friends on holidays they will pay for over the next eighteen months, with boyfriends who may well not be on the scene by the time the last bill rolls in. A few plates of food – some too healthy, some a ticket to a cardiac. Nothing that's halfway capable of dispelling the images of the severed arm I'd carried across the rocks. Nothing to put me to sleep.

Work then. I think. I'll sift through a few of those early TED Talks. See if I can learn anything interesting. So I set my laptop high on a chest of drawers and type in *Tim Henderson 1980*. The clinic opened in the eighties, but it wasn't until the nineties that it started to get results. The nineties was Henderson's heyday, before the fire, before he shut himself away from the world. I find an interview he gave in the late eighties. He looks younger, a little more hair perhaps, and dark brown, not the silver streaks he's sporting now. But still, the years have been exceptionally kind to Henderson. Whatever his secret, one thing's certain: money holds back the hands of time.

The clip strikes me as odd. There's something a bit 'off' about his manner, and I can't quite place what it is. I watch the video again. What is it that I'm missing here? He's younger, but he's got that unmistakable superiority, even though he hasn't done a great deal yet. He's talking casually about Grayling and their continuing plans for the clinic. He leans forward and takes a glass from the table, and then I see it. Pressing pause, I skim back and zoom in. There it is again. His hand. I enlarge it one last time – when he reaches for the glass, his hand shakes. It's just a fraction, not so as you'd notice if you weren't looking. But I am *looking*. I rewind and view, again and again and again. The camera doesn't lie. Henderson's showing signs of early-stage Parkinson's. Just like I'd thought this morning. I must go through twenty videos, from the eighties and nineties. In every single one, there's some telltale shake or slur. On one occasion he even fails to smell something in the studio. But there's a piece of the jigsaw that just doesn't fit: Henderson has early-stage Parkinson's now – forty years on. It should have progressed. Something's not right. Or, and I can't help but suppress a smile, perhaps something is brilliantly right. What if Henderson's found a cure? I'm grinning ear to ear, the horrors of the night forgotten. This story could be massive. If there is a scale somewhere of lives lost, lives saved, with this breakthrough I would tip my scale back into balance. Still wearing a smile so wide it's cutting long-term wrinkles, my exhausted brain switches to sleep mode as soon as I hit the pillow.

I'm back in the canteen. Only it's different. The strip lighting always seemed way too bright, but now it's painful. My eyes hurt. There's no coffee cup, but my fingers are still that odd luminous pink from having held something too hot. I rub my hands together, trying to get some kind of normal colour into them. Somewhere at the back of my mind, I remember I do have a problem; my skin's been turning different shades recently. Grey patches, I think, some kind of rot. I should see a doctor. I look up, and Dara's there. She wasn't there a minute ago.

'I don't have much time,' she says.

She's the same age as she was before, which is odd. She should have aged a bit, shouldn't she?

'I heard you left?' I said. Because the grapevine had at least delivered me that little snippet. She'd handed in her notice shortly after me. People got wind of her death-clock predictions.

There was an investigation; they couldn't pin anything on her, but any kind of investigation, when you work for the NHS, can prove difficult to shake off.

'I was a good nurse,' she says.

And she was, but the death thing was creepy.

'I failed big time on the doctor front,' I tell her.

She shakes her head, like it's not important. 'I came to warn you.'

A shadow passes around the room and I get the oddest sensation; my flesh begins to crawl like it's shrinking up over my body, sure as heated bubble wrap, yet Dara seems oblivious.

'You're in danger, Sophie.'

'What?'

Somewhere far away, I think I can hear something, something... running? Something big with massive laboured breathing.

'Whose story is it?' she asks.

'What?' I don't understand. Then the other noises, the normal ones: all the sounds that keep the canteen going, the air con, the heaters, the fridges, the hum of the coffee machine. All those signs that life is ticking merrily along, everything seems way too loud.

I glance around me, there's a dark shadow always just chasing off out of the corner of my eye, like the burning crawl on a strip of 8mm film.

'Whose?' She asks again.

'My story,' I say. But there's no answer. 'Dara?'

When I turn back to face her, she's gone.

A sharp haunting cry shatters the room. The darkness rushes towards me, and one massive swirl of black inky nightmare, a great hole cut for its screaming mouth, swallows me up.

I sit bolt upright. I'm in bed, gasping so loud it's like I've been punched in the stomach. Did I hear a scream? Was it in the dream or... I'm not sure. Peacocks? And Dara? I hadn't seen her since...

At the time I'd thought her pronouncements were spooky. Not suspect, she didn't do anything odd, I'm sure of it, but thinking back, her *gift* – guesswork? Probability? A rational explanation could rustle up the same kind of mortality odds. This was intensive care, not A & E. Everyone knew it wasn't a day at the spa. Then when the bomb happened, maybe Dara saw the TV screen with the blast, noticed it just before me? Maybe all the psychic intuitive stuff served some kind of personal purpose – made people think she was special and she liked that, but then again, maybe not. And now she was warning me about... I wasn't sure, and something, something hideous, my own fears perhaps, or had something really been screaming into the night?

I push open my windows and step out onto the balcony. Obediently, the clouds pull back, letting the full moon do its thing, but as it does, I hear footsteps. Glancing down, I can just make out a figure running across the paving stones towards the north entrance.

There is nothing I want to do less than go into that labyrinth, but I'm wide awake. I have no idea what's going on here, and one thing's for sure, Henderson's not keen on straight answers. So I dress quickly and make my way down through the darkened house. There might not be any CCTV cameras, but when I get to that central entrance hall, with its wide blank windows, I feel like a lab rat about to turn a million-dollar trick. It feels as if the house is watching, waiting, biding its time.

'*My door, Sophie, is open all night. My guests are free to wander the labyrinth if they wish.*'

Henderson's words come spinning back through my brain. 'Free to wander,' I wonder, or are they pushed? This is a man who believes in the power of myth: the need for stories to control. But hand on handle, I don't feel so brave. I'm remembering that beast as it shot down the tunnels. Thud, thud, zeek, zeek. Its huge horned head casting shadows. Standing at the threshold, I remain motionless, then it dawns on me. I'd felt the mask could well have something to do with my monster, and there's one sure-fire way to prove it.

———

When I get to the artefact room, I see the plinth standing empty: the mask gone. Somebody is playing games, and maybe trying to drag me into the funfair. It's the unknown that terrifies people most. The human mind has a capacity for horror that would give Stephen King a run for his money. But I've nailed my beast – one of the guests is wearing the mask. Alfred had said it was some kind of key. Like Ariadne's ball of string, it would lead the seeker to and from the centre and their true self. It looked like at least one person was taking Henderson and his labyrinth up on the offer.

———

I find the garden of the moon without any problems. There's a small alcove with a bench, hidden in shadow. I figure I'll just hole up and see what happens. I wait for around an hour. Despite being well prepared, I'd thrown on my leather jacket and jeans before leaving my room; I also wisely commandeered the throw from my bed, but I'm still cold and oh-so tired. It's been a long, very strange evening. Would any of it go in the biography? I have no doubt that it wouldn't find its way into Henderson's memoir. Henderson liked to be in control. But there was too much good stuff to leave on the slush pile. I know I have to do something with all of this.

Suddenly a child's anguished cry rings out sharp and clear through the cold winter night. This time I know it's not a peacock. It sounds utterly bereft. I've never heard anything so chilling. I may not be any closer to solving the mystery, but I am sure now that the cry is human and terrified.

The moon shifts and I move myself to another alcove; whatever is going on, I want to see it before it sees me.

I know deep down that if I hear the scream again, mystery or no mystery, book deal or no, I'm out of here. But the night has switched once more, it's now mercifully still. Sometimes I think I can hear running, sometimes hooves, sometimes heavy breathing. Mostly I think I can just hear the residue of an overactive imagination. I tell myself there's an explanation for everything as I press back into the alcove and wait.

Just as I'm beginning to think this is never going to happen, that maybe the person who stole the mask has found another exit, I hear it, a shuffling, dragging noise coming from the tunnel opposite.

The sound of heavy breathing fills the air, and I shrink back even further, as out into the moonlight stumbles my Minotaur. With antlers, it must stand at almost eight feet. Its sorry eyes stare out into the night. Its head hangs, overlarge and forbidding. But its feet are bare, not cloven, or hooved. Instead they're painted. The toes – a gel-glitter green.

The figure drops down by a bench, resting its heavy head, before two thin white arms wrap around the antlers, and with an audible wince of pain, the mask is removed, revealing a bloodied, tortured face.

'Mia?'

She jumps, startled and afraid. At first, she doesn't see me; I'm still hidden in the shadows.

'It's me, Sophie.' I step out into the light.

'Oh.' She sniffs hard, and I realise she's been crying.

'What are you doing?'

'I could ask you the same thing,' she says defensively.

'I heard someone crying. I thought it was a child.'

'A child?' Suddenly her eyes turn manically bright. She glances around wildly as if expecting to see a ghostly image of some kid standing in the moonlight.

'But it must have been you?'

'I don't sound like a child.' Irritated, she gets up and begins pacing around the garden, looking in the shadows for... something?

'No, but...'

Her mascara's smudged into full panda circles and there's a thin stream of blood trickling down over her forehead.

'You've cut yourself,' I say, but she must know that because the blood's running into her eye.

'We should get you back to the villa.'

She doesn't bother wiping the blood away. I see the mask, abandoned like a cheap toy by the side of the pond, and realise. 'You cut yourself wearing that thing.'

'It's worse for me. I have a small head,' she says pitifully.

'Mia, to be honest, I'm not sure anyone should be wearing that.'

She looks at the mask lying beside the pool, its large empty eyes staring up at the moon.

'It's very valuable,' she says but doesn't move towards it. 'You definitely heard them?' she asks a note of the clinically deranged in her voice that makes me shiver.

'Them?'

'The children.'

'I thought...' But now I'm uncertain. 'Henderson says it could be peacocks.'

'But it wasn't. I thought no one else could hear them. Looks like it's only us two. What do you want then?'

'Sorry?' She's lost me, but she doesn't bother to elaborate.

It's getting cold.

'We should go back,' I say. I'm not enjoying where this conversation is going. I don't believe in ghosts, but there's something eerie about that child's tortured screams. My rational brain is working overtime to keep panic levels at bay. The scream, it was so otherworldly, as if wrenched from some dark Hieronymus Bosch pit. Besides, I know that we still have to make our way back through the serpent's belly towards the house. Suddenly I'm freezing.

'I can't go.' She reaches for the helmet. 'If you're hearing them too, then they must be close. This is my chance.'

'I'm sorry, Mia, I don't understand.' I wonder how much she's had to drink. It can't have been a lot more than I'd had, but what with the accident I'd had to sober up fast.

'Let me carry that for you?' I reach out for the mask, but her grip tightens, and she pulls it towards her.

'Oh, you'd like that, wouldn't you? I've spent four years, four years looking for them. Then in you waltz and get everything.'

She's lost me completely. 'I'm sorry? Look, Mia, it's late...'

'Not for you. How old are you? Just turned thirty I'll bet. Immune. That's what everyone thinks. *I'm only mid-thirties*, all the time in the world. But that clock it ticks. It ticks whether you like it or not. Before you know it... it's all too late.'

Her mood has taken a psychotic leap from whimpering and wet to deranged warrior woman. I need to be on my guard.

'He'll be playing us off against each other next.'

'Henderson?' I say, confused.

'Do you want children?'

She's obviously *out of her tree*, as my mother would say. Where did this even come from?

'Not yet,' I say.

She eyes me fiercely for a moment before her features soften just a little, as though giving me the benefit of the doubt. 'Good. At the centre, there's a chapel. I know it. Got to be a chapel. To Aphrodite.'

'Goddess of love and fertility?'

She shoots me a look like I'm seriously stupid. 'Love? I'm not interested in love. I just want the baby. Don't you understand? I just want the child.'

And with that, like a wounded animal, Mia pulls the mask back over her head, lumbering off into a tunnel, leaving me staring after her bewildered. None of this makes any sense. If it's just a child that she wants, if that's what's driving her to distraction, surely Henderson has contacts. He could have referred Mia to some of the best clinics. He must even know of people who could act as surrogate. This man who could so easily have done something tangible, something good, has instead let a distraught, fragile woman loose in a maze to wound herself. *What's the great man like?* I remember Jed's text. Well now, I'm beginning to frame up a few answers.

17

THE SECRET

Next morning I'm up early, too early. Nothing about this place makes any sense. I am lying in this opulent *Homes and Gardens* bedroom, while my waste bin in the bathroom overflows with blood-soaked clothes. I feel utterly exhausted, and would seriously love to sink back down under the duvet, forget breakfast, cancel a day but I've got work to do. If I swim first, maybe, maybe that'll help get me in gear. I grab the thick towelling robe from the bathroom, a pair of Henderson-monographed flip-flops, and stroll through the empty house, all the time working things over in my mind. Last night wasn't just traumatic, it's turned this whole island paradise upside down. I need to think clearly here, because Mia, the labyrinth, even the boy, all of it could be a side-track. I've discovered a scoop which might just set me up for life and I have to hold on to the prize. If Henderson has found a cure for Parkinson's, and say he's using himself as a guinea pig, he would want to do the most extended trial possible. He'd want to be absolutely certain. There have been 'breakthroughs' before, but nothing resulting in anything like a cure. This could be the real deal. In which case, everything else in my life needs to go on hold. Maybe I've stumbled across my own personal Barry Marshall.

Before Marshall, ten per cent of the male adult population suffered with peptic ulcers. The kind of ulcers unpleasant enough to make the average life an unmitigated misery. The regime was constant medication and, a lot of the time, drastic surgery. Medics could see the ulcers with their fancy new machines, but the machines tended to be in the cities, so they made a connection between high-stressed city dwellers and peptic ulcers. But Marshall wasn't convinced. He felt the ulcers were the result of a bacterial infection. He did tests, tests that turned out to be pretty conclusive, so he tried to publish his findings. But the pharmaceutical industry wasn't having any of it – they were making a killing selling antacids and medication. Ulcers were a cash cow. Frustrated that people were in pain and dying from something Marshall felt was curable, he cooked himself up a broth of Helicobacter pylori, (the offending bacteria) then swallowed it. Sure enough, within less than a week, he's showing symptoms. So he puts himself on a course of antibiotics and just like he'd been saying for years: the antibiotics cured the ulcer.

Perhaps Henderson's also been self-medicating but then, for whatever reason, he's unwilling to share the breakthrough. If so, how long has he been doing it? It could be well over thirty years. That's one hell of a conclusive trial.

I dive into the pool, ploughing up and down, cutting uniform lines through the water. Swimming is my thinking time. Some people like meditating, or slipping out for a walk, but for me, there's something about the rhythm of my hands pulsing in and out of the water, and the constant pattern of my breathing as it forms large bubbles across my cheeks. It always puts me in the right place emotionally. It seems to engage my brain. Once in the pool, I lose all sense of time. So maybe my parents were right all those years ago to avoid beachside holidays; set me in the water in Cannes and I might well end up off the Algerian coast.

This morning, however, I can't help feeling that finally, I've found my true direction; this discovery about Henderson is going to make my name on the journalism front, as well as paying back a shedload of the karmic debt I fell into after Sally-Anne's death. In the light of recent discoveries about my host, the personal histories market is looking more anaemic by the minute. It may have been my initial ticket out here, but the scope of this story has grown. There is, however, a slight problem; I have to get Henderson on board. This is a man who can't be bothered to organise fertility treatment for someone who's been working for him for the past four years. The non-disclosure I'd been asked to sign before I even got on the plane, had pretty much tied my hands in silken handcuffs, but there's so much more on the table now. Now we're dealing with an item of genuine public interest. It isn't something that can be 'sat' on. Being here on the island, it's easy to see how Henderson might become oblivious to the outside world, but there are people in pain, families and lives shattered by a condition that might, with Henderson's help, be cured. And, if I handle it right, if I put on the charm, and get out my kid gloves, maybe, just maybe, Henderson will ask me to do his official biography.

I picture myself sitting in Waterstones, surrounded by stacks of books: Henderson's photo front cover staring out at the world.

Smiling, I pull myself from the water. A towel hits me sharp across the face – Cal.

'It's not compulsory, you know – this naïve glee about the millionaire's island.'

I take the broad stone steps out of the pool, wrapping the

towel around me as I head for the patio heater. 'Maybe not, but it's genuine. You know there's a word for people like you?'

'Just one?'

He's got a point.

He bends down to take a test of the water as if weighing up the possibility of a swim, but I can tell by his face as his fingers rest momentarily over the surface, he's more of a jacuzzi man.

'Freezing.'

'At eighty degrees? It's lovely. Better than Putney.'

'The squalor of gentrified living.'

'This time of year, England is all squalor.'

'So we whisked you away and put you on Prospero's island.'

'Who gets to be Caliban?'

'I'm sure we can find you one.'

'I hope not.'

Cal strides up the steps, handing me my robe. I slip it over my shoulders.

'Have you heard anything about the boy?'

'Doing well, so I'm told. The arm looks like it will be okay, but it's early days. Dad's flown him off to some private clinic.'

I feel a sense of relief wash over me; if the boy's doing fine, I can move on with my game plan. It's not just one child's life that's at stake here. Henderson's going to be a lot easier to get in a good mood if he's not dealing with an island tragedy.

'I should try and find your dad. This book won't write itself.'

'Don't worry.' Cal looks up towards the house with its blank empty windows staring out impassively at the world. 'When he wants you, you'll be found.'

'Cal?' I know I've tried once, but I decide to give it one last shot. I go for decisive. 'How long has he had Parkinson's?'

This time it's obvious: I've stumbled into a number one conversation killer. Cal turns away but there's something that doesn't quite sit right. If the disease had recently been diagnosed, then I could understand – there would be an element of shock or denial from the people close to Henderson. But from the way Cal's attempting to shut me down without comment, I get the feeling he's known about this for a while.

'Cal, listen, your dad looks like he's in the early stages, small tremors and a little slurring on his words, but if you watch the TED Talks from the eighties, he's in the early stages then. Okay, it's true that the symptoms are varied, and the way it progresses is unpredictable. But even taking all of that into account; it should have progressed much faster than it has. It's degenerative. The disease doesn't get better.'

'He has money to buy the best medication.'

This is a brush-off if ever I heard one.

'There is no *best medication.* Look, is he keeping something to himself?'

Cal's walking up the steps, as if trying to get away from an irritating fly but I know this is my chance. I hurry behind. Keeping my voice low, I grab hold of his arm. 'Listen, if there is some new medicine the wider world is in the dark about, if there is something which might help, shouldn't people know?'

'Your field of expertise?' His voice is laden with sarcasm.

'Not exactly.'

'Oh, I forgot. Sorry, you're a journalist, astronaut, medic – Jack of all trades, master of none.'

'I've got a medical degree. Not that that makes me an expert.'

'Just a know-it-all then.'

'I wasn't saying it because I wanted you to believe that I was an expert. I'm just someone with an informed opinion.'

Cal turns his back on me and starts to take the steps two at a time. 'Yeah, well...'

He's heading for the house. Once he's inside, I'll lose him.

I grab my clothes and hurry after him. 'Cal, listen, please? This is big. It's not about us bickering.'

He stops. I've got him. Quickly, I climb towards him, so I'm eye level. I want to be able to see his thoughts, judge his reactions.

'It is Parkinson's, isn't it?'

Cal glances awkwardly towards the house. There's no one in sight. He leans in. This is it, I think, he's going to confirm everything.

'My father...' he draws the words out, stopping to give me a flash of his blue eyes. 'Doesn't like people who snoop.' He shoots me a wide grin.

He's playing with me, but I can't let it drop. 'Look, Cal, if he has made some kind of breakthrough, however small, he needs to release the information. Maybe your father's afraid it's not stable, not fully tested, but with the help of the medical establishment, all of that can be done. In the UK it's around one in every three to four hundred people who've got it. Your dad's research could make an enormous difference.'

I stare deep into Cal's eyes, feeling sure that if he were to intervene, if he were to talk to his father, we would have a real chance of getting this story out.

But Cal throws back his head and laughs. 'You have so overestimated my father's feelings for his fellow man.'

'How do you live with that eternal negativity? Your father was amazing last night. He saved that kid's life.'

Cal just shrugs. 'He likes to play the hero, what can I say?'

I'm stunned at the sheer bitterness in his voice. I've never encountered such a sour, spoilt human being. I'm about to take him on when I hear a soft, heavily accented voice calling me from above.

'Miss Sophie. Miss Sophie.'

I look up to see Ellie leaning out over a balcony. 'Mr Henderson would like to work on the book.'

So Cal was right – when Henderson needed me, I would be found.

'Coming.' I clinch my robe tighter, knotting its belt. 'Does it matter, Cal?' I spit out at him as I climb the steps. 'I mean does it matter if your dad likes to play the hero and saves a kid, or if he is an actual hero? The net result is the same.'

That's shut him up, I think, as I continue up the terrace.

'Sophie, you're forgetting something.'

I don't think I am, but I turn back anyway so he can deliver another nugget of bitterness.

'It was his yacht.'

'So? And your point is?'

'Why was the kid sticking his hand into the propeller in the first place?'

'I don't know, cleaning it?'

'A kid?' There's a note of scorn in Cal's voice.

'Maybe a game then.'

'Game.' He nods, and I expect him to come back with a snide comment. Instead, he just raises his hands in a you-got-me gesture, but it's not convincing. Cal's hinting at something. Sadly, I have no idea what.

18

_____

BENTHAM

'The older I get, the more I believe society must be run on utilitarian principles.'

I'm in Henderson's office, surrounded by dark wood-panelling and heavy-looking furniture. In short: the place is ridiculously male. Henderson's been chatting away for around half an hour, and I still haven't mustered up the nerve to discuss the Parkinson's. There is a slight problem: the man is looking the picture of health. I could be totally on the wrong track here. Either way, I know I've got to pick my moment. If he has got the disease, and he's not ready to reveal it, I could be up for a quick return flight, no questions asked. So, for now, we're stuck neck-deep in ethics. It's not where I want to be, but by the state of his ready responses, it seems like something Henderson has a lot of opinions on.

'All societies,' he tells me, 'are anarchic at base. Think of them like bacteria; given the opportunity they live to destroy the host cell; take it down from the inside. Human beings often, for some reason, find this idea compelling. Young people particularly, they want to sign up to a cause. Need something to live for, something to die for. Doesn't matter what cause, they'll sign up anyway. Life has to have a sense of purpose beyond the individual. People thrive on fear and reaction. If there is nothing to be afraid of, they'll find something. Myths, legends, threats conjure up frameworks that can hold a person's imagination. Make the "story" compelling enough, and you have a method of control. You see, Sophie, there needs to be a membrane – a band around society, that can keep social interactions contained and functioning. Within this model, utilitarian principles could prove effective.'

I am so lost now. He seems to be advocating restraints on society, but these restraints are from the outside: imposed not organic. So, is he suggesting that society should be governed by some kind of superior hierarchy? The myth-makers? The storytellers? A hierarchy that we don't even know is present? *Storytellers* makes it all sound very romantic, but my guess is that this may well be just another name for old rich white guys.

I could do with Jed here for this; philosophy is a tricky bugger, and it sounds like Henderson's got a pick-and-mix approach. Which is bad, because I, on the other hand, only have a hastily grabbed smattering of the subject to keep me afloat.

'But utilitarianism, that's normative ethics? The moral action, and therefore the correct action, is the one that maximises the "greatest good", for the "greatest number of people".'

Henderson nods dismissively, not impressed with my brief stab at categorisation.

'In a nutshell,' I add.

'Nutshells, by their very nature, tend to miss out the meat of the matter. Utilitarianism may not be attractive as a *truth*, more as a tool.'

'I'm not up to speed on philosophy.' I might as well come clean. 'As part of my first year, I did a component on medical ethics.'

He doesn't look that interested. Understandably perhaps, after all, we're not here to talk about me. But even as the words leave my mouth, I realise that there's a touch of sadness about them. They bring back memories of a different time in my life, a happier time. My first year; that quick course in philosophy, that was when I met Jed.

It was a day trip to Cambridge, organised by a few of the Russell Group unis; a rare treat away from the hospital grind. I always put my name down for any of the jollies, away from sickbeds. The lecture was on biomedical ethics and the status of the foetus. I'd planned to get some shopping done in the town later. I was looking for a handbag to match a pair of shoes I'd bought in a sale. The lecture overran, so I decided to fake sickness. I could have chosen anything; a train I had to catch, a dinner engagement with a friend. I'm a lousy liar but the one thing I do know is that people unpractised in the arts of deception tend to overblow their hand. So I kept mine simple. It was just a passing comment as I flew out of the lecture room, thrown to this tall skinny undergrad with bright blue eyes; the guy who had been standing sentry on the door, ushering in, ushering out.

'Sorry,' I whispered. 'Not feeling too good.'

And he followed me out. The look on his face bursting with such genuine concern that I felt I had to keep faking. So, we sat on a bench in the sunshine, and he fetched me a glass of water. The lecture had just got to the subject of termination. Apparently, he'd been warned that sometimes people, for *people* I guess they meant women, can find this subject distressing. I wanted to assure him that my story was simple; something along the lines of a dodgy curry from the night before. I didn't think the idea of a cheap handbag lying dolefully in one of the local shops was going to cut me any slack. So, I launched in with how the foetus was just a cluster of cells, not a human until its first cry.

I'd been through this before: the whole justification thing, only on a *for real* front, rather than as a *hypothetical* luxury. It was just before I started uni. A close friend got 'caught-out'. So that day of the abortive abortion lecture, I told Jed exactly what my friend and I had told ourselves: abortion should be as easy as having your hair cut. The foetus was not a child, but Jed wasn't so sure. He pointed out that some actions have bigger consequences; they have ripples.

Turned out, Jed was an unwanted cluster of cells himself. He was literally the baby left on the vicarage doorstep. Only it was a nursery school in Jed's case. He still carried a key ring with a thread from the blanket he'd been wrapped in. Despite his shaky start, or perhaps because of it, Jed turned out to be one of the most grounded people I'd ever met.

Difficult decisions, he claimed, were an essential part of life. In fact, they were what life was all about, and he brought me back to my initial throwaway line – *having your hair cut* – shouldn't have life-altering consequences. I think it was then that I fell in love with him, sitting on that bench in the Cambridge sunshine as the shops closed their doors on the last customers, pushed around the hoover, and turned off the lights.

I went on to miss the bus home, and eventually I would go on to *miss* getting an extra credit for the course. But none of that mattered. In Cambridge, all those years ago, Jed smuggled me into his halls. When I woke the next morning to the sound of bells, my body wrapped loosely in his old shirt, and tea being cooked on a Primus stove, I thought to myself – this is it.

After that first date, we met up most weekends. Or at least those when I didn't have to look after sick people, or get roped into A & E slave labour. He took me along to a couple of lectures at the Royal Institute of Philosophy. Most of them made my brain ache. I like concrete problems to solve, not angels dancing on pins, hypothetical cats in boxes and trees falling in forests with nobody around to push or hear. But I liked him. No, I loved him. Love him? So why did I break the whole thing off? Because I'm not that woman anymore – after I saw Sally-Anne die because of my stupidity, I changed. I had to. I had to stop feeling; feeling is dangerous. It's unpredictable. If you feel too much you leave your soul raw. I built a protective wall around me and shut everyone out. Especially Jed. I stopped feeling so effectively, that now (leaving aside one quick Lambretta jaunt around the island) I'm not sure I even know how to start again.

Besides, Jed is somehow bound up with all the rubbish, all the sorrow. I want to cut away the dead in me, all the canker-infested bad bits, but they're in him too now.

I suddenly realise I've been sitting in Henderson's man cave, notepad in hand, curiously absent.

'I have a friend who studied philosophy,' I bluster, lamely: the word 'friend' catching in my throat like a large brick. I've reduced Jed to a generalised nothing, but I needed to excuse my silence. I have to get on with dissecting Henderson. This is my job. This is very much part of my *fresh start*. So I throw in a philosophical curiosity for good measure. 'I met Mr Bentham once.'

A smile flickers across Henderson's face. Is it amusement?

'Mr Bentham was a man after my own heart – unwilling to leave the party.'

'That's one way of describing it.'

Jeremy Bentham: philosopher, 18th and early 19th century. Tutor to John Stuart Mill, and founder of the philosophical school of Utilitarianism. He was most definitely a man unwilling to 'leave the party', as Henderson so neatly put it.

After his death, Bentham had his body embalmed and exhibited at University College London.

But… and suddenly the cogs in my brain begin to whir. Maybe there's something deeper here. I wonder if Henderson's idea of *not leaving the party* refers to his own ability to stave off Parkinson's? This is my chance. I lean forward in my chair, about to ask my *Times* bestseller question – how has he put the brakes on a disease that has no known cure?

'A tad macabre though: Bentham, locked in a glass case.'

We're back on Jeremy. I have to follow through. 'I guess when you've contributed so much to life, I suppose it becomes difficult to…'

'But the important thing is, he has no active voice.'

I realise with a sudden heart-sink that we're back on philosophy. Existentialism, if I had to take a stab.

Like a man who has all the time in the world, Henderson moves slowly towards the floor-to-ceiling bookshelf running one length of the study walls and takes down a large volume.

'Of course, there are his books.'

He places a first edition of Bentham's *On Liberty* in front of me. I flick to the front pages. It's a first edition, signed, but then that's kind of what I would expect on a no-holds-barred island.

'The books are now used as a platform for debate, a learning tool, a stepladder. Whereas, Bentham's body contributes… nothing. He has lost his voice.'

Flicking through another book, Henderson finds a page with a picture of Jeremy in his glass cage, leaving it open on the desk in front of me – a guy with a long face wearing a frilly shirt, plus fours and a straw hat.

'He has become an oddity.'

Henderson has a point, Bentham is looking the personification of *odd*, but I have to say, I do feel a bit sorry for him. It must be difficult to know what to wear in that kind of... situation.

'Is he the only person to be...' and I struggle over the word, it seems so inappropriate, 'stuffed?'

Henderson shrugs. 'No doubt there are others, hidden away in people's attics. The Victorians had a passion for taxidermy. There are a few Buddhist monks, apparently. He's certainly not unique.'

I stare at the picture again, the overdressed middle-aged man sitting in a TARDIS-like box with a Mona Lisa-style smile hovering somewhere around his lips.

'You have to admit; he looks pretty good for... How old is he now?' I ask casually as if asking the age of a favourite uncle, 'A hundred and fifty?'

'In his current form, thereabouts. Not his own head though, and that does give him an unfair advantage.'

'Buying youth and immortality,' I say, wondering if Henderson will bite.

'But reducing yourself to an object.' There's a note of disgust in his voice. Then he smiles knowingly. 'Soon there will be people who live longer than others.'

Yes! I think. This could be what I'm waiting for.

'It's a good thing, Sophie, a very good thing. It will allow for a more stable society. But...' Henderson nods thoughtfully to himself, ' ...this extended life will not be through random genetics or bizarre circus tricks.'

I notice there's a hard edge to his voice, a kind of bitter entitlement that would have got right up Bentham's nose.

'So who?' I ask, but I think I know the answer to that already. I just need him to spell it out. Maybe this is why he's so reluctant to broadcast his *potential* cure. Henderson's not interested in the masses. His utilitarianism doesn't include him as a participant, more as a benefactor perhaps? Is he advocating some kind of power-elite skimming off the best from the minions below?

'People are already living longer, and do you know what single overriding factor all these people have?'

'Exercise and diet.' It's out of my mouth before I've had time to engage my brain: one of the mantras we were taught at med school.

Henderson looks at me with a note of derision in his eyes. This is not a man who likes rote answers. Derision or disgust? I'm not sure, but my trite reply may have, in fact, worked to my advantage. Perhaps I have said the 'wrong' thing, but I've pushed him out of his shell, and he's going to want to show off. He may be a recluse, but I get the feeling Henderson is a man who likes an audience.

'Money, Sophie. It's only ever about money. You, for example, your good diet, the fact that you exercise, you look after yourself, you could have bought yourself an extra fifteen years more than your Glaswegian, fried Mars bar-scoffing, sofa-surfing doppelganger. But there's only so much more elbow room you personally can gain. For those who have unlimited funds, on the other hand, they can expect a doubled lifespan in the next thirty years. So, say that takes me, for example, to one hundred and forty.'

I wonder if he can still eat the fried Mars bars and get the same results? But know not to comment.

'Yes, a hundred and forty easily. Unfortunately, I shan't be sharing my retirement with intellectuals. No, sadly not. I will be sharing it with business entrepreneurs, Russian oligarchs, a few celebs and…' he sneers in disgust, 'the third-generation wasters: the uneducated, unworked, filthy rich.'

People like Cal? I wonder.

'Luckily,' and a smile breaks out over his face, 'I have always selected those I let into my inner circle. This little island of mine, Sophie, it's so much more than meets the eye, always has been. Greece has a tradition of sorting the weak from the strong. Take the Spartans: once a year the Spartan youths were given license to cull as many of their slaves as they chose. Actively encouraged. Purge, isn't that what they call it in that terrible film? Only this purge was for real.'

I'm amazed he's heard of the film. I can't think that popular culture would be his thing, but I say nothing.

'Take those much admired ancient Athenians, they left their sick babies outside of the city to die. And of course Minos had his games. His beast *might* be mythical, but I'm willing to wager the tradition of brutality isn't. People claim Greece is the cradle of democracy, but that *democracy* was highly selective. Some of us are *more equal than others*, isn't that right?'

He knows his Orwell.

'There are always worlds within worlds, Sophie. It's inevitable. Perhaps that's why I love this island so much; if you want to control something, you need to start off small. Here I can create my own perfect world. Test those who want entry. I have wealth at my disposal and a long life ahead of me.'

He fixes me with hard steely eyes. 'I shall need some source of entertainment.'

'But money can't buy you life.' I find myself blustering the blatantly obvious. 'It can buy you comfort. It can buy you the best medical attention. But love and life, that's beyond its remit.'

He looks amused. 'Money, Sophie my dear, will buy a person anything.'

I'm about to cite Steve Jobs; I think he'd have an opinion on all of this, when Henderson holds up a single finger to silence me.

'It's true some people will be unlucky, drop out of the game early, but for the lucky few... provided a person has enough money, and by enough, I mean more zeroes that most people can hold in their heads, life, the world, the universe perhaps, it's your oyster. Imagine what you could accrue, Sophie, if you doubled your lifespan, the knowledge, the real estate, the power.'

I'm not entirely sure where this is going, but from a journalistic point of view, he's giving me more solid character foibles and quirks than I could have got from throwing him into the *Big Brother* household.

Carefully, he puts Bentham's book back on the shelf. 'Of course, there was a reason behind Mr Bentham's little stunt. He led the way for modern surgeons; placing the human body, not so much on a pedestal as on a dissecting table. Southwood Smith's experiments in mummification were primitive. Hence the missing head.'

I shrug. 'Everything has its price, especially immortality.'

Henderson smiles, a thin, tired-looking smile, and suddenly he looks pale, almost luminous. 'I get so worn down by stupid people, Sophie.'

I'm a medical dropout, a journalistic failure and my personal life is in as much coherent shape as a failed dockyard development in Ipswich, I'm hardly an ally against *the stupid*.

'I'll take that as a compliment,' I say, brushing the praise under the carpet.

'You handled yesterday evening well.'

Did I? I guess so. The boy's all right after all.

'I can always do with good people on my team and your medical knowledge...'

'I don't practice anymore.' It comes out of my mouth like a freight train: too suddenly and way too insistent.

He shrugs as though my reluctance to practice holds little relevance. 'But to work with me, Sophie, to be part of my team I need total commitment.'

Hadn't I heard that somewhere before? Commitment. 'Well, to write a biography, to...'

'Not in that capacity.'

'Then what?'

'The commitment comes first.' He smiles. 'A small demonstration of your loyalty.' And with that, Henderson comes to stand beside me, placing one hand firmly on my shoulder. 'A sign. A small mark.'

Is he flirting with me? I try to repress a shiver of disgust. I don't like the hand on the shoulder, although it doesn't feel like flirting. No, more like... possession. Suddenly, Alice's bizarre idea of Henderson as ringmaster flicks through my brain and I turn my body slightly so that the hand falls away.

'I think sometimes you like to play games.'

He looks at me shrewdly, his eyes narrowing.

'Your sister told me about how you went to the circus as kids.'

His face cracks into a bitter smile. 'The ringmaster story?'

I nod.

'And you think that my...' He pauses, as if searching for the word. Though my guess is he knows exactly what he's going to say. 'My wanting to be that *character* means I enjoy playing games? Wrong track, Sophie. Not my style. To be honest, I thought better of you.' He gives me a long hard look, the kind that makes a person want to crawl under a chair and take cover. 'In fact, my early years were notable more for their absence of the usual childhood games.'

I know he's getting at something but whatever it is, it's going way over my head. I steer things back to safer ground. 'I appreciate the offer, the job offer, but to be honest, I'm enjoying the contract as it is.'

'Time, Sophie,' he sighs, 'has a way of winning people around.' His mood seems to have changed. His words are

163

shorter. I get the feeling he doesn't want to play anymore. He takes the seat opposite me once again, a little heavier this time, but when he glances up at me his eyes are steady: fixed as if boring into my skull.

'When the time comes, Sophie, I hope you will find yourself able to commit. Terrible waste if not.'

I go to protest, to ask for more information, but he holds up one hand once again: we're finished.

'For now, I have work to do.'

I notice that his hand is shaking, barely perceptible, but then I'm actively looking for just this kind of thing.

Does he want me to commit to the story? His Parkinson's. To help get the discovery out? Is that why my medical training is somehow relevant?

'We can catch up later,' he says. His voice barely audible. 'Think about it, Sophie. I can offer you... everything.'

I close my pad, stuffing my pencil through the binding. I feel odd, sullied in some way. Almost as if I am being sucked down into the lost passageways of the labyrinth, dragged into something sinister, something too dark for Henderson to voice, something not wholly human.

'Did you know that Mia goes into the labyrinth at night wearing the mask?' I blurt.

He shrugs like it's no big deal. 'As I said, my door is open.'

'She seems to think there's some kind of fully functioning temple to fertility in there?'

'The island has a history.'

'Oh?'

'Your *true self, Sophie*. Just sitting there at the centre. Different for all, one would assume, and who are you, Sophie?'

'Sorry?'

'Your true self, what's written there?'

Sadly, I don't have to search my brain for answers. I know

exactly what kind of a mess of a person I am. I also know, I have no intention of telling Henderson that.

'I'm not sure,' I say.

He smiles to himself. 'Oh, but you are. You must be honest with yourself. For some people that's very difficult. But once you understand your raw human needs, your needs, Sophie, not anybody else's, life becomes simpler.'

I'm not convinced that's working in Mia's case, but I say nothing.

19

GEOFF

When I get back to my room. I pull a chair to the window and, feet curled under my body, go through my notes. Underlining words or sentences that stand out, pausing for a moment when I get to – *island has a history*. I guess that should be easy enough to get to the bottom of. There was, after all, a resident archaeologist – Alfred. I continue on, scanning through my hastily scrawled shorthand. *Utilitarian*, but not socialist. 'Society must be run...' Henderson's words make him sound more like a dictator than a liberal. For someone younger, someone less experienced, less media-savvy than Henderson, I might perhaps have attributed the word *must* to a slip of the tongue, but Henderson's not naïve. He's old and educated enough to have refined his views on life along with his vocab. Every word that comes out of the man's mouth is calculated. *Must* was the word he used. Must was the word he meant. A power elite then, that's what he'd been advocating. Then there was the commitment thing, what was he asking me to commit to? Clara: that's where I had heard it before. She said she'd committed, but to what? I make a mental note to ask her at supper.

I appear to have way more questions than answers. This villa I'm cocooned in feels as if its foundations are entrenched in a web of mysteries, and it seems as if that's the way Henderson likes it. I stare out over the courtyard to where the mouth of the north maze gapes silently, and I can't help wondering about the tunnels: the sounds of a child screaming. I must have heard it because Mia claims to have heard it too. If we were both hearing it, then there must be children up here at the complex. And why not? Staff workers with children, village kids, it happens. But if so, why did Henderson try and fob me off with peacocks? Both Clara and Cal had hinted that there was some kind of story linking the labyrinth to children. There may be no CCTV cameras, but I have the feeling Henderson's aware of everything that goes on. So if he knows about the children, why is he so intent on denying it? I have to tread carefully. He has a reputation for shutting down. When the clinic closed, it happened virtually overnight.

I'm brought back to the present by the buzzing of my phone. It's Geoff. It feels so weird to hear that soft disembodied voice, with its dependable East End tones. Suddenly, despite the rain, and the threat of a Christmas holiday with my overbearing mother, I find myself missing home.

'Sophie!' he exclaims. 'Hadn't expected to catch you.' There's a warmth, a generosity in his voice, which I suddenly realise is a quality totally absent from Kairos.

'Geoff.' I hold on to the humanity in his name like a drowning woman who's just been thrown a life vest. 'Having a break from interviews.'

'I won't keep you,' he says, in that self-deprecating, ultra-British way – unwilling to intrude. 'I was wondering when you were going to be getting back. Thought I might go visit the kids over New Years.'

'Course.' I glance at my notebook with its smattering of

disjointed thoughts containing more doodle than direction. Nothing on this story is going anywhere fast. Besides, now Henderson appears to be offering me something else, a different kind of a job? Provisionally, my flight had been booked for the 24th, but there had always been an element of doubt. 'I can't see me being able to get to you between Christmas and New Year. I'm not even sure I'll be out of here myself by Christmas.'

'Not a problem, Sophie. My life story's waited this long, it can hold on for a few more months.'

'Thanks, Geoff. You have a good one.'

'I intend to...'

And then suddenly, it's out of my mouth before I can stop myself...'Geoff?'

'Yup?'

'Would you do me a favour? I was wondering about the fire. Henderson's clinic, how it burnt down? Would you...' And I can't believe I'm asking him this, but with his training, his contacts, it's too good an opportunity to miss. 'I've googled it, but... would you mind having a dig for me?'

Geoff laughs. 'Oh, you wouldn't believe how many years I've been waiting for someone to say that. I'll grab my spade out of the closet and get back to you just as soon as I can.'

I put the phone back into my pocket, half wondering what the hell it is that I think I'm up to. What do I expect to find? But I can't help feeling satisfied. I'm taking things into my own hands, digging around for a story I know is here. I'm just not sure what it is, or how to access it. There's something about the fire that bothers me. Why did Henderson never rebuild the clinic? I could ask him directly, but I've seen how adept he is at switching the subject. Geoff, on the other hand, with his old boys-in-blue network, might have a more direct way in.

I gaze out of the window; it's still early. I need to find out more about Parkinson's. I start typing into the search engine.

Suddenly, my hands freeze. In my head I get an image of Trevor on Tech, sitting comfortably somewhere in this vast building, mug of tea in hand, snooping on my every virtual move. Maybe Geoff's savvy enough to be slipping under Trevor's radar. No doubt Geoff will be VPN'd up to the eyeballs. Working for so long with criminals, his paranoia barometer is permanently set to overcautious, but my tech is a whole different story. Someone could easily be looking over my metaphorical shoulder, scanning my search history. I need to stay one step ahead. It's late morning already, but I could easily make it to Athens. They'll have a library and terminals that aren't under Henderson's watchful eye. It's a plan.

20

ATHENS

Getting to Athens might not be straightforward but at least I know now that there's an easy way through Kairos' core: I take the lift. It must be my lucky day because, miracle of miracles, Achilleas' boat is nestling by the pontoon.

'Achilleas!' I shout over the sounds of the sea clawing relentlessly at the cliff.

His face breaks out in a wide grin. 'Sophie. How are you? You are good?'

'Yeah. Yeah, great. I was just wondering... could you take me to the mainland? I want to go to the library.'

Achilleas suddenly looks uncomfortable. 'But there is internet here?'

'Newspapers,' I say, quick off the mark. 'I need to look back through Mr Henderson's arrival in Greece. Not sure it was all digital then.'

Achilleas glances anxiously around as if he's looking for approval but the hesitation lasts only a second. Maybe it's not even there because in an instant he's smiling as he takes my hand, and the light in his eyes is full-beam friendly.

'Of course. Of course. Let's go.'

Once on board, with Kairos receding into the distance, I realise I haven't exactly come dressed for an adventure on the high seas. My jacket's great, but my head is freezing. I go down to the cabin and grab a scarf.

'It's okay to borrow?' I say, clambering up the narrow stairs to the deck, indicating the brightly coloured slip of silk. Going by the Prada label, it must be one of Alice's. He nods, disinterested.

I tie the silk ends neatly behind my head. 'I must ring the house, tell them where I'm going.'

Achilleas smiles in that effortless way that he has, an amused look playing lightly over his lips. 'Done,' he says simply, before returning to what appears to be his never-ending job of staring out at the sea.

Odd, I think to myself. He barely had time to make a call. Then it hits me, an uncomfortable feeling that maybe it's a priority for Henderson to keep in the know: pegging his guests' movements as though we're all pins on a war-room map. Somewhere deep in my subconscious, I have that same uneasy feeling that I'm getting all too familiar with – is Henderson simply being the good host, or is there much more to it? He owns *the land, the sea, the fish, the sky*', Achilleas had told me that first day. But the most haunting bit to me now was how he followed it up. '*And you?*' Achilleas had asked. Does Henderson own you? A cloud passes over the sky. I shiver. Am I in over my head here?

It's then that my phone buzzes. A text from Geoff.

What about Kara Jarvis?

That's it. Sometimes cryptic clues can drive you insane. I try texting back, just a question mark, but Hermes seems to have shifted his attention. My text is going nowhere. Kara Jarvis, whoever she might be, will have to wait till the library.

We moor in Piraeus: a large private space too big and baggy for our small boat. I walk fast along the port, dialling home as I march. Funny, I hadn't wanted to ring Jed on the island. It's as though Kairos is a world to itself; it doesn't need or want outsiders, but here in Piraeus the real world is up close and personal. Everybody hurrying, busy with lives and jobs. I stick out my hand, and grab a taxi.

It might seem odd that the first person I ring is my ex but, like it or not, Jed is still the central pillar in my 'real world'. When you've been in a relationship for as long as we have, the roles of friend and lover are entwined. Break one, and the ghost of the other still hangs on; like a severed limb that you can't help wanting to scratch.

'The whole set-up is seriously odd,' I tell Jed. 'And Alfred...'

'Alfred?' I can hear the pinched tightness in Jed's voice all the way from England.

'He's old, academic, married.'

'Like him already.'

'Alfred's the archaeologist. The island has a resident archaeologist.'

'I guess if you have your own private labyrinth...'

'... You need your own private history boffin, and there's more – everyone here doesn't so much have a name as a purpose, like Accountant, or Doctor or... God knows what else.'

'You know it can only be a maze or a labyrinth, right?' Jed switches so easily into lecturing mode. He hardly realises he's doing it, but this is a point he's not going to have.

'No, seriously, it can be both, just not at the same time. Or maybe I mean not in the same place?'

'You're not making much sense, Soph.'

'Nothing here makes *much* sense. And the biggest thing is...'

I hold on to my seat as the taxi skirts its way in and out of traffic, attempting to second-guess the whims of other drivers. Horns blare as I stick one finger in my left ear so I can hear better. 'Jed, you're not going to believe this... Henderson's got Parkinson's.'

A brief pause, then a tone filled with resigned sympathy.

'Poor guy.'

But Jed's missing the point. 'No, no, Jed, that's not what I mean. Henderson's got Parkinson's, but it's not progressing. Henderson's got a cure.'

This time the phone goes really quiet. So quiet that, at first, I think I've lost the connection.

'Jed...?'

'I'm still here. Has he told you this?'

'No. But I mean it's self-evident, and somehow he's keeping it at bay.'

'Really?'

I know that tone all too well. It's Jed's sceptical tone. The one I find oh-so irritating. Why does he never let me win the argument?

'Watch the TED Talks from the nineties, even some of the ones from the eighties, just watch them. Thing is, he's no worse now – this is at least thirty years on.'

'I don't know, Soph, it sounds...'

'Amazing,' I cut in, not willing to entertain even a hint of disbelief. When you've got a story, you have to sprint with it till *it* runs out of steam or you do. At the moment, me and the story are both fully fuelled. 'Can you imagine how big this is going to be? *He's* got a cure, and *I* uncover it.'

'Bigger than Christmas.'

Now it's my turn to go quiet.

'Soph? Sophie?'

'Jed.' My voice dries as my body jerks forward in the seat, the taxi coming to a sharp halt as a three-wheeled delivery truck rattles past. But it's not really the truck that's slowing me down; it's facing the truth, facing Jed's disappointment. 'Of course it's bigger than Christmas. Christmas comes along every year regular as clockwork. You couldn't stop it if you tried.'

'So you won't be taking that flight on the twenty-fourth.'

'I'm not sure, it was only provisional, besides… now…'

'Yeah.' His voice sounds flat. 'Look, I got to go, Soph.'

'Jed? I can't come back now. I can't leave this.'

When he speaks again his voice carries double the diction: he's spelling out meaning in a way that I won't be able to avoid. 'This was supposed to be a personal history. Nothing major. You could easily have done it and got back home before Christmas. It's my only holiday till summer.'

'Jed,' and I take a deep breath, 'we're not together anymore.'

Silence. The brooding kind.

'Then what the fuck are you doing phoning me?'

'Because… Because…' And I'm desperate not to use my own F-word back; the *friend* word, which is even more insulting than the fuck word: packed full of patronising thoughts and fob-offs.

'Because I miss you,' I say, and despite everything, we both know it's true. That's the curious thing about all of this. I genuinely miss him with all my heart.

Quiet again.

'Yeah.' There's another pause.

The taxi pulls towards the pavement. The driver indicating the fare with one hand as he simultaneously points down the road ahead. It looks like I have to walk from here. I get out of the cab. I close the door. I stand on the street. I do all of this without saying one word into the phone. It's not just that I miss Jed. No, it's so much more than that – it's because I can't actually imagine a life without him, but I just can't give up this story. It's too important.

'Where are you now? On *Fantasy Island*?'

And I remember the odd eighties TV show we used to watch on the internet. An improbable premise, coupled with a bizarre cast. You went to this island, and all your dreams would come true. Only you didn't know what the best *dream* for you was. You had to discover that part for yourself. Very Socratic. Suddenly I'm reminded of the labyrinth, with its hidden centre that can drive a person to distraction, *their true self*, and a cold chill runs through me.

'No. Not *Fantasy Island*. I headed off to the mainland. I wanted to do some research.' I spot a sign for the library and set off in the right direction. 'Not entirely sure Kairos is functioning normally today, there was this... incident last night.'

'Oh?'

'Just some kid got hurt.' I have no intention of telling Jed more. I can't make sense of it myself; Cal's throwaway comments about the reason the kid was down there in the first place have left me feeling uncomfortable, yet I'm not sure why.

'It doesn't matter.' I sigh, coming to halt at a major junction; taxis weaving in and out of cars, bikes, people. Everyone is heading home for Christmas, and it feels like they're all going in the exact opposite direction to me.

'Jed?'

'Yeah?' He's doing something as he's talking, washing down the counter with a cloth, or sorting through piles of paper: documents, bills. I can picture him so clearly.

'I miss you. You know that, right?'

He stops doing whatever he was doing. Again there's silence.

'Come home soon, Soph. We need to talk.'

And he's gone. Of course, we do. We need to find out where this is going. No, that's not it. It's me. I need to find out where this is going. Sometimes I wish I were Jed. He may be hurting, but at least he knows what he wants. Me? I'm stuck in limbo.

Every option seems painful. All I really want to do is run away from everyone, but especially myself.

––––

By the time I arrive at the library, I know I'm going to have to put the UK and all its complications behind me. I want to find out more about Parkinson's, and I'm curious as hell about one mysterious Kara Jarvis.

The library doesn't disappoint on the visual front: exactly the kind of place an ancient Greek city should have. It's the dreg-ends of the afternoon, a dull winter's day. The giant torch lamps standing at the bottom of the curved stone staircases are on, shining warm perpetual flames of knowledge into the gloom. Despite its grandeur, the square in front of the building is virtually empty. Looks like people have already hurried home to their families. They'll be safe and warm in their houses. Many will have broken up for the holidays. For now, at least, the libraries of the world are forgotten, but I have work to do. The library building towers like an ancient Greek temple above me, and as I move quickly up the steps, I can't help feeling like some small insignificant mortal in search of answers from the gods. If only I had more time. Let's hope the gods answer in a quick burst of revelation.

The inside of the building is equally awesome: a cathedral to books and knowledge. I'm soon encased in a high room packed floor-to-ceiling with bookshelves. A wall of spines, bound in leather and inscribed with gold. Above me there's a great chunk of the ceiling missing, replaced by a large rectangular sheet of glass. Clouds skitter across the heavens.

A few hardcore academics cluster around bench-like tables, unimpressed by the approach of Christmas. They're flicking through books that look as old as the building itself. Under different circumstances I would love to sit, idle away my time; wait for serendipity to shoot a few arrows of inspiration, but the information I want is a different kind of a beast. It's not going to be here. I'm interested in the shoulder-padded power eighties and beyond. I search around for a less aesthetic enclave, a room where monitors protrude like glassy virtual windows out of every desk. I'm not disappointed. There's a small dark chapel to the digital hidden away at the south corner. I've been given a login code at reception, so pull up a chair and type in the code.

Luckily the internet is fast, much better than anything I'm going to get on the island, and no Trevor snooping over my bookmarks: Henderson might not like some of the research I'm about to do but I'm enjoying the feeling that this time I'm the one who's ahead of the game.

So, Parkinson's? In short – there's still no cure. I flick through a couple of recent articles in *The Lancet*. I have to sign up, renew my subscription, but that's all okay. I'm earning enough from Henderson; my bank account doesn't protest at the direct debit. Besides, I don't have a choice – I need answers. I scan through a ton of articles. Luckily, I'm good at speed-reading. There are drug tests, physical therapies. There's deep brain stimulation, not claiming to be a cure. Besides, it's been around for years. There's a possible link to calcium, but nothing I can sink my teeth into; who could resist the pun. Then I see it; a pattern begins to emerge – there are some new treatments using stem cell technologies.

I isolate a few periodicals, leafing through them till I find one that makes my fingers freeze over the keyboard. They're not using just any stem cells. They're using foetal stem cells. Because foetal stem cells have no antigenicity (cellular fingerprint), which means that there's no need to use drugs to suppress the immune system. In short, the immune system isn't going to kill off the newly inserted cells. They should (in theory) adapt. It's not a cure, and they're not claiming it as such, but what they are saying is that it appears to halt *some* degenerative effects.

Foetal stem cells? It's surely too much of a coincidence, although there's no denying that Henderson would have been in an excellent position to get access.

It must be almost four: my fellow researchers are beginning to leave. Time is slipping through my fingers, but I'm nowhere near done.

I watch the last guy pack up his notes, bundle them in a bag and head for the door before I punch Geoff's number into my phone.

I can picture it all so clearly; the small London flat, the fridge with its high-pitched whine. The photos of (some) of the people Geoff loved clustering the sideboard.

'Thank God you rang,' he blurts, not even bothering with bare-bones greetings. 'I'm beginning to smell a rat.'

'What?'

'Sophie, are you alone?'

I glance around me again. 'Totally, I'm not on the island.'

'Good. Good. Now listen carefully – this is important. For starters,' Geoff says, 'the fire. The police official line has it as an electrical fault, but I spoke to one of the guys who worked the case. He felt it was arson. All the files on Henderson's floor, well most of them had been cleared out. It's odd. The wiring had blown, that's what "caused" the fire but...'

'So you think someone wanted to destroy something?'

'Or make it look like things got lost in the blaze. But that's not the main reason I get the feeling something odd is going on here.'

'Kara Jarvis?' Why does that name ring a bell?

'Yeah. One of the guys, just out of the blue, he said how weird it was me asking about the clinic, because of Kara Jarvis.'

178

'Sorry, still not getting it.'

'Kara Jarvis, Sophie. You must remember, it happened a few weeks back. Google it.'

I type her name into the search engine, my fingers rapping hard over the keyboard.

'You got her?'

I click through to images. Kara's head and shoulders fill the screen: large blue eyes and a smiling face, acres of dark wavy hair. She's pretty, around my age, beautiful even, and that smile, so all-embracing as if she has the world at her feet. But there's more – I've seen this photo before. Something about it is beginning to unsettle me. I click on a link. 'TRAGEDY IN THE IONIAN' – a headline in the *Times* dated a few weeks ago. That's what Kara Jarvis was, a tragedy. Not a smiling, pretty girl full of hope. Her entire life has been reduced to this one sad sound bite.

'Well?'

'I'm reading it, hold on a second.'

She had, so the article tells me, everything to live for. Yet she suffered from depression. She was working on an internship the year before her death. Anecdotally it was reported that all had seemed good. She went on a holiday to Athens one weekend, a city break. She didn't tell anyone she was going. That was when it happened. There was a text home to her parents. It just said, *I'm sorry*. Suicide by text – so short it could even have been tweeted. So short that it leaves an entire mountain range behind of everything left unsaid; something for her friends and family to pick over for the rest of their tortured lives.

I look once again at the picture, and I remember it now. I saw it that day at Geoff's when he was binding up his old newspapers. It is a tragedy. But... I can't quite see the connection. This kind of thing happens every day. Someone with their life all laid out ahead of them, someone with so much to live for thinks maybe they'd rather not. The location is exotic, but the story's the same. Geography doesn't make it any better or worse.

'Sorry, I'm not getting it.'

'Kara worked for Henderson.'

Suddenly it's as if the temperature in the room has dropped. I flick back through the article. There's nothing. 'It doesn't say anything about that here.'

'The internship, that was for Henderson. Only for six months. London based. Doing some kind of research. Mythology, I think? Anyway, that was all they found, notebooks full of stories.'

'Did you see the notebooks?'

'They belonged to your Mr Henderson. He'd commissioned them. The guys at the station said there was nothing in there anyway. Just Greek myths and monsters.'

Monsters? The word unsettles me; fear and monsters to keep society in check. Isn't that what Henderson was advocating? I think of the labyrinth, the mask, poor Mia and those children screaming, but this isn't the time. 'So Henderson took the notebooks away?'

'Not him, someone called for them on his behalf.'

'Can you get me more on Kara, and anything more on Henderson?'

The line goes quiet.

'Geoff?'

'You know what time of year this is?'

I glance around me at the room, which is mercifully free of tinsel, just one large tree in the grand atrium.

'Yeah, sorry, but do you know if she went to the island?'

'Nothing confirmed. She arrived in Athens. She was working for him, so it seems likely there was some kind of contact. And as far as I know, you don't have passport control on that little island hideaway. Anyone can come, anyone can go.'

'I can ask back at the house. The staff would have known. Most of them have been with Henderson for years.'

'Up to you, but...' He hesitates. 'I'd be a bit careful.'

There's something about the way he says the word *careful*, that tells me he really means it.

'She had depression,' I say.

'Don't we all. But we don't all kill ourselves. She had a lot to live for.'

'Doesn't always follow.' I'd done six months in a psychiatric unit. I know that having *a lot to live for* can actually make things worse. 'Was Henderson questioned?'

'Yeah, squeaky clean.' I sense the doubt in Geoff's voice.

'Oh?'

'Maybe... too clean. Sometimes stories can be too... neatly woven; all the surfaces wiped just that little bit too spotless. It's possible to remove every single fingerprint from a crime scene, but the removal of fingerprints only ever tells you for dead certain that a crime was committed.'

I sigh, lowering my voice just in case we're overheard. The library is pretty much empty, but I'm taking no chances. 'Even if she was working for Henderson, it didn't happen on the island. It's the Ionian. We're in the Aegean.'

'We?'

'You know what I mean.'

He's right of course; I'm embedding myself pretty deeply into Henderson's world. I remember Cal's warning about fairy tales and perfect lives. Maybe I'm waking up just in time.

'Aegean, Ionian. It's not so *far-fetched*,' Geoff says cryptically. For some odd reason, he's putting emphasis on the *far* and the *fetched*.

'Okay, Geoff, maybe it's best if you spell it out.'

'Kairos is right by the Calypso Deep.'

I'm none the wiser. Henderson's boat is called the *Calypso*, but Calypso Deep sounds more like a dance routine.

It's then that I notice Achilleas. He's hanging back in the outer room, half in, half out of the shadows. He must have just got there because I'd scanned the place before I called Geoff, and I'd been keeping an eye out. Despite myself, I feel a hot flush of guilt flare across my cheeks. Guilty of what? Surely there's no crime in calling home? But I've overstayed my exeat and get the feeling I'm being reeled back in like a fish on the end of a line.

'I've got to go, Geoff.'

'Well, think about it.'

The phone goes dead, and I wonder what it is that I'm supposed to be thinking about? Soon as I get back to the UK I'm going to tell Geoff we've got to put an end to the whole cryptic thing. I'm going to take up something easier: sudoku will do. When a girl's been (possibly) murdered, it's no longer fun and games.

Seeing the phone go down, Achilleas moves cautiously forward. He looks out of place in this grand palace. He's a character from the outside world, from nature, all tanned and windblown. The library with its formal lines, and hushed air, is pushing him way out of his comfort zone.

'We should go.' His voice is quiet, despite a sense of underlying urgency to his words.

I nod and begin to collect my things. I can do more research from the island. It's only stem cells and Kara Jarvis that I need to be careful with; I'm not so sure how those topics would go down with Henderson. Which suddenly reminds me...

'Just one thing.' I hand Achilleas my bag and quickly log back in, typing *Man with no face*.

Achilleas sees the words in the search engine, and shifts

slightly, looking towards the door. Is he worrying about being late back, or my search?

'Oh, it's silly,' I explain, aiming for a dismissive note in my voice. 'I keep seeing this man, but I never quite see his face. It's always in a reflection, always distorted.'

'Where did you see him?' Achilleas' voice sounds tight, as he continues to scan the library anxiously.

'No, not here. On the island... and...' I remember the strings of lights going up in the street back home, Santa's smile and the shadowy figure hugging the darkness, always keeping just out of sight. 'And I thought I saw him in London. It's stupid but...'

But it doesn't feel stupid. It feels like a threat: the monster was on my doorstep: outside my flat even before this island.

'He's skinny,' I say. 'Dressed all in black, and his face... I just never see his face?'

When I glance back at the screen, my heart sinks because there he is. The image of a Slender Man looming out of the monitor: dark suit, stick-thin angular body, no face. A modern-day monster, created in a Photoshop competition. Users were invited to edit photographs, making them look paranormal. One single competition and a horror for our age is born. A featureless, suited man, an abductor of children: my faceless stalker?

Achilleas leans forward and presses the off button. His fingers barely balancing on the keys, as if they're somehow infectious.

'We should go. It is late.'

I can't quite believe what he's done. I feel like a child who's been given their IT quota for the day. He can't have meant the gesture to be so paternalistic. I try and catch his eyes, but he's deliberately avoiding my gaze. Then I realise why: he's frightened. He's seen the faceless monster too.

Back on the boat, Achilleas seems upset. He keeps staring out nervously at the darkening sea, as if expecting the horror to rear its ugly head.

'You ever heard of a Calypso Deep?' I ask as the damp air seeps into my clothes.

He nods. 'Part of the Hellenic Trench.'

'Sorry?'

He stops, forehead creasing into a frown as he struggles with his English.

'Is like big valley in sea. Very big valley. Underwater.'

I gasp. It's difficult to dull my excitement, to keep it under wraps, because – if there's a trench, if there's directed movement of water, then there could easily be directed movement of a body. Which reminds me: Kara's not the only body in the water, there was the lad with the severed arm. It had been pitched as a success story. The boy was safe, his arm saved, he'd gone to an expensive clinic, but what proof did we have?

'Do you think the boy will be okay?' I ask, as Kairos' dark shadow looms into view.

Achilleas looks blank.

'The kid that got hurt at the taverna. His arm got caught in the...'

'I do not know,' he says, but he's avoiding eye contact.

Since we got back on the boat it's been like talking to a brick wall, sadly I have too many questions to keep quiet.

'Achilleas?'

'Mr Henderson will handle it.'

'And that man, the one without the face? Can Henderson handle that too?'

He looks forward at the horizon.

'The picture on the screen, Achilleas. I know you've seen that man before?'

He shakes his head, but it's not really a denial, more reluctance: he doesn't want to speak about it.

'On the island?'

'Sophie, you must not ask so many questions. It's bad luck.'

He doesn't look at me, just keeps gazing straight ahead, not giving anything away. Is this a kind of loyalty towards Henderson, I wonder? Or perhaps fear? But now there's a dead girl involved. I need to get the whole picture. 'Did you know a Kara Jarvis?'

His cheeks flare red, even under all that weather-tanned skin, they're flaming. I say nothing, hoping to prod him into conversation with my silence. Eventually, he shrugs, still not looking towards me.

'I don't think so.'

I don't need him facing me to know that he's lying. 'That's funny...' Achilleas is the person who brings people to and from the island. If Kara had visited Kairos, chances are Achilleas would have ferried her there. 'She worked for Henderson.'

No recognition.

He puckers his lips as if trying to get rid of a sour taste. 'A lot of people work for Mr Henderson. I don't remember them all. Only you, Sophie, I won't forget you.'

It is such a transparent attempt at dragging the conversation off-topic, but this is serious. I have no intention of letting it drop. 'She committed suicide.'

'Yes,' he says flatly, turning away again.

'You met her, didn't you?' It's not a question. I'm saying it as if I have evidence to back it up. I'm bluffing, but it works.

'Yes. Ah... Kara.' The fakery is transparent. The way he says the name, stressing the K, offering a slightly different pronunciation. As though it was the way that I'd said it that somehow created the confusion. 'Of course, Kara. Now I remember. It's so sad to talk of the dead.'

'Yes, but...'

Achilleas turns, fixing me firmly with his eyes, and this time his voice holds a harsh edge to it, one I haven't heard before. 'And... bad luck to talk of the drowned when you are on a boat.'

A chill slithers down my spine as I glance around me at the wide watery darkness. I can understand his reluctance; to talk of the drowned while floating precariously on a thin piece of wood seems a little like an open invitation to Poseidon to reach up and grab us down to the bottom of the deep black sea. The blue waters have long disappeared with the afternoon, leaving nothing but a dark grave of water and a black shroud for a sky. I decide not to push any further, not now anyway.

It's late by the time we arrive back on the pontoon. I'd been so desperate to escape earlier in the day, now I feel nothing but relief to be back on the island. The twinkle in Achilleas' eye, his warm friendly smile, all of that has vanished. He doesn't seem to like women who ask questions. I gather my things, returning the scarf below deck. As I do the boat rocks awkwardly, buffeted by angry waves that have found themselves trapped in this small bay. The hull lurches. A cupboard falls open. Suddenly, my heart misses a beat. Hanging in the closet, lurking at the back, I see a black suit.

I close the door tight shut, scrambling quickly up the narrow staircase, my breath sticking in my throat. What the hell is Achilleas doing with a suit like that? Surely it can't be him – the man in black?

As I race up the stairs out onto the deck, a firm hand grabs my arm. I feel my heels losing their grip on the shiny wooden boards. I'm going to slip. I'm going to tumble back down, smash my head on the beams, lose consciousness, end up in the deep, black water. But no, the hand pulls me back. There are arms holding me tight.

'Sophie?' Achilleas looks puzzled.

I have to get away. 'Seasick... I...'

He helps me from the boat, but there are still no smiles, and his grip is too tight.

'Sophie,' he says, leaning towards me so even the waves can't hear his words. 'No more questions.'

I'm not sure if it's advice or a warning. Either way, I don't wait for clarification. I walk from the boat as quickly as I can without breaking into a run.

Crossing the rocks, I take the lift back to the villa. What kind of perverse satisfaction can Henderson have got that first day, in forcing me to climb alone up the cliff face? It's already late by the time I get back to the house. I would, just about, have time for the old dressing for supper routine, but I haven't the heart for it. I tell Ellie I'm not feeling well: seasick. It's halfway true. Clutching my stomach as though to demonstrate my plight, I head up to my room. I need to sleep. Need to rest. Need to get away from all those other people with their false smiles and posh frocks. Ensconced behind my closed door, I push the beautiful clothes Sylvie's left out for me deep into the wardrobe. I'm in no mood for partying. Instead, I stare out of my window at the darkened courtyard below. No one moves. Not even the leaves dare to fall in the wrong place. My little jaunt to Athens has left me with not only a shedload of questions but one hell of a creeped-out feeling. I thought I could trust Achilleas, but if he has that suit on his boat, I'm pretty sure I can't.

21

CASTELLANOS

Thankfully, my night at the villa slips past without incident. If there is screaming happening, I'm too exhausted to hear it. I wake the next morning feeling rested and wanting to get answers. Someone, Ellie? Has left a tray outside my room. Nothing fancy, cereal and orange juice, but it does the trick. I stand in the window overlooking the terrace, bowl in hand, trying to work out how to move forward. Here at the villa, I feel like a goldfish in a tank. If I'm to get a true picture, I know I need to get out. The boy's mother, I think to myself. If she's still on the island, it would be worth paying her a visit.

I could go down to the pontoon; Achilleas might be there, but the memory of the black suit hanging in his closet sends shivers down my spine. Besides, hadn't he warned me last night about asking too many questions? I'll just follow the road I took with Cal.

Sylvie's in the hallway when I come down, standing in a sea of foliage, making one of the largest flower arrangements I've ever seen. A mass of bold reds and bright greens cluster around twisted silver branches – an uber-tasteful, understated nod to Christmas. Not a Santa, fairy or bauble in sight.

'That is so beautiful,' I say, as I wind around the staircase towards her.

'Hmm.' She doesn't look up, her delicate hands are held out in front of her, framing the broad face of a burnt-red sunflower. 'I take no credit for nature's beauty. She does it all by herself.'

'But you're the one who puts it in place.'

Sylvie shrugs. 'The beauty comes first. Are you feeling better?'

'Yes. Fine, thank you.' I squirm uncomfortably. 'Do you know if the boy's okay?' Then I realise Sylvie might not know anything about the carnage at the Taverna; she wasn't there. 'There was an accident the other night when we went out for supper,' I explain.

She shifts awkwardly, and I sense that she's heard the news. But her voice, when it comes, is dismissive, cold even. 'Sometimes there are accidents.'

'He's gone back to the mainland?' I ask.

'I would expect.' There's something in the curt way she delivers her words, in the way that she refuses to look at me; a kind of glazed-over appearance that tells me she doesn't want to talk about it. I glance at the windows. Eyes, I think, and not for the first time: are we looking out? Or is someone looking in?

'And what about his mother?' I say, reluctant to let it drop.

'Still on the island, so I am told.'

'Didn't she want to go with him?'

'Sophie.' Sylvie lets the flowers droop in her hands, and turns to face me, a frown creasing that perfectly poised face. 'Why would you think anyone would tell me?'

It's kind of light-hearted, but I'm left under no illusions: my interest is pushing our friendship out of its comfort zone.

'Not sure. I just thought...'

'Too much thinking, it's not good for a person.'

I can't help myself, an image of those early phrenologists

pops into my head; the oddballs who believed that if women used their brains, the brain would become enlarged. Woman would become unattractive and the entire human race would be wiped out.

'To be honest *thinking*, it's kind of essential.' I start leafing through a stack of flowers by the stairs. 'Part of being human, I'd say.'

'Well!' she puffs, gathering some stems into her arms and pushing them down into what looks, from the tangled foliage, as though it must be the discard pile. 'Go be human with someone else. I have work to do.'

'Can I take these?' I hold up some of the abandoned red sunflowers.

'You think he will like flowers?' There's a playful note to her voice.

I look at her curiously, not following her line of thought. 'He?'

'Our young Achilleas. Weren't you out with him all day?'

'Sylvie!'

But Sylvie just laughs, in a conspiratorial way. 'Don't worry. I tell no one.'

Of course, she's right; any sane woman would fall for Achilleas. That is, before he squeezed their arm off, and they discovered he had a monster outfit dangling at the back of his closet. In truth, Achilleas was never really my type. So, does that mean Cal is my type? Surely not, and yet, oh-so annoyingly even thinking about him makes my heart run quicker.

My arms stuffed with flowers, I walk past the parked cars, their gleaming, waxed bodies glinting in the low winter sun. I bet the engines are just as clean. These cars must barely hit the road. Shop window, I think to myself, it's like all the treats are laid out in a shop window.

The villa is soon lost behind me, even the odd little turret sinks into the landscape, and I feel myself absorbed into the peace of the island. Like a speck of grit in an oyster shell, my edges are being smoothed over. I strike out, only the sound of my shoes hitting the tarmac for company.

There are tangles of paths leading away from the road, meandering off through olive groves in every direction – some made by footsteps, others, no doubt, by animals. I've never liked walking on tarmac. It gives your spine one hell of a jolt, but I'm not sure where the paths lead. There are no markers, no colour-coded trail signs. I suppose this is a private island and I get the feeling that visitors either know where they're going or are not exactly encouraged to stray. I stick to the road. It's pleasant enough. There's no traffic, and the incline, though steep, appears to be steady. I'm feeling brave now. I have a mission. I'm going to drop in on the boy's mother. I want to get the low-down on what actually happened at the taverna and where the boy is now. She might also know something about Kara. Maybe. It's worth a shot.

I've walked about a mile when I hear a faint sound ringing above my footsteps, a kind of tapping. I stop. There's definitely the sound of metal against rock: a series of small, high-pitched repetitive strikes, and I can make out voices floating up from the woods to my left. One male. English, I think? I stop, close my eyes, and listen, tilting my head into the sun.

Again there's that tap, tap, tap.

'Bring it up carefully. Carefully.' I recognise the voice instantly. It's Alfred.

'Alfred?' I stare into the tangled thicket. 'Alfred?'

The hammering stops.

'Sophie? Sophie, is that you?'

I walk off the road onto a small dusty path that winds down through the groves towards the sea. Although it's not the season for olives, there are nets cast over the ground, and I find myself having to watch my step; the earth is cracked and slippery where it's riddled with roots.

'Sophie. They're a pest,' Alfred says, emerging from a bushy outcrop, grinning, 'the nets,' he continues. 'The locals leave them down all year. You develop a sixth sense for the things. Come, come.' He beckons me forward.

Just behind a mesh of undergrowth, there's a clearing and a dig in progress. Two Greeks I haven't seen before are excavating a small trench. They glance over at me with a mixture of alpha-male distrust and a smattering of curiosity.

'Welcome, welcome.' Alfred beams, oblivious to the cool looks I'm getting.

I smile, glancing around at the day camp; a canvas tent, a few folding chairs, tools neatly lined up on the parched ground.

'We've just had a bit of a find.' He holds a fragment of pottery towards me, soil still crusted to its edges. 'An amphora.' He smiles excitedly as if from this small piece of clay, he can reconstruct an entire civilisation. 'Not the biggest piece we've had, but I'd say it may well be one of the oldest.'

'A good day then?'

He nods with childish enthusiasm. 'I should say so.'

Then, without pausing, he launches into a string of Greek words leaving me far behind.

The men look me up and down, before climbing slowly out of the trench and wandering off; dragging their heavy booted feet across the grove towards another pit at the far side of the clearing. Their movements are lumbering, like weary oxen. Without a flicker of any expression, they lower themselves down into the earth once more and continue to work.

'I shall excavate this later myself.' Alfred nods towards the original trench. 'Needs concentration. It's just a small dig. Mr Henderson lets me explore the island pretty much unchecked, and today I found something. It doesn't happen every day, but today...'

He stops for a moment, as though suddenly realising he's been blustering on, before glancing at the flowers in my hand.

'Oh, I thought I'd take something to the lad's mother; the boy who got hurt at the taverna.'

'I see.' Alfred looks nervous. 'Mr Henderson asked you to?'

'No, I just thought...'

'In my experience, it's always best to let Mr Henderson authorise these things. Sometimes the locals can be...' He looks over at the second trench. The two men, their heads just visible, are continuing their work in sullen silence. 'Well, let's just say that the locals... they don't always like strangers. Will you stay for tea?' he asks, indicating a makeshift camp stove.

He clears some bags from a mossy stone for me to sit. His enthusiasm wins me over. It's so genuine. Like a kid keen to show off his new den.

'Actually, Alfred,' I say, settling into my pew, 'I have a few questions.'

'Oh?' he asks, and I can't help feeling that there's an edge of nervousness to his voice.

'Yes... Did you know a young woman called Kara?'

He looks blank.

'I think she may have stayed on the island?'

'No doubt. We get a lot of people passing through. I'm afraid I don't take much notice.'

'Dark hair, my age, past month or so?'

Perhaps Henderson didn't bring her to the villa. It was a possibility she never even came to the island.

'So sorry, Sophie.' Alfred smiles indulgently. 'People are not really my thing.'

Or newspapers it would appear, but Alfred continues oblivious. 'It's the island that interests me most. Young women, that would be Cal's department.'

I don't doubt that for a moment. Then Henderson's words come back to me. '*The island has a history.*'

'About the island,' I say. 'I was curious about its past.'

The nervousness evaporates. Alfred's face beams. 'Then you, young lady, have come to the right place. Hmm.' He smooths his chin as if running his small delicate fingers through an imaginary beard. 'It's difficult to know exactly where to begin.' He shoots me a wry smile as he sets to work pouring tea from the can into an enamel cup. The liquid is boiling. The cup, no doubt, heading in the same direction.

'Fingers...' Alfred says helpfully, 'wrap them in your jumper.'

I do as I'm told.

'Let's... Okay...' Alfred settles himself on a matching boulder. 'Let's try the early part of the last century. That might work.'

I nod, happy to get any bearing he's able to give.

'Well, at that time Kairos was, on the surface, your typical sleepy Greek island minding its own business: the men harvesting the seas, the women and children tending to the olives and the home front.'

And I can imagine it, as the sun warms my back: the idyllic, timeless nature of the place.

'Like so many of the smaller islands,' Alfred continues, 'history moved at a snail's pace. Traditional farming methods, ways of living, well, they hadn't changed for hundreds of years.'

I glance around me at the olive groves, at the sparkling sea below us, which I notice has switched back to its customary blue. It's easy to picture that kind of age-old existence. Even today, few scars of progress have managed to muscle in.

'But the island idyll, well...' And Alfred's forehead creases. 'That was all before the arrival of a man called Castellanos.'

'Castellanos?' It's not a name I've heard before. 'A Greek?'

'Mmm...' Alfred sucks in his bottom lip. 'To be honest, not exactly sure on that one. In point of fact, we can't be entirely certain that Castellanos was even his real name.'

'A man of mystery.'

'Certainly that. You see, despite all my efforts, which have been pretty considerable over the years, I can discover no evidence of the man's existence before he set foot on Kairos.'

'Surely birth certificates, parish records?'

Alfred simply shakes his head dismissively. 'The man with no history just seemed to *arrive*. Like Aphrodite from the waves.'

'I suppose a lot of admin must have got lost in the war.'

Alfred nods, but it's half-hearted as if he thinks this is not really the answer.

'Records could indeed have been lost, but he didn't appear to be Greek. His name might suggest that he was Spanish? And although his Greek was fluent, so I understand, it was edged with a strange accent no one could quite place.'

'A different Greek dialect?'

Alfred nods once more, as though it's possible. It's certainly something he's thought about, but again, he doesn't seem convinced. 'He arrived in the 1920s, a wealthy man. Though how he made his money is unclear. But perhaps why he chose Kairos rather than the other islands is more to the point.'

Alfred takes a moment to draw in a long breath before continuing. 'You see, many say the other islands are prettier, and at that time had better infrastructures, certainly they were closer to the mainland.'

'Maybe he just wanted to get away from it all?'

And who wouldn't? I think. This kind of feeling of eternal peace, it's priceless. I've swapped the constant smell of diesel fumes for the scent of wild thyme filtering through clear salty skies. The house may feel oppressive, but here... I feel more alive than I've felt for years.

'Solitude is a motivator, perhaps.' Alfred takes a sip of his tea, and I wonder how he can drink it; it's scalding hot. Archaeologists must be born with asbestos lips.

I raise my own mug to my mouth and blow.

'He tended to keep himself to himself, but over the years he embarked on a major building project. Initially, it was the house. The site currently occupied by the east wing of Henderson's villa. But as soon as this relatively modest structure was finished, he engaged builders to work on a series of tunnels.'

'The labyrinth,' I say. 'So he's responsible.'

Alfred smiles, nodding slowly, hinting that there is so much more to this story. 'Well, in part. The island had always had a series of ancient tunnels, no one's certain why, but for Castellanos they became a ... well, an obsession. Did he come here for the labyrinth, or did it take his fancy after his arrival, we're not sure. But he developed a passion for the structure. A passion in which it seemed imperative that he not only excavate the existing mazes, but build more. He housed the builders in a camp close to the villa. The men were brought in from the mainland, even though the islanders expressed interest in working on the project, and the majority of the builders had no formal training. They were just labourers. So the islanders would have been perfectly capable of the work but Castellanos was... reluctant to employ locals.'

'Maybe he didn't want them to understand the structure?' I offer. 'I mean, if it's a maze or labyrinth, part and parcel of the structure is that sense of mystery?'

'Exactly so, Sophie.' He takes another sip of his tea.

This time I join him. It tastes more of hot water than tea.

Not really my style. I like a good caffeine fix, but I feel it would be ungracious not to drink.

'But back to Castellanos.' Alfred's eyes sparkle as he returns to this favourite subject. 'Every three months or so, the gangs of labourers would be replaced; the old workers sent back to the mainland and fresh hands brought in.'

'To ensure secrecy?'

Alfred looks doubtful. 'Not just that I think. You see... although the project went on for many years, the speed of the work seemed to be of the utmost importance to Castellanos, and fresh workers work harder, are more enthusiastic. There are some notes in a site manager's journal; so we may assume the sentiment is reliable.'

'How many years did it go on for?'

He draws in a deep breath as if the air itself might carry him back through time: give him a better understanding. 'Till the beginning of the occupation in 1941. So just under twenty years.'

'That's a lot of tunnels.'

'Oh, believe me, there are a lot. The villagers were happy enough with the arrangement. Castellanos kept himself to himself. The constant influx of workers had advantages. The small taverna in the town was always full. Not the one we went to with the jazz band. There's another village around the other side of the island, abandoned now. But island life was thriving. Labourers that caused problems, those who became overenthusiastic with fists or flirtations, well they were simply deported. No fuss. No questions. Besides, the islanders were kept busy with the new dynamic: the men fishing for the workers' hungry appetites and the women taking in washing, mending, that kind of thing.'

'And then...?'

'Ahh...' He smiles to himself. 'Of course, Sophie, there has to be an *and then*...'

A light breeze blows across the clearing. A speck of dust falling into his cup. He stares after it, like a gypsy intent on divining some connection with the Fates.

'Well, as hindsight tells us, the first half of the twentieth century has the seed of change embedded into every story. Our story is no exception. Some said that Castellanos must have been a government official all along and had gotten wind of the turbulent political times ahead.'

I can tell from Alfred's tone that his bet's not on this as a theory, and sure enough, he continues.

'But the start of the tunnels was too early. There was no way he could have known about the German occupation, or had any idea that the civil war would follow. It seems... unlikely that anyone could have known. Nobody could have foreseen what was about to happen, all those sets of circumstances lining up. Some said that he must have been a mystic: able to see the shadow of disaster written in the sky, or in the leaves of his tea.'

Alfred stares at the offending speck in his cup. Then, with a curled finger, fishes it out, wiping his wet hand on a cushion of moss.

'Like myself, he was famous for his billycan.' Alfred smiles fondly at the stove, as though it's an old friend. 'He was notorious for wandering cup in hand in the evenings, examining each dig.'

'It takes more than a teacup to make a mystic.'

Alfred smiles. 'True. And those not fond of mysticism said that there was only one possible answer to the question of Castellanos' true motives.'

He smiles at me, a childish glint in his eye.

'And that is?'

'He was a pirate.'

REAP WHAT YOU SOW

I laugh, conjuring up some Jack Sparrow image in my head.

'Not so funny, Sophie. These were different times. We're not talking picture-book pirates: pointy hats, skull and crossbones. We're talking thieves, pure and simple. Some of the workers spoke of tunnels that led directly to the sea.'

'On an island, where would you expect a tunnel to lead?'

Alfred shrugs, like he'd got there already on that one.

'Over the years the complex here became more elaborate. The need for a purpose for the tunnels became less necessary, and the myth began to take hold. It was said that he was building a labyrinth that would make Minos himself envious. Perhaps it would be a tourist attraction? Perhaps it was simply a curiosity?'

'Maybe just employment. You've heard of the Williamson Tunnels?'

Alfred nods. 'Joseph Williamson, 1810 to 1840, created subterranean passages beneath Liverpool. However, unlike Williamson, Castellanos appeared to have no philanthropic tendencies. There was only one thing that the villagers could all agree on.'

'Oh?' I ask.

Alfred smiles. 'That he truly was a man with more money than sense.'

I laugh. 'So it's just a folly? A tourist attraction?'

He raises his arms around him, reaching them out into the wide empty space. 'But for who? Legend has it that, one night in the taverna one of the builders who had a smattering of archaeological knowledge and had done a little research on the mainland before taking the job, said that this could be no labyrinth, at least not in the true sense. It had four entrances. A labyrinth has only one. And the four entrances led into a maze of circular chambers, which twisted and turned. With false starts that could keep a man lost for days. The circular chambers, so the worker claimed, were reminiscent of the four stomachs of a bull. Get beyond the 'stomachs', and you should reach one long labyrinth leading to a mysterious inner chamber.'

Suddenly I think of Mia, searching and searching in the dark.

'Have you seen it?' I ask.

'Not me, no. And there's a catch. Just like the old – *be careful what you wish for*. The villagers said that if you were ever to find the centre, you would find your true self. Yet in doing so, you would be driven to insanity, because sometimes your true self is an ugly thing to behold.'

'Human nature,' I mutter to myself. Alfred looks at me, quizzically.

'Oh there's this curious quote in Virginia Woof's *Mrs Dalloway*; a character's struggling to keep hold of his sanity and he says "Once you fall... human nature is on you... Human nature is remorseless". Like it's some kind of rabid animal.'

Alfred nods in understanding.

'And you, what do you think the purpose of the labyrinth is?'

He smiles. No doubt he's spent years thinking up answers to this very question. 'Monsters, dragons, curses, they're all useful devices employed by the wealthy to protect themselves. Just like people have security alarms on their buildings now, but don't connect them up. Perhaps all the mystery, all the secrets and myths were just a diversion coined by Castellanos to keep the locals away from the villa. And whatever it was, it worked. Even today the villagers don't like to come to the house.'

I remembered my first day, being dropped in the shelter of the elephant cliffs, and Achilleas' reluctance to linger.

'Did Castellanos ever finish it?'

'Well,' Alfred shrugs, 'after twenty years, the builders stopped coming from the mainland, and it was assumed that the tunnels had been completed. During this time the villa had also grown in size. The modest east wing was still there, but the larger central portion of the house, with the grand staircase and upper floor...'

The fish tank, I think.

'All this had also been installed. However, despite the size of the building, Castellanos continued living on his own. The island fell into the doldrums. Castellanos had no real visitors to speak of. If the man had friends or family, they didn't appear to keep in touch. The occasional academic would arrive, fuelled on by the mysterious stories heard on the mainland of a fantastic underground labyrinth. Mostly, they would be turned away on arrival. The villagers fell to gossiping – the size of the island simply didn't warrant the amount of traffic that Castellanos and his folly drew. And there was a problem: the islanders had grown up with two decades of families being supported by Castellanos' extravagance. People would joke when their homes became overcrowded with children. Offspring welcomed in by the sense of plenty that the lucrative labyrinth-building days had prompted. The locals would say that perhaps they should move into some of the spare rooms at Castellanos' villa. But of course, no invitations were forthcoming, and in truth, none of them wanted to get too close to the place. Many people felt, feel,' he corrects himself, 'it has a... curious ambience.'

I knew exactly what he was talking about; that sense that somehow the house is actually not bricks and mortar, but some kind of creature climbing angrily out of the soil.

'In the end, time managed to find a use for Castellanos' grand scheme, and it turned out that it was indeed fortunate he had extended the house. Because in 1941, when the Germans arrived, the villagers were thankful that at least they were able to maintain their own homes. The villa, with its grandeur and infrastructure to house so many, seemed fitting for an invading army. At first, the Germans left Castellanos to himself, more or less. The officers inhabited the grander main body of the villa. The soldiers were billeted in the outhouses where the workmen had once slept, and Castellanos was allowed to remain in the east wing. It was almost as if he had known. The structure of the compound seemed to fit the invading army as perfectly as a glove.'

'The villagers told you this?'

Alfred looks down at his cup. The tea is cold. He pours it onto the hungry ground and watches as it soaks away into the cracked skin of the earth.

'People don't like to talk about it, and the original villagers are of course no longer with us. There were a few documents that survived. One of the clerks had the good sense to preserve correspondence and files in a metal strongbox, which proved efficient in fending off the ravages of time and...' he hesitates, 'anger. Most of the documents were inventories; lists of grains, vegetables, citrus fruits imported from North Africa. The diet would have been predominantly fish caught for the army by the locals. The villagers had very little say as to how their time was spent. Records indicate that the soldiers were well fed and supplies easy enough to come by. I'm not certain this was always the case for the locals however.'

'And Castellanos?'

Alfred smiles sadly. 'We know very little. There are a few third party, so to speak, letters. In one Castellanos is described by a German officer as a "remarkable man" and "highly skilled".'

'Skilled in what?' I ask.

Alfred shakes his head. 'That's not stated. Although, some of the documents are of a...' and he hesitates, glancing for a moment at the two locals who are continuing their work in a sluggish, reluctant fashion, before lowering his voice, '... a disturbing nature.'

I suppose he's giving me the chance to get out, but I know I have to follow that golden thread right to the centre. 'In what way?' I ask.

'The people of Kairos were, understandably, not happy with the takeover. There were reprisals, but the Nazis had no intention of walking away. Kairos may not be the prettiest island in the Aegean or have the most desirable infrastructure, but geographically it's a gem. An ideal "stopover" for resistance movements, or the Allies coming in from Turkey, Cyprus or North Africa. The Germans were keen to discourage any kind of succour that might be given to the Allies. So despite the reprisals, or perhaps because of them, the Nazis put a new... tactic in place. It was felt that the best way to keep people on your side was to keep them in fear.'

'Henderson.'

'Sorry?'

'He spoke of society needing myths, gods and fear to keep people in their place.'

Alfred nods. 'It's an effective tool: the politics of fear. If a person is scared, they need something, someone, to protect them. Neo-conservatism and the politics of paranoia. If someone wants you to be afraid, they'll be wanting to manipulate you. Sadly, fear is a force so much stronger than common sense, so much more...' He searches for the word. 'Instinctive. And the Nazis were well versed in it. But if people are to be cowed, the gods or at least the men who have been allowed to rule, must feel... superior. There was an instruction from Germany stating that the people of Kairos should be *dehumanised*.'

I'm beginning to feel uncomfortable, but Alfred's not stopping as if he knows that if he pauses for too long, he'll never have enough momentum to carry him over to the other side of the horror.

'It's very difficult for most people to kill another human being. Thankfully, we all know it's wrong. But if you stop thinking of someone as being human, if you erode that status... The Nazis made a habit of making some people, "less than". They used Kairos, this island, as a training ground for brutalising, or desensitising if you prefer. Here...' He fishes in his canvas messenger bag for a moment, taking out some crumpled papers.

'Just photocopies, you understand. The originals are back at the house. Henderson has a collection. He had these copied for me when we first arrived. He's not quite so... helpful now. I sometimes feel that we may perhaps have overstayed our welcome.'

I flick through the papers; the intricate letters and records of people long dead sit beside plans of the labyrinth. Alfred looks intently over my shoulder. Though I'm betting he's looked at these documents so many times he could draw them from memory. Squirrelled away in the right-hand corner of one map, I notice a hastily written annotation. I squint, trying to focus on the words. They're German.

'*The labyrinth game has proved...*' I stumble; my German is not good. '"*Most effective in eroding the perception of the islanders as human beings.*" What does that even mean?'

'In short, kind of what it says on the tin. How they did it now... that's another matter. The Nazis began to regard the islanders as – *less than.* To think of them more like one might think of a dog, or cat, than an actual human being.'

'But game?' I say, flicking quickly through the papers. 'It talks of a game?'

'This is when the past becomes... even less... pretty. When myth becomes reality, it tends to lose its charm.'

Despite the fact that Alfred must have told this story many times, I can tell that he's still not entirely comfortable with it. The fact that it's in the past has done little to dull its horror.

'The Nazis would take small children, sometimes even newborns.'

And as soon as he mentions the children, I feel a sickening sense of dread; this must be the story about the children Cal referred to.

'You have to remember,' he continues, 'Kairos had been a prosperous island with the help of Castellanos. The families in the fishing villages had blossomed. There were many young children.' He sighs, reluctant to move on, glancing nervously over at the workers.

'And?'

'The Germans would take a child and leave it in the maze. The parents would have four hours to locate the child. If they were unsuccessful, the child would be removed from the parents.'

'What?'

'Sadly,' Alfred hangs his head, 'if it's possible, it does actually get worse. Legend has it that the children were...' he looks around him anxiously, before lowering his voice, '... sacrificed.'

This has to be a part of the myth machine, some tale spun for naughty children and revolutionaries, veiled threats to make them behave. 'You're joking, right?'

Alfred says nothing, and I know, with a sickening jolt in my gut, that he's not joking. Of course, there were the concentration camps: the horrors of what had happened to the Jews, but to incorporate killing into an actual game?

'You mean they killed the children?'

Alfred shrugs, as he flicks on through more papers, as if a definitive answer might suddenly come to light. 'Sacrificed? That part is unclear. It's what the stories say, and as you know, say a thing enough times, and it becomes so deeply embedded in the psyche it *becomes* true. It's the popular belief. But even for the Nazis, it doesn't seem entirely their style. Not sanitary enough. Perhaps the young people were taken away to the mainland? It's possible that they were all transported back to Nazi Germany. They weren't Aryan but could be brought up as soldiers, as *cannon fodder for the cause*. I like to think that's what happened. It's a little better than the alternative. But the myth maintains that the children were slaughtered. Only one thing's for sure: not one of them came back. All these years, and not one returnee.'

I stare around me at the peaceful olive groves, the same trees that would have witnessed these atrocities. In the bright winter sun, it's hard to believe such things could have happened here on this sleepy island.

'And this...' Alfred unfolds a piece of paper with a neatly composed accounts table etched on it. There are about fifty entries. Around twenty-five per cent have a black mark after them. He points to a small black circle next to a name – Spiros.

'This is where the parent was unsuccessful. So, as a game, as a lesson in dehumanising, and with a purpose of kowtowing your subjects, bringing the island to order, we must assume it was...' he hesitates, 'effective. To this day, legend has it that when the wind blows in the right direction anyone who carries a guilty secret in their soul or has lost a child, will hear the sound of children crying out in fear.'

Could that be it? Could that be the sound I'd heard? My own phantom returned to haunt me? Sally-Anne, my 'lost' child.

The wind moans as it edges through the trees, pushed in from the sea. I feel so cold, so alone; someone's walked over my grave.

Alfred leans towards me, takes the dregs of my tea and

pours it onto the ground. When he talks again, his tone is lighter. As though the fireside stories have been put to bed.

'Of course, I always think most people don't need a mythological structure. Guilt will track them down eventually. It's a hard beast to shake off.'

In my mind, I can see the darkened labyrinth, hear the child crying out into the night and the shadowed beast crawling down the passageways. I shake the thought from my head. There is nothing otherworldly about my tragedy. It was brutal and short and pointless, but there was no game involved, and the only monster was the man who planted the bomb and me – a monster of stupidity.

'Did you know Mia goes into the labyrinth at night?' I can't help myself. It shouldn't really be any of my business, but if Alfred knew, perhaps he could do something.

A look of sadness crosses Alfred's face, and I realise he's all too aware of Mia's night wanderings. 'I wish she wouldn't,' he says simply, staring out towards the blue sea.

'For me, it's an archaeological journey. I'm a historian, and the labyrinth is a point of interest. For her, it's become some kind of arcane ritual.'

'She claimed there was a temple at the centre, kind of like a fertility temple?'

'In one of these it describes...' Alfred's hands shuffle back through the documents, searching for something that can throw light on the subject and take us safely away from the personal. He rolls open a scrolled map, a photocopy, not the original, so it's difficult to guess at its age.

'This is much later. After Castellanos the island was uninhabited until the eighties.'

'Don't you mean the house?'

Alfred shakes his head. 'The whole island. No one wanted to live at the villa, and without that, there was no work. Then

Mr Henderson bought the place and started the refurbishment.'

'Of the house?'

Alfred smiles, amused by my understatement: 'Of everything: one of the fishing villages, the houses, the taverna, and yes, of course, the villa, but also the tunnels.' Alfred suddenly looks weary. 'Mr Henderson does know where the centre is, but he's not giving anything away. Once he said...' Alfred tilts his head back, narrowing his eyes as if trying to retrieve the exact words Henderson used. 'Something like... to find the centre...' He shakes his head, exasperated. 'No, it's gone. It was so odd, like a...' He rummages through some of the papers. 'Ah here, I scribbled it down after he said it.'

Alfred hands me the document. At the top left-hand corner are a few words in pencil. 'Agree to put money on the roll of a dice.'

'Gambling?' I ask. 'Did he want you to gamble with him?'

'It's certainly a possibility. Mr Henderson's the sort of man who...' Alfred hesitates, no doubt not wanting to seem disloyal. 'Well, he likes a bet. But myself, I'm useless at all that kind of thing. Perhaps it's a dare.' Alfred's brow creases. 'Mysteries. Mr Henderson does like his mysteries.'

I stare at the document. It's some kind of ground plan. 'What is this?' I ask, turning it around in my hands, trying to work out which way is up.

'That is the best map I have. It gives a kind of hint as to how the maze and labyrinth might fit together. It was drawn up by an archaeological team in the seventies, when the island was vacant, but it's incomplete.'

At the edges of the diagram, I can see the four entrances. A short way down from one entrance I make out a square courtyard: the quadrangle garden with its moon pond.

'I've been there,' I say eagerly, pointing to the courtyard on the map in a smug, proprietorial way, but Alfred's not impressed.

'That's the easiest one to navigate. The Garden of the Moon. These are more tricky.' He points to the other entrances. 'And this one here...' He raises his index finger before bringing it neatly back down on the north entrance, following the tunnel along till it reaches a circular garden. 'I've called it the Sun Garden. There's a sundial in it. It's relatively easy to find.'

He flicks his finger towards the other entrances.

'But these I'm not so sure. And as you can see...' He indicates the large blank centre in the very middle of the diagram. 'This is a mystery. This is where the children were left, we must suppose – at the heart of the labyrinth. I've looked for it, but it's confusing in there. I'm not even sure the Germans knew where the exact centre was. Maybe it was just Castellanos.'

I pull out my phone and take a quick photo of the map, not bothering to ask permission – better to ask forgiveness.

Alfred makes a grab for my phone. 'You shouldn't do that.'

'Why?' I hold it out of reach.

'This map... it's not for publication. It took me two years to get it out of him, and this is just a copy.'

'I won't make it public. It's only for me. I promise.'

Alfred looks uncertain, but it's all too late now. Unless he physically tackles me to the ground, the image is on my phone.

'Well, don't let Henderson see that you've got it. He likes to...' Alfred suddenly looks awkward, glancing nervously at the two workmen. They've taken out sandwiches and are settling in for a break. 'Our host likes to drip-feed information. He doesn't ever give anyone the whole story, only fragments, and of course, these may be just the fragments that he wants me to uncover. The fragments for you might be entirely different.'

'Sorry?'

Alfred's looking uncomfortable, as though he realises he's already said far too much.

'You should go if you want to get to the village. Besides, I have work to do.'

The moment is lost. Recording evidence for prosperity unnerves people. Once it's been snapped and stored in a digital cloud, it's not just Alfred's mystery anymore; it's partly mine. And Alfred's right, I've already spent too long here. My flowers are beginning to wilt, and the workmen have lost all interest in their task. I make my excuses and set off once again, walking back through the olive groves towards the tarmac road, careful not to trip on the nets or the roots running like serpents under the soil.

Moments before I reach the road, I hear footsteps closing on me from behind. I turn to see Alfred's hurried, dishevelled frame, hobbling awkwardly over the broken ground.

'You forgot this,' he says, handing me a handkerchief, a nervous air to his manner. He keeps looking back through the trees, as if the workmen may be following him, lurking in the shadows. I take the handkerchief, which I know full well is not mine, and as he hands it over, Alfred leans forward, so his lips are almost touching my face and whispers.

'Maybe keep it to yourself, what I told you. Keep it all to yourself.'

22

MONSTER

I walk on alone, the sounds of Alfred's dainty hammer fading behind me. Soon, all signs of human life have been gobbled up by the dense, twisted trees. This landscape hasn't changed for hundreds of years. The tarmac road may be new, but take that away, and Jason could easily have strolled down these very paths with his Argonauts on their boys' trip out. Jason's antics seem comic-book clean compared to the horror that Alfred's just related, but is it just a story?

There's nothing I like more than a puzzle. I did a bit of investigative journalism on my MA. Even medicine can be like some kind of riddle: you're trying to figure out what's going wrong. All the stories that I'm being told, I wonder where the actual truth is with any of them? It's as though the island means something different to everyone.

By the time I reach the village I'm dog-tired. The square is eerily quiet, tumbleweed central; like a film set when the actors and crew are all engaged somewhere else. Nothing seems real. The houses stand with their vacant eyes staring out at me. There are no cars, no villagers. Nobody sweeping steps or putting out washing. My footsteps echo off the buildings, ringing out my arrival, but no one comes to see.

Achilleas' boat is moored at the jetty. It doesn't look quite so pretty anymore. I cross the deserted square towards the taverna. As I round the curve of the building, I see the manager, sitting outside on the steps hiding behind a cloud of cigarette smoke, his arms rested on his ample belly. He looks up as I approach; as if he's an automaton suddenly wound into action.

'Καλή μέρα.' I use my phrasebook Greek.

He nods his head in a silent greeting.

Good day is about as far as my Greek gets me, so I continue in a loud overly-expressive pidgin English.

'The boy, he was injured? His house?' My words come complete with hand gestures, gestures that I would normally be mortally embarrassed by. But the manager seems keen to continue the mime routine. He nods, and points across the square towards a narrow house precariously sandwiched between two much taller villas. The windows are covered with black curtains as if the house is already in mourning. It's a meagre-looking building, but scrupulously neat. The front step swept clean, and a dirt-filled window box promising flowers, sometime. It doesn't look large enough for a family, so I'm guessing that maybe the injured child is the only son?

The manager, I notice, despite pointing, hasn't looked in the direction of the house. Instead, he keeps his eyes fixed firmly on me. He's not attempting to hide his curiosity, which is about as naked as curiosity tends to get. I'm guessing that he has high hopes for me – I must be the entertainment for the day. From somewhere deep inside the taverna I hear someone call a name, presumably his, because he sighs, stubs out the cigarette, pulls his jumper down a little further over his basketball stomach, and round-shouldered as a kid called in from the street for bath time, wanders back into the building.

Once again, the stage is empty. I cross the square, but as I do, I get a strange feeling that I'm being watched. The manager? I know he's still inside the taverna. I glance around, looking up at all the windows, and as I scan across the house fronts, a curtain in a room above the restaurant falls back in place. Someone was there, but then, is there anything so strange about that? The village has witnessed a series of arrivals. Not all of them welcome. There was Castellanos. Then the Nazis, and now Henderson and his entourage. An invasion that of course, I've unwittingly become a part of. If I lived in this village, perhaps I would stare.

The memorial is directly ahead of me: the one that I noticed from Cal's bike. It sits in the centre of the square, a simple unassuming construction: a vertical stone pole pointing up high, with a small plaque on it and an inscription in Greek. I take out my phone and log into Google Translate, but then stop. I have no idea how to type in the Greek characters.

I switch to camera mode and take a photo.

Στη μνήμη εκείνων που αρνήθηκαν να παραδώσουν τις ψυχές τους.

Someone can help me translate it back at the villa. Then it strikes me, there's something a little odd about the memorial. I must have seen hundreds of these things. Let's face it, every village back home has one, but this... The style seems contemporary. The lines and angles are just a little too rounded. I slip the phone back into my pocket and glance around again. All is quiet. The window with the swinging curtain appears cold and empty now. Turning back to the stone, I let my hand trail over the carved inscription, guessing it's the usual thing – *to all those fallen. In memory of...* but it looks different in the Greek alphabet, more meaningful somehow. As if the words have power. As though the island is asleep, and this inscription contains some magical spell; an utterance that will awake all those taken in action and set them walking again.

I continue towards the house, heading up the stone steps to the front door, clutching my flowers tightly. Although they must have been fresh this morning, the thick stems are beginning to smell like rotting cabbage, like death. I should have wrapped the ends in wet paper, but it's too late now. The heels of my boots strike echoes into the quiet, hollow air. I am alone. I can see that. But I still get this odd, uncomfortable sense that people, many people, have their eyes trained on me. Despite the bright cold sun, I shiver. Perhaps it's not just curiosity that's making them look; maybe it's malice. All these invasions throughout the years, and yet not one person was invited.

I knock. Lightly at first, even so the sound rings out into the emptiness. Echoing around the square, mocking me loud and bold as a woodpecker. I wait for a moment, but there's nothing. The square sits in stony silence. I shouldn't have come. What do I hope to get out of this? Why am I here? I realise, as I ask myself this question, that I'm not entirely sure. But something about the incident with the boy makes me uncomfortable. Not just the fact that a child was hurt. Was the child really okay now? And Cal's words keep gnawing into my brain – 'Why was the kid sticking his hand into the propeller in the first place.' The crew member mentioned a 'game'. Then today, Alfred... Alfred had said that the Germans had devised a *game*. So I know what I'm doing here – I want answers, and the only way to get answers is to ask questions.

I lift my arm once more and am about to knock when suddenly I hear something from deep inside the house; the sound of someone, somewhere, dragging themselves slowly into action. I feel the sudden desire to turn and run, but I'm out of time. The door pulls open, and there she is, the grieving woman from the taverna. Harrowed and pale, even smaller and thinner than she looked when I saw her at the taverna; as if all the air has been crushed out of her.

I hesitate, unsure where to begin. Words evaporate in my brain, till all I can manage is a solitary, 'Sorry.'

I'm ready for tears. I'm ready for remorse, and as her lip begins to tremble, and I remember just how much I hate emotion, I begin to ready myself for an explosion of grief. In a vain attempt to stop it, I move forward with the flowers. 'These are for...' Instantly I regret closing the gap.

The woman opens her mouth and lets out the most piercing, heart-wrenching wail. I stumble backwards, but she's heading down the steps after me shouting in a language I don't understand, and it's anger that's pushing her forward, not distress, but raw anger. 'Téras, Téras.' She keeps repeating the word over and over, shaking one hand madly in the air, thrusting the other toward me, fist clenched.

'I'm sorry...' I gasp, barely audible, stumbling, tripping down the last step, my arms flailing wildly through the air as I fall towards the hard ground. But she's right over the top of me, and I swear she's going to lash out. She balls one hand, and it's all I can do to defend myself, my arms flying instinctively over my face. Yet the blow never comes. Another heart-wrenching wail racks her body, and she slumps for a moment as if grief is dissolving her from the inside out. Then wearily, she hauls herself back to her feet, lurching up the stone steps and pulling the door firmly shut behind her.

The street is quiet again. There's no curtain twitch. There's no manager on the taverna steps but there's not a doubt that everyone saw.

23

LONG WALK

Humiliated, I pick myself up. The flowers lay scattered, petals crushed, stems broken at my feet. My ankle hurts, twisted from my fall and my clothes are covered in dust. I feel like a kid abandoned by a bully in the playground. The bell's been rung, and nobody's interested, or at least not in a good way.

To get back to the path I'm going to have to cross the void – the dusty, empty square – under the silent eyes of the village. This is ridiculous. It's not my fault but I'm not sure that matters to them. I was mad to come. Henderson was handling it. I'm crap at this kind of thing: patients, relatives, any kind of trauma. I've done it all before, and it doesn't work for me. It's like you end up wearing a bit of their grief, it rubs off on you, and I have enough. Besides, deep down I know my motivations hadn't really been to *support*. I'd been egged on by the *need to know*, which is an ugly thought, but at least it's an honest one.

I could go to Achilleas' boat, but I can still see that suit swinging on its hook. Was he warning me when he squeezed my arm as I was leaving last night, or was it a threat? I'm not sure, and to be honest, I don't want to find out. I hope to God he didn't just witness my public humiliation.

I'm close to the winding cliff road I took with Cal. The island is small: surely I can navigate it without going back through the village?

I must look a state, limping across the harbour wall, broken flowers clutched tight in sweaty palms, the reprimands of a village still ringing in my ears. I had nothing to do with the accident. I'd helped as much as I could. But perhaps… It's as if there's this sense of resentment on the island, running deep and unfathomable as ley lines, or labyrinthine tunnels. Me and 'my kind' are invaders who arrive in a tidal wave of extreme wealth and arrogance, just another part of the exploitation machine.

No. That's not right. Whatever the boy's mother might think, I need to keep hold of the facts. I'm already carrying one child around on my conscience. I refuse to add a second. Besides, I need to keep focused. As I begin the long climb up the hill, I start to run the facts through my head, because nothing on this island is making any sense. Why is there so much hate, so much raw emotion? This place should be paradise. I need to get things sorted, process it all and come up with some answers: I have an absurdly rich man with a disease that he's halted. But he isn't just any man; he's a world-famous geneticist. The condition I know can be arrested by foetal stem cells. And who but a renowned geneticist would have better access to such things? I have been told horror stories about children. I've even heard something like a child screaming out in the night, and a young boy has been hurt, almost fatally. Rumour has it he's now at a private clinic somewhere. He's certainly out of sight. Then there's an actual dead woman: the lovely lost Kara, who may have died on the island and been washed away on the ebbing tide, carried so conveniently from Kairos, and awkward questions by the Calypso Deep. Kara was the same age as me. Is that important? I remember the date on the entry pad – the year that I was born. The year Cal was born? Meanwhile, I am bound to an island where myths seem to permeate the very air. Old tales of journeys into labyrinths with monsters, they're existing side by side with new horrors of faceless Slender Men that steal children. *Stealing children*, isn't that exactly what the Nazis did?

My ticket home has been provisionally booked for the 24th, in the evening. It had only ever been provisional. Jed knows it's unlikely I'll be back before Christmas. I could extend. Today is the 21st. I have barely three days, will that seriously be enough time to gather all the information I need? If Henderson gets wind of what I'm up to, there's a good chance he'll try and stop me, because somehow his cure for Parkinson's, I'm damn sure, has something to do with his clinic. Is this where this notion of *commitment* comes into play? Is that what he was hinting at? My silence buys a job for life, not as a journalist though, as a medic. Why would anyone want me to step back into that role? Yet somehow, I know medicine is at the core of this problem. So maybe I'm right – he did steal from the clinic. Stealing sensitive biomedical material is illegal. Could this be why Grayling fell out with him? Why there was a fire? Suspected arson, Geoff had said. Perhaps Kara discovered the connection between Henderson and the stem cells? If so, that means he's willing to kill to keep his secret quiet. I could be putting myself in danger here. And why has Achilleas got that black suit on his boat? Realistically, he can't be my stalker: wrong size, wrong shape, and when he saw the picture in the library he was scared but there is someone following me. I'm sure of that now. He was outside my flat, at the airport, on the cliff path, and maybe even at the taverna; lurking outside the windows the evening of the accident – the guy with no face.

As I walk beneath the tepid winter sun, I could kick myself for not grabbing a bottle of water before I set off. My mouth feels like someone's crawled in there and died and I'm hungry to boot. I stare out at the sea. I could phone someone to come pick me up, but I don't. Instead, I phone Jed. It's his answerphone.

'Leave a message, and I'll get back to you when I get in.'

I phone again.

'Leave a message, and I'll get back to you when I...'

I phone one last time, just in case.

'Leave a message...'

I don't leave a message. Far below me, I see the beach I visited with Cal. It looks like a different place now: no longer paradise. The sea looks hard and cold. Maybe it is time to leave. If Kara was murdered, I seriously am in danger. Rather than extending my stay, shouldn't I be thinking of getting off the island? I could go back to the house, make my excuses. Tell them my mother was sick. Some emergency came up. Anything. The ticket is transferable. So, yes, I could extend it, but wouldn't I rather leave early? Henderson's already paid for the tickets, the fancy clothes, the food, not to mention the fifty grand sitting in my bank account, but if it's just the pretence of an all-gloss memoir that I'm supposedly working on, if that's the only thing holding me here, I have what I need. Then again there's that spark of life that I haven't felt for years, that curiosity; the Henderson story, it is just so big, and every day I spend on the island, another piece seems to get slotted into the puzzle. Can I seriously afford to walk away from that?

Funny how you never really notice how far things are when you're being driven. They say that the route back is always quicker. Maybe it's because on the way out you're concentrating harder. The route's less familiar so you're remembering the landmarks. On the way back, you're not forming those new memories. So everything takes less time. I've also switched transportation, and looking at the tarmac stretching out in either direction, I realise this is going to be a long job. Again, I wonder about phoning the villa. Cal wasn't exactly booked wall to wall. He'll probably have heard I went off on Achilleas' boat yesterday, and he'll have noticed I wasn't there for lunch. Knowing his juvenile mind, he would no doubt put two and two together and come up with sex, and I just can't be bothered. So Shanks' pony it is. There are no road signs, but the sea is my guide; I just have to keep it over my left shoulder, and all will be well. And all does go well, until the coastal road fizzles out into a small car park overlooking a deserted village. It must be the second village Alfred told me about, the one that had been abandoned. There are a few houses down there, the roofs fallen in. Skeleton struts exposed to the sky. Then I notice smoke coming from one of the chimneys: a thin grey trail leaking into the air. Kids maybe? I look closer. There's a little skiff, a motorboat, pulled up on the beach. It's been covered with branches so it's hidden from view, but one of the branches must have washed off in the night, and a fibreglass hull pokes out. I smile to myself; Henderson hasn't quite got total control of the island. The thought gives me a hint of pleasure.

At the back of the car park, there's a small path leading away into the olive groves. I look behind me at the road back, back to the beach, back to the village, back past the distraught mother of the injured boy. No, I've come this far. I've got a good two hours before it gets dark. I'll be fine.

I follow the path into the groves. It's well maintained. The island can't get enough traffic to keep the foliage down. If someone is looking after the path it must lead somewhere important, and there's only one place of importance on the island – Henderson's villa. The olive trees here are older than the ones by the compound. Before, I felt like I was walking through an ancient grove, but here I feel almost as if the trees are somehow woven into the sky and earth, as if this landscape is part of the fabric of time. Continuing on through the wood, I feel that intense feeling of absolute calm again. Could this island really have witnessed such horrors during the occupation? Another Greek myth comes hurtling into my mind: sirens and blocking up your ears. The Venus flytrap might look pretty, but it's a well-camouflaged trap.

After walking for well over an hour, my throat is so dry it feels like I've swallowed a knife. I'm starving and my boots are beginning to rub. The ground is uneven, laced with roots running riot through the hard soil. There's still no sign of the villa, and I'm beginning to lose faith, when suddenly I come out of the wood into a clearing with a small stream. The water's crystal clear. I'm so thirsty I drop my bag to the ground, lunging eagerly towards the brook. As I move into the clearing, I see that the water is travelling through a little grotto. A series of granite-grey boulders, gnarled and creased, stand sentry; stacked one on top of the other and reaching to around eight feet high. A 'seemingly' natural rock formation leading into what looks like a normal cave. But, I remind myself, on this island it's difficult to know what's natural and what's not. You can't trust anything, not even the eyes in your head.

The actual mouth of the cave is about five feet by four. Smaller than the entrance to my moon terrace but it has to be one of the entrances. I take my phone out of my bag and scroll through my photos till I find the one I took of Alfred's map. I can easily make out where the moon terrace is. I'm guessing I'm on the east side of the island, so this could be the eastern entrance? I move closer to the cave and shine my phone into it. The phone gives me about six to eight feet of light, but not one clue. All I see is a tunnel leading off, sloping gradually down. With my sensible head on, I'm unwilling to go potholing through mysterious Greek tunnels. Especially when no one knows where I am. I pick up a stone and throw it into the cavern. It skitters out of sight, but the sound of it falling is intermittent, as if it's dropping down a series of stone steps. I take a photo of the grotto and the cave. I'll talk to Alfred, maybe ask him to give me a tour but for now, I have something more pressing on my mind. Thirst. I drop down beside the stream and raise the water to my nose in cupped hands. There's a faint mineral smell, not unpleasant. Besides, how could this water be any worse than the stuff we get through our taps back home? It tastes delicious. Cold and fresh, like it's mixed up with air and soil. So raw on my teeth, it makes them tingle. I go back for more, the water running down my palms into my open sleeves.

Satisfied, I relax in the grove, leaning my head back against a mossy outcrop. I glance at my watch. It's already half past three. I reckon I have another half an hour until I need to start panicking. I'll walk just a bit further. If I don't manage to get anywhere familiar, if I don't recognise the surroundings, I'll simply jog back to the car park at the entrance. Cal will know where it is. He'll pick me up.

I stare into the sparkling water of the grotto. Then it dawns on me: Castellanos/Castalian – the spring at Delphi. It's where pilgrims washed before going on to visit the Oracle. Not Spanish at all, but Greek. I set off walking once again. So Castellanos may not have seen himself as the ruler of his domain, more the guardian? That was why he built the smaller house. That was why he was so ready when the Nazis arrived. He was waiting for someone, or something.

When I come out of the next block of woods, only a few minutes later, I find myself on a high clifftop. I drop my bag down by the side of a gnarled olive tree and walk cautiously to the edge, keen to get my bearings. This is going to be the point at which I continue on, or go back. I need to make my decision. The wind blasts cold and fresh on my cheeks. This side of the island is as high as the villa side. But, unlike the elephant path from the villa, an open track cuts down through the cliff below me towards a rocky cove. There's another pontoon, much smaller and empty. This track has no walls, no tunnels, just a metal cable swinging in the wind. Even looking at it makes me feel queasy. I pull away, making a mental note to avoid this exit at all costs.

The light is beginning to fade, leaching out of the landscape. I really don't have much time. I should call the villa, make my way back. If it gets dark, and the battery on my phone goes dead, I'm snookered. It's then that I hear something behind me in the woods, and out of the corner of my eye, catch sight of a shadow flickering through the tangled darkness.

'Hello?'

Whoever it is, they're not feeling chatty.

'I know you're there.' But again, nothing. Perhaps they don't speak English? But would they need to? *Hello* is kind of universal, and it's not exactly as if I look threatening.

I take a step towards the wood, but as I do, I hear the snap of a twig. Someone really doesn't want to be seen.

'Are you following me?'

Could it be one of Henderson's men, or perhaps one of the surly villagers?

I take a few steps, backwards this time, towards the path; if someone does lurch out of the darkness, I may need to run. Suddenly I realise I'm a very long way from anywhere.

'What do you want?' I mumble. As if in answer there's a sudden explosion of noise.

I jump from my skin, as a pheasant lifts itself into the air with a ricocheting burst of wings. Then I see it, because I'm not the only one to have been startled: on my left, in the dark foliage, the bushes have moved just enough for me to catch sight of a figure. I feel a lurch of blind panic because I know who it is:

the stooped skinny gait, the black clothes: the faceless man. Everything seems to be running in slow motion, and this time I manage to get a good look. His face is half covered in shadow, but he's staring straight at me. He knows he's been seen, and he's not trying to get away. The skies open and a shaft of light falls across his face, and as the harsh sunlight hits, I'm left in no doubt. What I see fills me with horror. It's as if the skin has melted away. And there's a look of such anguish and terror in his eyes: eyes that are pulled down as if dragged by dissolving flesh. I want to run. My heart pounds in my chest, in my ears, but my feet seem rooted to the spot. Then he does something so awful I feel my breath catch fast in my throat: he steps towards me holding one hand out as if he wants to touch me. I shudder, but my feet won't move. I'm frozen. He's getting nearer, stepping out of the darkness, those fingers clawing at the air, every moment getting closer and closer. A blast of wind ruffles my hair. In that moment, it's as though my whole body unfreezes. I let out a scream and the horror disappears back into the wood.

Within moments there's the sound of heavy footsteps running towards me from the opposite direction. I feel a wave of relief as I realise it's Cal.

'Sophie? You okay?'

I nod, but I'm not, I'm visibly shaking. 'I thought I saw someone.'

Cal glances into the woods. The light is fading fast.

'It's possible. Dad has this area patrolled. It is right by the pool.' He indicates to what I now realise is a high overgrown wall just beyond the line of trees. Hidden behind swinging creepers, I can make out a gate standing open after Cal dashed through. I'd practically been home and dry. But who, or rather what, had been following me? I look nervously into the dark woods, not sure that I want to see *it* for a second time.

'This wasn't a security guard,' I say, feeling a little irritated that Cal's downgrading what can only be described as my terror. 'I've seen him before.'

Even though Cal is everything every good mother would warn her daughter against, I feel much more confident with him at my side. So much so, that I move back into the wood in search of the melted man. Perhaps I can make out which way he went.

Cal's behind me, though he's sticking to the glade, reluctant to step off the path. 'What were you doing here anyway?'

'Long story.'

'We have a lot of guests, they sometimes...'

'No.' I shake my head, as I scour the trampled brush. 'It's not like that. This guy isn't the *guest* type. It's not just...' I'm not really sure how to explain it: if Cal would even believe me. It all seems so far-fetched. 'I keep bumping into him,' I say, thinking that this is not really the whole truth, but close enough. 'It's like he's watching me.'

Cal looks uncomfortable. 'I hate this area. It's creepy.'

I don't disagree.

'We should tell Dad about the guy. He likes to know who's where. What did he look like?'

I shake my head dismissively, as if it's not important. I don't want to describe him. To be honest, I don't want to think about that face again. And I wonder if this island doesn't have a monster for everyone – a Minotaur for Mia, a Slender Man for me, and perhaps more to the point... what had been on the cards for Kara? I have no intention of asking Henderson about the man. Maybe if it is Henderson's *game*, maybe I just don't want to play.

'There was something wrong with his face,' I say, hoping Cal will either know who I'm talking about, or drop the subject.

'If the face doesn't fit.'

'No, I mean really wrong.'

Cal glances up into the sky. It's getting late, and besides, he's not really interested. 'You sure you saw someone? The island kind of plays tricks on people sometimes. We're a long way from the village.'

'The island plays tricks, or is it your dad?'

Cal shrugs, like how would he know?

'Islands don't play tricks, Cal, people do. And I'm positive the guy I saw, he's not from the village.' I carry on, beating around in the undergrowth looking for any trace. 'His dress was too formal. No one in the village dresses like that.' I think of the suit hanging in Achilleas' boat. Maybe I'm asking the wrong questions. 'How long has Achilleas worked for your dad?'

'Always.'

'Does he ever take trips? Go away, like England or something?'

Cal laughs. 'You're joking. He barely steps off that boat of his.'

From the way the foliage has been crushed, I'm standing at the exact same spot where the man stood. I've got a good line of sight to Cal, who must be in the same kind of position as I'd been in.

'Why would he follow me?'

'Achilleas?'

'No, this guy, the one I keep seeing?'

'Pretty English lady, trying his luck.'

I run my hands over the trampled branches, then look over my shoulder into the undergrowth. Is he still there watching from the darkness? I'm always dubious about people relying on senses; the idea that you *know* someone is there just because you can *sense* them. It all seems too... mystical, more the kind of thing that people want to believe, than the kind of thing that actually happens. But silence is a good indicator, and there's not a breath of movement coming out of that wood. The man has gone.

'He wasn't following me because he fancied me.' I sigh. 'Is that all you ever think about?'

Cal shrugs, slipping his sunglasses over his eyes even though the sun has headed off for the day. *Fancied me* – of course, that is all Cal would ever think about. I'm about to head back to the path when I see something caught in a tangle of brambles: a black-and-white picture of a young woman. I pick it up.

'Found something?' Cal asks.

'No,' I say, pushing it quickly into my pocket. 'I dropped my watch,' I lie. I'm not exactly sure why.

'We all wondered where you'd disappeared to, especially after your no-show at supper last night.'

I clamber back out onto the path. 'Thought your father would have known?'

'Knowing and telling aren't the same thing.'

'I went to the mainland with Achilleas, yesterday. I was tired. Today I've just been exploring the island.'

I don't tell Cal I visited the boy's mother. I wouldn't really know how to explain any of that. Besides, he doesn't ask, just nods like *why not explore*? Nothing more normal in the world. There is, I suppose, an unwitting camaraderie between the two of us simply because we're the youngest here.

We follow the path towards the gate. My little adventure 'done'. *The kids are back together*; that's what the others will think. Then I realise it's not true, we're not the only *young ones* on the island. In fact, we're surrounded by young people. There are pretty maids serving breakfast, turning down beds, and muscled young men tending to boats and buildings. I've fallen into the rich person's trap, and it is so easy to slip into that I'm stunned, and slightly disgusted at myself – I am unable to see the people around me, the mere mortals. Somehow, I've managed to manoeuvre myself into the world of the elite, and we are the only ones that count.

'It can get...' Cal hesitates for a moment as if needing to choose his words carefully, '... claustrophobic on the island. Next time you're going to the mainland tell me, I'll tag along.'

After seeing what Achilleas has on his boat, I don't think that's going to be happening any time soon.

'Christmas is coming,' I say breezily. 'Everything's closing up.'

'Not here. Here time just carries on.' He eyes the wood anxiously behind us. 'Didn't find any Minotaurs then? Or maybe your stalker was part bull.' He laughs. 'Bull as in BS...'

'I got it, Cal. Besides, surely the Minotaur would stick to the tunnels?'

Cal shrugs, holding the gate in the wall open for me so I can slip through. 'I guess monsters can do whatever they like, depending on the leash they're on.'

He eyes me curiously for a moment; my dishevelled hair, my dirty jeans. 'You've got some work to do before supper. You got away with skipping it last night, but I wouldn't push it again, and you know the Great Man doesn't tolerate lateness.'

'Don't worry. I can scrub up quick.'

We step through the gate, and sure enough find ourselves back on the wide pool terrace. The pool lights are just flickering on. I really had been that close.

Cal leans back into the door and pulls three large bolts across: no one is getting in that way.

'Cal? Do you know what the war memorial in the village square says?'

'It's not a war memorial.'

'Oh?'

'No. It looks old, but it went up about five years ago. Dad was away for the summer, and when he got back...'

'So what does it say?' I ask, reaching for my phone in case he needs the text in front of him.

'I don't know. Something like, *In memory of those who refused to surrender their souls?*'

'So it's about the occupation?'

He glances at the image.

'In memory of those who refuse to surrender,' he reads.

'Refuse?'

He looks blank.

'Is it refuse or refused?'

He glances again at the text. 'Odd. Refuse, I think, but don't quote me. My Greek's not brilliant, and history's really not my thing. Maybe you're right... Course you're right. It must be refused. I know Dad wasn't happy about it. But to get rid of the memorial, well, that would just draw more attention. So he leaves it there. People forget if you leave something in full view. It just becomes part of the furniture.'

24

REAL STORY

One major downside of being ridiculously rich is that there's no such thing as solitude. Having people waiting on you hand and foot has its price; there's always someone doing a mysterious 'something' in a person's personal space. When I get to my room, my door is open. Inside, Sylvie is draping the bed with the latest haul of dresses.

'You!' she exclaims, dropping her bundle onto the cover and taking my face between her hands. 'Out with the Greek boy, no?'

'No,' I say, perhaps a little too forcefully.

'Well, this is your mistake, and you look such a mess. I will call someone to run the bath.'

'I can run the bath myself,' I kick my boots off by the door.

'You do that, and you steal someone's job.' Sylvie is pragmatism personified. 'There are people paid to run baths.' She looks at me in exasperated affection, like a kind schoolmistress with a favourite naughty pupil. 'Sophie, you run me around in knots. Now sit.'

I don't need a second invitation. I fall back on the bed.

'I'm exhausted.'

'You have no time to nap.' She runs her critical eye over me. 'We must try and detangle that hair, or there will be birds nesting.'

She takes what looks like a phone from her pocket and presses a button.

'Pager, for Ellie,' she explains. 'Stops me shouting the house down. My room is all the way up in the tower, so... she has younger legs.'

I remember the curious tower I'd noticed on my arrival. It seems fitting somehow, the beautiful Sylvie living in a tower like a forgotten princess.

'Now you sit straight at the mirror.'

I do as I'm told.

'What have you done with this?' She asks, raking her fingers through my hair. 'Get tips from Medusa?'

'It's the sea air. I met up with Alfred today. He was digging.'

'That man is always digging.' Sylvie sighs, picking up a brush from the dressing table and tackling my locks. 'Leaving his poor wife all the day. Is no good for a marriage.'

'People do it all the time back home. Breadwinners commuting into London, while other halves get stranded in suburbia.'

'Other halves?' She looks curious.

'Partners.'

Sylvie laughs. 'Like nobody is whole?'

Suddenly, a look of complete sadness crosses her face. The brush goes limp in her hand. I'm just about to ask if she's okay, but when I glance in the mirror again, the look has gone. Maybe it was all in my head because she's off once more, all French smiles and cheeky charm. 'Anyway is not the same. Back "home" there are things to do. Here, the mind, it runs away with a person.'

I remembered the broken Mia walking through the maze at night, blood running down her forehead.

'Is not good.'

I had to agree with Sylvie on that front. 'Are you worried about Mia?'

Sylvie's eyes dart quickly away, and I get the distinct feeling that, as far as Sylvie is concerned, she has said too much already.

'Nothing that happens on this island is any of my business.'

It's almost as if Sylvie's granted herself a stock get-out-of-jail clause. Her brush-off was all too quick, too seamless.

'What do you mean?'

Sylvie just shrugs: the discussion is over.

'Alfred told me something about the history of the island,' I say, trying to change the subject. Because it feels as if Sylvie is walking on eggshells this evening.

'Ah ha, the island – Castellanos?'

'Yes.'

'Is a good story, no?'

'And the German occupation.'

'Hm,' she sighs, 'is not so good.'

'I went to see the boy's mother today.'

Sylvie looks blank.

'The one who got hurt.'

'Why?' Her forehead creases into a frown. 'This is not necessary. *This* is not your business. Mr Henderson, he has everything sorted.'

'She called me something – *téras*. Do you know what it means?'

Her face clouds. 'Oh, Sophie. The woman was upset.'

'Yes, but I just wondered, what does it mean?'

'It's stupid. She was angry.'

'Yes, but... Sylvie?' I'm not going to let her give me the verbal slip again, and this time she knows it.

Sylvie lowers her eyes. 'Monster,' she says, her voice barely audible. 'It means monster.'

It's only a word. How can a word carry any weight at all? As soon as it's said it should be lost but of course, it isn't.

'Why would she say that?'

Sylvie shrugs. 'Her boy, he is hurt.'

'Where have they taken him. Will he be all right?'

'Of course.' She laughs, a little too enthusiastically.

'What's going on here, Sylvie. I mean really going on?'

'You ask too many questions.' She puts the hairbrush down firmly on the dressing table, as though marking an end to the conversation. 'I told you, Mr Henderson, he has everything covered.'

'Sylvie?' I glance around me, checking we're alone. Ellie's somehow slipped into the bathroom while we were talking. The taps are on, thundering into the porcelain tub, but I still go to the door, pulling it closed. I want this to be said in confidence. Yet when I turn to face Sylvie, I get the distinct impression that she's not in the confidence business: the closed door is making her nervous.

'I think someone's following me.'

A flicker of fear, so quick it would be easy to miss but it's definitely fear that I see. When she speaks again, however, her voice is under control. Clear cut as though she's reading from a rule book. 'Mr Henderson has security on the island. It's for your protection.'

'No, you don't understand. I think someone followed me from London. It's not Henderson's security.'

'Then you should tell Mr Henderson.'

'But...'

She raises one eyebrow sternly. 'You do it, or I do it for you.'

It looks like I don't have much choice.

'To be honest, Sophie, I think you are worrying over

nothing. The security here is excellent. We don't always see it, but it is always there.'

'No.' The idea that the man is just *security* won't work. 'He doesn't fit the type,' I insist. 'There's something wrong with his face.'

At the mention of the man's face, Sylvie stops dead in her tracks.

'What do you mean?'

'It's kind of...' And I stumble over the words. 'It's kind of like it's been melted. Maybe an acid attack?'

Sylvie looks awkward. Instead of answering me, she goes to pick up her sewing basket. I get the impression she's keen to make an exit. I grab her arm.

'Sylvie, what do you know?'

'Nothing,' she hisses. 'I just work here, and I want to carry on working here. I know nothing.' There's more than a hint of impatience in her voice as she shakes her arm loose. 'You tell Mr Henderson, or you don't. Up to you. But for me... keep me out of it.'

'Sylvie?'

'You talk too much.'

And she's gone. But I know I've stumbled on something. Someone is following me, and whoever, or whatever it is, struck a shaft of fear into Sylvie. Maybe there really is a monster on the island. I let out a long, low sigh. None of this is making any sense. I glance down at the beautiful dresses; a petrol blue, a delicate nude, a jade-green silk. It would be so easy to sell your soul on an island like Kairos. You could sell it without even realising you'd stepped into the auction house. Suddenly I remember – the photo I'd found in the woods. I take it out of my back pocket and gaze at the face smiling out from a different time. Going by the hair and clothes, I'd place her early 2000s. I flip the photo over. There's a name printed on the back in neat cursive script: Susanne Millar 2006. I grab my phone and send a text to Geoff.

Susanne Millar – mean anything?

———

I've got work to do before supper. I grab my computer and go straight to Google. I hadn't had enough time at the library yesterday. I'm still looking for something on my faceless man, and I've got to remember I'm in the realm of myths here. I'm after some kind of monster, some kind of entity, older than the Slender Man and boy do I find it. I flick past the Wiki entry I had in the library. There are so many articles: the Celts have farriers, the Japanese have faceless spirits. In fact, here's an international army of faceless men in black chalked out through the ages. They stalk and traumatise people, mainly children. But... I also get the feeling that these are horror stories created by people who want to fuel fear and superstition. It might be parents needing to keep control, or some kind of power elite. Just like my Minotaur, I'm convinced that there is nothing supernatural going on here. There's a rational explanation. All good mysteries have a point at which they unravel. I just have to find the right end and pull. As soon as Ellie's gone, I ring Jed.

'So you're saying this creep is following you?'

'He was at the airport.' I don't tell Jed about the night I thought I saw something in the road outside my flat. Besides, it doesn't make sense: how could my pursuer have known where I lived?

'He was at the airport, then by the pool, and at the restaurant...'

'So... maybe he's on some kind of holiday there?'

'It's not that kind of island, Jed. And today he was way out in the woods.'

'Soph.' Jed's assuming that irritating, sensible, I'm-the-grown-up-here tone. 'You know this is all nuts, don't you? Labyrinths and now this faceless creep.'

'I know.'

'And then the thing about Parkinson's?' He sighs. 'I mean, Soph, you're all over the place.'

'And don't forget Kara.'

'What?'

As soon as her name is out of my mouth, I regret it.

'Kara Jarvis,' I mumble.

At this point there's a pause so loud it's in danger of bursting my eardrums. Too late, I remember – Jed doesn't know about Kara. Well, he doesn't know that Geoff and I have discovered some kind of link from Kara to Henderson. Jed must have seen her name in the paper. So he knows that her body was found in the Ionian. Jed can probably cope with the overinflated ego of a billionaire living on his own private island. He can possibly even cope with mixing myth with reality. But as soon as there's a dead girl floating in the mix, Jed's hackles are up.

'Soph, you should come home. I want you to buy your ticket.'

'I have an open ticket. It's not that. I haven't finished the memoir,' I interject lamely.

'We both know this is going way beyond coffee-table tat.'

'Jed.'

'You can do a memoir with a day's contact. You're digging up dirt, and there's already one young woman dead.'

'And you are being melodramatic. I've thought about it. I've got a ticket for the 24th anyway.' I'm so regretting having told him. Why on earth did I have to mention Kara? 'Look,' I say, keeping my tone level. 'I've got to get this story. It's what I do. Besides, if I can get the research, if there's even a shred of truth in my Parkinson's theory then...'

I don't need to fill in the rest; he knows that if I can help people, ease suffering, then maybe, maybe, I can finally kiss Sally-Anne goodnight. Make some kind of atonement.

'Okay. Okay then, I'm coming out.'

'Jed!'

Despite myself, I feel such a rush of joy. For the first time in two years, I realise, actually Jed is the only person in the world that I truly want to see. But... 'You can't just arrive on the island. You have to be invited. It's not like a normal island.'

'Tell me about it.'

'I mean, there are no hotels. No places to stay.' But I so want him here. I so need him beside me.

'Then I'll get to the mainland. You can make your excuses, and I'll meet you in Athens.'

When he says it like that it feels so right, so exactly what should happen. It also means that my time on Kairos is ring-fenced, which is what I need. It'll focus my investigation and chivvy Henderson into getting on with that memoir. I get the distinct feeling that if Henderson doesn't have some kind of deadline, I could well just end up on the payroll indefinitely. Or until he gets bored with me, and I've seen what happens to people who have served their purpose. I don't want Henderson offering me any more job extensions, asking for any more *commitment.* Jed's right. I need to get out.

'Great,' and I mean it. I genuinely do. I'm even getting butterflies at the thought of being with Jed again. I'm beginning to feel. Then, irritatingly, my mind stumbles over the spanner in the works.

'Hang on, Jed... you might find it really difficult to get a flight. It's Christmas, remember.'

'Let me worry about that. I'll close this place, it may take a day or so, but then I'm on the first plane out there. I'll sort the cat.'

I hadn't even thought about the cat. Jed really is the most unselfish, considerate man I've ever met. I'm lucky, so lucky.

'Okay. When you get your ticket, you text me.'

'Sure.'

'I'll try and meet you at the airport in Athens. If I can get there, I mean. But I'll try...'

'Thank you, Sophie.'

Such simple words, but they contain so much.

'And, Jed...'

'Yeah?'

'I'm sorry. I'm really, really sorry about taking you for granted. I never meant to. I just wasn't in a good place.'

'I know, Soph.'

'I think I've had enough on the adventure stakes to last me a lifetime.'

He laughs. 'The big wide world not all it's cracked up to be?'

'You got it, and Jed... I love you.'

And that's it. There's a silence both sides. A pause to let our hearts soar. Jed is exactly where I need to be. We both know that. No more games.

I put the phone down, taking a moment to glance around my beautiful room. This is all coming to an end. I will take my research; I will write up my story somewhere else. I will spend Christmas with Jed. Maybe, probably, the rest of my life with Jed. We'll start a family. Perhaps a little girl. I'll call her Sally-Anne so that I never forget: never forget that we have to keep finding hope in this world, keep building something out of the wreckage.

It's seven thirty by the time I get to the tub. I sink back into a sea full of bubbles scented like an English garden. Tonight, I'm looking forward to supper. Not just because I'm starving. I'm desperate to chat to the other 'guests'. See if I can find out just one bit more of the puzzle without having to ask the big man himself.

I dry off quickly, put on the nude lace dress, and tie my hair in a simple ponytail. It's unfussy, but the dress is doing so much work I can get away with 'unfussy'. Maybe I'll take this one when I go? I could even get married in it. Married – now there's a thought. I haven't thought about being *married* for a long time. I paint my lips, not bothering with the habitual dab of blush for my cheeks. The day has gifted me some great colour in my face; outdoor life always agrees with me. I look good enough for any table. It's then that the thought begins to niggle. *Good enough for any table?* What does that even mean? Henderson doesn't appear to be interested in getting this memoir sorted. So, why am I here? There are better journalists, better biographers, better company, way more beautiful women. Am I here for Cal? There had been an attraction certainly. How could I help it, he's a good-looking guy and it kind of went two ways. Only... now I think about it, there was something more than just attraction from my side. Something I can't quite put my finger on. Cal had obviously felt it too, what had he said when he met me? *Christmas suddenly got interesting.* Was I the entertainment? The fresh meat? It's not just a niggle that something's not right anymore; it's a full-blown warning bell as I stand there trussed up in the latest offering – Kara Jarvis, same age, found floating.

The dress doesn't seem quite that appealing anymore. And why had Cal been so close this afternoon? I had been walking through the woods. There was no one around, then suddenly, two people? It all seems more than a little convenient. Was there enough time for Cal to have doubled back? I didn't see the two men together. Was it a face that I saw melted and disfigured, or could it have been a mask? But if so, why? Then I remember: the photograph. I grab my phone and pull up Geoff's thread, still no reply.

I've spent so much time chasing monsters on this trip that my judgement's becoming clouded. I should just try and work with the concrete, not go off on a wild goose chase. Work with the facts. I've got time to put in one last call before supper. I grab my notebook and find the place where I scribbled down Grayling's number: the other partner at the fertility clinic. If there are meaty stories to be had about the clinic, he'd be the man to talk to.

I don't really expect to get through. I'm guessing I'll have to book a time for a conference call. So, I'm taken aback when I find myself speaking to the man's wife. She has one of those old-fashioned formal phone voices, answering as if she's just stepped out of a sixties sitcom.

'Grayling residence?'

Not even my mother does that anymore.

'Hello, it's Sophie Williams here. I'm doing a memoir on Tim Henderson.'

If it's possible to feel ice flow through a phone, I would swear that is exactly what I feel when Henderson's name slips from my tongue. 'If I could just talk...'

'No comment.' The voice from the other side is hard, clipped and inflexible.

'But...'

'If you call again I shall report you to the police.'

The phone goes dead.

I know the Grayling/Henderson relationship had been strained at the end, but there was something in the woman's voice that went far beyond a mere falling out. She was scared.

I sit down on the bed and pull on the kitten-heeled shoes

that have been left for me, feeling oddly reassured by the fact that they pinch at the back – not even extreme wealth can buy extreme comfort in a pair of high-fashion shoes. Although the thought only amuses me for a moment – why would Grayling's wife be scared? I can't call again. She'd made that clear, threatening me with the police, but I have no intention of just letting this drop. Back on the web, I flick quickly through a group of emails claiming to be registered to Grayling. He's got everything: BT, Google, Mac. I try them all. I send a standard letter:

`I'm doing a piece on Henderson and the clinic. I would welcome the chance to talk with Grayling. The conversation would be entirely private and confidential.`

I pause. I need more. I need to entice him out of his shell. I place my fingers back on the keys and type:

`I want to set the record straight.`

What might prompt Grayling to talk? He doesn't need money or fame. So, there's only one good reason I can think of to get those vocal cords lubricated – a grievance. Offering to 'set the record straight', is exactly the sort of hook that just might get him engaged.

I glance at my watch. Five minutes to go. I type in Google Images, download the BBC logo, and add it to my letter. The email wouldn't have the BBC address, but lots of producers work freelance. The logo will suffice. I click send. If there's no reply, I'll just have to hook up with him when I get home. Because just maybe the mythology element is a red herring, a smokescreen to mask the real story: the story of the clinic.

25

FEAR & GREED

When I arrive in the dining room, I feel a tsunami of disappointment – Clara and Numbers have gone. Numbers I can do without, but Clara? Their seats are now occupied by a man, not much older than me. He's accompanied by a young woman; her face so long and sombre it's unnervingly equine.

'No Clara?' I ask, hovering somewhere by the entrance to the room as though I might just back out.

'Had to leave suddenly. Gone this morning.' Alfred sounds chirpy. Perhaps he didn't like her? Clara was probably a bit on the brash side for him. Besides, I imagine he's seen a lot of people come and go.

'Oh?' I continue to hesitate. It looks like Alice has deigned to give us her company. It all feels a bit too... musical chairs for my liking.

'Going to join us?' Beavis walks past me into the room, his eyes shining small and sharp as stones inside that tight skull.

Then I remember. I remember the misted bathroom mirror at the taverna, and the conversation with Clara as she leant on the sink, dragging her finger across the steamed mirror –

LEAVE NOW. I feel a creeping panic crawl up my spine. She'd tried to warn me. How could I have forgotten? So much had happened after. But Clara's warning, was it something to do with Kara Jarvis?

'Feeling better after last night?' Alice asks, though I get the impression she doesn't really care.

'Yes. The boat ride back from Athens must have,' I hesitate, 'upset my stomach.'

She smiles a thin smile. 'Unfortunate. If you had been here you would have known about Clara's imminent departure. Sometimes, people do have to leave us suddenly,' she announces casually, taking a seat at the head of the table. Raising a glass of wine to those dry red lips, she shoots me a hard look.

I get the uncomfortable feeling she's got something on me. Maybe she's not buying the fact that I pulled a sicky last night. Then it hits me. Of course! In my mind, I picture that closed bathroom stall of the taverna. Had Alice been in there when I followed Clara to the bathroom? I scour my brain, running through fragments of memory from that disastrous evening. Had Alice been sitting at the table when I left for the washroom, or was she on the dance floor? I can't picture her there: meaning... she could easily have been in the cubicle. As I'd left I'd seen Clara wipe the mirror, wipe all traces of her message, but marks on mirrors don't come out completely without a touch of vinegar. They reappear like ghosts every time a bit of steam is applied.

'Clara had demonstrated her commitment,' Henderson sneers. That word again. 'But loyalty is part and parcel of the deal. No loyalty, no true commitment.'

What on earth can he mean?

Beavis suddenly looks uncomfortable, pulling his sleeve down over his bad arm. *Commitment*. Clara and her damaged leg. I glance around the table. Mia and her insistence on self-harm. Is that what Henderson means? To enter the inner circle, you have to demonstrate your commitment, actually hurt yourself in some way; carve some kind of sign on your body?

They're all seated now, like an always-eclectic dinner party at the 'Hotel California'. I need to play the next few hours very carefully. Keep my cards close to my chest then I seriously do need to get the hell off this island. As if he's read my mind, Henderson pushes the chair beside him out from the table. My place yawns before me; like a grave cut neatly into fresh soil. He says nothing but locks me in a long steady gaze. Does he know I've found out about Kara? About his Parkinson's? About *commitment*?

'We're just lucky that Elliot and Portia could make it at short notice.' Alice smiles pertly, and I know I've guessed right about Clara's message: Alice had seen it.

The evening is off to one hell of a bad start. I needed to be ahead of the game, but it feels like I'm continually three steps behind, stepping into squares that have been left purposefully open for me. To make matters a whole lot worse, Portia, I soon discover, has a laugh to go with her look: all horse. She gives us a quick trill and is just about to launch into something mind-numbingly sycophantic when Alice goes for the kill:

'Goodness knows how we'd manage without a constant stream of nobodies to entertain us.'

'We missed you on the road back, Sophie,' Alfred says, doing his best to dilute Alice's sting.

'I took a detour. I wanted to get more of a... picture of the island, maybe figure out a little bit more about Castellanos.'

'Castellanos?' Henderson's voice booms out over the table as Alfred pales, and I remember, too late, I'd been told to keep our conversation to myself.

'Fascinating man.' Henderson's voice carries clear as a bell over the clatter of silver-serviced lamb cutlets. The bones hit the plates as the guests lick their lips. My own entrée appears to be something with beetroot, a vegetable that bleeds.

'Yes, I stumbled on a few articles about him before I came out here.' Luckily I've been raised in the school of flying-by-the-seat-of-your-pants. Unfortunately, I now have the full attention of the table. Not exactly what I'd wanted.

'Oh, which articles?' Henderson asks, and the blood in my veins freezes. What would it be? *National Geographic*? *History Today*?

'Oh, er,' I stumble.

'Archaeology,' Alfred cuts in. 'The *British Museum Magazine*?'

'Ah, that must have been it.' I nod.

'Yes, that one carried a lot of speculation as to why Castellanos built the labyrinth.'

'Exactly,' I say, toying with my napkin. 'And I was interested as to where he came from. I was wondering...' I think we're safe now. 'I thought perhaps he might have been Greek, but from a region with a different dialect?'

Henderson eases a finger around the lip of his wine glass as though casting a spell. 'Well, dear Sophie...' He draws out his words, so they sound long and tortured, not exactly genuine. 'You have an expert here.' He gives a half-smile and nods towards Alfred.

'Oh, hardly that.'

'You've spent four years researching the man. If you're not the expert, who would be?' There's a taint of distaste in Henderson's voice.

'Perhaps his name isn't Spanish,' I continue. Hoping I haven't sunk Alfred neck-deep in trouble. 'The name might not be his own. Maybe he took it from the Castalian Spring?'

Henderson nods, and I get the feeling he's already got this far in the puzzle.

'Castalian Spring?' Portia looks blank.

Alfred steps in helpfully with an explanation. 'Where the pilgrims stopped before going on to see the Oracle.' He's not looking convinced.

'This was what made me think of it.' I take out my phone and show Alfred the grotto.

'Ah... the east entrance.'

So I was right.

The phone is dutifully passed around the table, to a range of mixed reactions. Alice doesn't even feign interest. I find myself wondering what it would take to get Alice engaged.

'That is one of the most difficult entrances,' Alfred offers up to the table at large. 'It's got a myriad of tunnels.'

'That thing we came up through was bad enough,' Elliot, the new Numbers, is aiming for a degree of levity, but his voice sounds a little strained.

'Sophie did it very quickly.' There's an odd proprietorial note to Henderson's voice, and I realise he's trying to pit me against the new arrivals. He doesn't want friendship. Friendship can lead to honesty and secret sharing, and I'm beginning to see that Henderson is in fact a big fan of blind confusion.

'But why would anyone build such a thing?' Portia asks.

Henderson leans back in his chair, bones abandoned on his plate, a few scraps of lamb sitting in a pool of blood. 'You know what the two most underestimated motivations of humanity are?'

'Love,' Portia offers naively, and I feel an instant wave of pity for her. She is so out of her depth.

'Fear,' I say. I've got a good idea where this is going.

'And?'

'Greed.' It's Mia who speaks. She'd been so quiet I'd almost forgotten she was there. It's a good answer, despite the fact that she's slightly inebriated.

She remains looking down apologetically, her eyes fixed firmly on her plate. 'With fear and greed at your disposal, you can conquer the world,' she says, barely audible. There's something truly chilling about the way she delivers her line. Not an ounce of emotion. As if the writing is on the wall; our fate is inescapable.

'Exactly.' I'm not sure if Henderson's failed to notice Mia's tone, her broken demeanour, or if it just isn't important to him because he's instantly spring-boarding into his own theory anyway. 'Castellanos understood the importance of these two elements. He used the greed of the locals – they needed him. They needed the jobs. They needed the trade. And the true beauty of money is that the more people have, the more they need. Then there was the labyrinth. Fear. Make yourself a myth, and if you promote it well enough, the whole world bows down before you.'

26

BREAKING IN

My plans to tell Henderson I was heading home didn't quite pan out. He was on his own personal power rant, and I didn't get a look-in. Nobody did. I make a vow to get my announcement in early over breakfast. When I arrive back at my room, I find a text from Geoff telling me to call. I do the calculations. It's ten o'clock at home. I go into the bathroom, run the taps and dial.

'Sophie, what's that noise?'

'The taps.'

Geoff laughs. 'You're becoming quite the detective.'

'It's Henderson,' I say, irritation lacing my words. 'He's a control freak. I swear he's onto everything.' I stand looking at my reflection. Was it really a mirror? Or was there someone sitting behind it monitoring me even as we spoke? No, that's madness. I need to keep a grip.

'Yeah, well. No harm in being cautious.' Geoff's voice comes back calm and clear, the voice of reason. 'Henderson, he's had his fingers in a lot of different pies over the years.'

'Susanne Millar?' I ask, as I open the drawer in the

bathroom cabinet, lift up the towels and take the photograph I'd found in the bushes from its hiding place.

'Worked for him ten years ago. Found floating in the Med.'

Another drowned woman. What the hell was happening here?

'Don't tell me this Hellenic Trench can get you to the Med as well?'

'To be honest, all you need is a boat. A private boat will get you and your dead body just about anywhere, very few questions asked.'

Henderson certainly had a boat. 'Geoff.' I take in a deep breath. I'm stepping right out of my comfort zone here. 'I think Kara and Susanne Millar were onto something about Henderson. I think...' And I pause awkwardly because it all sounds so far-fetched in my head, that I'm sure it's going to sound doubly mad when voiced in the open.

'Go on,' Geoff says, and I realise I've got to try.

'I think there was something odd going on at that fertility clinic.'

'As in?' Geoff wants all the evidence before committing to a reaction.

'I think Henderson was using foetuses in stem cell research.'

There's a brief pause. Thinking time. 'No doubt it's heavily regulated, but provided he had consent, it might not be illegal.'

'Maybe not. But my feeling is... he may have been using stem cells to help cure himself. He's got Parkinson's.'

For a long moment Geoff says nothing. I get the sneaking suspicion that he's also smelling a rat.

'Susanne Millar and Kara... Maybe, somehow, they got wind of what he'd been up to and he got rid of them. To lose two members of staff, it just doesn't sit right.'

'Four,' Geoff says. 'I found two others: Bobby Gainland and

Ed Marchant. Also employees. Marchant 2008. Gainland 2003.'

Men? I don't know why, but this surprises me. 'In the sea again?'

'No. One was a building accident. Three months after Marchant worked for Henderson. Happened in Piraeus. He'd been taking some time out. He'd got a job working on a site as a labourer. Just casual stuff. A slab of marble became unsecured.'

'Ow!'

'Yeah. Poor bugger. Didn't stand a chance.'

'I suppose these things happen. Construction sites are dangerous. Most likely, he had no training.' I'm playing devil's advocate. I have to. I know that – I need to test the story. 'It's tragic, but I guess he wasn't actually working for Henderson at the time.'

'Well...' I note the scepticism in Geoff's voice. 'The construction site was owned by a friend of Henderson's, an M J Beavis.'

'I know him.'

'What?'

'He's here. He's a doctor.'

'And a property developer?' Geoff's sounding dubious at this.

'And Gainland?' I ask.

'Road accident. Hitch-hiking in Cyprus. Happened two weeks after he'd finished his placement. His placement with Henderson.'

'Hitch-hiking can be risky.' But I'm just doing lip service now. I'm not sounding convinced.

'Seems that way.' Geoff's tone is drier than a bone-dry Chardonnay. 'Hit and run,' he adds, just so I'm fully in the picture.

I feel a cold sensation creep over my body. 'Could be a coincidence?'

'In your file on how to be a detective, next to running taps as a precaution for bugs, make sure you put a warning note beside the word *coincidence*.'

'So I'm not wrong?'

'That I don't know. First things first, young lady, you need to be careful. Whatever Henderson's hiding, he's more than willing to kill for it.'

'Should I call the police?'

'And tell them what, exactly? These "accidents", the paperwork's all been filed, done and dusted years ago. There are no loose ends. People like Henderson are canny bastards. They hide the truth so deep the only way you can find it is to trip them up.'

'But if Kara and the others had found something, why didn't they go to the police?'

'Kara doesn't look like she had much of a chance. The others may not have even realised what they'd stumbled on. Or maybe one of them, or all of them, were trying to blackmail Henderson.'

'So what do I do?'

'Best advice? You get yourself home tonight.'

Silence.

'Funny,' Geoff comes back. 'That's exactly what I thought you'd say. Okay,' he continues. 'You need to find Henderson's secret. Sounds like it's got something to do with the clinic, something to do with stem cells, something to do with his illness.'

'Thanks for the summary,' I say sarcastically. 'But where do I start?'

I think about the island: its myriad of secret treasures and the strange cast of people that switch and change before my eyes.

'The others were all working as interns. So, unlike you, they were office-based. It could be in his files. You need to find it, then get out quick.'

'Easier said than done.'

'Whatever it is, wherever it is, he'll keep it close.'

I remember Henderson's man cave: all that thick wood panelling. It's got to be in there somewhere.

'What about his partner, Grayling?' Geoff asks.

'No joy so far. I've tried to get hold of him, but he's not interested.'

'Don't give up hope. People will often open up to a pretty face.'

Maybe the comment is sexist, but I'm not above taking a compliment. Besides, he's old school.

'Thanks, Geoff, but it's a phone call I'm after, not a date.'

'The point is, just because you come to one brick wall, doesn't mean that you can't get around it in a different way.'

I think of my earlier foray into forgery this evening: attaching the BBC logo to my emails for Grayling.

'Already there,' I say lightly, though in my heart I'm feeling a sense of absolute dread. 'But there's a big difference between googling bits of information or sending the odd email and actually snooping around your host's office. Especially when there's a body count on the board.'

'Good to be cautious,' Geoff says.

I'm about to put the phone down when he cuts back in.

'Oh and, Sophie, how did you hear about Susanne?'

I stop dead. So much has happened that I haven't even told Geoff this bit.

'There's someone following me.'

Geoff says nothing but I can tell he's not happy about this latest nugget of information.

'Or at least I think there is. He may have even followed me from the UK. The photo of Susanne was his.'

'He gave it to you?'

'Not exactly. He kind of keeps in the shadows.' I think of his melted face, those dark, sorrowful eyes. Does he mean to harm me? If Cal hadn't appeared when he did...

'Sophie?'

'Yeah, sorry. I thought at first he was one of Henderson's entourage, but now I'm not so sure. The photo must have fallen out of his pocket. So it was just a lucky...'

'... coincidence?' Geoff finishes my sentence. I'm fully aware of the irony.

'Yeah.'

'Oh and, Sophie, another rule of policing... depth? Out of? You have to wonder.'

To be honest, I didn't have to wonder. I'm a swimmer, my innate sense of depth could be used to pilot a submarine. I know that I am way down deep in something that I do not understand. But if I come up too quick, I'm likely to get the bends or have Henderson exit me through the gift shop like the others. Besides, just like almost all other journalists I know, I'm a pushover for a puzzle. So that's why – at three o'clock in the morning – my alarm wakes me.

The house feels like it's holding its breath, and I wonder just what secrets it's hiding. Geoff's last few comments have got me thinking. Why would a man who's stalking me leave me a clue? It must have fallen out of his pocket, but the image is immaculate, not a bend, not a crease. This photo has been lovingly carried. Not the kind of thing to be dropped carelessly. The faceless man doesn't seem to fit with Henderson's carefully staged image. I just can't figure it out. If he is an outsider, why is he on my tail?

At the bottom of the stairs, I walk quickly towards Henderson's office, my bare feet chilled on the cold marble floor. I glance up at the corners of the room yet again. There really are no cameras. Henderson is one hell of a confident man – confident or arrogant? And I can't help but wonder where the tipping point is.

There may be no cameras in the hallway, but his office could well prove a whole different story. My mind starts ranging over excuses, ranging from the decidedly daft to blindingly bizarre. *I left my pen in your office – I sleepwalk.* None of it sounds even part-way plausible. Besides, the truth is burning a hole through my gut so loud I want to scream it out loud – *I'm just snooping, Mr Henderson. I think you've been up to no good and I'm keen on doing a centre page spread in the Sundays.*

I turn the handle. The door swings open slowly in front of me. I could go back now. Climb up those stairs, pull the duvet over my golden curls and fall into blissful sleep. But there's a story, a growing graveyard of dead peers stacking up behind me. I take a deep breath, step over the threshold and into my first dalliance with vice.

The room is much darker than the hallway. The wood-panelled walls seem to emit shadows, absorbing any light foolish enough to trespass in. I go to activate the torch app on my phone, then realise this is ridiculous. If I get caught, it's better to get caught with the lights on. It looks less shifty. I press the light switch and the shadows retreat.

I go straight for his desk. Surely that's where he would keep any keys? I try the top drawer. It's locked. I try the next drawer down, same story. I could force the lock, but if I do, he'll know someone's been here, and I would make a sizeable bet that I'd be high on the suspect list. The wall cabinet. It's got no locks on, no handles. I run my hands across the smooth wood. When I press it, it sinks in a little. It must be one of those hidden catches. Running my hand down the seam, I press gently till I find the sweet spot. The door slides open. So far, so good. There's a filing cabinet in the cupboard, only a small one, just one drawer. I'm willing to bet that's where he keeps anything sensitive. I look for some kind of combination lock, but there's nothing. Puzzled, I give the drawer a gentle tug. It slides open straight away. Wow, this guy is so sure of himself. Although, the next hurdle is not so simple. There's a locked drawer inside the cabinet. This time it has a regular keyhole. I go back to the desk and try the top drawer again. The key to the filing cabinet has to be in here. Okay, so maybe he's not quite as laid-back as I'd supposed. The joins in the desk are tight. I'm never going to get the drawer open without marking it so badly that I might as well take a sledgehammer to it.

I sit down in the chair behind Henderson's desk and rack my brain. If I break the lock on the desk, first thing in the morning, he's going to see. This is where he sits, but how about if I go straight for the filing cabinet? I cross the room once more and run my fingers along the top edge of the drawer. There's a hint of dust, just enough to let me know this drawer isn't opened very often. If I open the drawer and somehow stick it back, it's going to take Henderson a while to realise someone's been meddling. Maybe forever. Maybe he'll never realise. Doesn't matter, all I probably need is around thirty-six hours.

To jimmy anything open I'm going to need the right tool. There's a ruler on the desk, but the metal isn't thick enough. It'll just bend under pressure. Then I spot it. Beside a monographed writing pad there's a silver letter opener. It's heavy, expensively made, the blunt blade virtually growing out of the handle. Bingo. It'll be able to withstand the strain. Barely breathing, I ease the blade carefully into the gap at the top of the cabinet.

When the blade's three quarters in, I push gently up on the handle. A cracking sound rings out loud into the silence. My heart drops. I wait for a moment, not daring to look, or move, or breathe. Nothing. Glancing down at the drawer, a smile flits across my face – it's open. No splinters of wood. Almost there. I ease the knife in once more, but this time it's just to guide the drawer out, and out it slides. It's only the lock that I've damaged.

Before even looking at the files, I want to check the drawer will go back. I have no intention of gloating till I'm on the home straight, tracks covered. The drawer slides neatly back. There's no visible damage to the front, although I'll need something to stick it shut. A piece of card might do the trick: if I make the gap smaller, it should hold the drawer in. There's a tray full of business cards on the desk. I find one, and tear.

It's all good. Now I need to get on with the job in hand. I'm spending valuable time thinking of logistics: of how to cover my tracks, but I badly need the evidence that's going to make covering my tracks worthwhile. I sigh. I'm stalling, and I know exactly why. It's because I have no idea what it is that I'm looking for.

I flick through some employee records, but the names I'm after, the Jarvises, the Gainlands, not one of them is here. Then it dawns on me. He must have some kind of HR department somewhere in the building. I could kick myself. I've broken into the wrong place! This is not where Susanne or any of the others would have worked. I've spent all this effort, risked being caught, for nothing. Then just as I'm about to give up hope I see a file marked 'clinic'. It's twenty years since the clinic closed, but maybe this drawer was for the sensitive stuff. For Henderson's eyes only.

The clock on the wall chimes the hour, and I realise, to my horror, this is all taking me way longer than it should. If the morning brigade are up at four thirty, I'm on borrowed time. I only need one person to decide to rise early, and the game is up. I take photos of the documents, trying my hardest to keep my hands from shaking and hold the picture in focus. It takes me a full five minutes. Then I put all the documents back in the file, and the file back in the cabinet; sliding the drawer in and wedging the folded bit of card into the corner. It should hold. Done, I think to myself. Though what is *done* I am still none the wiser since I haven't had a chance to absorb any of the information; it may well amount to nothing.

I hear noises from outside, so hit the lights and duck down behind the desk. My breathing sounds so loud that I find myself cupping my hands over my face as I listen into the darkness. Nothing. My heart beats hard in my chest. Then suddenly from outside I hear it again; a soulful cry that makes the hairs on the back of my neck stand on end. I creep to the window. The terrace is bathed in moonlight and shadows. The entrance to the maze stands open like a toothless howl. I shiver. What would possess anyone to enter it late at night? And I think of poor sad Mia wandering around, searching or lost, I wasn't sure. Was she braver than me? Or just more disturbed? I wait for another five minutes, but there are no more cries.

Putting my phone in my pocket, I creep quietly out of the office, shutting the door carefully behind me. The villa is still cocooned in sleep. I pad through the empty rooms, only daring to fill my lungs when I reach my bedroom door.

For a good minute, I don't move, just stand on the inside of my room, back to the door in a state of adrenaline-fuelled paranoia. I listen till it feels like my ears are pulling themselves in knots. Not a sound; no one has followed me. I'm safe.

The first thing I do is open the windows. If I hear that cry again, I will leave the safety of my room and enter the labyrinth. I'll go in there and try and talk Mia down. Talk her down and... I realise, pick her brains. I don't want to hear the cry again. I'm happy with the silence, but I'm so short of answers; I need to follow everything up. Thankfully, whatever or whoever it is that cried out, appears to have moved on. I close the windows tight and pull the shutters. Placing the night and its monsters firmly outside. I have work to do.

Grabbing my notebook, I curl up on my bed and flick through the photos on my phone. I'm not really sure what I'm looking for. The lists of names blur in front of my tired eyes. There are, I guess, over 50,000 patients for the thirty years of the clinic. I'm staring at a spreadsheet of hope and disappointment; would-be parents desperate to conceive. All those names linked to tiny crosses or ticks; marks that look so innocuous but must have contained such suffering or joy. Because I'm guessing that the ticks resulted in a valid pregnancy. The x's? Failed pregnancies and perhaps more; perhaps the x's were used in Henderson's experiments. Did the parents know? These kinds of treatments don't come cheap. Not all of it would have been on the NHS. Some of the parents might be tempted to turn a blind eye if fees were waived.

Five o'clock is ushered in by the clock in the hallway. The names of clients from the clinic are now not just swimming in front of my eyes, but doing aqua aerobics. Beyond the success or failure of a pregnancy, I can't really see how this information can help. If Henderson was doing an 'off-the-record deal', it was most definitely 'off record'. So what was it that Kara, Susan, Bobby and Ed discovered? Was I even on the right track? Was I looking in the right place? I sigh wearily, rubbing my eyes. I could send it all back to Geoff, perhaps his trained eye... I'll send him everything I have. All of it, even the things that aren't making sense. It's just as I'm sending the last file that I stop dead. Suddenly I'm wide awake – Jarvis. Melinda and Adrian. Two strikes, one tick, and I know exactly what that tick stands for – Kara.

27

ACCIDENTS

Breakfast turns out to be a quiet affair, which suits me fine. I'm not in a chatty mood. Besides, I'm dog-tired. Yesterday was way too full on. Thankfully, most of Henderson's cronies have already worked their way through the chafing dishes. No doubt Alfred is out digging somewhere. I'm not sure what Mia gets up to during the long days? She's pale as a snowdrop, so it's certainly not sunbathing. Perhaps she's studying Alfred's notes, trying to work out where that mysterious temple might be? I hope so. I hope she cracks it before it cracks her.

There's a stack of plates left neatly on the table; more than you would need to feed a small army, with cutlery to match. I wonder if Cal has been processed already. I'd like to talk to him. At least he answers questions. I stare up at the house with its wide, empty windows. It's sending me no clues as to where he is. Perhaps it's best. If I start asking about the four missing interns, Henderson will get wind of what I'm up to. I flip the lid up on one dish. It doesn't even look as if it's been plundered yet. Rows of grilled tomatoes smile up at me.

I grab an orange juice and raise the shiny stainless-steel lids of the three remaining dishes. There's scrambled egg inside one, mushrooms inside another and potatoes cooked with red onions and chilli in a third. Well, at least I won't starve.

'Hungry?'

It's Henderson. I try very hard to look normal and realise *looking normal* is almost impossible to do when you're *trying*.

'I've always had a good appetite,' I say, ladling out a double helping of scrambled egg. I have so many questions colliding in my brain, I just can't figure out which should take priority. One thing I do know is that not one of them should be aimed at Henderson. Not if I want to get to the bottom of this.

'We should work on the memoir today; if you have time,' I say as casually as I can, affecting an easy come, easy go attitude, which even I'm not totally convinced by. 'I may need to get back home sooner than I thought.' I let my bomb slip.

'Oh?'

A young woman dressed in house uniform brings Henderson a mug of coffee. I can taste its bitter, acrid smell in the air and realise, sadly, that I'm trapped till he's downed his drink and I've eaten my meal.

'Yes. I mean I can get a lot of information from the web, and we've had that one session. And of course, I've got a good sense for how you're living now.' As I say the words, in my new carefree tone, I can't help feeling there's an irony to that last phrase. How he's *living now* – courtesy of a batch-stock of foetuses from a defunct clinic. Is that why Grayling won't speak to me?

'Today we go out on the yacht,' he says, dismissing my plans as if they're of no real consequence, gazing instead out towards the water.

'Actually, maybe I'll give that one a miss.' I think of the women found floating in those clear blue seas and Geoff's comment as to how easy it is to dump a body if you have a boat.

'If I spend the day at the villa then I should be able to get an outline for you by the end of this evening?'

'I'm in no hurry. We must all go. After all, we are a party.' His voice might be jovial, but there's a little too much of the passive-aggressive in it for my liking. I'm in no doubt that I'm not really being given an option.

'Okay,' I say with a lightness I'm not feeling. 'All of us?'

'Show the new recruits around.'

Well, at least that's something. He can hardly dunk me in the sea when his entourage is on board. I might not be fond of Horse Woman, but I can't imagine that Mia, Alfred or the new Numbers are the type who enjoy seeing someone abandoned mid-ocean. As I'm clinging to this thought I suddenly remember: the boy and the propeller – there are, of course, always accidents.

28

SWIMMING

In the safety of my room, I flick through the photos I'd taken of Henderson's documents. Each of the parents of the four interns are here. All parents ended up having one child but had a series of miscarriages. I'd sent the files through to Geoff, even the ones that don't seem relevant. I wanted him to have every last bit of information. After all, he's the detective. I check my phone. He hasn't got back yet. I text another note, spelling out that all interns had parents who underwent fertility trials at the clinic. This could mean that a) the parents were still friendly with Henderson. Perhaps he offered them work placements? Or b) that he actively targeted them. He wanted to have them working for him – because?

I knew that stem cells from foetuses could prove more effective in the treatment of Parkinson's. The four couples under scrutiny – Jarvis, Millar, Gainland and Marchant, had all experienced at least one mid-term miscarriage. So perhaps he had used something in the miscarried foetus, something that he could match with the adult carriers? I need more answers.

I remember Geoff's words about coming up against brick walls and finding ways around. I've got to be a bit more bullish.

Which seems ironic, considering I'm sitting on a labyrinth. I ring Grayling. This time there's no answer, just the machine. I'm about to hang up, then realise the machine might work better for me. I can get my story across.

'Hi, I'm working for the BBC.' The guardians of truth, I think to myself as the lie slides from my tongue. I really am getting good at this. 'Sophie Williams. I hope you got my email. I'm doing research on the fertility clinic you ran with Henderson, and I've found some... anomalies. I would welcome the chance to talk to Doctor Grayling confidentially.' I leave my number.

I'm feeling so tired after the previous night's exploration, and I'm far from enthusiastic about the whole 'boat trip', but orders are orders. I'll just have to stick close to the others. Safety in numbers, etc, etc.

There's a pair of cream slacks and a sailor-striped Henley laid out on the bed. The idea that I'm being dressed like a doll is beginning to stick in my throat. I go straight to the small drawer which contains my regular clothes and grab my jeans – I'm not playing anymore.

I've been told to take the lift down to the pontoon when I'm ready. I throw a jumper into my bag, grab my jacket and check my phone has charge. I'm also looking for messages from Jed. I'm not disappointed. He's closing up the club. The flights are full, but he's taking his chances at the airport. Tomorrow then, he'll be here by then. I'll make my excuses and get to the mainland but I can't trust Achilleas. Not after I saw the suit on his boat. I'm not sure how he fits into all of this, but the thought of that man, his dripping face, those tortured eyes. I need to give Achilleas a wide berth. It might be awkward on the trip. Then again, he's staff. The distinction suddenly seems useful.

When I arrive at the jetty, I realise we're not taking Achilleas' boat. *Calypso* is moored at the end of the pontoon, looking stark as a fibreglass shark. Mia, Alfred, Portia and her accountant husband are already being helped up onto the deck. Unfortunately, Achilleas is also on the pontoon but luckily not destined for our little jolly. He's talking to the chef, getting orders for the evening, I guess. I can avoid him if I'm careful. I head quickly towards the boat, but I'm not fast enough; he's spotted me.

'Sophie. Sophie.' He jogs down the pontoon in my wake.

'Oh, hi,' I say, my voice sounding two turns too bright.

He flashes me one of his stock smiles, but this time my heart's not going for it.

'Sophie, is no big problem. But please, don't go on my boat without me.'

'I didn't, wouldn't...' I stammer, not sure what he's getting at.

'Sophie.' He flashes me a knowing smile. 'You left something...'

'The scarf,' I bluster. Feeling the colour rise in my cheeks. 'I think that was Alice's.'

'No, was a black suit thing. You must have brought it with you.'

This is news to me, but I go with it, letting Achilleas fill in my silence. '... and then I think you must have come back to collect?'

Is he double bluffing?

'Sophie, you know you are always welcome on my boat, but maybe... would you check that I am on board before you...'

So he knows nothing about the suit. It's not his. I feel a wave of relief wash over me. Our relationship might be odd, but at least he's someone I can trust. Perhaps No Face may have been stowing away on the boat?

There's no time for figuring things out now. Achilleas is waiting for a reply. 'Sure. Sorry.' I don't bother giving any explanations. 'Look, I may need a lift to the mainland tomorrow morning, could you?'

'Of course.'

He flashes me another smile. I'm not sure whether he's flirting now, or if he just can't help himself.

'I have a plane to catch. Have to get home.'

Still the smile. 'No problem. If it's okay with...' And he glances up at the *Calypso*.

'Course,' I say. I'm going to have to talk to Henderson about it. Achilleas isn't taking me anywhere without the Henderson's say-so. 'Can't see there'll be a problem,' I say brightly, repressing the urge to cross my fingers behind my back.

───────

If Henderson notices I'm not wearing my 'outfit', he makes no comment. All of the other women, I note, are all dressed immaculately. Designed by Sylvie's ever-tasteful eye.

I'm told that we're going to another island for lunch, before swimming from the boat. There's a shallow bay where the water is always warm. I'm not totally convinced about the warm bit, but it looks like I have no choice in the matter. I take a seat on the deck beside Portia, hoping to get off on a better foot, but her shrill laugh and vacuous questions soon wear me down. *How long have I been here? What am I doing? Isn't this paradise?* I can see all too clearly now how I must have irritated Cal when I first arrived. After forty minutes of Portia's glowing eulogies about the island, I make my excuses and corner Henderson, explaining to him that I'm keen to get those last few details for the memoir. My mother is ill, and it does, indeed, look as though I will have to return to the mainland tomorrow.

'And you're sure you have all the information you need?'

His bright blue eyes burn, so clear, so sure, and I can't help myself – I get the feeling he's mocking me.

'Oh, I think so. I can always mail you if I need more.' I keep my tone light, carefree. 'Do you think Achilleas might be able to drop me over in Athens? He said to run it by you.'

'When's your flight?'

'Not booked yet, I wanted to check it was all okay.'

'You may have problems getting a seat.'

I can't help but note that his tone seems more than a little smug.

'Well yes, but... I'll just kill time in the city till I manage to get something.'

He nods. 'I'm sure Achilleas will be delighted.' His voice rings out, so very sarcastic.

I don't care. My ticket home is in sight.

It's early afternoon before we get to the swimming spot. The waiters lay food out on small foldaway tables in a neat corner of the deck. A light snack, presumably so as not to interrupt our scheduled dip: grilled vegetables, a little cold meat for the carnivores and fruit.

'We were in New York before. But Elliot's been working for Tim for some years now. This seemed like such a good opportunity.' Portia's taken to boring Alfred. Who simply nods, smiles then turns his attention away.

It seems as if once you're on the payroll it's very hard to get off.

'Sophie, I hear you're leaving us tomorrow?' Alfred says sweetly. I genuinely think he'll miss me.

'Yes, home for Christmas, that kind of thing.'

'Got your flight booked?' Alice's haughty tones float over the gathering. She's sitting, sunglasses on, eyes fixed to the sky.

'No, I...'

'Unlikely you'll be leaving tomorrow then.'

'Well, I thought I'd just...'

'Tim, put the girl down,' Alice's voice rings out, cutting me off.

For a moment, I'm not quite sure what she means, then I see out of the corner of my eye, Henderson feeding a reluctant Mia strawberries from his hands.

'You people shouldn't eat if you don't want to drown,' Alice barks. But I'm not sure that's exactly what her initial point was. 'Is the cabin made up?'

One of the waiters nods, dipping his head obsequiously low.

'Well, give me a shout if anything remotely interesting happens.' With that, Alice peels her body from her lounger and disappears inside.

'Is the water cold?' I ask, removing my jumper. I have my costume underneath, a black one-piece, brought from home. The jade polka-dot bikini that Sylvie laid out on the bed is exactly where she left it.

'Well, it is winter,' Alfred offers helpfully. 'But Henderson's right, the water temperature in this particular cove is often a little warmer than elsewhere.'

Mia pulls her cardigan tighter around her shoulders.

'You wouldn't catch me in there this time of year,' Portia says simply. Her excuse neatly delivered.

'Oh, I hate the water.' Mia glances nervously over the side. 'It's my contact lenses, I think. It's horrible not being able to see properly. And I was thrown in as a child.'

'Well, no one would throw you in here. The ladder is very stable.' Henderson taps it gently as if to prove that this is indeed the case.

'Not tempted, thank you.'

But there's a note of nervousness in her voice, and an awkward pause in the conversation which, to my surprise and disappointment, Alfred breaks.

'Oh come on, Mia. Be a sport.'

'She doesn't want to.' I can't help myself, the words are out of my mouth before I've given my brain a chance to engage. But no one backs me up. In fact, Portia, perversely, has a look of goblin-like delight etched into her features. I knew I was right not to like her.

'I really think...' Mia starts, but Henderson stares hard at her, and whatever it was that Mia *really thought* dies on her tongue.

We stand on the gleaming deck, watching as poor Mia lowers herself down into the sea. I'm amazed that no one, apart from myself, has said anything against the idea. Then again, a part of me can't quite believe that Mia, a grown woman, doesn't refuse to play this 'game'.

'You don't have to do this,' I say.

Yet with her body visibly shaking, she continues on down the ladder.

It's painful watching her descend, like witnessing a disaster waiting to happen, one you are totally unable to stop unfolding.

'Henderson... What the hell...?' I turn on him.

Alfred catches my arm, hissing in my ear, 'You'll only make it worse.'

Mia reaches the bottom and, gasping from the cold hit, lowers herself in. Her shaking shoulders submerged, she's finding it hard to catch her breath. The cold waves slap at her face, circling around her like dark, angry crows. Was this what happened to Kara?

'You've got to let go of the ladder,' Cal shouts down at Mia.

Mia's knuckles are white and boned where she's clinging to the steel rungs.

'If you don't let go, we just might yank it up,' Henderson says, coldly.

'Mia,' I say, leaning out over the boat, trying to catch her eye. I don't care what Alfred said, how can this get worse? 'Mia, this is stupid. You don't have to do anything you don't want to.'

'Go on, sweetheart.' Alfred's voice carries a note of tension, as though he wants the whole sorry business to be over but knows that the only way to get it done is to bite the bullet.

'Mia.' That's all Henderson says, just one word, and Mia lets go of the ladder.

I don't go in the water. I don't want to prolong this any more than I have to. I don't even bother holding out a towel for Mia as she clambers back onto the boat shivering and cold, as the others clap and whoop their applause. I don't pat her on the back. I don't bother to say *well done*. I think of Athens and the airport and Jed. All I want to do is go home.

29

THE CHAMBER

That night, I have absolute zilch enthusiasm for the old dressing-for-dinner routine. The itsy-bitsy polka-dot bikini has gone. Instead, three cocktail dresses lie teasingly across my bed, but I'm in no mood for teasing. I feel sick to the stomach. The day's events have shown island life in all its rot. It's like staying too long in a nightclub after the lights go up, all the cobwebs and cracks are out in the open. Rather than fraternising with the hairdryer, I'm onto the internet scouring for flights. Infuriatingly, Henderson et al. were right, there's nothing available for tomorrow. But Jed will be here soon. We can stay in Athens for a few days: spend Christmas together. Then when the celebrations are over, we can get a plane, or train, or bus, we can get anything. In short, we can just get the hell out of Greece and away from Henderson. I pull open the wardrobe and reach for my faithful black jersey. It's not there. I look through my drawers. There's nothing left of me in here, just the jeans I arrived in and my jacket. Bastard, I think.

I don't have much to say at supper, but then Portia seems to have slotted neatly into the vacuum I've created, and I wonder if that's always the way: the old and disillusioned being replaced by something fresher. *Something* that doesn't realise it may well somehow end up being the next course. We navigate slowly through the meal, time dragging to the point where I feel I'm going to scream. I just want to go. I'm amazed Mia's been able to pull her shattered ego back together in time for the feast, but perhaps, like the swim, she has no choice.

'You're very quiet this evening, Sophie?' Henderson's helping himself to some cheese.

It stinks. I have to wrinkle my nose from the inside. Parkinson's, I think. Has to be. I guess all maladies have their upsides.

'I'm just tired,' I say, although actually, my feet have electricity pulsing through them: I want to run. I flex my toes into the floor, hoping this might hold me, and prevent the fidgets. 'It was a long day.' I don't bother to look him in the face.

'Sophie intends to leave us tomorrow.'

I'm not keen on the way he uses the word *intends*, but I let it pass.

'Oh?' Portia says.

'Sick mother, so I understand.' Henderson's voice sounds so sceptical, it's bordering on hostile. 'Yes.' He smiles a quick lizard smile. 'Which is a shame, as really the fun is only just beginning.'

I notice Mia's finding it hard to digest her food. She's raising her fork to her mouth, but somehow it never appears to go in.

'A great shame. You've been good company, Sophie.' He holds his glass up in a toast. The others follow suit with varying degrees of enthusiasm and interest.

'To Sophie.' My name is mumbled around the table.

'Perhaps there's still a window,' he says looking smug, 'a way I might persuade you to stay?'

'I'd love to, but...'

Henderson holds up one hand, arresting my words.

'Because, I don't feel we've... discussed all that we needed to...' He wipes his mouth on the linen napkin. '...discuss.' A waiter hovering in the shadows moves closer to fill his glass, but Henderson drops his other hand, so it rests over the crystal. 'I think Sophie still has a lot of questions about the island.'

'I don't know...' I mumble, 'I think I'm beginning to get the picture.'

'Besides, you haven't heard my proposition.'

I don't like the sound of this. Curiously, from the look on his face, neither does Alfred.

Henderson, however, seems oblivious. 'Friends, you will have to excuse us for this evening.' He lets his eyes fall on the other guests.

Mia seems to be going for a no-eye-contact, blank-face policy. In contrast, Alfred's face is the exact opposite – whipping neatly through enough expressions for two; they're being dismissed, and Alfred's not happy.

'On our little island, we like to have a kind of hierarchy. Time buys many...' and Henderson hesitates over the word, 'privileges.'

'But I've been here a very long time,' Alfred says, a churlish note to his voice.

Henderson shoots him a withering glance, and Alfred sinks back from the table, like a snail retreating into its shell.

'Well... I guess... I am a little exhausted anyway,' he blusters.

'Actually, you know what...' I say, scrunching my napkin into a ball and pushing back my chair. 'I think I'll call it a day too. I have to pack.'

Henderson smiles, his reptilian smile. 'Ahh, but, Sophie, maybe you don't?'

'I'm leaving tomorrow.'

'One last evening for me to win you over then. Besides... would you really want to give up on the "*story*"?'

'We should be hitting the sack.' The new Numbers breezes in easily.

Portia looks disappointed, till her husband takes her hand gently but firmly, leaving her in no doubt – they have had their marching orders. She raises her eyes in irritation, but obediently gets up.

I glance nervously towards Mia and Alfred. Poor Alfred has the appearance of someone who would dearly love to burst into tears. He's been here before I guess, seen people admitted to the 'inner circle', if that's what this is.

'I should make my excuses as well.' Beavis wipes his wet lips on his napkin, placing it decisively on the table.

Henderson nods. 'Tomorrow will be a busy day.'

Busy? I wonder what they have on the agenda. I'll be gone by then. Whatever Henderson thinks he's going to offer me, it won't be enough to keep me here. Tomorrow's business has nothing to do with me but still, I'd like to know. Chairs are pushed back, napkins abandoned, and as we stand from the table, I accidentally drop my purse. My compact goes skittering across the floor. Beavis reaches down to get it. His face momentarily reflected, just an eye, the nose, half a smile: those full wet lips. And I get that same unnerving feeling as he pulls the compact back, straightens his spine, and smiling, hands it over to me; I have seen this man before. That feeling keeps haunting me. I know him from somewhere – somewhere before the island. Before I'd even known of its existence. If only I could remember. I'm sure that somehow if I knew, I'd be able to unlock a large piece of this jigsaw. But Beavis is soon gone, leaving me alone and irritated with myself. There's some part of this puzzle in the dead zone of my brain, lurking there like a taunt, but I just can't sink my teeth into it.

Henderson's already moving towards the door.

'Alfred,' I mouth, catching his eye. 'Sorry.'

Alfred shrugs, resigned. The plan, whatever it is, is going to go on without him yet again.

'Come, please, keep up,' Henderson calls back over his shoulder, and I set off behind him, trotting like a brainless dog after its master. I don't want to follow. I don't want to be put in this position, but still I trot.

'I hadn't planned it like this, Sophie, but actually, I'm beginning to think it all works rather well. You know how I love stories, myths, legends, modern and ancient. And you see, Sophie, you're so like me. You're a storyteller too, a journalist.'

Does he know I'm onto the whole Parkinson's thing? Is he going to try and somehow buy me off? Is that what happened to Kara and the others? Was there an offer which didn't quite work out?

'Our society needs its myths, wouldn't you agree, Sophie? It needs fear to function.'

We arrive at the circular room with its artefacts all out and on display.

'Alfred is uncovering his truths with his little hammer but you, Sophie, you're the journalist – our myth-maker.'

'Not sure most journalists would be too happy to be described that way. I think we're more after truth.'

'Truth?' He weighs it up. 'Perhaps it's overrated and... in my opinion... difficult to come by. Now myths and stories, on the other hand, these have a very specific role.'

'So you've told me,' I mumble.

'They are what is needed to keep mortals in check.'

Mortals. There's a note in his voice when he says the word, something that I'm not wholly comfortable with, as though he's not personally standing underneath the mortality umbrella and maybe... instead of *mortals*, he should really be saying insects.

'Fear is one of the most expedient tools that we have.'

Fear again. I think of the labyrinth, of the children whose lives were lost.

'We need to maintain and relive old myths, but we also need to create myths for our new age, and indeed the ages to come.'

The faceless man?

Henderson lets his hand rest gently on the mask as we pass, and I can't help but shudder as I think of the spike waiting like a snake behind those empty eyes, a snake with an ever-ready bite. I feel a rush of blood rising inside me, and know that if he attempts to put the mask on me, no matter what it's worth, I'll smash the damn thing to pieces. But there's no need, Henderson moves on through the house, through the wide sweeping hallway and down a long narrow corridor leading away to the right. I haven't been this way before. I'd imagined it led to the staff wing. It's a little darker than the other passageways, older. But then I notice that the walls are hung with expensive art, Picassos, Hirsts, Emins. The plaster in this place must carry more money than a few world governments, and still no CCTV.

'This was where Castellanos lived, more modest than the villa. I like to think of him as... the curator. He was waiting you see, Sophie, getting everything ready.'

So I was right. 'For the Nazis?'

Henderson stops in front of a large iron door, a smile flickering across his face. 'Maybe he had even more foresight.'

For Henderson? Is that what the man thinks: Castellanos was waiting for him?

'The tunnels below us, Sophie, they are from a different age. They run through this island like veins, stretching back to the beginning of time, linking us to something so much more fundamental. The original structure is not even man-made. Castellanos was the curator for something far more... eternal than merely the German occupation, or possibly even myself.'

He takes a huge key from his pocket, it must be six inches

long, but then hesitates. 'Before we go any further, I must insist not a word of what I am about to show you goes off this island. No social media. No books. No journals, Sophie. Not even in conversation. You are my guest, and my employee.'

I feel a flush of embarrassment as I get the sneaky feeling that I could very easily be trapped in a rabbit wire of my own making.

'And I expect discretion,' he continues. 'If you genuinely feel this may not be possible, then perhaps this is the moment for you to retire.'

So I have a choice? Somehow I'm not so sure. This is an odd kind of a deal. Besides, I'm not convinced I'm going to be able to keep my end of the bargain on the *no talking* front. As far as I'm concerned, where crimes are committed the obligation to keep secrets doesn't hold fast. Then again, I have an uncomfortable feeling that this may be the least of my worries.

'Where are you taking me?' My voice sounds cracked, unpolished as a schoolgirl's. 'Is it the centre of the labyrinth?'

'No, not the centre, close though. It's where the Nazis thought the centre was, but they were off by a few metres. It's the...' And Henderson pauses, waiting for the silence to press in and give his next words maximum impact. 'It's what they called the Sacrificial Chamber.'

It's just a name, I think to myself, just a name. It has no power. All the same my skin crawls, and God, I wish it was called something innocuous, something like the Blue Grotto, or the Kairos Cave, anything, anything but Sacrificial Chamber. But I just nod, and wonder too late if in offering up my silence I'm somehow selling my soul. Henderson fits the key snugly into the padlock. Poor Alfred, I think to myself. This will be even more insulting for him when he does eventually get initiated: he's been hunting around in the dark for years, and all the time

Henderson had a staircase to the heart of the labyrinth from the villa.

The door swings open with a heavy metal creak, stale air flowing out through its dead, gaping mouth, and I shiver. I don't know why, it's not cold, but there's something about the 'breath' that comes through the doorway. An odd kind of energy. The sort of thing you feel when you stand under an electricity pylon. The kind of feeling that sets your fillings on edge and rattling in their calcium cradles: something at the edges of human experience.

'After you,' Henderson says.

In this instance, I'm not convinced it's the kind of thing a gentleman would say, but I move forward anyway, into the damp mineral stench.

'Hold on to the handrail, Sophie. We wouldn't want you to go having an accident.'

There's something about the way Henderson's been looking at me all night, a kind of cold, hungry glint in his eyes, that makes me think I'm an essential part of this particular game, this strand. Perhaps this 'treat' had been planned for later, a few weeks or months down the line, when the proposed memoir failed to get signed off. My impending departure may have pushed Henderson to rethink. All of this should be conjuring up warning bells, but to be honest, I've had a few too many. My amygdala, that almond-shaped cluster of nuclei employed as the early warning system for the whole flight/fight, scared/safe routine has been soused: I'm feeling Bacardi brave.

'After you, Sophie,' Henderson says again, indicating the dark hellhole in front of me, and this time it's unmistakable, it's a *command*. He's trying to scare me. Like a good little sheep, I allow him to shepherd me anyway, and in this crypt-cold environment, where the ancient rocks close in above us, I can't help thinking about some of the monsters Henderson's conjured up. Is the faceless man a new myth, something that he's intent on creating? If so, why is the creature interested in me? Am I the witness, the person meant to promote the myth, to get the ball rolling? Or is it all a test that Henderson's setting – a part of that *commitment* he talked about?

Clunk, clunk, clunk, go my shoes on the metal grills. Three Billy Goats Gruff, I think to myself. Who will I sell downstream – myself or my brother? Isn't that the only way that the goats survived?

I pick my way carefully down the spiral staircase. The light from the doorway behind me pales to an insignificant speck as I pull out my phone, switching it to torch mode. I wish Alfred was here, but then at this point I'd even settle for Portia. The steps are dark, uneven, tight, and the beam from my phone seems to have a reverse effect: making a single pool of light ahead but darkening the surrounding shadows into deep wells of inky blackness. My shoes are not suited to archaeology and adventure. Was this deliberate? Was Sylvie encouraged to provide me with footwear that would make me unsteady, push me into the role of hapless heroine? There I go again putting myself centre story and creeping myself out. I seriously need to get a grip.

The staircase seems to wind forever; an infinity corkscrew embedded into the very earth, and that electrical buzz. There's no sound, but I can feel it. I can actually feel it thrumming at the base of my skull. I remember my insistent words to Jed as we stood on safer ground, my flat, before any of this. I'd said, *Maybe it's my time.* The words claw at my brain now with cold fingers as if fate is trying to get her hooks in. *My time.*

I pull at the flimsy shoulders of my dress, needing more of a covering than my evening gown is offering. It's as cold and damp as a grave down here, but unlike a grave, if you were to die on these steps, your soul could easily get lost, sucked into the black.

Suddenly I stumble and lurch forward out of the darkness.

'It's flat,' Henderson states, too late to be useful.

'This is the bottom?' I hope so. I really don't think I can go any further. I'm so glad I couldn't see how far down it was from the top.

Henderson waves his torch ahead, making the shadows grope out of the darkness; sending spiralling phantom arms to catch at us.

'Henderson, are we here?' I say, shuffling a little, unwilling to step forward, reluctant to leave hold of the staircase.

But Henderson remains quiet as a rock. I take a step back and wish I hadn't. The ice-cold wall behind strokes wet fingers down my bare back, and I stumble, my hands coming to rest on planks of wood. I turn, sweeping the beam from my torch behind me. I'd walked into some stacked crates. Curiously, they have German writing stamped across them. War relics?

'This way.' Henderson pushes forward, marching into the darkness. 'Keep up, Sophie.'

I follow his voice as it drifts off down the coal-black passage. He's walking fast now. I don't want to lose him. A cold blast of air hits me; there must be another passageway to my left. Alfred was right to be wary; a person could easily get lost in these tunnels. The sound of our footsteps ricochets like goblin laughter from the walls. It's difficult to know if we're coming or going, if we are alone, or surrounded by ghostly strangers, and all the time that odd feeling thrumming at the base of my brain, like trapped energy. After a few minutes, Henderson stops, and I hear the sound of a second key being inserted firmly into a lock.

A heavy iron door creaks open. No blast of air this time, instead a hollow kind of stillness, as if something is waiting, crouching, cowering just out of sight. I stare into the wall of black. My breathing fast and shallow. All my bones on edge. People say that it's possible to get a feeling from a place, a gut, intuitive understanding. When you buy a house, it feels right or wrong. No doubt there are hundreds of subliminal signals that we're not even aware of. Signals we're continually picking up on. Most of them are surface. A summer's day in a bandstand might make you think the place is joyful, switch the weather, put in a storm blown in from nowhere, and that same place can seem haunting, menacing. But there are those that believe some places have a darkness running through them like indelible ink threaded through veins. Do I believe that? I hadn't, not really, not before. But this place, Henderson was right, it's like it exists somehow outside of time, on the edges of civilisation. In short, I don't like it. My legs are reluctant to take me into that darkness because I know, I feel, there's something in there. Something older and nastier than anything I've come across before.

Henderson hits a switch. Light spills out. Even though there's no fear to be had now from the unseen, from the shadows, I can't help feeling that the light is no more than a sticking plaster hastily applied over a run-in with a chainsaw.

On the face of it, it looks as normal as a cavern a few hundred feet underground can look. A vast chamber, like a bunker or maybe a warehouse? Probably that's what the Nazis had used it for. Currently, it's filled with containers. Small versions of the kind of things you get on the back of a lorry.

'What are these?' I move into the room, reaching out and touching the cold metal. How did he even get them down here? Is there another lift?

'These are dreams, Sophie,' Henderson says, striking out across the room.

Dreams? I hurry after him. I have no intention of letting him out of my sight.

'I understand,' he says, not even bothering to look back, 'that Alfred told you a little of our history. A little about Castellanos.'

'Well, you were there at supper when he...'

'No, Sophie.' Henderson sighs. 'I do find it so tiresome when people deliberately try to deceive. Alfred told you the entire story at the dig.'

There's no point in protesting. Henderson's obviously got some inside track – the two workmen?

'Well, it was fascinating.' It feels a bit lame as a comeback, but better than floundering about with some weak denial.

'*Is* fascinating,' Henderson returns. 'Castellanos was the man who discovered the labyrinth and set it working once again.'

'Working?' He's talking about some kind of geological feature as if it's a clockwork toy. 'But the initial labyrinth... you said... I thought you said it was natural? So it can't have had a purpose?'

'Nature does nothing without purpose.'

There's something about the way these container obelisks are placed, something random but uniform. It reminds me of archaic standing stones, all linked in patterns holding long forgotten meanings.

'This room has changed a great deal. It was enlarged initially by the Nazis, and then I had another go at it. They thought it was the centre: used it sacrificially.'

'But the Nazis didn't advocate...'

And then I see it, and my blood freezes, because in what I assume is the centre of the room, there's a large stone slab. A sacrificial stone, complete with a grotesque tortured face: mouth open wide in a scream, blank eyes staring out at the watchers. The watcher. Me.

'What the Nazis did *advocate* or didn't is neither here nor there. This island works on its own rules. Rules much older than anything known to man.'

He extends a hand towards me, helping me onto the raised dais.

'However, they were right about one thing, something that humanity is too afraid to voice.'

'Oh?' I stare at the room behind me, all the containers standing closed as tombs, their rust-grey bodies looking strangely inert. Apart from the closest container, which is still a bright factory yellow.

'Society has two stratas,' Henderson says. 'Ask Plato. Philosopher kings, the enlightened, as opposed to all those creatures that continue to live in the shadows of existence.'

'And, let me guess,' I say, because I'm beginning to see where this is going. Let's face it, he's even got Plato's shadowy cave here: the one Plato used to illustrate how mere mortals never get to understand reality. How all they can see are shadows on a wall, whereas actual reality, the thing that really exists, is the thing making the shadow. 'My guess is... you would be on the philosopher king side of the line, or maybe even a god?'

He smiles a thin wry smile. 'Sophie, you flatter me, but perhaps something along those lines. I told you, we are already buying immortality.'

'By the truckload,' I say, indicating the containers. 'You said they were dreams?'

Henderson nods. 'The other kings and queens. The people I have allowed in to the... idea.'

He takes a remote from his pocket. One side on a container, the yellow one, collapses with an almighty crash that makes my heart jump. I clutch my ears as the sound thumps around the cavern, bouncing angrily into all corners. My God, this place is vast.

'Dreams,' he says, when silence has once again got a foothold, and he walks slowly down towards the open container.

Cautiously, I follow. It's seriously weird. I can't quite believe my eyes. Inside the container is what looks like a small office: a desk, a chair, and row upon row of display cabinets and drawers.

'These are pods,' Henderson tells me. 'Investment pods. Everyone gets one. The chair, the desk, those are really just icons. The dreams are packed inside. Please, feel free.'

I step into the container and randomly pull open a drawer. Inside are pictures, paintings. I'm not sure who the artist is, but they're beautiful.

'Those are Ivan Prostel. Russian contemporary artist. I bought up all his work. As a stock, they're rising at a rate currently twenty times inflation.'

I open other drawers, there are gold bars, actual gold bars, and neatly bound portfolios of what looks like lists of stocks.

'This...' I say, flicking through the paperwork, wishing I could take my phone out and grab a few snaps. 'It's some sort of time capsule for investment?'

He nods. 'Exactly. There's a team that manage the portfolios. I can't have my kings and queens wanting for anything. We have a long future ahead of us.'

An uncomfortable feeling dawns on me. 'Why are you showing me this?'

He smiles, pulling himself out a seat at the desk. 'Because, Sophie dear, I'm offering you the chance to join us.'

'But?'

'Why?' He raises an ironic eyebrow. 'I think you know things that I'd rather not have out in the public domain just yet. And I'm... having to adjust my game plan slightly. This is not what I expected to be saying to you on our last evening together. Not initially that is. However, I'm looking at all the advantages here. You were a brilliant doctor once, showed enormous potential.'

Brilliant? I'm not so sure, besides… 'That was a long time ago.' I don't want to revisit this, especially not with him.

'Two years give or take a few months. You won the Longbow Award for most promising medic in your cohort. Isn't that right? And had a full scholarship.'

'I really don't want to…' I'm so tired now. I can barely breathe. I need to get out. I start to walk away, not even sure where I'm going, I just have to put some distance between me and… me and my past.

'And then the bomb.'

I stop dead in my tracks, just like it's exploded all over again.

There's a long pause, where the damp air eats into my body. I haven't talked about this to anyone for so long, not even Jed.

'And the overdose.'

Henderson knows everything.

'Sally-Anne Jennings. Pretty girl.'

'A lot of people died that day,' I mumble, even though I know that only one matters to me.

'What happened?'

I say nothing. I can't. I just can't go back there.

'My guess is…' Henderson continues for me. 'You were at the end of the team. The others went on ahead. You were probably tired. You may have already perhaps put in a full shift at ICU.'

He knows. He knows everything. He's playing with me.

'So, you arrive at the scene. You can't see anything, the air's thick with dust, debris. Then you hear something, a child? You look around, and sure enough there's this little girl caught under some bit of concrete? Girder? Wooden beam? Something heavy, pinning her in place. She seems fine, she's awake, she's talking, but she's so scared.'

My God, why doesn't he just shut up?

'You can't see the others, but you've got to get the child out. You lift the pillar off.'

I say nothing, as the whole incident flashes through my mind, just as fast as the blood would have rushed through her body.

'Internal haemorrhaging.'

'What do you want me to say?' Tears slide down my cheeks.

'I want you to realise – the child is dead. But you, Sophie, you're still in the land of the living. Throwing away a career for what? A good career, a promising career.'

'I couldn't go back to it... seriously I...'

'No, but you could work for me.'

'What...' I am so confused now I want to scream, 'writing?'

He throws back his head and laughs, the noise echoing off the containers, making it seem like there are forty Hendersons, fifty, a hundred.

'Forget that, Sophie. I know my own story. I certainly don't need some third-rate journalist to...'

'Sorry?'

'You're a medic, not a journalist. Do what you do best.'

'I can't.'

'Of course you can. All that training, it's criminal to waste it.'

I had heard that line so many times.

'You'd be rich, Sophie. This pod, this dream, this investment capsule; this one is yours.'

Confused, I stare back into the pod. The portfolios are still lying on the desk; the drawer with Ivan Prostel's beautiful paintings standing open. Mine?

'We can put in a few personal touches,' Henderson says, looking down at the gold bars. 'You get salaried as well, of course. Three hundred thousand a year, and a place to live.'

This is ridiculous. 'For just running around after you, after your guests?'

'It's slightly more complex.'

Three hundred thousand pounds, can he be serious?

'Of course, you have to think like us – philosopher kings. Put yourself above the rest of humanity.'

'I couldn't... I...'

'Course you could, aren't you better than most of them, most of your colleagues? Top of your class, Sophie. And you know it. If one person had to die, you or the little girl, who would prove the greatest loss?'

'But that's not...'

'You know what the Nazis did? You know the games they played here to prove that there was a difference: that there is a hierarchy?'

'Obscene. It was...'

'Or practical? There *is* going to be a master race, Sophie. There *is* going to be a group of people who live longer than anyone else on the planet: a group that can accrue knowledge, wealth, investments. You know some of the story... You've guessed about my condition.'

So he was onto me.

'But you don't know the whole thing. I'm asking you to join us. We have a position with your name on it. An investment portfolio. A living. If you want it.'

I think of Jed, heading over the seas towards me. How would he feel about all of this? Could I really do that to him? Would he be sitting at the table with the rest of the *kings*, or perhaps waiting at it, the new maître d'. A couple like Mandy and Trevor on Tech. Was that how it worked? But maybe Jed wouldn't want that. Maybe I didn't want that. Then again... could I put Sally-Anne to rest? Could I do more good here

REAP WHAT YOU SOW

somehow. Turn the whole tragedy around if I had more time, more influence?

'Think about it,' Henderson says. 'A life without want.'

I nod. Maybe I should. Maybe having me on board might tone down his delusions. Maybe I could somehow persuade him to get his cure out. Being on the inside, it's a powerful position to be in.

'Sleep on it, but first... I need to be sure you know the implications. Look in that drawer there, on the right.'

Puzzled, I slide open the top drawer of the desk.

Inside is a sketchbook. Its pages fall open in my hands revealing a monster. Large wings fill the page. It's part Minotaur, part devil. The pencil work is frantic, scratchy and erratic. The picture is not in the same league as those by the Russian contemporary artist. This is almost schoolkid stuff: good, but not professional, and seriously disturbing. As if it's fighting to get off the page, fighting to warn me. I look closer at the beast, at eyes that seem to stare right back at me. There's something familiar about those eyes, something... I glance up. Henderson is looking at me, smiling. The exact same eyes staring at me for real. He's the monster in the picture. I look back at the drawing: the smoky, scratchy ball of hate and fury, and then I notice in the bottom right-hand corner a set of initials. KJ. – Kara Jarvis.

'Everybody, Sophie dear, has their price. I'm keen to know yours. Each person admitted into the circle, well they must show commitment. Make a sign on themselves that demonstrates to all... that they belong.' I remember Mia on the boat, Clara's leg. The Doctor's disfigured arm. Had Kara died accidentally in some bizarre ritual marking? Whatever had happened, Henderson was warning me that part of my price had to be silence.

He's not a philosopher king, no, not Henderson. He most

287

definitely sees himself as God, and we are all just toys for his cruel amusement, invited to mark ourselves with commitment. Write his name on our mangled bodies – the man without a face. My God. Even that!

I'm about to tell him what to do with his proposal when there's an almighty crash from the other side of the altar.

I hear a small voice. 'Sorry, I'm so sorry.' It's Alfred.

Glancing around, I see Alfred being strong-armed onto the dais by a large guy in black: security. Where did they even come from? Sylvie was right when she said Henderson's men were never far away.

'Found him snooping, sir,' the security guy growls.

Henderson sighs wearily as if he's being presented with some naughty puppy. 'Oh, Alfred. Really?'

'I just wanted to see...'

'And now you have. Too early, Alfred. Not your time.'

I notice Alfred's clutching something tight in his palm.

'What have you got there?' Henderson asks.

Alfred pushes his hand forward, I take an instinctive step back – it's a grenade.

But Henderson hardly looks fazed. In fact he looks bored.

'This was outside the chamber, bottom of the stairway. A pile of them. They're old but they could be dangerous,' Alfred stutters, as though suddenly he's on the Health and Safety board, and trying really hard to be helpful.

Henderson looks irritated. 'I know exactly where they are. They're left over from the war. They're fine as long as people don't mess. They're artefacts, Alfred. I collect artefacts.'

Alfred lowers his head in shame. 'I can just forget it... forget what you were saying.'

'I think not.' Henderson draws out his words making them sound cold and inflexible. 'Actually, I think we need a little chat.

Jones.' The security guard takes a step closer. 'See that Ms Williams gets back to the villa.'

The guard nods.

'I'll deal with our intruder.'

'I'm sure he didn't mean...' I mutter, but Alfred shoots me that please-shut-up look. Anything I say will only make it worse. Besides, I have no intention of hanging around. Walking three paces ahead, I let Jones escort me out.

30

ESCAPE

What's my price for silence? That's what he's asking. Henderson wants me silent on the Parkinson's, silent on his little plan to produce a master race, silent on Kara. In return, I'm set up for life, but what exactly did happen to Kara? Henderson appears to have a warped, sadistic idea of commitment. Insisting people harm themselves, mark themselves in order to demonstrate their loyalty. Is that what went wrong for Kara and the others? They made commitments that backfired?

At the top of the stairs, I say goodnight to Jones, the security guy and pretend to be heading up to my own room, but I double back. I'm not interested in Henderson's offer. Tomorrow I will most definitely be leaving the island, and I want to corner Cal while there's still a strong likelihood of an evening's alcohol loosening his lips.

I find him on the terrace. The heater's on. He's wrapped up tight in blankets. Somewhere far below, I can hear the sea clawing hungrily at the rocks. That constant rumble that so often feels reassuring, but now only serves to make me feel more isolated and alone.

'You didn't want to come on the tour?' I ask, pulling up a seat beside him.

'As you know... it wasn't meant for me.' Cal pushes a bottle of brandy across the table.

I take a swig, and he smiles, as if I'm instantly part of his club.

'Alfred's down there.'

'Down?'

And I wonder if he knows; if he's even been to the chamber? 'Is your dad always like this? Always trying to make people do things they don't want to?'

Cal shrugs. 'Pretty much. Absolute power with absolute dosh, and so it goes, and so it goes.'

I grab one of the cashmere shawls placed in baskets for the guests and wrap it around my shoulders. All this luxury, but I can't wait to trade it in for perpetual rain and boredom.

'I had a question.'

'Oh?'

I'm guessing Cal probably likes being in the limelight a little. It must be difficult growing up in the shade of someone like his father. 'You said that your dad got angry with you?'

'Maybe I'm just that kind of person.' Cal smirks, shooting me a wry look.

He's been drinking up here on his own since supper. Self-pity and arrogance have settled hard on those broad shoulders.

'You said it was just once. I... I'm curious.'

'You know what happened to the cat.'

'Nobody knows what happened to the cat, isn't that the whole point?'

Cal nods, amused.

'Tell me anyway, about your dad – what made him angry? I'm going tomorrow. My last wish.'

Cal laughs. 'Okay, Sophie, why not? My parting gift. I'm HIV positive.'

I put the bottle down sharply on the table. I can't help myself. It's involuntary.

He smiles, amused. 'It's okay. You can't really get it from...'

I know all of this. I shouldn't have reacted in the way that I did, but... 'I'm so sorry,' I say.

Cal smiles wearily. 'I've been healthy enough so far. The drugs are better than they were. My prognosis is good. Good enough. We're all going to die.'

'It probably wasn't anger. Most likely, your dad was concerned.'

Cal puckers his lips in an ironic manner. 'Looks like you still don't know him.'

'He's your father.'

'Biiiig daddy,' Cal says and dissolves into fits of laughter. 'You don't know how funny you are, Sophie.'

'I'm just saying...'

'Biiiig daddy.'

'You're drunk.'

'Of course. Biiiig...' he calls out once more, shattering the night. 'You see that's the thing, Sophie. He is the big daddy. I'm not his only kid. There are loads of us. Promiscuous doesn't even begin to describe what he was.'

Suddenly I begin to feel sick, really sick. The world is spinning out of control. Cal flashes me a long, blue-eyed, lopsided smile, and I think I'm going to vomit. His smile. The reason why, despite all his arrogance, I can't help liking Cal, can't help having an affinity with him – he looks like Jed. Jed and Cal, there are so many similarities.

'I've seen a couple of the siblings. They come, they go. But you, Sophie, you're different, not like the others. Are you sure you are one of his?'

'It's late,' I say, getting to my feet.

That was why Cal found my appearance curious, why the young visitors were always brunettes: the genes were stacked that way.

He grabs my hand.

'Stay, Sophie, stay. Don't let the HIV put you off, and I'm pretty sure we're not related.'

'I need to get some sleep,' I blurt, but that's the last thing on my mind. I'm finding it hard to breathe.

'You okay?'

My whole world is crashing down around my ears. I cannot believe how stupid I've been. Henderson was never after me. I'm not the centre of this story. Jed told me that day at the airport how he'd been invited to run some bar in Greece. It was always only ever about Jed. I don't know why yet, but I do know I've messed up big time.

'Fine. I'm fine,' I call back over my shoulder as I stumble from the terrace towards the villa.

I dash through the entrance hall, knocking a picture off the sideboard as I go. Dropping down to pick it up, I see the smiling images of Henderson and the Doctor... only... the Doctor has a beard. The thin-lipped, wet-mouthed doctor has a beard. That's it! Of course. That's how I know Beavis. The guy on the train; the man who suggested I do personal histories, the Doctor, they're the same man.

I hurtle up the staircase. I may not know what Henderson is up to, but I do know that people, young people, are dying because of it. I grab my phone. There's a text from Jed, an old one by the looks of it, there's a delay.

At airport. Arrived.

No. I hadn't even realised he had got a flight. I text quickly back.

Don't come. On my way. Stay where you are.

I have to get off this island. If I can just get myself to the village, I'm guessing Achilleas could take me to the mainland. I stick my phone on charge. Whatever happens, I'm going to need to be able to communicate with Jed. Grabbing my case, I start hurling my things in. My phone buzzes – an incoming message. It must be Jed! I jump on it. But no, it's an email from Grayling's office. I skim the content, trying to ignore the bits about confidentiality. Looking for facts that might make sense of all this. Then I see it.

`Henderson may have replaced some of the semen samples. I flick down further. Many of the samples contained the same genetic material.`

Realisation comes flooding in on a tidal wave. My God! They're all his, Kara and Susanne and Bobby and Cal, and yes – Jed. How could I have been such a self-centred idiot?

My case packed, I pull the evening dress off and tug on my jeans. I don't want anything that's not mine. Not one thing. I'll find Sylvie. She'll help me get away; I know she will. Then I realise, I have no idea where Sylvie's room is. She'd told me it was in the tower, and at least I know where that is; I've seen it from the outside. I'm not sure how to get there, but decide to go in the opposite direction to the guest rooms. I'm guessing Henderson would keep guests and staff separate. I run a mental picture of the building through my head. The tower is to the south. Provided I stick to the outside wall and work my way to the upper floors I should hit it.

My boots barely make a sound as I step across the landing, walking quickly towards what I think must be the *servants'* quarters, looking for a staircase.

Sylvie must have some kind of transport, a motorbike, maybe a car? She might even have a boat. I climb a short flight of stairs. Surely these must lead to the tower? As I climb further, I can just make out music floating down from a room above: *Lady Sings the Blues*. The soundtrack. The sugar-sweet tones of Diana Ross. That's got to be Sylvie.

Gently I knock on the door.

'Sylvie?' No reply. 'Sylvie.' Still nothing, then a long low moan. Her voice. It's enough.

'Sylvie...' I push open the door. 'You've got to help. I have to get off of the isl...'

But nothing has prepared me for what I see. The beautiful, calm, sophisticated Sylvie sits on the bed. At first, I think she's painting her toenails. Then I realise, she's got a hypodermic aimed neatly between her toes. As I watch, the amber-coloured liquid leaches from the plastic tube and Sylvie's shoulders slump. Eyes blank in ecstasy, she raises her head, noticing me for the first time, and gives me a lazy what-the-fuck look.

'We all have our price, Sophie. Didn't he tell you that? Or is it just that you didn't listen?'

She slumps back on the bed.

I rush towards her, gripping her shoulders in both hands. 'I need to get off the island,' I say, shaking her hard, her head lolling from side to side.

'Too late.' She lets her heavy lids close sleepily over her eyes. 'All too late.'

'Sylvie!' But she's gone. Her body is as soft and lacking in muscle as a rag doll. I let her drop gently back onto the pillows. This is hopeless, but I need to think. I can't afford to panic. The only way I'll get out of this situation is by using my head.

My phone buzzes in my pocket.

Thanks for sending the car.

It's Jed. Everything is happening too fast. What's Jed doing getting into a car? I picture the smiling toothless goon, the doors opening, Jed entering the trap.

I text back.

I didn't. Don't get in. Don't come.

I see my warning fly off into the ether. Why isn't he listening? Why is he ignoring my texts?

I need to get out of here fast. If Sylvie has car keys, they'll be here in her room. I open all the drawers and empty them onto the bed. There are Chubb keys and door keys, but nothing that looks even remotely like it would fire up an engine. She'd said that she didn't get out much, and here was the proof. Then I see her phone. Maybe she has Achilleas' number?

It's a miracle. The phone's not locked. I guess the security here is so high, why would she need to? I flick through her contacts. Yes. Achilleas, he's there.

I dial the number. It's late. I'm not even sure he'll answer. It clicks through to answerphone. I disconnect then try again. The answerphone clicks in once more. He has to answer it! I phone again.

'Sylvie?'

It's him.

'Achilleas, it's Sophie, I need help.'

There's a pause.

'Sophie?'

'Yes, yes. I need to get off the island.'

'But... is late?'

'I know. My... My mum's sick. Really sick. I need to go now. Can you meet me by the pontoon?'

'But Henderson, he says this is okay?'

'Yes. Yes,' I mumble frantically. 'Just be quick.'

Achilleas' voice sounds sleepy, confused. 'Normally Mr Henderson, he phones?'

'He's not feeling well.'

'At the jetty?'

'Yes.'

'Now?'

'How long will it take you to get here?'

'Hmm.' I can hear him weighing it up mentally. 'Forty minutes?'

'Okay. Quicker if you can. See you there.'

I put the phone down and glance at the comatosed Sylvie. Her limp body fills me with sadness.

'Sylvie, you need to get out,' I whisper and kiss her gently on the forehead. 'Don't leave it too long.'

The house is silent as I pick my way back down the spiral staircase. I think of Alfred far below in Henderson's macabre labyrinth. What will Henderson do with him? I'm not sure. I only know one thing – when people make their own worlds, they should avoid making them in their own image. They should take the best bits of humanity and leave all the fucked-up bits to rot. Crossing the landing, I grab the case from my room. All I need to do is get myself into the lift, then clamber over the bridge, and the rocks. I've done it before. I know the codes. If worst comes to worst, I can swim to Achilleas' boat.

I come out of the room, dragging my wheelie case, and suddenly realise how ridiculous this looks. All I really need is my phone and my purse. I open the door to my room again and abandon the case back inside. There's nothing valuable in there. The most valuable thing in my life is heading towards me, hurtling through the night, walking straight into a trap that I've helped set for him.

Quietly, I go down the steps. I don't have a lot of time. I can hear people talking. Cal and the accountant, I think. Cal's voice is too loud, too drunk, his words a series of loud guffaws. The new Numbers sounds equally inebriated. I imagine them hugging the brandy bottle between them; they're not going to come looking for trouble.

I skirt down the corridor, through the circular room with its artefacts. My heart sinks when I see the mask is missing again. I hope it's not Mia, but who else would it be? I get into the lift, pressing in the code. I can hear voices. Henderson, I think. Sounds like he's heading down the passage towards the lift. I press the button again, press it again, press it again, hoping the doors will slide shut. His voice is getting louder and louder. Any moment he's going to swing around the corner and see me, and it'll all be too late. To my relief, the lift doors slide shut, and I allow myself the luxury of breathing again.

Now I just have to get down that corridor in the basement, out onto the bridge and across the rocks. Glancing at my watch, I figure I have around twenty minutes.

The doors roll open and to my absolute joy, Achilleas is standing there filling the doorway. Lurching forward, I grab him into a hug.

'Thank God, Achilleas. I need to get out.'

'Sophie, what's wrong?'

There is no way I can even begin to explain.

'Later. On the boat. We need to leave now.'

Henderson had been so close to the lift, he may well have heard the doors close. We don't have a moment to lose.

My phone vibrates in my pocket. It could be Jed. I pull it out.

Soph? I thought we were meeting in Athens. Why the boat?

'No.' I can't believe it. What's happening? Why isn't he getting my texts? 'Wait.' I hold my hand up to Achilleas to stop him from moving away. We need to go, but this message is more important. My fingers fly over the keys.

Don't get on boat. Coming to you.

Again I wait and watch. It's going. The message definitely went.

'Right, we need to shoot.' I grab Achilleas' hand and launch myself forward into the corridor, but there's a sudden tug backwards. Achilleas has his feet planted firmly on the floor. My face crumples when I turn to see him. It's so obvious. He has no intention of going anywhere.

'I'm sorry, Sophie.'

Humiliated, I stand beside him as the lift goes back up to the villa.

I can't even look him in the eyes.

'Henderson's a monster,' I mutter like a sullen child.

Achilleas simply shrugs. 'My boat, you know how I got that boat?' He's not really looking for an answer. 'The propeller game.'

So that was Achilleas' commitment. He was just lucky, not maimed. He doesn't have to wear the game like a badge of honour. Instead, it's etched into everything he will ever do for the rest of his life.

As the full weight of his words sink in the lift doors open and standing in front of me is Henderson.

'Sophie, you can't leave now. The fun is just beginning.'

31

MILLAR

On Henderson's orders, I'm taken to my room. The shutters are drawn and bolted. The door is locked. There's no way out. As Henderson's men prepare my prison, I can't help feeling like Persephone; locked in the underworld because I got taken along for the ride: enjoyed the rich trappings just that little bit too much.

'I'd been trying for years to get your young man to come visit,' Henderson tells me as his heavies sweep my room for anything that might prove remotely useful in an escape.

'But he always declined.'

I remember Jed talking to me about the job offer in Greece. If Henderson is trying to make me feel even worse, he needn't bother. I'm up and overflowing on my full quota of guilt and self-loathing.

'You can't just abduct people,' I say bitterly.

'Oh, Sophie.' His tone suggests that I am in fact a halfwit. 'The world is a big place. People get lost all the time.'

I'd like to hit him. I would seriously like to do damage to that smug, arrogant old face. Then the door opens. In walks the Doctor and I can't quite work out who I'd like to hit first. Even without the beard, I can see it all now clear as day. He is so obviously the man on the train; the one who told me about his friend making a mint doing *personal histories*.

'So what was your price then?' I sneer at him, I can't help myself, part of me is actually curious. Although I know that whatever it is, it will never be enough.

He shifts his sleeve awkwardly over the skin graft on his arm. 'I'm a collector. We share...' and he glances towards Henderson, 'interests.'

'You're getting the picture now I take it, Sophie?' Henderson says.

I don't bother to reply.

'Everything's prepped,' Beavis tells Henderson. 'We just need the content.'

He smiles at me, and I feel a sick lurch in the pit of my stomach. By *content*, does he mean Jed?

In my pocket, my phone vibrates. I am trying so hard not to look at it. Perhaps they'll forget I have one. It's a wild hope, but wild hopes are what I've sunk to.

'What will you do to him?' I'm shocked by the sound of my own voice. It sounds broken. Henderson has won; the bastard's won.

He shrugs. 'A painless procedure. I know you've established a link between Parkinson's and stem cells, Sophie. We have access to all your searches, your communications.'

Trevor on Tech, I think, with his all-smiling PR wife.

'And having your own genetically matched stem cells works best, I'm guessing?'

Henderson nods. 'Something like that.'

'Kara and the others, they've been keeping you alive?'

'You overestimate the efficacy of the process. At the beginning, we could get away with every other year. That worked well. Now it's every six months. The donors rarely survive past two procedures.'

'And then you throw them in the sea?'

Henderson raises his eyes in amusement. 'Now that would be careless. When you have your own island, there are a million ways to get rid of a body. The ones you know about, they got jittery before I'd really worked them into the program. A bit like yourself. It won't happen again.'

I feel an overwhelming sense of desperation. 'Please, take what you need from Jed, then just let us go. We won't tell anyone, I promise. You've bound me up in ND forms. I'm up to my neck.'

'Yes but...' he pauses to suck in a breath, 'up to your neck in concrete guarantees a more... trouble-free future.'

Tears flood silently down my cheeks, not just because I'm terrified, but because of my stupidity.

'Oh, Sophie. Can't you see? This is important, what I'm doing here, having the space to do it, the time. The world needs guardians, older guardians, wiser guardians. People who can see the whole picture.'

'But not this. Nobody needs this,' I sob. 'You can't...'

'Ah, but actually, Sophie, I can. I really can, and in fact... I have.'

One of the heavies who's been scoping my room nods, satisfied it's clear.

'I've left you some sleeping pills,' Beavis says, putting a small bottle by the side of my bed.

'You've slept through it this far.' There's a sickening edge of amusement to Henderson's voice. 'Why not continue in the same vein? You know I meant it when I said you could have come on board.'

'You seriously think... I'd...'

'If you had committed before, perhaps, but now... Now I think it is all too late.'

He's smiling, but as he raises his hand to his face, I notice it's shaking.

'Was it all part of your plan, the fertility clinic?'

'No. Not at all. A fortuitous accident. Although I've always believed that if you have a machine which you value, car, house, body, it's a good idea to have a full stock of spare parts.'

The heavies have left. It's just me and Henderson. I could try and overpower him, but I'd never get out. I haven't a doubt in my head that the Doctor would love to slam a hypodermic into my arm and then I'd be useless, utterly useless. Right now I need to think.

'Shame.' Henderson leans forward and touches my cheek. 'Eventually, I'll run low on my foetus stock, and you could have worked well on that front too.'

I pull away in disgust. The man is hideous.

He takes a moment to enjoy my reaction. 'Goodnight, Sophie. Such a shame.'

I feel nausea rising in my chest as Henderson pulls the door closed, and for the first time, I notice that it's inches thick. There's no way I'm getting out through that unless it's open.

'Oh, and your phone...' I hear Henderson's voice through the sealed door.

I can feel the phone's outline in my pocket. He's going to ask for it back.

'There's no outgoing signal. You can, however, receive texts. You will get all Jed's notifications until we... deactivate him. But he can't receive anything from you. Nobody can.'

I run to the door, hammering against it, my shoulder shooting a sharp pain through my body as it comes up hard against solid wood. 'You can't do this, you bastard.'

But this world runs on its own rules. I should have known

that from the start. Hadn't Clara tried to warn me? On my trip to the mainland, instead of playing the journalist I should have been running through the streets, flagging down a taxi to the airport, getting home.

The sound of male voices evaporates from the corridor outside. They've gone. Bereft, I sink down against the wall and take my phone from my pocket.

There's a new text:

Soph, is this all okay?

It was sent an hour ago. Even though it's useless. I send one last text back.

No. You are in danger. Get out.

The message flies off. I imagine it cropping up on Trevor's computer somewhere in the villa; on a terminal manned purely for Henderson's amusement.

I cannot give up though. I mustn't give up. The others got out. There has to be a way. I leap to my feet, cross to the windows and begin to pull at the shutters; they're locked tight. This wood is so thick. God, why is everything such goddamn high quality here? Suddenly I hear something. From somewhere far below, I can just make out the soft diesel chug of *Calypso* as she pulls into the bay. Jed. He must be arriving.

'*Deactivate.*' Deactivate Jed? The idea haunts me. I stare at my phone, at the dead thread of texts. Then I remember my Kindle. They'd taken my laptop, but my Kindle? I hadn't used it whilst I'd been on the island. It had been beside my bed. I'd knocked it off the table that first night. Could it be... I hadn't seen them remove it. I feel down the side of the pillows, thrusting my fingers into the gap between mattress and headboard, till my hand hits on something hard and loose. Grabbing hold of the small, hard plastic rectangle, I draw it up into the light – my Kindle. I know they've blocked my accounts, but could I sign in using an alias email? I had a couple set up before I'd decided on my company name, just dummy addresses, but they were all functioning. Maybe one would still work. If I could just get a message out.

I switch it on, so thankful that I got the 3G model. I won't have to connect to the wi-fi. They'll spot me, but if I can just work quickly enough I might be able to slide one last message out under the radar.

history4U@gmail. The old account is still there. I'm about to send a message to Jed: *Your life in danger. Get out.* Then suddenly I stop, hesitate, my fingers hovering over the send button. That's not going to work; they've got him. I only have one chance at getting a message through before they trace the signal and block it. I type in Geoff's address:

Send help. Urgent. Life in danger.

The words are all squashed tight into the subject line. Will he know it's me? I'm not sure. I attach my signature, press send and pray. It goes. The email switches from outbox to sent, but that doesn't mean... Suddenly the room lights stutter, then snap out. Henderson's cut the power. Punishment? They've seen the email, but... did they manage to stop it? I stare at the dark light fittings. Maybe, just maybe that one message had got out and the lights going off is a sign from Henderson. It's to remind me that he's still in control. He's trying to scare me. He needn't have bothered on that front: I'm beyond scared.

I hear a scraping noise: a key going into the lock. Without even thinking, I grab the heavy lamp from the bedside table, dragging the plug out from its socket, and duck behind the door. They're coming in, but coming in to do what? To take the Kindle away? Surely they don't need to bother. They'll have traced the signal. They'll have blocked it. One email was all that I had. My one last chance and it was gone. So, maybe they're coming in to teach me a lesson? The handle turns hesitantly. I hold the lamp high over my head. If there's a way in, there's a way out. I'm not going to lose this chance.

The door creaks open. For a moment, whoever it is just stands there in the doorway. I'm barely breathing. My right arm aches from holding the lamp so high. Whoever it is, they need to step forward. Step just one foot into the room and I've got them. Please. Please. Please.

'Sophie?'

The voice is quiet, male, barely audible. Not a voice I recognise.

If he doesn't enter, I'll have to startle him. Run at him with all my might, but that's going to draw attention. He just needs to take one step, just one more foot into the goddamn room.

He's in. I push the door shut. The lamp comes down hard on his head.

It doesn't smash, but it does the job. He's on the floor. Not unconscious, but groaning, clutching his skull between his hands. It's dark so I can't see his face. I find myself praying that he doesn't get up.

'Move, and I'll kill you,' I say. I have no idea how I'm going to do the killing, but the lamp goes up again as if I mean business.

'Ughh.'

The groan is pitiful. Small and hurt like a wounded animal. Not at all what I would have expected from one of Henderson's goons. I should really take him out, but it's not that easy. I've never knowingly harmed anyone before in my life. The lamp is still hanging precariously above his head. I will have to smash it down with more force next time. Much more force if I want to knock him out. My arms go up, to give my swing more momentum.

'Please,' he says.

There's something irresistible about politeness, an instinct that runs so deep in the British psyche. Something which seems strangely arresting and out of place in Henderson's world. With my free hand, I reach into my pocket for my phone and shine the torch in his face. I wish I hadn't. The phone goes clattering to the floor. It's No Face, and he's even more horrific close up, a mass of molten white flesh.

'My God.'

'Please.' His voice is calm and slow. 'We don't have much time.' I can see the shadow of his hands reaching out towards his bag.

'Hang on. Wait. Stop.' I pick the phone up again, shining the light back on, trying to avoid looking at that face. 'What's in there?'

He leaves the bag where it is, hands up in an attitude of surrender. 'I came prepared... I've tried to break in before.'

'In? I don't need to get in. I need to get out. My friend, my boyfriend, Jed, they're bringing him here.'

He looks puzzled.

'Henderson is using kids from the clinic.'

'I know.'

I stop for a moment, draw a breath. He believes me. This whole thing is so fantastical, but No Face believes me. 'You work for Henderson?'

He shakes his head. 'Not anymore. We need to get you and your friend out.'

Suddenly it doesn't matter what he looks like. He's the first person I've met on this island who is genuinely on my side. I push the bag towards him. 'Who are you?'

Clutching at his bag, he stumbles awkwardly to his feet. He's not so young, sixty I'm guessing. I don't let go of the lamp but lower it a little.

'Susanne Millar was my daughter. I did work for Henderson, but a long time ago.'

I stare at his face in the torchlight. I've seen photos of staff at the clinic, but there was no one with a face like that. I would have remembered.

'The fire, were you in the fire?'

He shakes his head. 'No, the fire... I'm pretty sure Henderson started that himself. He wanted to get rid of the records. I worked for Henderson, just a lab assistant. Nothing grand. Me and my wife, we'd been desperate for a child, and Henderson, well he said he'd do the fertility treatment for us as a favour.'

I can't help but notice there's a touch of bitterness in Millar's voice when he says the word favour.

'It didn't work?'

'No. It was successful. We had a beautiful baby girl.'

'Susanne?'

He nods sadly. 'Years later, an invitation came for Susanne to do an internship. A great opportunity,' he snorts ironically. 'The clinic was closed, but there'd never been any problems at work. Grayling and Henderson had fallen out, but these things happen. Susanne had studied anthropology at uni. Looking into Greek myths, the internship, it was all right up her street. Too good to be true. Turned out, that's exactly what it was. She got whisked off to Greece. Well, she was a... We thought she was a grown woman. Then one day I bumped into Grayling, and he... he expressed concerns about the fertility clinic. At the time, I didn't take much notice. Put it down to professional rivalry. But it kept worrying away at me, gnawing into our "perfect" little life. Grayling said that the...' And Millar hesitates.

'Yes?' I ask, but I'm pretty sure I already know where this is going.

He draws in a deep breath. 'Grayling suggested that the majority of the children from the clinic were sired by Henderson. No doubt Grayling had forgotten I had a child through the clinic. Maybe he wouldn't have told me if our treatment had all been on the record. Anyway, at first, I dismissed it, but... I was cleaning up her flat. She was coming home, only had a couple of weeks left, and I saw her hairbrush. I wasn't planning on it. I... well, I took a few strands, sent them to a lab. It was just to stop that niggling doubt that Grayling had planted. I didn't think for one minute she wasn't mine. It turned out Grayling was right. Henderson had switched things up in the lab. I didn't know why. Only thing I did know was... Well, besides the heartbreak... What he did, it had to be illegal. Susanne was in Greece. Henderson wouldn't return my calls. She didn't have a mobile. So, I got here under my own steam. I should have known that I wasn't going to get onto the island without being seen. The guy who brought me over on the boat turned me straight in. Henderson said I could have her back if I did a...' He hesitates.

'Made some kind of *commitment*?' I ask.

Millar nods. 'It was bizarre, as though he thought he was some kind of God. I had to wash my face in...'

And with a sickening lurch, I know. The thought fills me with horror. 'Acid?'

He nods again.

Suddenly it's all making sense, or at least as much sense as it can. Henderson told me in his study how his childhood was notable because of its absence of game playing. 'He's a psychopath,' I say.

'Exactly.'

'But really he is.' How could I have missed it? He'd virtually told me himself.

The one thing psychotic personalities all have in common is that they don't play the usual childhood games. Sadism, cruelty to animals, maybe the odd whip-cracking ringmaster, but none of this stuff is anywhere near normal. Henderson's spent a lifetime working up to the ultimate power game. One that at every step reinforces his idea that most human beings are beneath him, but I don't need to tell Millar any of this.

'Then he wheeled me out in front of her,' Millar says, unable to meet my eye, 'like some... some nightmare. She didn't even recognise me. I... I managed to escape through the labyrinth. Got lost in there for days, but eventually, I got out. Stole a boat.'

'Why didn't you go to the police?'

'I did. They said that Susanne had left the island. There were reports of her living in Peru. Though I'm not sure she was ever there. According to some official records, she even went into a police station. Claimed she didn't want to come home. She "said",' he stumbles, his eyes full of pain. 'She claimed I was an abusive father.'

He turns his sad gaze on me as if asking me to look into his soul; to witness how ridiculous this is. All I can see is love and pain. Millar shakes his head slowly. 'Then Susanne, or whoever was claiming to be her, just went under the radar. When they found Kara Jarvis, I knew Henderson was up to something. You see, I remembered the Jarvises from the clinic.'

'So you followed me?' This doesn't seem to make sense. 'Why me?'

'You tweeted. You'd hashtagged *Henderson* and *fertility clinic*. You said *Christmas in paradise*.'

That sounds so sour to me now. 'Why didn't you try and tell me this before?'

'I had to be sure you weren't attempting to flush me out. Henderson's been trying to get rid of me for years. I thought you might be some kind of plant. I couldn't find any records that tied you to the clinic.'

'No,' I say bitterly. 'Henderson's after my boyfriend, Jed. But hang on a minute... how did you get the key to my room?'

'Sylvie, she has keys to all the rooms. Sylvie... she tried to help me before. She... but then she saw what he did; my face... and...'

Suddenly there's a noise from outside; heavy feet: someone walking down the length of the corridor. I put one finger to my lips, Millar nods. We barely breathe as we listen to the footfalls passing my room. We need to get a move on.

'I've got a motorboat.'

I remembered the abandoned skiff I'd seen on my walk yesterday. Its prow poking out from a hasty camouflage of branches. So that was Millar. 'At the abandoned village?'

He shakes his head. 'It was. I've moved it closer now. It's on the beach by the east entrance to the labyrinth.'

I'd seen the bay by the eastern entrance: the steep sloping path with its flimsy, single rail of cable. The path I had sworn to myself I would not be going down. 'What about Henderson's yacht, couldn't we...?'

'It's out of action. The motorboat's good.'

Something about the way he says *out of action*, makes me think that maybe he had a hand in making sure the *Calypso* was taken out of the equation. All music to my ears – in a race between a two-bit motorboat and *Calypso*, it was easy to know who would win.

'And Achilleas?'

Millar looks blank.

'Your clothes, I saw them on his boat.'

'I stowed away, one night. Was lucky to get off alive. The abandoned village is better. No one goes around that side of the island.'

A stowaway, of course.

'Look, Sophie...' his voice sounds heavy with the weight, the hopelessness of the situation, 'I have to get into that lab. Find out exactly what Henderson is doing.'

'He's using some kind of stem cell engineering to stave off Parkinson's.'

Millar's eyes light up, as if finally everything is making sense for him.

'Of course. Parkinson's. There was a brief clinical trial years ago. It was a chemical called...' he searches his brain, 'Tridopoline. They were hoping it was going to be safe for IVF patients who had Parkinson's. We had two women at the time, so... I mean, it was all very new and had to be clinically tested. But for a while, it was looking good. Then, a few of the lab technicians started noticing side effects in the rats.'

'Side effects?'

'Antisocial behaviour. The rat taking the drug would eat the others.'

'That is so much more than antisocial.'

He nods. 'But that's how they termed it. Come morning, there would only ever be the one rat left in the cage. They said...' again he searches his brain for the exact term, 'it was a... megalomania.'

'You think Henderson could have taken the drug, tried it out on himself?'

'Officially we never had it on-site. We were just interested in its development. These pharmaceutical companies, they guard those kind of secrets better than the Crown Jewels. A cure to an illness like Parkinson's would be priceless.'

Maybe not for a man like Henderson. Seems as though having all the money in the world can sometimes get you into a hell of a lot of trouble. It was the philosopher's stone all over again. People who searched for it, who tried to create it, Newton and the others, it always ended up killing them. Mercury poisoning, delusions of grandeur, or some such 'treat'. There is no quick fix for immortality.

'And when the drugs didn't work for him, Henderson

moved on to harvesting stem cells.' A cold chill passes over me. Maybe it was already too late. His personality type, coupled with the Tridopoline; he had become the rat that ate everything else in the cage.

'I've photographed some documents. We can use them as proof, but I have to get my boyfriend out. There's an operating theatre...'

Millar shakes his head. 'He preps people somewhere else. Somewhere secret. Does it all himself. I know because it irritates Beavis.'

'The centre, the labyrinth centre?'

'The museum? The place with the sacrificial altar?'

'No.' I grab my phone and flick through the diagrams Alfred showed me of the labyrinth.

I scan the images, feeling nothing but frustration. Something is not stacking up here. According to Alfred's main map, I've been to the centre. It's the place Henderson took me with the containers and the altar.

'Here.' Millar points to the exact same chamber.

It does look central. There's surely nowhere else that the centre could be. There are no other rooms down there, but it wasn't the kind of place you would prep someone for an operation. There's the medical facility, but Henderson's doing this in secret. Away from Beavis. I run my eyes back and forward over the plan. It's hopeless. If the centre eluded the Germans, Alfred, and all the archaeologists over the years, how on earth are we going to find it now? I see the pencil marks in the top corner of the map. Alfred's hastily written notes. 'Agree to put money on roll of a dice.' Another game: the obscure clue set by Henderson. Suddenly it hits me. It's been staring me in the face all this time. I remember Alice's story, her brother as ringmaster, always controlling the action, cracking the whip to guide his animals along well-trodden paths. But in reality, it's not just about control; Henderson's desperate for the dumb beasts to break out. To find the escape key, to prove that their existence is not simply some kind of bovine joke, and he just can't pull himself back from showing off. When he gave Alfred the clue, he was handing him the key.

'It's cryptic.'

Millar draws in a tired breath. 'Perhaps but...'

'No, you don't understand. This clue *is* cryptic. Like a crossword puzzle.'

He looks confused. 'What makes you think...?'

'Look, this isn't grammatically correct. If it's a sentence, it needs more. It would say something like "we should agree to put money on the roll of a dice". Its brevity gives it away.'

'Well, say it is.' Millar's not looking convinced. 'Even if it is a cryptic clue, what does it actually mean?'

'Okay...' I draw my lip in, hold it between my teeth. I need to think. 'Cryptic clues are normally either charades where you get two words put together, anagrams with letters mixed up, or anagrams where words are spelt backwards. Sometimes a mixture. You always have a definition. That's normally at the beginning, so the definition here is *agree*.' I point to the word on the photo image. 'Money could be...'

'Drachma?' he offers.

I shake my head. 'Simpler. Money is...?'

'Notes,' he says. 'Coin?'

'Could be. Hold on to that. Now the roll, in *roll of dice*, that could be an anagram indicator. You *roll* the words. So if we look at the word *dice*.'

'Coin cide.'

'Coincide,' I say excitedly, staring at the image on my phone. 'And to coincide is to exist simultaneously. Look. Look at that line!' I point eagerly at the centre of the image.

The line around the sacrificial vault is indeed different. It's thicker than the others. I zoom in, and suddenly it's all oh-so obvious: there are two lines banding the sacrificial chamber. There's a room within a room.

'It's underneath. Henderson had said that the Germans didn't find it, but that they were only off by a few metres. He meant metres down.'

Like a child; it's being carried by the other room. We've found it.

'I can get us there,' Millar says. 'I'll leave markers on the wall, but in fact, if you see the markers, you know you need to turn back. It's just a trick to try and get Henderson and his men following the wrong lead. That should give us some time.'

I'm beginning to like Millar more and more. 'We need to go.'

He nods. 'Leave your phone...'

'I can't... All the document images are on there.'

'They can track you. You might as well be carrying a neon sign with *get me* on it.'

'But the images are evidence.'

He shakes his head. 'Not really. It's useful, yes, but it tells us nothing about what he's doing here. Taking the phone is too risky.'

I remember Geoff. 'I sent them to a friend.' Of course, Geoff will have everything.

Millar nods. 'Hopefully, if something does happen to us...' He shrugs, leaving the sentence hanging.

And I know that we are staring down our own mortality here: chances of us getting out are slim.

'I'll also try and get evidence when we're at the centre. Just in case. There has to be something incriminating in that room. He guards it too well.'

I abandon my phone, grabbing my leather jacket from the cupboard. I'm still haunted by the bone-chilling cold I'd experienced on my last visit to the labyrinth.

'Ready?' he whispers.

We listen at the door, holding it open just a fraction. There's no one pacing outside. They are so arrogant; they're not expecting me to get out. Millar takes the lead, and right now I could not be more relieved.

We walk quickly towards Sylvie's staircase. I think maybe we're going to go up to her room, but no. There's a small narrow stairway, almost hidden to one side. Millar disappears down it and, with my heart thumping, I follow.

There's no light, only shadowy darkness and damp, cold bricks. Cautiously, we wind our way down the steps, not wanting to alert Henderson or his heavies. It's just one floor down, then the clean night air assaults us. I feel an overwhelming sense of panic. I want to run off into the dark night and not look back, but I know I can't do that. I have to get Jed out. I have to go back into that labyrinth, into the very place that I never want to see again in my life. Thankfully, there's very little time to think. Millar is pushing on. Keeping in the shadows, we run silently across the pool terrace. Millar opening the gate in the wall for me, and we're out.

We sprint through the wood. I know where we're going now. We have to get to the clearing with the grotto but although every step is taking us further from Henderson, we're far from safe. I see the eastern entrance at the edge of the wood. It's at the other side of the grove, through the clearing. Nobody looking for us yet. The alarms haven't started to ring. Hopefully, our path will be clear. I can hear the soft burbling sound of the stream, jabbering on as if none of this is happening, as if this is just another evening.

What had been going through Jed's head, I wonder, as we dash through the shadowy trees. What had he thought when they grabbed him at the airport and brought him here? What feelings of despair when I failed to reply to his texts? Did he think I'd abandoned him again?

'Down in that bay.' Millar points from the cliff. 'The boat's there.'

I remembered the bay. How could I forget? I don't need to look. I can recall in graphic detail the steep path down and that flimsy handrail shaking in the wind. I shudder. I have to be brave.

'We can get out through the labyrinth at beach level,' Millar says.

I feel a sense of relief wash over me. I won't have to use the path; we're going down through the labyrinth.

At the tunnel, Millar hands me a torch. I'm getting used to his face now. It's horrible, but the initial revulsion fades, once you realise those scars are because of love, because of selflessness.

Millar rummages in his bag, pulling out a pen, a Sharpie. Then grabbing the torch back, he heads off into the tunnel, light swinging in front of us as he drags the Sharpie along the wall; leaving a luminous snail-trail of yellow in its wake. The trail, I remember, is just a decoy. This is my way in, but it's not my way out. Beach level, that's what Millar had said. He must have been planning this for years. Despite myself, I start counting my route; thirty steps down, twenty steps left. Surprisingly, the numbers help. It feels like I'm putting order into this nightmare. I'm just going to count. I'm going to follow Millar and keep those numbers running through my brain and try not to think beyond, to the place where the numbers run out.

Alfred was right, this part of the maze is really confusing, paths ducking, diving and splitting away from us into the darkness. But, Millar explains quietly as we walk, there are only ever two real options. One circles back on itself. As long as you know which route not to take, you can find your way. We must be heading down to the shoreline; the descent is so steep. The smell of salt water mixed with a heavy, metallic taint of minerals fills my nostrils. We are getting closer. There's a sense of purpose to this tunnel, as if it's heading to the heart of everything. It's so steep that it must, I think, be going close to the Sacrificial Chamber. I wonder if Alfred is still there? And then underneath the chamber, surely it has to be underneath, that's where we'll find some kind of hidden room; the heart of the labyrinth, and Jed. But will we find Henderson too? My skin crawls. I remember those arrogant eyes. Say they're working on Jed tonight? Maybe not – the Doctor had been drinking at supper. He won't be going into surgery tonight. Besides, I'm not convinced that Beavis even knows where the centre is. It's Henderson's special place. The dark place he returns to, and I'm guessing he always returns alone.

After what seems like an age, the tunnel flattens out. Millar turns to me and nods; I'm guessing we've reached ground zero. He walks on, keeping his Sharpie against the wall. The line is intermittent; he doesn't want it to run out, but you only have to take a quick look at the wall, shine a light on it, and you can see the trail.

'Get out! NOOOOOOOOO,' a terrified voice screams into the night, making me leap out of my skin. I stop dead in my tracks.

'NOOOO.'

'Your friend?' Millar hisses.

I shake my head. No, it's not Jed's voice. Then who? Alfred. It's Alfred. Has Henderson locked him in the chamber he was so keen to discover? Is he being taunted by ghosts, real or imaginary?

Find your true self. Sometimes it's not that pretty.

'We're close,' I say.

We come to a fork. Millar hangs back and indicates for me

to look around a corner. Immediately I have my bearings. It's surreal. We've been descending for twenty minutes, half an hour, through ancient ruins, a passage that seemed to be spiralling, crawling into the very earth itself. Yet in front of me, I see the white clinical corridor, strip-lit and 21st century; the lifts standing ready and waiting at the end. This is the operating theatre; the place we came with the boy.

'Out that way: over the rocks to the other beach,' Millar hisses.

I nod. I've got it. No going down the cliff face; we just have to crawl around the headland. Low rocks and an angry sea I can cope with.

Millar points in the opposite direction, back down a darkened winding tunnel, and despite myself, I feel a sudden sense of awe. So this is it. This is where the true labyrinth begins, but there's a problem. Because the thing about labyrinths is – they only have a single entrance, one that doubles up as an exit. If we meet anyone we're done for. It's a risk we're going to have to take. Millar puts his Sharpie away and takes out a grenade.

'If we need it,' he says. 'I found a pile of them in the labyrinth. Not sure if it'll still work.'

I pray to God it will. If it comes to it, I hope this small oval object will bring the whole thing down on everyone's heads. This is serious, life-and-death serious. There are no comforting illusions to hide behind: if they find us, they will kill us.

32

JED

I'm convinced we're going to get caught. We're walking so fast: fuelled on adrenaline, like ants that march until they drop or bees that work until they die. It's as though we have no choice. Round and around the tunnel we go, so fast I can almost imagine meeting myself coming back the other way. We drop down a little, the passage levelling out. I figure we must be skirting around the Sacrificial Chamber now. Through the rock, I can hear Alfred moaning. It's as if every inch of this stone wall contains pain, humiliation and fear. I wonder if our footsteps are serving to terrify him even more.

'This is hopeless,' I hiss. There is no centre.

'It has to be here.' Millar speeds up in front of me, moving so fast I feel he's going to break into a run.

'Wait.' I grab hold of his arm. 'Go that fast, and we'll miss it. We have to use our heads. This is a puzzle. It's a room within a room.'

'But it can't take up the same physical space.'

'No,' I say, stealing a moment to lean against the wall, and fill my lungs with damp air. 'It can't be inside, but it could be above or underneath.' I shine my torch up at the ceiling. It's vaulted. 'I don't think it's above. That ceiling has been there for maybe fifty years. We're looking for something older. The room has to be under us.' I draw my boot across the floor. 'We're looking for a trapdoor. Walk too fast, and we'll miss it.'

Millar's on edge, itching to move forward. There's a kind of energy in the tunnels, and that feeling: the standing beneath pylons feeling, it permeates everything. It's raw, chaotic, relentless even. Desperate to drive a person on.

'Okay,' he says reluctantly. 'You first.'

We shuffle forward much slower this time, Millar following behind me. I'm inching my feet cautiously out in front. I've got to stay alert. I can't afford to miss the merest hint of an opening. I'm looking for uneven flagstones in the floor, anything out of the ordinary. I keep one hand on the wall as I move slowly forward.

'This could take hours.' Millar sounds irritated.

I know he's right, but I refuse to give up. It's Jed's life that's at stake. I'm not going to abandon him, even if it means I get caught trying to get him out. I shine the torch over the walls. Then I see it: a line of Millar's bright-yellow highlighter. We've been here before. My heart sinks as I gaze at the continuous strip. Only then it hits me, it's not continuous. The line is broken slightly. I move my hand against the rock. At the break in the line, there's a small ridge. We can find the door using the pen.

'Millar, keep the Sharpie against the floor, any gaps in the flagstones, and we'll know.'

He takes the lead. His body bent awkwardly. We walk forward again, inching into the darkness.

'I'm not sure this is going to work...' he mutters. 'It's just flat. We don't even know...'

Suddenly, the Sharpie jumps.

He looks back towards me, his hands held over the point

where the line broke. I don't wait for an invitation. I'm down on my knees, digging my nails into the ground. My fingers slip inside a trench. I follow it around. 'It's just a flagstone,' I say, my voice near to tears.

'No.' Millar shakes his head. For the first time since I've met him, he lets a smile spread across that strange haunting face of his. 'This has to be the door.'

Dropping to his knees, Millar joins me, tracing the edges of the indent.

'There must be some kind of lever,' he grunts.

'And stairs, the access has to be easy; Henderson's over seventy. He never lets anyone into the centre. If he can get in alone, it can't be too difficult.'

We grope blindly, looking for some kind of catch, and sure enough, something gives under my fingertips. We flatten back against the wall as the rectangle below our feet slides open.

The change is immediate. My eyes are blinded by a flood of bright, white light, like a spaceship about to take off. But worse, the energy, whatever it is, that sense of standing under an electrical freeway, it's so much stronger here. It's as if we're walking over a generator.

I give Millar a triumphant look but we don't have time to congratulate ourselves. Underneath the door is a small, brightly lit flight of steps. I go first, Millar close behind. I don't know what I expected to find. Something like the chamber, perhaps? Something macabre. Well, it's certainly that. The room below is smaller and more basic than the operating theatre, a cross between sacrificial temple and hospital. I glance around me. There are inscriptions carved into the wall, religious I think, predating Christianity. Symbols that I've never seen before. This is the place where the spores started to reach out into the real world. To carry veins of hatred slowly up towards the surface. This is where the seeker finds their true self. And it's horrible. Every inch is hatred and futility. A sense of so much more anguish than one person can possibly bear.

Then I see him – Jed. He's stripped down to his pants, pale as a ghost and stuck all over with monitors; a drip containing some kind of clear solution feeds steadily into his arm. This place is literally poisoning him, little by little, drop by drop.

For a moment, I freeze. It is all my fault. Yes, I can see my *true self* here, in all its horror; I am selfish and stupid. I've destroyed the only good thing in my life. But as I sink deep into self-pity, Millar doesn't hesitate. Not for a moment. He dashes to Jed and pulls out the drip.

'What!'

'He's healthy. Whatever it is they've got going into him, he doesn't need it.'

Millar's right. I'm soon beside him, tugging off the wires.

'We don't have much time. You need to get him out. I've no doubt that all of this will be hooked up to some kind of control centre.'

Somewhere in the complex, machines will be beeping. We've taken away their victim, and they won't be happy.

'Jed? Jed?'

He mumbles, incoherent and woozy. I bend my knees to give my body some kind of momentum, then with all my might, I attempt to pull him up. It kind of works, he's half sitting, half slumped. I shake him gently.

'We have to go,' I say, biting back the tears.

'What? Sophie? What?' His voice is so confused, so trusting, so hurt.

God, I hate myself. I swing his legs off the plinth. 'Can you stand? You need to stand.'

I look around for Millar, but he's busy taking photographs, opening drawers, looking for evidence. He flicks through files so quickly. His trained eye scanning the details. Suddenly he stops. 'Susanne.'

'What?'

'This must be her. There are no names but the dates match. Her blood type. Everything.' His voice cracks. His eyes are filled with such pain and exhaustion. 'It states everything that he did to her.'

There's a whole chart. Twelve months of invasive procedures, recorded for prosperity and pain.

I feel a tug on my arm; Jed's sinking back down onto the stone bed.

'Jed, you need to lean on me. We have to get out. Millar?'

Millar pushes the file inside his jacket, then he's beside me. He swings Jed's arm over his shoulder and lifts. Jed's standing, but only for a moment. We're just not strong enough. He's sinking back down onto the plinth.

'Jed!' I scream. 'You have to wake up. You have to.'

'On three.' Millar grabs Jed's arm again and is levering it back up.

We get him standing. He's swaying a bit, but with support I think we can make it.

'Shit. This is going to take forever.'

Millar looks at the woozy Jed. We both know it's not going to work. We'll never get him back down the tunnel like this and even if we did, we're not fast enough to outrun Henderson's men.

'Sophie, I have to get this evidence out.'

I know Millar's right. I know this is hopeless.

'Okay.' I nod, trying not to let panic seep too far into my voice. 'You get everything you need. I'll handle this,' I say, letting Jed drop gently back down. If Millar wasn't here, I'd have to do it on my own. I can do this on my own. I need to calm down, use my brain not my muscles. I'm a doctor for

Christ's sake. I'm in an operating theatre. Emergency – what would I do? First thing. First thing is always – what's the patient taken? I scrabble around on the floor, looking at the markings on the drip. No clues. I empty the bin. It's Benzodiazepine.

I go straight for the fridge. 'I need Flumazenil.'

'What?' Millar's looking confused, but he's not stopping he's emptying documents into his bag like he's on *Supermarket Sweep*.

'I've got to try and wake him up.' I go through the drugs, pulling them out, scattering them over the floor, till my fingers clutch a small vial. I read the label. Brilliant. I need a syringe.

'Syringe, Syringe.' I'm talking to myself. My eyes flicking around the room like a madwoman.

'We don't have time,' Millar says. 'This evidence, it has to...'

'You get out,' I say. 'We'll join you. I promise.' I grab a syringe. 'If we don't make it, then...' But I don't need to say the rest. I don't need to add that if we don't get to the boat, Millar has to go on without us.

He nods, then, clutching his backpack, races off down the tunnel.

I puncture the vial with the needle, pump a vein in Jed's arm and inject the Flumazenil.

'Ow! Soph.'

'Jed.' I take his face gently between my hands. 'I'm so sorry. This is all my fault.'

He shakes his head. The movement is too wide. He nearly knocks himself off balance again.

'Jed. Listen.' I hold his chin gently between my fingers, staring into those sad blue eyes, maintaining contact, willing him to keep holding on. 'You need to stay awake. We're going to get you out.'

He's still unsteady. The Flumazenil could take a while to

get into his system. It may not even work. This is not an exact science.

'We don't have much time. Lean on me.'

He's heavier than I could ever have imagined, but determination is making me strong. I think of all those stories I've heard about mothers lifting cars off their crushed children or stopping raging bulls with their bare hands. When someone you love is in danger, you have to find that inner strength, even if your track record isn't really skewed towards heroic.

Soon we're stumbling up the narrow stairs out of that terrible place. I can hear Millar's footsteps ahead in the darkness. My eyes are finding it difficult to adjust after the bright light of the central chamber. The fact that they're stinging with tears doesn't help. The edges of my vision are blurred into a shadowy mass. But I can't cry. Not now. This is not the time for emotion.

'Soph?' He can hardly speak.

'Quiet now, just concentrate.' Tears, these goddamn tears. If I focus on self-pity, I know we won't make it. The only way is forward. We limp down the path of the labyrinth. I have to keep talking to Jed, trying to keep him awake. Just like I've done so many times when I was training with concussed patients. I did it with Sally-Anne. Even then, when it came down to it, there was no team at my side. I continue to talk to Jed. Half the time I'm not even sure what I'm saying. It's just a mixture of reassurances and apologies, but it seems to help fuel us forward.

At the end of the labyrinth, there are two turnings. I know I need to stay calm. I've got to think rationally and not panic. I shine the torch down the first turning. The yellow marker illuminates. This was the way we came in. I remember where I am. I need to go in the other direction, get out down that white sterile corridor. Go across the rocks.

Suddenly there's an earth-shattering BANG: an explosion.

The passage I was about to enter fills with smoke, as I'm blown off my feet. Choking particles fill the air. I'm coughing. I can hardly breathe. I've lost Jed. My eyes sting, clogged with dust and grit. Jed's nowhere, blown away from me in the blast. What just happened? And then I remember – Millar's grenade. The conversation we had. Would it work? Well, it obviously did. I'm not sure if the explosion was an accident or deliberate, but I do know it's a warning. Our planned exit is out of bounds. Millar's trying to buy us time.

I spit the debris out of my mouth. My tongue is coated in a thick layer of plaster. I wipe it with my palm: also covered in a thick fur of dust.

'Jed,' I splutter. Nothing. 'Jed!'

I hear a cough. It must be him. I grope in the darkness. My fingers closing around the small torch Millar gave me. It's barely enough; the air is so thick with dust that the beam of light simply bounces back at me. I've been here before: with Sally-Anne it was the same – the thick dust blocking my airways, the smell of concrete and stone. I stumble around, throwing my hands out into the milky darkness. Suddenly I touch something warm, something soft – Jed.

'Soph?' He coughs.

'Yes. Yes.' I clutch him to me, burying my head in his hair. Kissing the top of his head again and again. 'Are you okay?'

He says nothing, but I can feel him nodding. He takes my arm, pulling it down to his body. There's rock, a great slab of rock sitting over his torso.

His eyes are open. He has a smile on his face, a weak one, but still a smile. Tears prick my eyes. I've got to be careful because I've been here before. I took the girder off Sally Anne's body, and that was when all smiles stopped.

'Soph?' He coughs again.

'Mhhmmm.' I can't talk. What do I do?

'You need to...' he says, not finishing his sentence. But I know now.

I don't have a choice. Maybe I never did. I take a deep breath and haul at the slab of rock that's across his chest. If it happens, it happens. Sometimes the choice isn't between right and wrong. Sometimes that's a luxury you just don't have. Sometimes you just have to do your best, and your best has to be enough.

'Jed.' Nothing. 'Jed!'

'Soph?'

He's still breathing. A rush of emotion surges through me. He's not dead. Not yet.

'Come on.' I pull him to his feet, pushing his palm over his mouth, covering my own mouth with my hand. It's not a perfect solution, but it helps. He's alive. We're moving. We limp along the tunnel. It's exhausting; every single one of my muscles is screaming out in red-hot pain. There's barely enough air, but we're managing to stumble on. My ears still ring with the blast, but I can make out other noises: shouting, running. Is it ahead? Is it behind? Is it above? I don't know. Another fork. Left, I think. I had counted us down here. I can count us back. We continue on. A hundred steps, there's another fork. I have no idea where I'm going. I pick the furthest left, and we limp off again. More voices. Muffled calls. Closer. I'm not sure where they're coming from. I flatten Jed and myself inside a small alcove. It's lucky that the air is cleaner here, but my lungs are still convulsing with dust. The footsteps pass, but no people. They must be above us? Or below? I don't know. I'm getting confused. The only thing I know for sure is that we don't have a lot of time. The explosion has bought us some, but they know we're out. They can't be far. I grab Jed's arm and pull forward, but he's so heavy. During our stop he's slumped into the alcove, taking on its shape as if he's begun to grow out of the rock.

'No, Jed, this is no good.' I pull again.

Suddenly more footsteps and this time, shooting. I lurch Jed forward, and my heart sinks as I see in the beam of the torch – three more exits! I thought there were only ever two passageways? Hadn't Millar said...? I fall towards one, shining my torch into the darkness. Then I see it; the yellow marker. It's in front of me and behind me. We are going the exact same way we came down. Just what we wanted to avoid, but now it's a godsend. At least I have a sense of where I am. I need to be faster than they are. Jed's too heavy, but if we can only get to the surface, maybe the fresh air will wake him. We have to keep going. We continue climbing steeply up the path.

'We've got to hurry. You must go faster.' I repeat the same thing over and over again. Pulling Jed along. He's holding one arm against the wall for support. He's trying to help. One more right turning. Then I hear a scream, and my blood runs cold. Millar. He's warning me. They've got him. We have to get out now: we are the only evidence.

'Quick, Jed. Please, quick.' We lurch forward. I keep thinking I hear those footsteps; above us, behind us, in front? I pray that it's anywhere else but in front. We push on, there's another turning. I turn right, and suddenly I hear something that makes my heart sing – the sea. I let out a gasp of joy.

'Jed, we're almost there.' He's so heavy, but we can't give up now. Behind us, from the belly of the beast, there's a second explosion. No dust this time, it's too far away, just the sound reverberating, storming through the walls of the labyrinth like a giant's sneeze.

There's a small window ahead; a cut-out circle of midnight-blue sky. We can do this. We stumble forward. I'm mumbling the whole time, 'Left foot, right foot, left foot, right foot.' Like it's some sort of catechism.

With a great yawn, the tunnel opens up wide around us.

The cold night air slaps my face, welcome as an overdue kiss. We are out. I allow myself a single second's relief before I'm scouting around for the path.

I try not to think of that flimsy metal cable that'll be edging our descent, swinging in the wind, because even thinking about it makes my hands sweat. I need to get a grip, and please, please, please don't let my knees go.

If only it was dark. If it was pitch black, then I wouldn't be able to see the cliff below me, but a large moon shines down on us.

'Jed, you need to walk carefully now.'

'Carefully? Sophie?'

'I don't have time to explain. Trust me?'

He nods.

Trust me, the bitter irony is not lost on me; that's what got him into this trouble in the first place.

I'm going to have to go backwards down the path. If I look down the cliff, I'll freeze. Backwards is the only way. We can't afford me dissolving into a gibbering mess. I'm going to look at his face, the face of the man that I love, the face of the man that I am determined to save. I'm going to count my steps and walk down that path.

So that is exactly what I do. All down the cliff, between each shuffling step that I take, I talk to Jed, coax him, and most of all, apologise. I tell him again and again how I'm determined to get us to safety. As I shuffle backwards, the sound of the sea gets closer and closer, and I carry on counting, counting my steps. Feeling the cliff wall at my left shoulder. Making sure my feet slide back slow and sure. No room for slipping. Each foot will take me one step closer to the bottom.

They must have gone to the other exit. They may think that Millar was acting alone. It's a possibility. The labyrinth entrance was pretty blocked, it might take them a while to realise Jed is gone. There are no sounds from the clifftop above. We have a little time. Not much, but maybe enough.

Suddenly, my foot slips on scree, and my body goes rolling down the path. Jed crumples into a heap on the ground.

I lie there for a moment, my breathing coming fast and erratic. It can't be much further now to the sea. Surely? I turn, sneaking a look. I'm right, twenty feet and we're done. Twenty feet, it's just a short shuffle.

'Jed, one last push,' I whisper. 'We're almost there.' But he makes no movement. 'Jed, please.' My words sound so pathetic in my ears. So lost, so small.

'I'm tired, Soph,' he mutters, and I kiss him again knowing full well that we don't have time for this. I look at the beach below; it's so close. I stand up, and my feet slip away from me once again, but this time I don't fall.

'Damn it!' I shout. This whole place is against me. The skin on my wrists is torn to shreds from where I slipped. I am exhausted, every muscle in my body is screaming at me to just curl up somewhere in the dark and sleep all of this away. There is no way I can support Jed down the rest of the cliff. I pull my coat tighter around me. Then I remember... *Always best to leave a little leather on the road, rather than a portion of skin.*

My jacket. It's crazy, but it could just work. I strip the jacket off and lay it on the ground beside Jed.

'Jed, I need you to roll over onto this.'

He grunts.

'Jed.' Damn it! Why isn't the Flumazenil working? It should surely have kicked in by now. What the fuck have they done to him?

I take a deep sigh, bend my knees, balance my body, then grab his arms and lift him up for just a second; sliding the jacket underneath with my foot, before lying him gently back down. It's kind of worked. The coat is mostly under Jed's body now.

This is my last hope; I pick up his legs, ankles held in my hands, and pull. The stones roll underneath him as he jerks forward. The jacket stays in place. I pull, and he rolls. I pull, he rolls. It's working. It's slow-going, but working. On we go, shuffling down and down. Till my arms ache from holding his legs up high, and a trainer comes off in my hand, but just at that moment, miracle of miracles, my feet flatten out. We've made it!

I scan the beach and true to Millar's word there it is, bobbing about six metres out – a motorboat.

'Just this one last bit, Jed.'

I throw cold seawater over his face.

'Sophie.' But the protest is short-lived. He lurches, heading for the water.

'Jed?'

He's like a bull in a china shop – full tilt forward. He wades knee-deep into the cold water, but he is so unsteady. I need to get him to the boat. What's he doing? Suddenly he stops, sways, then bends his head into the waves, plunging his face into the water. He's coming around, I think. He knows he's got to snap out of it. I dash to him, resting my hands on his shoulders.

'Better?' I say.

He sighs and nods. 'Okay,' he mumbles.

Nothing more, just that one word, but I can work with *okay*. We manage to walk him forward through the waves. He's still heavy, but the fresh air and the cold water are waking him little by little. The dark, brooding island is behind us, each step we take towards the boat I feel that somehow it's losing its grip on us.

Soon we're waist-deep. 'Almost there,' I say, grabbing the boat and bringing it towards us. I shove his body forward, taking the wooden prow with both hands. He's kind of leaning into it, managing an 'ow' as it butts him, which seems like a good sign. I bend down shoulder-deep into the water, grab his legs and lift them, kick them, wedge them, up and in. He's not lying neatly, but that's not important. I lever myself up on my arms and hurl myself after him.

I don't have time to congratulate myself. I need to start the motor. My fingers fumble around the outboard, and my heart sinks: there's no key in the engine. Millar must still have the keys. I look around the boat frantically. There's one oar, just one. For an emergency, I guess. Rowing around in a circle is not really an option. Then I remember my D of E course from oh-so many years ago. The boat may have a recoil starter. I feel around, find the cord and tug. The engine splutters. The sound carrying; echoing off the tall cliff walls sure as if it's been plugged into an amplifier. Anyone standing on the clifftop will have heard, but I can't worry about that now. I pull the cord again. This time I'm in luck. Above the noise of the outboard, I can make out shouts from above. Keeping low in the boat, I angle the rudder around, and we head out into the wide darkness.

I hear what I think might be a shot, then another.

'What?' Jed tries to sit up.

'Down.' I push his head into the well of the boat.

We're still far from safe. *Calypso* might be out of action, but Henderson must have other fast boats. Perhaps my best bet is to skirt around the island. Go to one of the other bays, hide for a day or two, try and get word back home? But I don't turn the rudder. I keep it fixed, heading straight out into the oily night. We are running. The only thing my body will allow me to do is put distance between Jed and the monster that is Henderson.

'Are you okay?' I ask, my voice sounding thin and far away, as it fights against the outboard.

But there's no answer. Jed's asleep, and I am alone skimming along on a small plank in the middle of miles and miles of empty darkness, with a devil in my wake.

It must be well over an hour before I allow myself to relax a little. There's been no sign of pursuit. It looks like Millar really had taken Henderson's yacht 'out of action'. Achilleas has his boat, but when I called him, he got to the house too quick. He can't have had it with him. Perhaps all that they had at their disposal were small boats, the same kind of thing as I'm in now. Maybe they didn't have radar? Just maybe it's as difficult finding me in all this sea, as it is for me to work out where in the hell it is that I'm actually going. We're all lost.

Just as I'm beginning to wonder if we'll ever be found I hear a loud BANG. I look up into the sky. There's a glowing red ball of fire mounting into the heavens. At first, I think it must be a flare. Too late I realise it's not meant to illuminate, it's meant to obliterate. There's a second explosion. Only this time, I'm inside it. For a moment, everything is blinding white, searing hot. A chaos so sudden, so loud that it cancels out everything else. I am falling. Falling backwards into the cold, black water, the blast still ringing loud in my ears. Then, almost as suddenly, the light is gone, and I'm in complete darkness, darker than before. Darker than I ever thought life could be. The world around me is eclipsed. I tread black water in a sea full of splintered wood.

'Jed!' I call. My voice sounding strange in my ears, as though it's coming through muffled speakers. 'Jed.' But there's no answer.

He must be here. I know that. He was so close to me in the boat. If I just reach out our hands will touch, but they don't. Terrible images fill my brain, of the man that I love sinking silently into the cold dark water just a fingertip out of my reach. I dive below the surface, all the while carrying the sound of the explosion with me. Under the water, I am blind. All I can do is feel, and there's so much debris; some of it sharp, some of it angular, not one piece of it Jed. He could be right beside me in all this darkness, sinking silently, and I would have no idea.

—

I'm not sure how long I dive for, an hour, maybe more? Tears clog my airways, making it difficult to breathe, difficult to swim. In the end, I grab a piece of wood and just hold on.

33

LISTEN

When the coastguard finds me, I'm given hot coffee, blankets and sympathetic looks. There's a language barrier as big as the Calypso Deep itself. Eventually, I discover that a message came through from Scotland Yard – Geoff. *A woman is in trouble.* The Greek police had been on their way to the island.

Back in Piraeus, people become increasingly uncomfortable when I voice my allegations. There's no sign of Millar. No sign of Jed. I'm attempting to rock the boat – causing trouble for a local celebrity. The police contact Henderson. He's 'living' in South America. He claims he's been there for over a month. He has witnesses. Multiple witnesses of good character, including one judge. I don't give up. There is a connection between the dead woman Kara Jarvis and Henderson. It can't be ignored. Warrants are applied for, which is a long, drawn-out process, especially with the grind-to-a-halt break for Christmas. It's more than a week before I'm able to return to the island with my police escort. The villa is empty. Only a handful of staff left to maintain the property; not one person I recognise. The pool has winter leaves floating on its surface. The heating is off. Some of the gawping French windows stand open as if guests and staff left in a hurry.

The key to the labyrinth door, the one that leads directly from the house, is nowhere to be found. I venture in through the northern entrance and sit on one of the hard, stone benches in the moon terrace. In broad daylight, all its mystery is laid bare. Someone is even cutting the lavender as I watch. Eventually, the *someone* wanders off, and I take a moment to hold my eyes tight shut. I can hear the soft gurgling of water, but nothing else. No children crying out. I walk into one of the dark tunnels, the same tunnel the 'beast' had chased me down. It's silent, innocence itself. Not a remnant of the terror I had experienced before. The screams in the night, were they really the sounds of ghostly children? Without Henderson and his myth-making bandwagon, it doesn't seem possible. In fact, it feels more likely that I brought the ghost here myself. That it was Sally-Anne all along; the young girl that I've been carrying around in my head since that terrible day when I made my wrong decision. Seems like I'm good at making wrong decisions. I place my hand on the cold tunnel wall. If it was Sally-Anne that I heard, I want to take her back with me. I want to take Jed too. I don't want to leave their souls trapped in this place.

On my return to Athens, I keep the pressure on the police; dragging my weary bones into the station every day. Concerns are expressed about my sanity. My therapist in the UK is contacted. Old files get opened. My details may be confidential, but I have a history and that's more than enough. Lines are drawn between dots that don't even exist. I'm no longer a reliable witness. The link between Kara Jarvis and Henderson seems to evaporate under the scrutiny of the authorities. The sympathetic looks from the police become less tolerant, more wary. No one believes me. It's Henderson's word against mine. He's a renowned doctor and I'm... well, no one. They tell me to go home.

———

Besides, there are no bodies. Jed and Millar have simply disappeared. The police are not even looking for Millar, who went off the radar years ago. Apparently, Jed handed his notice in at work only days before Christmas; leaving abruptly since he couldn't get time off. One of his waitresses told the authorities he'd seemed distracted. Unstable. Possibly suicidal. I'm unable to contact her. Conveniently, she handed in her own notice shortly after giving her statement. Paid off, no doubt, by Henderson.

I hire a local with a motorboat and scour the coast. We find nothing. My mother says she can't make it out to Greece. She's sorry, but she has a full diary of events booked – theatre, friends, Pilates and besides, she's never been fond of Athens in the winter. I tell her there's no need anyway; I'm doing fine, and I'll be home soon, but I have no intention of going anywhere. I discover a chat room which mentions the island and take to scrolling through it most days. People on yachts sailing close to those stark elephant cliffs have reported hearing the sound of a child cry out, in fear and pain. One brave soul even pulled up at the abandoned jetty and conducted a search, but no one was discovered. An archaeologist added to the thread, stating that the wind had been known to play tricks – howling through the tunnels at night, sounding remarkably like a lost child. I know differently. I know about all the children who were lost in those caves. I know that they don't want to be quiet, and I know more:

there's something on that island, something calling to the broken and the guilty; the people who are already haunted.

I move out of the hotel I'd initially hauled up in and take a cheap room in a townhouse. It's unglamorous. The curtains are too thin. There's no heating. The washbasin tap drips all night. The toilet doesn't flush and the footbath in the communal shower never manages to get rid of its customary swill of grey water. I stop taking showers, staying in my bed, the thin curtains drawn. Eventually, I stop looking at the chat room, but I don't stop thinking. My brain feels like it's on speed. My mind has become a labyrinth, carrying the ghostly echoes of all the people I've lost.

One morning I wake to hear an argument in the hallway. There are a lot of arguments; the place is falling down. It may be cheap, but people have limits. I press my face into the coarse mattress that smells of straw and sweat, pull the pillow over the back of my head and groan. I can't go on like this. I think about the clear blue water only a mile or so away and the possibility of swimming out into it. Swimming till the cold freezes every organ in my body and feeling is not even a possibility anymore.

Then I get the most curious sensation, wet sandpaper against my skin. Rubbing again and again over a small patch of bare arm. I pull the pillow away from the back of my head, raise my torso a little and squint into the light. There's a cat. My cat?

'It took me bloody ages to get all the paperwork through for that.'

And Geoff!

'Time to come home, Sophie. We need you.'

I burst into tears as Geoff holds me, telling me it's all okay. It wasn't my fault. I got caught in somebody else's game, but now it's time to shift the power.

And so, in rain-soaked Putney, I take my engagement ring out of the bathroom cabinet and thread it onto its chain. Initially, I thought the fact Jed's body hadn't been found was a good sign. Despite everything, I'm still holding on to that thought. Geoff's alternative is way more difficult to digest. Geoff explained that without a body there is no murder. He thinks that most likely, Henderson scooped Jed's lifeless limbs from the water and got rid of him; disposed of him so thoroughly that Jed will never be found. Even though this alternative is better than persecuting myself with the idea of Henderson living off Jed's body like some kind of hideous parasite, part of me still refuses to abandon the last glimmer of belief that Jed could still be alive. According to the Greeks isn't that always the way; the only thing left in Pandora's box after all the nightmares have flown is simply – hope. Although, most days I try not to think about any of that. Because whatever happened to Jed, I can't afford to sit at home licking my wounds, or watching the clock tick away at my life. I've managed to notch myself up an even bigger debt on the karma front and surprisingly, taking action is easier to live with than self-pity. Emotionally, I'm not out of the woods. Maybe I never will be, but I get up when the alarm goes. I see my old therapist twice a week. I've even gone back to the pool. Financially I'm doing okay; I still have the money Henderson gave me. Spending it is the one thing I don't feel guilty about because it will give me the freedom to track that monster down, nail him, but there's something I need to do first. I need to put the brakes on Henderson's warped harvest. So at the moment, most of my day is spent with Geoff, trawling through records, searching for addresses linked to the clinic. We write letter after letter, and each and every one by hand. Because I cannot erase my stupidity, but perhaps, just perhaps I can save someone. Maybe I can save you?

You don't know me. We've never met, but I wanted to warn you that your life is in danger. If something happens to you, some kind of invitation, some kind of gift from the gods that seems too good to be true, it probably is.

THE END

ACKNOWLEDGEMENTS

With special thanks to The Bloodhound team, Tara Lyons, Betsy Reavley, Ian Skewis (editor) and Shirley (proofreader).

A NOTE FROM THE PUBLISHER

Thank you for reading this book. If you enjoyed it please do consider leaving a review on Amazon to help others find it too.

We hate typos. All of our books have been rigorously edited and proofread, but sometimes mistakes do slip through. If you have spotted a typo, please do let us know and we can get it amended within hours.

info@bloodhoundbooks.com

Printed in Great Britain
by Amazon

24952036R00199